FORTUNE'S KNAVE

FORTUNE'S KNAVE

The Making of William the Conqueror

A Novel

Mary Lide

St. Martin's Press
New York

Library of Congress Cataloging-in-Publication Data

Lide, Mary.
Fortune's knave / Mary Lide.
p.   cm.
ISBN 0-312-09293-8
1. William I, King of England, 1027or 8-1087—
Fiction.   I. Title.
PR6062.I32F67   1993
823'.914—dc20   93-18410   CIP

First published in Great Britain by Headline Books Publishing PLC.

First U.S. Edition: June 1993
10 9 8 7 6 5 4 3 2 1

To F. R. C. – with love and thanks

List of Characters

William, Duke of Normandy

Herleve, William's peasant mother
Fulbert the Tanner, William's grandfather
Walter, William's uncle, Herleve's brother
Herluin, Vicomte of Conteville, Herleve's husband

Robert, Archbishop of Rouen, William's great-uncle
Ralph de Gacé ⎫
Richard   ⎬ the archbishop's sons, William's second cousins
William   ⎭

Mauger, Archbishop of Rouen ⎫ sons of Papia of Envermeu,
William, Count of Arques   ⎭ once Duchess of Normandy;
                              William's step-uncles

The Monk Nicholas, son of Duke Richard III of Normandy,
    William's cousin
Guy of Burgundy, claimant to the duchy of Normandy
Grimoald of Plessis, a supporter of Guy of Burgundy, would-be
    assassin

King Henry I of France

Yvres of Bellême, Bishop of Sées

Count Gilbert of Brionne, William's guardian
Osbern, William's steward
Turold, William's 'tutor'
Golet, William's 'jester'

Matilda of Flanders
Count Baldwin of Flanders, her father
Adela, sister of King Henry, her mother

Chronology

Family Tree of Dukes of Normandy

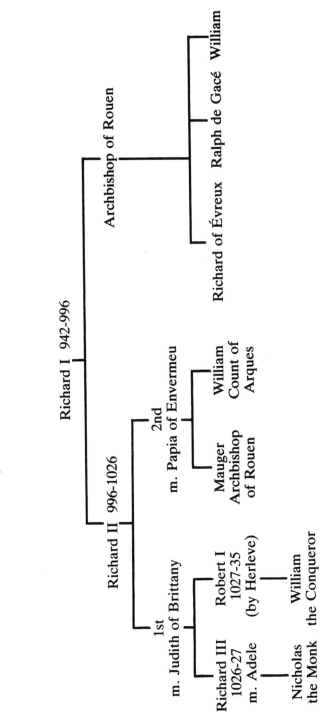

Richard I 942-996

Richard II 996-1026

Archbishop of Rouen

1st
m. Judith of Brittany

2nd
m. Papia of Envermeu

Richard III
1026-27
m. Adele

Robert I
1027-35
(by Herleve)

Mauger
Archbishop
of Rouen

William
Count of
Arques

Richard of Évreux Ralph de Gacé William

Nicholas
the Monk

William
the Conqueror

[William] excelled in wisdom all the princes of his
generation . . . he was outstanding in the largeness of his
soul . . . he was never daunted by danger. So skilled was he
in his appraisal of the true significance of any event that he
was able to cope with adversity . . . Great in body and strong
he was also temperate. . .

Excerpt from a monastic record, translated

FORTUNE'S KNAVE

Chapter 1

The great courtyard of Falaise smouldered in the heat of the day. It was high noon. The year was 1035, the time August. Beyond the castle walls the rich harvest fields basked in the sun, ripe for harvesting, and beyond them again, the surrounding woods lay thick and still in their dark summer foliage. The guards on the battlements leaned on their shields, yawned, scratched themselves lazily, chatted in low tones, not as meticulous in their guard as they would have been had their lord, the Duke of Normandy, been in residence. From time to time a servant stared out from behind a door, too hot to cross the yard to fetch water from the well, or bring wood for the fires that day and night burned within the castle keep. Even the hounds slumbered on their paws, occasionally yelping as they dreamed of chase and hunt. In all that sleepy tranquil world only one thing moved.

For its size it showed astonishing agility, this whirling ball of dust from which a pair of skinny legs and arms and a tousled head projected at irregular intervals. Dressed in rough homespun of russet brown that complemented the tangled curls, the legs encased in rough hose already torn and scrapped, the child who emerged from the dust cloud was a boy of some eight years old. Slight of build but remarkably quick, about his waist he wore a thick leather belt meant for someone twice his age, and in his right hand held a wooden sword with which he flailed some invisible adversary. Behind him he dragged the boss of a shield, the dangling strap alone almost his length. The broken part had come from an old round shield, unlike the triangular ones his father's guards leaned upon. When he had tired of inflicting damage with his sword the boy wound the strap about his wrist and used it to heft the boss in fighting fashion.

Some of the guards were watching him as he advanced upon his selected enemy, an old deer-hound that slumbered close to the inner gate in a favourite patch of sunlight. As if aware of professional scrutiny, the child now lunged forward, dropped to one knee to make a telling thrust, and stabbed close to the sleeping hound's side with his sword before leaping back and straightening as if to parry counterblow. Although the weight of sword and shield would have hampered any ordinary child, the boy was too proud to let his arm droop or in any way show signs of weariness. The reddish fair hair stood on end, matted with sweat; dirt and heat mottled the fair skin; but he paid no heed to these minor inconveniences, and from time to time let out a shout surprisingly loud for so slight a child. It was a warrior shout, the cry of his ancestors keeping time with his attack, *'Maslon, Dix aie,'* all the while whacking the hard ground with the wooden blade as fast as he could until more clouds of dust flew. On the battlements above, his father's men clashed their spears in encouragement, and grinned.

'Go to, *mon gars*,' one yelled, then, at his neighbour's surreptitious nudge, amended it to a 'my lord', drowned in a fit of coughing. If the child heard either epithet he paid no heed, the words lost in the sound of his panting. Without pause he thrust and lunged with all his puny force until the sleeping hound, too old and wise to want to hold its ground against such attack, lumbered to its feet and retired. Only then did the child pause, lean on his sword and wipe off the sweat. A pair of extraordinary sharp blue eyes surveyed his victory. Then, in a swift slide back to childhood, the lad plumped himself down in the hound's place, back to the wall, looking very pleased with himself while he fished for something in the inner folds of his tunic. Producing an apple, he began to munch it, pips and all, his eyes shut against the heat of the sun, his feet, in torn stockings, stretched out with sword and shield propped between them.

From inside the great square keep two other people watched; one with the sort of love only a mother feels, the other with equal intensity, but with no love in his regard. The mother could perhaps be excused. This was her pride, her only child, her little William who had stolen her heart as he had stolen the hearts of the castle guard, as he had those of all the dukedom. The other was his grand-uncle, Archbishop Robert of Rouen, chief churchman to many dukes and veteran of many wars. The archbishop's stocky figure was hunched under his episcopal robes, for although the day was hot the interior of the stone keep was cold, and his glance was keen. The sight of that youthful energy made him sigh several times as if despairing of harnessing it, and when his hostess gestured to a serf to stir up the fire while she herself replenished the old man's wine, he waved her ministration aside as if he too had greater things in mind.

Keeping his goblet clasped in his hand he continued to stand the right and might to make good their claim.

As if he guessed her thoughts, the archbishop stirred restlessly and played with his ring of office. He glanced down at her slight figure. Perhaps for the first time he glimpsed something of Herleve's spirit, for he moved uneasily as if he found her silence unnerving. And because at heart he was not a wicked man, merely one to whom the ambitions of the flesh were more important than the dictates of the Church, he could not resist adding, 'And so I warn you. Without a mother's family to act on her behalf, without benefit of status or noble rank, the safety of mother and child must both be at risk.'

After he had taken his leave, in his usual heavy, ponderous way, scrupulously polite but without warmth or feeling, heaving himself up on his horse in the manner of a Norman knight (for being a duke's son he had also been raised as a soldier and was trained to soldiering), Herleve was left alone. 'Here's a predicament,' she thought, and went out onto the castle walk to call her son.

William came reluctantly, no doubt remembering too late that he had been dressed in his best clothes expressly to meet the archbishop. Herleve heard his ingenuous pleas without comment: that 'twas not his fault his clothes were torn; that the archbishop had been so slow in greeting him he had had the time to become dishevelled; that the archbishop had passed him by without a smile, with only a curt nod of the head and the archbishop's ring to kiss; that the archbishop had shown him grave discourtesy, all excuses she shook her head at disapprovingly although she secretly agreed. But when she sat him down to eat she let him perch in his father's chair – even when kneeling on a padded cushion he could scarce reach the table top – and though in his father's absence they usually dined without ceremony, she had him served with dignity, albeit with merely bread and milk. She berated one serf for chattering, and chided another for dropping a knife, the sort of scolding unusual in her; and while William spooned his dinner up, careful not to spill a drop and if truth be told a little awed by the novelty, she sat beside him and considered the gravity of their predicament.

The archbishop's logic had summed up fairly her lack of influence, her unmarried state, her son's youth and illegitimacy. These were things she could not deny; they were all quite evident. But what the archbishop had set aside, or chosen to set aside, was equally important, and perhaps to her eyes more so since it alone made sense of all the rest: the love the duke held for her and for her son. She had no need of oaths or witnesses to swear to that. It was the lodestar of her existence, kept deep in her heart's core. And while the duke was gone she held his son in trust for him. And that also was something the archbishop did not count upon.

The duke had asked it of her, it was between him and her. Before he had left he had spoken of it, confided in her, the sort of secrets that husband and wife whisper to each other in the dark, the sort of confidences which are not spoken but which flow almost from thought to thought without need for words.

It had been nearly eight months ago, close to the year's end, that they had lain close entwined for warmth in the little ante-room, set in the castle wall, which from boyhood had been his. Although there were other, greater chambers for his use, he preferred its simplicity. From its window slit he could look down on the village of Falaise to the river ford where he had once seen her run barefoot. In this room she had first come to him, having ridden through the castle gates like a queen on her white horse, without subterfuge or shame; in this room she had dreamed of her child and the child himself had been born. '*Ma mie*,' the duke had said, smoothing her hair, winding it round his finger tips, '*ma mie*, for nine long years I have assumed the title and rank of duke although God knows and you do too, that I never sought it. But it has been an uneasy weight. For to my mind, although my brother's death was not of my contrivance, and came in strange unnatural wise, yet I had no part or say in it, but people have put its blame on me. And as God is my witness I wish no fraction of that blame to fall on my son, who in that matter is as innocent of any wrong as you or I have been. And I have wronged you too, my love, to keep you as I do. Oh yes,' for she had begun to speak then, 'I know that we ourselves are handfast, as they call it, in our eyes and God's eyes perhaps as closely knit as if we were in truth man and wife; yet in the eyes of the Church and the outside world we are not wed and so live in sin. For nine years then I have yearned to make a journey of atonement and prayer and now I see the time has come. My dukedom is at peace, not rife with anarchy and war as I found it. My barons are united and I can bend them to my will, which is more than my poor brother could, who used them for his own foolish ends.'

And when she stayed silent, knowing he would not be swayed from the task he had set himself, 'Listen then,' he said. 'I have a favour to ask. Keep you my son safe. And when I return then will we be married to make his inheritance certain and our happiness complete. I cannot marry earlier, not with my brother's blood upon me, even for no fault of my own.'

And after he had given her other assurances of love, passionately, ardently, with all the fervour of a young boy, then he had explained how he had issued a decree summoning all of his great and lesser lords to meet with him in council where he planned to require each in turn to swear an oath of fealty and obedience to her son.

'Thus in my absence, in all ways except by issue of lawful marriage, shall William be granted title of duke,' he had told her, smiling a little as she took in the seriousness of that fact. 'And God willing, I shall return to see it well fulfilled.'

He had laughed at her anxiety. 'But not until I myself am grown old,' he had joked. 'He is too small for such honours yet, and I too young to relinquish them. And in case he grows large-headed in the interim, you must cut him down to size.'

'*Ma mie,*' William's voice was imperious, his name for her borrowed from his father. It drew her abruptly back from that happy past into the present. '*Ma mie*, you aren't eating and I have already finished mine.' He showed her an empty bowl. ''Twould be waste you know,' he added diplomatically, pouring some from her plate to his. 'Brother Jehan says waste is a sin. He says too it is the heat that causes lack of appetite, but I don't notice it. I have noticed,' he went on between mouthfuls, his eyes bright, his chatter that of a precocious child whose place is secured and who knows of his right to it, 'that my pony seems the smaller the bigger I get. So if I eat more than is good for me shall I have a real horse when my father returns?'

She had no answer. 'He promised me a real saddle too, and a sword from Damascus with an inlaid hilt, and a suit of mail, made of shining rings – like my great-uncle's ring, but made of steel, all intertwined to form a mesh – a real guardsman's coat, with pieces extra to put in the sides as I grow in height and weight.'

She let him chatter, the words dropping like sun motes, all the lovely innocence of childhood contained in them. Only one sentence rang like a warning bell. 'When my father returns.' He was old enough to anticipate that. He remembered every detail of the departure: the stamping horses, the bodyguards, the rich trappings of men and beasts. And in their midst his father on his huge black horse, the ducal banner spread. A riot of colour and pageantry for a small boy to feast upon. ('Thus shall they take note of me,' the duke had explained at the time, laughing a little from embarrassment, for display was not to his usual taste. 'Why, the eastern emperor himself shall be impressed.' And then, more soberly, 'Even to largess in Jerusalem where I shall pray for our souls' grace, that it be granted us by a God who proves as generous.')

When their frugal meal was over, Herleve straightened William's clothes and had him change his shirt before winding her shawl over her head and taking him by the hand to lead him out of the castle and down towards the ford. She went on foot, without escort, as safe here in the heart of the dukedom as in a nunnery, although had she so chosen a dozen of the ducal household would have ridden at her command. But she did take one retainer, a dour, older man, Turold by name, a crafty man, equally clever with advice as with bow and spear, a member of the guard of the old duke, the present duke's father. Turold came from a noble line, had been selected deliberately by the present duke to be his son's pedagogue or tutor, when the child should be of age. Herleve was somewhat intimidated by the man's stern aspect, but she trusted her lord's choice and, more to the point, so did the child. William went cheerfully with Turold to the stream, which widened just below the ford into a series of pleasant pools of a depth for a small boy to paddle in, and had green banks for sitting on and fishing from, while she herself crossed the ford and entered the house of her father, Fulbert the Tanner.

Of all the men in Normandy, next to the duke, Fulbert was the one she most admired, although when she had been younger she had not always seen eye to eye with him. And, being her father, he had not always looked favourably on her alliance with the duke, like the archbishop in not wanting his name sullied by scandal. But all that had passed.

Herleve found Fulbert in his usual place, before the hearth in his workroom, in his hands a piece of leather which he turned and twisted as if he had forgotten the use for it. As often happened the fire was out, his tools were idle, and he sat deep in thought. He was a tall man, with scant red hair, and there was something in his brooding expression that spoke of deep disappointment or grief, long suppressed, which even now, when stilled, was perhaps not completely forgotten. He was a stubborn man, as Herleve knew to her cost, at times implacable, and something of that stubbornness may have passed to his daughter and through her to his grandson. She had no need to tell him of the archbishop's visit, he would already know. The village of Falaise would have turned out en masse to watch the spectacle of the great man's leave-taking. For the Archbishop of Rouen rode more as became a lord temporal than spiritual, having about

8

him his own bodyguards from the lands of Évreux, as well as monks from his abbey church, and in the duke's absence few visitors to Falaise came with such a noteworthy entourage.

Fulbert knew the archbishop, having in earlier times had dealings with him, not always of the most satisfactory kind, and having once for a short while been in his service in the city of Rouen where the tanner's skill had been in great demand. Like many men of his class Fulbert was suspicious of all lords, secular or priestly, and although he gave the present Duke of Normandy grudging respect, he had not shown much to previous dukes and he felt none for their chief bishop. He had been pondering the archbishop's visit, a rare occurrence even when the duke was at home, and had already guessed why the prelate had come.

'So daughter,' he began when she had kissed and greeted him and fussed over his sitting in so cheerless a fashion, 'what news from Rouen?' And when she did not immediately reply, too busy sweeping out cinders from the hearth, he added, 'Full of gloom and doom for sure, and after feathering his own nest.'

As a craftsman, Fulbert ranked not much higher than a peasant, and might have been expected to have been so far beneath these lordly affairs as to be ignorant even of their existence. But he had always been a clever man, and in his way as proud of his standing as any lord. Fulbert had taught his children, his two sons and his daughter, to be equally proud, since birth instilling in them an awareness of their rightful heritage as descendants of that Viking race who had first captured and settled Normandy. 'As Norsemen,' he used to boast, 'we are the match of any man. For when our ancestors came in their long boats, all rowed the same oars, swung the same axes, hefted the same swords, bound to each other by a common bond, comrades at arms, not lord or serf. Equals all, we shared the land, and gave it our name: Normandy, men of the North.'

He did not make his boast today. Age and his daughter's position had tamed his fire but he was still shrewd. And since her place in Falaise castle had been secured, his own standing in the village had risen so that among the village elders he had at last acquired the place from which hitherto his moody temper had excluded him.

'For look you,' he went on, 'while your lord's away they'll all be probing for weaknesses. Even the archbishop, although as regent he's sworn to act in your son's interest.'

He mused a while. 'There's been no love lost there in the past, and you know how the archbishop treated you. And how, in the first year of your lord's reign, when the duke besieged and exiled him, the archbishop put all of Normandy under interdict. Uncle and nephew may have given each other the kiss of peace; it does not mean they have become friends. Remember that beyond his archbishopric at Rouen he also controls Évreux. As Count of Évreux he wants to secure Évreux for his sons. And maybe more.'

Prompted by him, Herleve now spoke of the archbishop's warnings. 'Aye,' her father's reply was grim. 'There speaks a truth. For beside Rouen's sons, who else has claim?' He spread his large hand with its horny fingers, and counted. 'First, since we have mentioned them, the archbishop's sons, three, of whom Ralph de Gacé is called most dangerous: like his father he is ambitious and full of guile. But as Rouen hints, there are other claimants with more pressing rights who may be no less backward in stating them. In order then, foremost in rank, that young Nicholas, mentioned as being set aside, only son to the older brother of your lord. His friends will maintain that on his father's death Nicholas was supplanted by your lord, placed out of the way in the monastery of St-Ouen, to be bred up as a monk without interest in ducal affairs. And so, they say, he is wedded to monkish ways. Nevertheless, by *primogeniture*, that is by order of birth, he is the only son of an older son and if he will not stake that claim himself there are plenty who might do so for him. Thirdly, and again dangerous, the present duke has two half-brothers, his father's sons by a second wife, Papia of Envermeu's spawn – surely you have heard talk of them? Papia and her father, the Lord of Envermeu, had no love of your lord, were ever anxious to do him harm. She'll be as zealous on her sons' behalf now as ever she was when she was duchess here at Falaise. Why not? The old duke's unexpected demise robbed them of great reward; she'll have fed them on hopes ever since.'

He suddenly snapped his fingers shut. 'They'll pounce,' he said, 'like snakes in the dark.'

His summing up was lengthy and more detailed but it was no more than what Herleve had already assumed. And like the archbishop's, Fulbert's logic was precise and not to be gainsaid. Again, Herleve did not fault it but it saddened her. I want nothing for myself, she wanted to say, nor for my son, but what his father decrees for him. But she knew that was not true. Her ambition for William was great, as great as that of Papia of Envermeu for her sons, or Archbishop Robert of Rouen for his, or the supporters of that monk Nicholas for him, except without the wish to kill for it.

During the last part of her father's speech a man had come in through the door and settled himself down unobtrusively (for age and fame had given Fulbert the Tanner a certain pomposity that brooked no interruption). This newcomer was Walter, Herleve's older brother. He listened intently as his father talked, his grey eyes fixed, then rubbed his hand slowly through his thinning fair hair so it stood on end like a ruffled dog's. And when Fulbert had finished Walter stood up and shook himself as if preparing for action.

'I remember them as well as you,' he told his sister. 'Leastways the Duchess Papia's sons.' He scowled. 'A nasty thieving lot, the Envermeu, always after gain. Until the present duke put them in their place.'

From him that came as praise, and Herleve knew the truth of this as well as he did. Her lord had tamed the Envermeu as he had other factions in his lands; had won them to his side as indeed he had done Walter himself. For in his youth Walter had been an outlaw and had been pardoned after his sister's rise to prominence. And Papia of Envermeu was in the present duke's debt, so much so that she might be held in check. But none of those gathered in Fulbert's shed held much trust in that.

'If I were in charge,' Fulbert said, in the sort of tone that suggested he felt he should have been, 'I'd find some protection for the lad. Fine promises sound well,' he added scowling at his son – for as he spoke Walter had gone up to where Herleve was and had taken her hand in his with a look and smile that said, 'You can count on me' – 'William needs more than talk. He needs weight and substance. Where would he find that I ask? Not here in Falaise.'

His shrewd appraisal, again similar to the archbishop's, made his listeners pause. After a while he continued, 'For my part I'd send the lad where he'd be safe, even out of Normandy. Just for a while, to be sure, just until his father came back, to throw his enemies off the track.'

Herleve cried, 'No,' and wound her shawl about her hands in agitation.

'The English atheling sought safety here with us when he was exiled from his kingdom,' Fulbert went on, by his tone showing this was a thing he had thought over and deliberated with himself many times before speaking of it. 'And so have others of great rank, to be befriended by the duke and therefore stand in his debt.'

He looked sideways under his bushy eyebrows, 'Even to the French king,' he said.

'Oh, I know in the past the old king of France's been no

11

friend of Normandy,' he went on, 'but he's dead and gone. And although there's long enmity between the kings of France and the Norman dukes the new king owes his title to your lord.'

He added sagely, as if familiar with kings, 'Acceptance by the king would set a seal not easily broken, would enhance the rightness of our cause and confuse the opposition.'

Reluctantly Walter agreed but not Herleve. She shook her head. That past enmity was still strong in her mind. And although she admitted that the young king seemed of a different breed, and had shown suitable gratitude to her lord, she was obviously unwilling to trust him. 'There must be some other means,' she said, 'some other protection until my lord returns.'

But while they talked on, the shadow of their present difficulties merged with memories of former ones. Both Walter and Fulbert had rebelled against a previous duke and both had suffered for it. Herleve, by reason of her attachment to the duke, had become a victim of noble intrigue and spite, hounded by the French. Yet all these recollections paled against the fear, now openly expressed, that the present duke had been away too long. That, all Normandy admitted. The whys and wherefores of his prolonged absence were of course unknown, were the source of much pleasurable debate. They knew he had reached the Holy Land, had achieved the pilgrimage he had sought, should already be on the homeward track. He might have been delayed in foreign parts by desert storms, or by bad weather that closed the passes north; he might have been caught up in some foreign war or controversy, might even have been tempted to take part in such things, as his nature and warrior instinct might dictate. Herleve did not believe so. She knew he meant to hasten back. Neither she nor the other men dared think of the 'what ifs' that laced their secret thoughts: what if he were imprisoned on the way or held to ransom by some hostile lord – such things had happened before; what if he had fallen sick and languished in some lonely part; what if he never returned at all . . . ? Such catastrophies did not bear thinking on.

Beside the River Ante the primary object of the three's concern had tired of splashing after miniature boats. He had fashioned them out of leaves and sticks and sent them floating from the bank, bobbing along on the current like Viking ships towards the sea from which he knew he and all his ancestors had come. But the summer heat had reduced the pale brown water to a mere stream, a trickle over stones where the fragile crafts lodged and could not be prised loose. Thoroughly wet, William now came back to sit on the bank with his tutor.

In the manner of older men, Turold had seized the chance to enjoy the shade. All was quiet. Above the spread of beech trees the white 'felsens', the cliffs which gave Falaise its name, glinted in the sun, and above them again the great keep stood squarely against the blue of the sky in which puffs of clouds drifted like smoke. The tutor and the little boy sat together in companionable silence. Perhaps the tutor dozed; not so William. Although outwardly keeping still his thoughts went jumping about, grasshopper quick, turning again and again to the morning's events and the visit of his reverent relative.

'Sir knight,' he said after a moment or two, when it seemed to him Turold had slept long enough. He spoke respectfully, for since babyhood he had been trained in manners by the duke and had always had his mother's gentle courtesy as guide. 'Sir knight, why do you think Great-uncle Rouen came today? Myself,' he folded his arms across his chest as he had seen his father do, 'myself, I think it was to frighten us.'

Turold's eyes blinked open fast, but he didn't respond. 'For, look you,' William was continuing in his careful way, precise and sharp, a trait he had inherited from Fulbert, 'Great-uncle Rouen only ever visits when there is something to complain about. I heard my father explain it to my mother before he left. "The archbishop's a bully," my father said, "like a schoolboy in his own palace school." He was jesting to make her laugh, and she did, but underneath I know she was sad. And now she is alone, Great-uncle Rouen thinks he can bully her all he likes. But not with me to answer to he won't.'

He jumped up and knotted his fists. 'Besides,' he said, 'I don't like the way he looks. And his hand is cold and full of bones like a carp.'

He frowned, for a moment looking very much like Fulbert indeed. 'And the day before my father left, why did Great-uncle argue so? "He's only a bastard," I heard him say, not once but twice. He meant that for me, though it made my mother cry.'

Another bunching of the fists, a down-turning of the mouth. 'Turold,' he said, 'what is a bastard that we are so named?'

The use of the 'we' of ducal rank, the formal speech, sat strangely on the childish lips but was uttered deliberately, out of pride. It took Turold by surprise. Uncertain how to reply, the old statesman coughed to hide his embarrassment, and was saved by a white flurry and splash from one of the lower pools.

'Why now, my lord,' he said pulling himself up, 'there's that big trout I've been watching this past hour, see there, beneath

13

those rocks. Shall we have a look at him?'

Usually William would have been nothing loath, would have been clamouring for pole and fishing line, the big trout another well-known adversary he'd often tried to catch. Now he hesitated. 'We shall spare it yet awhile,' he said grandly, hands on hips, legs astride, the eyes unsmiling in the round, as yet unformed face. 'We shall save it for our father's return. It is our father's right as duke to fish it for himself.'

Again Turold was silenced.

'For our father will return,' William said, 'he promised to.' And a third time he balled his fists to brush the angry tears aside.

But even as he spoke, even as his mother, grandfather and uncle talked, even as the archbishop journeyed back to Rouen, it was too late. Robert, Duke of Normandy, known as the Magnificent, would never come back. All the penitence and prayers in the world could not turn the will of God. The duke was already six weeks dead, at Nicaea in Bythinia.

Chapter 2

That summer of 1035 Paris was in full flower, the river low but not so low that the stench of sewage was overpowering. The plagues and fevers usual to the hot months were mercifully in abeyance and consequently the king and his entourage remained in residence in his great palace overlooking the Seine. With time on its hands the court was receptive to every rumour, gossip and intrigue making their way through the palace doors as easily as through more humble residences. The main topic of discussion was the death of the Duke of Normandy, soon to be confirmed by the sad return from eastern parts of his men without him.

The manner of his death became the subject of detailed debate. Some said he died by poison, poisoning being a favourite device of the Normans. The poisoner was even named, a certain Ralph Mowin who had his own motives for murder, beyond the temptation of the ensuing vacant dukedom. Others claimed the duke had met his end naturally, that tainted water was the most likely cause, although since water in the desert regions was always suspect the duke had carried good French wine with him. Others again refused to believe either story, claimed that the duke was still alive and would one day come riding back in all his magnificence. His loyal companions, too grief-shocked to counter any gossip, spoke only of his cheerfulness even in the face of death, reporting that when through weakness he was carried by four natives of the region he had jested saying, 'Tell the world you have seen me borne to Paradise on the backs of four black devils.'

The death of a lord whose dukedom was so large and important could not be ignored, no matter how unpleasant. The king had finally taken action. Envoys were directed to those distant lands where the duke was reputed to have perished; formal letters of condolence were conveyed to the Archbishop of Rouen, the young duke's legal guardian. But to Herleve at Falaise the king sent an entirely different sort of message.

The king was not the same who in the past had crossed swords

15

with the Dukes of Normandy, but his son, Henry, the first of the name. And as Fulbert had suggested, King Henry had good reason to be grateful to Robert of Normandy. As a young boy Henry had fled to Rouen under the duke's protection when his mother, Queen Constance, had preferred his younger brother to him. Despite the attempts of Henry's father to protect the succession, the queen, a vicious meddling woman, had quitted the court and raised up an army on her younger son's behalf. It was only with Duke Robert's aid that the young Henry had eventually driven the queen's forces back and taken possession of the kingdom. Thus in a true sense Henry owed his position to the duke. But there was more to it than that.

During the period when Henry had been at the mercy of the duke he had come to know Robert well. Of Robert's fighting prowess he had no doubt; as Robert's feudal overlord he had sensibly called upon those skills. But there were other things in Robert that the young prince had come to respect – rare in days when force of arms was all men cared about. First was the duke's unusual sense of fair play, his instinctive willingness to see another point of view, even that of his enemies. That empathy had caused him to come to Henry's aid, repaying evil with good, without thought of revenge, even though in previous times the prince's royal father had shown no such mercy to the duke. Then there was the duke's idea of responsibility, a concept that Henry had never met before, and indeed in his own court now had difficulty in applying. For although as a youth he had vowed to model himself in all ways upon his benefactor, in actual fact he was overwhelmed by the role of kingship and too often allowed his nobles to go their own ways, unchecked.

The last thing however that the young prince had come to admire was the hardest to put into words and yet was the one he envied most. That was Robert's religious fervour, for all he kept it dampened down, hidden in himself. Henry had often been on minor pilgrimages to places within his kingdom, such as Martin-le-Tour and Notre Dame de Vezelai, but he had never been to the Holy Land. Many of his great lords had, the Counts of Anjou for example. Fulk the Black of Anjou had perhaps started the trend, but then Fulk the Black had committed so many crimes a thousand pilgrimages would scarcely win atonement. Secretly Henry admired Robert for going to the East, and for thus being counted among the blessed. Like the disciples of long ago or monks of the present, for a certain space of time Robert had devoted his life to God, by so doing gaining two-fold reward: reputation in this world and redemption in the next.

Henry did not believe the story that, like Fulk of Anjou, Robert too had atonements to make for heinous crimes. Nor did he condemn Robert's journey as feckless self-indulgence, as the Archbishop of Rouen had. If pressed Henry would have confessed that to his way of thinking only a man of Robert's strength would have made the momentous decision to go on a pilgrimage at all.

The duke's death saddened him as if he had lost a personal friend. And in the midst of his own grief it came to him in a flash that if Robert had done well by him, it was only fair that now in turn he should do well by Robert's heir, the little William, baseborn or not. For if Henry remembered his stay in Normandy with affection, he remembered Herleve and William more affectionately, although she came but seldom to Rouen and he had seen her and her son only once for a brief moment.

But it was a meeting he had never forgotten. He had been in the courtyard of the ducal palace, idly lounging in the sun, waiting for his horse to be brought out, when a clatter at the gate attracted his attention. A group of knights came riding through, their arms and equipment as well as the ducal flag revealing them to be part of the ducal guard. In their midst rode a girl on a fine grey horse: he had thought of her in those terms, even though part of him knew she was more than just a girl, with her long fair hair and wide-set grey eyes and a smile to win the world. She rode astride, her skirts hitched up, her slender legs encased in men's riding boots, and when she drew rein looked round her with unabashed curiosity. Beside her, sharing a trooper's horse, a small boy, held with difficulty around the waist, wriggled in excitement until a word from her quietened him.

The young prince had stayed where he was and watched, noted how the castle guards came running, eager to serve. Pleasure motivated them, not fear. He noted how they helped the child and held him still until his mother had dismounted. And he noted how the duke himself came to lift her down and held her for an instant longer than strictly necessary, laughing up at her while she blushed. And then the duke had come up to him, one arm easy about the woman, the child on his shoulders tugging at his hair. 'My lord king,' he'd said, in a tone that overflowed with pride although he tried to hide it, 'here is Herleve and her great son.'

The child had laughed and jumped up and down, fists buried in that crop of russet hair so that the duke had been forced to bend his head until Herleve stretched up to rescue him. Then she had bobbed a curtsey in a country style, and said in a country voice that to the prince's city ears flowed like running water, 'My lord, you honour us.' And she had smiled at him, a smile like quicksilver, so full of welcome he had felt warmed by it. 'I have brought you some apples, there in the saddle bags. Normandy is famous for its apples, my lord, and you must try these, the first from our new trees.'

And when he had tried to stammer thanks, she'd said, 'Call me Herleve,' still with that same luminous smile, 'everyone does.' To the duke who had tried to frown and yet had laughed at the same time, 'Even your son tries to,' she'd playfully chided.

They had left him then with wishes for a good day's hunt, and had wandered slowly through the crowded courtyard, pausing to speak to this one or listen to that, the woman still enveloped in the duke's grasp, the child still bouncing exuberantly. And while his horse stamped with impatience, Henry had continued to watch, overcome with some emotion that he could not name but which filled him with longing, as if he had received a glimpse of true happiness.

That same longing overcame him now as he thought of the duke. More than ever he felt the waste of his own life, the futility of it. He wished – what did he wish? – still to be without responsibility as in those days, to have the liberty to ride his horse wherever he willed, spur it through those Norman hunting grounds until in a quiet glade he could fling himself off to lie in the shadows; to be free to listen to the nearby brook, feel the sun, have time for dreams. And hence his message to Herleve.

The message was not a written one, for he himself did not know how to write and it contained thoughts which even his best-known scribes were not to be trusted with. And as he knew Herleve herself could neither read nor write, Henry preferred she heard his words as he himself would have spoken them.

His envoy was a chosen friend, a messenger of about his own age, a close-mouthed man who had followed Henry into exile and already knew the Norman court. The message Hugh brought was simply said:

'To the Lady Herleve I send my wishes. I think on her and grieve. What I can do as friend and overlord is hers to command. If she would have it so, my court is open to her and her son. Let her find shelter here a while, let William do obeisance for his father's lands.'

And so it was, while all of Falaise was numb with shock, while yet sad tidings from the East had not sunk in and all over Normandy the Norman barons debated their next move, the solution Fulbert had advised presented itself.

King Henry's messenger had steeled himself for tears and bitter mourning. A married man himself, he sympathized with Herleve's plight. He was no courtier by trade, but a simple man-at-arms, albeit loyal to his fingertips, a man instinctively to trust, and a bonny fighter. He found the Lady Herleve in the great hall at Falaise, not secreted in the woman's bower as he had expected. She was clothed in white, her head covered, her arms filled with white lily flowers that grew in profusion along the river banks. Her face and expression had not much changed from the girlish looks that King Henry had admired, but her eyes were dark pooled, as if sorrow lay in their depths too deep for finding.

She greeted Hugh gravely, listened to his discourse, thanked him, called for wine. 'It's hot for riding,' she told him with her simple courtesy. She held out the sheaf of flowers. 'We picked these fresh this morning,' she said, 'to lay in the chapel for Mass. He always liked them.'

It was the only mention she made of her dead lover until Hugh asked for the little duke. Then her pale cheeks flushed. 'He is sitting out there with Turold, look.'

She stood aside so Hugh could see through a slit in the walls down to a kind of inner courtyard where Turold and the little boy were seated side by side. The child was listless, his hands crossed, his feet still. He leaned his head against the old man's shoulder and said nothing. But from time to time when a sudden noise broke in upon their solitude, he would start up, then sink back to his former pose, with a broken-hearted sigh.

'William looks for him,' Herleve said, 'he does not believe he will not come back.'

Tears were rolling down her cheeks and she brushed them away with her hand as freely as a child. 'We will hold a service,' she said, 'but we can't have him back for burial. It seems hard, don't you think, to be kept for ever so far from home?'

Herleve smiled at Hugh through tears, and went her ways; he thought in all his life he had never seen anything so fair or sad. She made no answer to his master's offer, except those first thanks, but later that evening, Osbern, the castle steward, came to find him. He was accompanied by Turold and by an old peasant and his son, unknown to Hugh, who stood in the shadows.

He was immediately alert. He had been almost asleep, for he had dined well: the servicing of the castle, the comportment of the servants and the ordering of food and wine continuing without disruption; the strengthening of the castle guard the only open sign of tension. Osbern spoke first as was proper, a man of considerable rank and influence, he was himself a member of the ducal family whose loyalty, like Turold's, was well known and had withstood many tests in the last ten years or so.

'Tell the king, your lord and master, that the Lady Herleve expresses gratitude. As do we, the new duke's councillors here at Falaise. After due consideration we are of the opinion that to accept the king's offer would be in all best interests. But time is wasting. It is nearly two months since our lord's death; our enemies gather. To avoid delay the lady is prepared to ride out early tomorrow morn, she and her son. Among those to accompany her will be the young duke's closest companion, Turold, and this man,' he indicated the younger of the peasants, 'his uncle Walter. Both attend the duke at the lady's own request and by her direct command. In her absence I, Osbern, will undertake to keep Falaise castle, come what may.'

This long and solemn discourse, which Hugh heard in equally formal fashion, kneeling to receive it as custom dictated, was interrupted by what can only be called a snort of derision. 'And as the boy's grandfather,' Fulbert said, 'I'd say cut through this twaddle. More important than William's oath is the oath the king swears to him. When we are assured of the French king's support, only then should William go to Paris.'

Walter tried to hush him but he turned as fiercely on his son. 'All very well for you,' he said, 'you'll ride with him. 'Tis easily done, to go abroad into venture and danger while we old folks, long past such capers, must bide at home. But were I younger, you'd not leave me wanting.'

He was suddenly silent, perhaps remembering too late how once his son had taken blame for him, and in truth ridden into danger while Fulbert had stayed in safety. Osbern smiled at him good humouredly. 'There'll be work enough here,' he said. 'I shall be glad of your company, Master Fulbert, to hold the village steady. This unexpected death has hit them hard.' For a moment his voice faltered as he added, 'As it has hit all of us, God have us in His keeping.'

Recovering his composure, Osbern turned to Walter. 'As for you, Messer Walter,' he said, 'I have no doubt you will keep your nephew safe. But leave our guards something to do! We'll have a force large enough to send attackers flying. And if you ride fast, in secret as we intend, I doubt if there'll be need or time for fighting. As for what we Normans think,' his gaze now swivelled back to the messenger, 'with all due respect to you, Sir Hugh, and to your master, and no offence intended, to my mind that's better held within our own private thoughts than spread abroad to be a comfort, or a threat, to others.'

His rebuke was mild, yet he eyed Hugh carefully, his small dark eyes sharp and knowing, obviously not a man to trifle with. Before he left, he turned to speak.

'The duke's party would be glad of your company, Sir Messenger,' he said. 'In dangerous times another sword is always welcome. And when they reach Paris, they would be glad of your help to come quietly into the city. The Lady Herleve is not used to crowds, would not wish to have her presence known.'

He coughed. 'But you, as king's envoy, may wish to make better speed, seeking hospitality as your status gives you right. You may even have business in Rouen. They on the other hand shall journey in secret by slow routes, even to bypassing that city.'

The words were delicately expressed but the king's messenger understood their import well enough. The duke's advisors did not mean for the archbishop to be privy to their plans. And Herleve would not have her presence used against her son, nor have her lower rank act as deterrent to his new position. Yet for her son's sake she would put mourning time aside and travel with him even though, Hugh thought, she would be as out of place in that frantic Paris court as a gaudy bird in a Norman orchard.

Hugh nodded his head in agreement, stepped back to let his visitors leave. In due course, as he must, he would report on these things to his master. They were no more than the king had himself suspected, hence the very nature of Hugh's mission. But what a child, and what a woman to be left to the mercy of the Norman wolves! He shuddered. And before he slept he vowed to dedicate his sword and skill, such as they were and within the limits of his envoy, to the little duke's defence and the honour of his mother.

It was a crisp morning, having within it the promise of the coming autumn for all that it was still summer, when William and his entourage rode out from Falaise castle. The sun was not yet up but the faint red light on the eastern ramparts suggested that the day when it dawned would be fair. No one watched them leave: it was too early for the village serfs to be about their work in fields and byres, and only the castle guards had risen to lean over the castle walls, intent on their duty.

William rode beside Turold. He was mounted on a new pony, acquired for him the day before, larger than his usual mount and sure-footed if frisky. It was the little horse his father had planned for him, and so he had heard of it and mounted it with only a

21

token show of interest because to show interest would reveal how much he missed his father. The pony trotted briskly over the cobbled causeway and down towards the forest. Behind it clattered the ducal guard, all riding armed, their great shields slung over their shoulders with the markings turned inside. Even the ducal flag was furled which William thought a pity. William loved the great banner. It was called a gonfanon, and the snap and crackle of the square pennant with the three points attached was one of the most familiar sounds in Falaise when his father was in residence. But he forced his mind back from that thought. This banner was new. 'You shall order it unwrapped,' his mother had told him when she showed him it, 'see how the ladies of the castle have stitched it with red and gold. See how the leopards prance.'

She had smoothed the material carefully to display it to advantage. He knew that she herself had little skill at embroidery, which was a noble lady's occupation, or so she had often told him, but she could sew seams and mend holes and the new shirt he wore was of her making. He wriggled his shoulders, feeling the rub of the fine stitches against his skin. Over the shirt he wore a tunic embroidered with gold, and over that again a mantle of dyed blue wool, fox-edged, his best. 'Mind how you go with that,' his mother had told him as she had helped him dress in the dark. 'It's too nice for tearing.'

He peered ahead. There was still a ground mist and the forms of horses and men bobbed up and down as if they rode through waves. Two summers ago his father had taken him to Fécamp to look at the sea. First there had been a ceremony on the cathedral steps opposite the duke's palace. All of the Norman barons were there, and his father had talked to them. Then he had lifted William up and all the men had clashed their swords and shouted out, so loud a shout he had been frightened. But he hadn't let them know it. Afterwards his father had gone into the church and showed him the place where an angel had appeared to one of their ancestors. 'He was called William, like you,' his father had said, 'William Long Sword.' He laughed, ruffled William's hair. 'Not because his sword was long,' he said, 'but because he himself was short.' And as William's eyes had grown round at all these strange stories, 'But you'll be tall; no fear of your sword dragging on the ground. And after me you'll be duke; they have just sworn so.'

And when they had looked at all the other marvels in the church, and said prayers at the tombs of William's grandfather and uncle, who had also been dukes, he and his father had walked along the pebbled beach where the wind blew the spray into clouds.

The beach stretched out towards the limestone cliffs, studded with green upon the top where grass grew. His father hadn't looked at them, but pointed out across the sea which by turns changed colour as the sun caught it, sparkling blue-green like his eyes.

'Northwards,' his father had said, laughing down at William. His boots crunched through the flints; the salt made his hair curl with damp. 'Northwards,' he repeated, 'where we came from. Where there are many countries for the taking.' And looking down from his great height, 'Where one day we shall return to take them.'

Again William beat the memory down. It wouldn't do, he mustn't think. Like his mother he must endure. He twisted in the saddle looking now for her, but she was safe enough, with Uncle Walter to keep her company.

'Pay attention now to what I say,' she had told him last night. 'In the king's court you shall forget that I am there. Oh, I don't mean really forget, just pretend to, until we have done what we are going there for.'

She had hugged him. 'I shall remember for both of us.' She had explained that he would sleep apart from her, with Turold and Walter to accompany him. Others of his guard, men he knew, would stand watch outside the chamber door so he need not be afeared. And he must be on his best behaviour, must keep his clothes neat and clean and his own self likewise, must bow when spoken to and answer politely to do himself and her proud. And when he had done whatever it was that needed doing for his father's lands, why then they would ride home together and life would go on just as it always had.

But without my father, without my father, William thought. And without him nothing can ever be the same.

'My lord,' Turold spoke gently but insistently. 'My lord, when we get to Paris there are great things to look for.'

He went on explaining what an important city Paris was, and Rouen but a village in comparison. Paris had many gates and towers and walls that had been built originally by the Romans. The streets were stone-made but full of dirt, like a midden, and the river there was so large it doubled round almost back upon itself, enclosing gardens and orchards and fair palaces within its loops. And many other marvels, even to the marvel of his ancestor, Rollo the Viking, who when he had approached those same walls more than a hundred years before had so frightened the

French that their king had given him the whole of Normandy to ensure his withdrawal.

After Rollo the Viking had come William Longsword, Rollo's son, whose grave William had seen at Fécamp. And after him a whole line of dukes of which he, William, would now come next: William, Duke of Normandy. But only if the Church allows, he thought. For last night his mother had also explained that although at Fécamp the Norman lords had sworn to accept him as his father's heir, and shouted out their oath of fealty, there were difficulties which, now that his father was dead, had presented themselves anew. For although she certainly was his mother, and his father was undoubtedly his father, for reasons of their own they were not married, or at least not in a manner accepted by the Church, and it was this marriage, or lack of it, that would complicate his inheritance. And for that reason he must get up in the dark and ride to Paris to the king to swear to be the king's true and faithful vassal. And in return the king would swear to be his true liege lord and help him keep his dukedom against any man who tried to seize it in his place.

Last night, William, for whom the Church meant Great-uncle Rouen, had said, 'It seems to me that if there are problems as you say, then it is the Church's fault. And if Rollo could put fear into the French when he wasn't even Christian, perhaps we don't really need the Church at all and would be better off without it.'

His mother had put her hand across his mouth. 'That's blasphemy,' she had whispered. 'Pray God for forgiveness. 'Tis easy to blame God. But I believe,' she gazed at him intently, her eyes luminous, 'we ourselves make us what we are. And I have found – and, dear my son, I have had troubles enough in my life – that when we are at greatest need, then is when God shows Himself.'

She had hugged him then. 'This must last you a while,' she had told him, moving away. 'Until then, know yourself beloved. Stand firm, my lord.'

Her use of his title had impressed him. It sounded strange, as did the name of 'duke' that his father's men had given him. Again he looked around him. Directly ahead the outriders cantered along; in front of them, scouts went to spy the way; behind him rode his mother and friends; and all about him flowed the forest of Falaise. Beyond stretched the land of Normandy with its woods and fields and orchards, mile after mile of it, land his ancestors had fought for and won.

He gritted his teeth, gripped his legs tight against the pony's sides and kicked it into a gallop. His thoughts kept time with the pony's hooves. If I am to be duke like the others were, if I am to hold the dukedom as my forefathers did, whether my father married my mother or not, I will fight for it.

Chapter 3

In his palace at Rouen the archbishop was confronting his sons. For once he looked his age, his haughty Norman features peaked with fatigue. His beaked nose and high cheekbones had caved in upon themselves; dark shadows showed beneath his eyes; only his keen glance revealed intelligence. He knew what his sons were about, of course, what they wanted, nay craved, and had he been their age and of their disposition he would have craved it himself. But many years in holy office had taught him patience, and he knew better than anyone how to dissemble.

'My children,' his voice could be deceptively mild as many sinners knew to their cost, 'you are welcome here at Rouen. I see you come in haste. Had news of your visit reached us earlier we would have better prepared a greeting.' He smiled though neither mouth nor eyes showed mirth. 'Even to the fatted calf of biblical fame.'

In turn his three sons looked at each other furtively and shifted their feet. Booted and spurred, they were mud-spattered from hard riding, and had come bursting into his chamber unceremoniously. Their father's taunts stung even though they were grown men, and his grave demeanour, his aura of holiness, put them at disadvantage: still they fought against letting him see it. That he assumed his pose deliberately was all the more irritating.

The youngest and oldest brothers were tongue-tied, their father's presence always having that effect on them, although away from him they could swear and swagger with the best. They hung their heads, scrapped their spurs sheepishly on the floor to get rid of the mud, and let their middle brother speak for them.

Ralph de Gacé was a tall, heavily built man, very like his father in looks, with the russet hair of his Viking ancestors. Unlike the eldest, Richard, who would inherit Évreux (and seemed not to mind being treated like his father's bailiff), Ralph had long been dissatisfied with his father's plans for him, or – more properly – lack of plans. Being brash and not given to mincing his words, since early manhood he had challenged the archbishop over various matters of inheritance, not least those pertaining to his own future. That jibe about the 'fatted calf' was meant primarily for him, and he knew it. He bit his lip. Only matters of the gravest concern would have brought him here to his father's inner sanctum. When last they had met their parting had been so vitriolic as to make him vow to meet no more – and that too he knew his father remembered.

'Your Grace,' he said. He unfastened his cloak and threw it to the floor, and, feet apart, clasped his sword belt in both hands in the traditional stance of defiance. 'In Évreux, which my brother holds at Your Grace's pleasure [a subtle blow of his own], news has reached us of Duke Robert's death . . . I see 'tis so.' He had noted how the archbishop's face whitened at the words, and how instinctively his hand lifted to cross himself.

'If true,' he continued, 'then how is it that we your sons have had no direct confirmation of it from you, but have had to scrape and claw for scraps of news like dogs among the dungheaps?'

His scowl resembled his father's. 'Even now as we rode in we witnessed the departure of the French king's envoys. Surely their being here means a message of the gravest kind?'

The archbishop sighed, sank back into his chair, bided his time.

'And all the city is full of it,' Ralph went on, 'the citizens – cretins that they are – weeping, and calling upon God for help.' He burst out, ''Tis help they'll need in truth with only a bastard brat between them and ruin.'

The archbishop's brows creased. What Ralph said was no more than he himself had said, yet he distrusted his son, or rather he knew him so well that he divined the way his son's thoughts went even before Ralph did himself. That was another cause of quarrel between the two – whereas the archbishop went by stealth, feeling for footholds, his middle son hurled himself impetuously at matters without forethought or discretion.

Ralph warmed to his cause, throwing caution to the winds. 'For you know as well as I, my father, that Duke Robert had little claim to the dukedom in the first place, held the title in defiance of you, even to the besieging of you in your own castle. Why, he sent you into exile. [Another shrewd blow, one he knew would rankle.] His death is but God's confirmation of the illegality of his rule which should never have been allowed in the first place. For after the old duke's death, and the death then of the elder brother, there should have been succession direct.

'Now since the first grandson chose a monastic life, we are the next ranking of the line,' he went on, brutally frank now, straining for acceptance. 'I and my brothers, the oldest grandsons of the dead first duke. And, speaking for the three of us, I say we are agreed to act on this as one.' He drew a breath. 'To wit: that the eldest of us, Richard, is to have Évreux – when in course of time it comes to him – and, when in the same due course your bishopric falls empty, the youngest will have Rouen. Praying God,' he added, in a sardonic aside, 'that that time be lengthy. Then of us three I alone am unprovided for. For what is Gacé? A name only; nothing of value there. And since of all the old duke's grandsons,' he went on, modesty never a drawback, 'I am the most suited to inherit – capable of holding the dukedom intact, commanding more friends and influence – so do my brothers accompany me now to give support.'

The archbishop made a decision, stood up and moved away, his long furred gown sweeping across the rushes that lined the paving stones. 'And all that planned before breakfast?' he said mildly. 'Why child, you must be ravenous.'

He clapped his hands, and when a monk came, bowing, he gave orders for food to be prepared. 'Now then,' the archbishop said, still in that deceptively low voice, as if Ralph de Gacé was but eight years old himself, 'come to the truth. What else have you heard?'

Not only Ralph but his two brothers with him burst out with the other thing that had stirred them to action, namely the rumours of King Henry's secret envoy to Falaise and the imminent departure of the young William, details of which had been imparted by spies they had long had implanted at Falaise.

'By God,' the archbishop gasped, and was so genuinely overcome as to allow himself to sink back into a chair and fan himself with a corner of his gown. 'By God, to think that bitch capable of such deception.'

'Perhaps!' Ralph waved his father's comment aside. 'But how're we to stop her?'

He leaned forward, resting on his sword, the epitome of a Norman warrior. 'She must be stopped, of course,' he said. 'She and her son.' And his brothers nodded in agreement.

The archbishop took a gulp of wine. It wasn't often he was caught off guard. To himself he called Herleve all sorts of names, most too vile for a bishop's lips, conniving harlot being the least of them. Imagine her acting as if butter wouldn't melt in her mouth and then stealing a march on him! If he had been a younger man not all the cares of office would have prevented him from giving chase personally and dragging her and her wretched offspring back where they belonged. He drank, was revived, and sat listening while Ralph eagerly pressed his suit, dismissing other claims contemptuously, asserting his right to control the affairs of state, calling on his father to assert himself. In the duke's absence, wasn't the archbishop named as regent? The archbishop let the words wash over him, all froth and bombast. William out of Normandy, William off to Paris without a word of warning, without so much as a by-your-leave, or request for advice – there his thoughts were focused, there was humiliation at its most virulent. But what Ralph and his brothers were suggesting, what lay behind their ranting, was more than insult; it was treason, foul and rank.

Treason, usurpation, murder perhaps, was what they had in mind; and if not murder, then certainly some sort of confinement such as the young Nicholas had been forced into, or true imprisonment, possibly mutilation, to ensure the child never grew to challenging age . . . The archbishop crossed himself furtively without his sons noticing. Yet the other side of the dilemma – a William freed from the archbishop's domination, escaped to safety in Paris where he would have the king's support, where new alliances, new friendships, would counterbalance the archbishop's prerogative – all that was equally unacceptable. And contrived by a peasant slut without an inkling of the nature of the game she played. Or its consequences! The archbishop had good reason to curse his own shortsightedness, and the folly of his sons.

He hid these cares behind his bland expression, but beneath his downcast look, facts were being weighed and balanced. A little William docile in his care, a little William to mould and foster, while as regent he ruled instead, that was the future he had envisaged. William being a child who might yet not survive childhood, the odds were in the archbishop's favour and gave him power instant and complete. But to have his own son as duke, to have Ralph de Gacé lording it over him, running roughshod through the dukedom like a bull turned loose, the bishop shuddered, seeing disaster whichever way he looked. Yet if William were to be brought back, and that was the essence of the moment, and Ralph turned to that task and no further, there was still a victory to be snatched from defeat.

He cut through his son's discourse. 'Fool,' he said, rising up again to his full height, once more in control, a man of authority. 'Fool, to stand here nattering. Time's a-wasting. Do you ask permission to breathe? Of course we need William. Duke's heir or not, he can't go creeping out of the dukedom like a thief, with his mother's contrivance, as if peasants rule themselves. Of course go after him. But bring him back. Alive,' he added as if an afterthought. 'Dead he's another burden round your necks. For who wants to succeed a martyr? And that's what he will be called if you play him false. Alive, William the Bastard's a nothing, soon to be forgotten when we've done with him.

'The afterwards, that'll be my charge,' he added. 'The present work's yours, my sons. And if in the heat of the moment Herleve gets in a sword's way, well then, as far as I'm concerned, good riddance. . .'

As his sons now gaped at him, his own brutality by its very unexpectedness regaining all the ground he had lost, he pressed home his advantage. 'Quick then, to cut him off. How many men go with him? Did your spies tell you that? [A sneer he couldn't resist.] Even his mother won't leave without escort, but she may now know which men to take and which to leave to guard Falaise. And by which road? Surely not the direct one; they'll avoid Rouen and the Seine but they won't dare stray far for fear of losing precious time. Send then and seek or they'll be out of Normandy while you hesitate.'

It was then that Ralph de Gacé shot his last, most telling, bolt. 'We already know,' he said, 'we had him followed. He has slipped between us, has already crossed the Risle and is heading for the Eure.' And as his father, losing control, stamped and cursed, 'He'll cross somewhere north of Ivry. And at the Eure our men lie waiting in ambush.'

The archbishop's gauge of the ducal party's choice of route, or rather the conditions which would govern that choice, was sound. In normal times, the way to Paris from Falaise would go through Rouen. To avoid land controlled by Rouen or Évreux the little duke must be driven further north or south. Northwards would have hemmed him in against the sea and cut the party off from friends; southwards was further still, and kept them longer at risk. Before they left, Steward Osbern, who knew the region well, had planned a straight line east for Turold to follow; almost insultingly straight, relying on secrecy and speed to make the river crossing into territory owned by the French king, and therefore safe from Norman attack. And taking Osbern's advice, Turold had carefully timed their rate of progress to come upon the ford at daylight, for even at this time of year when rains were few, the river could rise suddenly, and the stony bottom was prone to frequent erosion, making a night-time sally all but impossible.

So far the journey had been uneventful, a succession of calm, halcyon days and cool nights. Turold covered their traces with care, avoiding all the natural places where they might have found shelter as was their due, such as abbeys, monasteries or castles of loyal barons who would be honour-bound to offer hospitality. Instead they bivouacked within the forest, sought lodgings where they could in humble villages, and gathered provisions along the way. As day followed placid day, they moved unopposed across the great wooded plateau of central Normandy and their spirits rose. Even Herleve felt secure enough to let Turold have his way in the matter of daytime travel. She herself would have preferred to move only by night: darkness held no terrors for her. It did, however, complicate the journey, cutting down their rate of progress and in one way making traditional escort more difficult. 'For look you, lady,' Turold had explained patiently, when at first she had remained adamant, 'if the dark hides you from your enemies, it also hides you from your friends. How will your men guard you if you are invisible?'

Added to his good-natured insistence was William's own preference. For as the journey continued so did the boy's spirits rise, and it did his mother good, as it did everyone, to see him forging ahead, his pony jumping every bush and stone in sight (even to his taking a tumble or two in the process): something which would have been impossible except by daylight. That his bodyguard and his uncle Walter were never far from his side, and that the king's messenger and Turold kept pace with William's adventuring were added securities which Herleve could not fault.

'Very well, then,' Herleve had agreed at last, 'we rest this last night. But as we have agreed, we must still cross the river at earliest dawn.' And on her own she had heaved a sigh of relief at the thought that safety was in sight – once across the Eure and out of Normandy they would surely be free from danger. Her prayers to God she kept in hand until that time was assured.

So it was that, on the evening that Ralph de Gacé's messenger came thundering up to where his ambushers were encamped – in a little gorge at the plateau's edge before its descent to the river bank beneath – the duke, his mother and all his party were ensconced in a simple hostelry close by, alongside the path that led across the river towards Dreux and beyond.

The ambushers were mercenaries, hired for this purpose, men without loyalties or faith. The message was simple, in Ralph de Gacé's own choice of words. His father's advice in the matter had been more complicated and therefore rejected out of hand, although Ralph had pretended to accept it as a means of keeping the peace between them. 'Hunt them down,' was what he actually said, 'grant no quarter. Kill the woman and boy, dispose of the bodies and disperse without a trace.'

And in his father's palace, while the archbishop still spoke of an 'afterwards' in which William would have played some part, Ralph and his brothers drank to a success in which there would be no William, no ducal party, and very possibly no archbishop!

They underestimated their father. He had means at his disposal unknown to them; as head of the Church in Normandy he had monks and abbots at his beck and call; systems of communication that were a secret of the Church; influence, as his oldest son used the word, that outweighed all their spies. And he knew his sons and rightly feared their violence. He knew they plotted to kill William; he wanted William alive. And yet if things came to the worst he still wanted a foot in either camp. Therefore the archbishop too undertook to have a message of his own delivered, to warn the ducal party of the attack. He could not stop it, could only hope to mitigate its brutality, and although the message went by devious, underhand means that even his sons would have disdained as being too lowly for their nobleness, at least this method took the taint of treason from him. So it was that on the same evening, a pilgrim – as his sandalled feet and cockle-shelled hat proclaimed – came knocking at the inn door.

The term 'inn' was too grand for such an establishment. Most of the time it was the simple farm its byres and barns declared it to be. Only in the autumn, during the horse fair for which the region was famed, did it open its doors to the many traders who came to buy and sell. The main building was narrow, with a high sloping roof of thatch in which birds had made their nests and upon whose ridge-pole small plants grew like tufts of hair. It was built of rough timber cut from the forest, packed with mud between the beams, and stood at one side of a rectangular courtyard edged with stables and barns. Beyond this inner complex however was a large outer yard, fortified by a high wall and secured by gates. At fair times this outer enclosure was used to pen the animals for trading, but now served the duke's soldiery as a camping place. They at once stopped the pilgrim, and would have sent him about his business as a matter of course had not something he said alerted their captain. He brought the holy man to where Turold was sitting with Hugh in the farmhouse kitchen which, in season, doubled as a dining-room. They were discussing the day's journey and planning the morrow's, but jumped up nervously when the ill-matched pair came in: the captain in all his armour, his coif pulled low over his forehead, his helmet with its nasal piece set firmly on his head; the pilgrim in his tattered old robe belted up so that his dust-caked feet in their worn sandals could be seen. Where the captain was armed with a lance and broad-bladed Norman sword, the pilgrim carried only his water bottle and staff for defence, and his face was meek, his demeanour humble, as becomes a man of God.

'He asks,' the captain's tone was expressionless, although the curl of his lip spoke volumes, 'he asks who be we to turn him away from shelter. "Hospitality's due to all," he said. "But there be others more amenable." And when I asked where: "Camped over yonder," he said, "they fed me well last night." ' And the captain gestured upriver with his thumb while his listeners looked at each other in consternation.

'What others?' they cried in unison, and heard the pilgrim explain again, becoming more and more confused as he talked for, seemingly alarmed now himself, the holy man kept insisting he couldn't tell one armed soldier from another thanks be to God: his life was one of peace, far removed from soldiering and battle. At the end of his mumbling he had revealed enough to put the duke's men at full alert, any troops encamped nearby must be a danger by their very existence.

And all accomplished without mention of the archbishop, his master, or the archbishop's sons! Just as the archbishop had intended. After he had been well rewarded for his pains, the pilgrim disappeared into the darkness to assume another role at another time.

Behind him, in the hostelry, the duke's friends prepared for the worst. They did not immediately warn the lady, as they called Herleve, but let her rest a while. Nor did they disturb her son, although they doubled the watch outside the chamber in the attic space and set bowmen on the barn roofs overlooking the outer yard. By common consent Hugh the Messenger took control. Although younger than Turold, by virtue of his royal office he was deemed of higher status, and being in the king's service was accounted familiar with war in all its aspects. When the guard had been called to arms, when the windows and doors of the farm had been locked and its owners bustled below into the cellars (where, overcome by the greatness of their unexpected 'guests' they squatted among their sacks of grain, terrified at the thought of further trouble), scouts were sent crawling through the rough uplands to locate the camp. The identity of the intruders proved impossible to establish; though the scouts were able to report on their numbers and mustering.

'More than forty mounted knights,' Hugh the Messenger made the count. 'Two to one in their favour. But ours are all chosen men, trained, dedicated: 'twill serve.'

'A hard match,' said Walter, but then he was not used to head-on conflict, and relied more on stealthy tactics, was at home only in covert actions such as outlaws employ.

'They lie in wait.' Hugh was grim. He tightened his belt as he spoke, for it had been loosened while he sat and ate. Now he worked the sword blade to and fro in its scabbard for easy drawing. 'Unnamed men, without device, camped in secret – they can have but one mission. So we plan one in return.'

Walter's eyes sparkled anew at that thought, he liked the idea of trickery. Turold, more cautious, waited to hear further before committing himself.

Hugh's plan was simple. 'Stay put,' he said. 'Pretend to be off guard. Then draw them in. And then, when they are truly on us, attack with arrows from above.

'They must know where we are,' he continued, 'if not in particular at least in general. If tomorrow we go on, they will catch us at the ford. Better they attempt us here than in the open; here we've walls and shelter. And the advantage of surprise.'

'And how draw them in?' Turold was sharp.

'A lure,' Hugh said, 'a lure no ambusher can resist: that while the little duke and his mother lie sleeping, our men carouse out of control, their captains helpless.'

'And who will be the lure?' Turold still sounded doubtful.

'I, I.' Two answered as one, Walter and Hugh contending for the honour. In the end Hugh was chosen. 'For, look you,' he said, 'a king's messenger carries weight. And with all due respect, what should I care for a Norman entourage or its well-being? They'll believe what I tell them.'

He allowed himself a grin. 'That's my profession,' he said. 'One I'm good at.'

After he had had his horse saddled and had struggled into his royal livery with the golden lilies, he rode away, shrugging off all thought of danger. His story was well prepared. He'd over-taken the ducal party by mistake, and had the misfortune to lodge with them until their drunkenness drove him out – swilling cider was not his pleasure; he had left them in disorder not two miles behind.

He'd chosen a slightly circuitous route to as to reach the ambushers' encampment from a different direction, thus distancing himself from the inn; in short, he would give the ambushers all the information they needed without seeming to; a tactic, had he but known it, very similar to the pilgrim's. 'And when my message's done, then look for me again,' he had said to his comrades. Once more he worked his sword blade. 'You may need my help.'

His departure taken, the others prepared quickly. They called in the scouts, and all fell back within the inner quadrangle where they took up defensive positions. The outer yard was virtually abandoned and the wooden gates were locked, though a few men volunteered to keep up the pretence of debauchery while a fire was lit and bedding rolls heaped to give illusion of drunken sleep. All was arranged in fact so that a cursory look would reveal what the attackers would be expecting: an ill-kept watch, a carelessly defended position, a vulnerable target. Within the inner yard, on roofs and rafters, the archers waited and, hidden behind doors among the stacks of hay, the rest of the ducal guards stood mounted and ready.

Herleve had long been awake, startled out of heavy sleep by the sound of footsteps. She had gone immediately to the door of the room where she and William slept, had opened it a crack, a little dagger given her by the duke in her hand. As she peered out two men sprang to attention, and Walter spoke from the shadows.

'Nothing to be alarmed about, sister,' he said, his strong white teeth showing for a moment in the grey dimness, 'nothing but farm rats and the rat-catchers waiting.'

He grinned again, and smote the wall with his broad hand. 'Stout Norman timbers,' he said, 'as strong as any keep. Stay you within, we'll hold you safe.'

'No,' said a muffled but resolute voice behind them. William was also peering out. Like others of his class he slept naked, but he was already struggling into his shirt and, as his curly head emerged, they could see how his eyes blazed, so like his father's that for a moment they were disconcerted, almost expecting to hear Robert's voice. 'No, that's my task,' William said. He held out his hand. 'But I'll need your dagger, *ma mie*,' he said. 'Mine's too blunt for man's work.'

Walter put his arm about William's shoulders and exchanged glances with Turold who had also come up. 'Very good, my lord,' Turold said after a moment. 'Guard you the window to this room. Let no one enter. If you have need of us we are outside.' He took the dagger from Herleve and set it firmly in the boy's hands. 'There my lord,' he said, 'to your charge,' just as if William were a grown man.

Inside the upper chamber, almost too humble a space to merit such a term, two beds had been made up of straw and drawn close together for comfort. At fair time perhaps twenty men would sleep there, crowded in rows like onion sets. Beyond the door a narrow corridor led to a wooden ladder; inside, the room was lit only by a rough opening under the triangular peak of the roof. The walls were high, rough cast, with sharp edges of flint sticking out from among the clay packing between the wood; overhead, black beams projected under the steep, sloping roof. It was the work of a moment for William to jump up on to the bed, scramble up the uneven wall, some ten feet high, then swing himself like a monkey across a beam. And there he perched at the opening, while Herleve begged him to come down.

The opening was rough, wide enough for a man to pass through and, on the outside wall, strengthened by a wooden beam that formed a sill. William leaned out and listened. It was dark but the camp fire in the outer yard gave light enough for him to see the circle of cloaks and blankets under which the troopers would normally have been sleeping, and he could plainly hear the yells and the discordant singing which punctuated the quiet. High up like this, had it been day, he could also have seen over the outer walls and down the valley towards the river Eure, which he knew they had to cross. He had been wondering about that river since he had first heard about it; in his imagination it had grown to a raging torrent, bristling with rocks and edged with cliffs in which great bears and wolves and other wild animals lived. Now it seemed worse enemies than bears or wolves were skulking nearby. He had heard Hugh and the others talking, had put his ear to the cracks in the floorboards and listened while they discussed their chances. He swore to himself; they shan't take me or mother, and he clutched the hilt of the dagger so tightly that it grew slippery with sweat.

As his eyes grew accustomed to the darkness he began to pick out the faint glitter of stars – most masked by clouds, the clearer aspect to the right where perhaps the land opened out into fields, the dark heavy shadows on the barn roof where some of his Norman archers were crouching. Sometimes his quick ears caught a rustle as their feet slipped a little on the thatch, and down in the stables he could hear the stealthy sounds of horses, being saddled perhaps or, more likely, already saddled and being held in check until they were needed. He was just thinking, I wish I could have been there on my pony, when a different sort of sound caught his attention. It came from the outer wall, a kind of clink as if some piece of equipment, armour or sword, had caught against the coving. He held his breath, staring closely until he thought he saw something move. It was barely a stir, a lightening or darkening, he couldn't be sure which, but some change of density, rather than colouring, against the roof-line. A second later, a blink of the eye later, and it was gone; he almost thought he had been mistaken. Yet the very fact that it was gone surely meant that it had been there.

'*Ma mie.*' His whisper was as light as a cobweb: it floated down to where she sat taut and silent beneath him on the little bed. '*Ma mie*, say they are coming, I saw someone on the outer wall.'

And while she departed swiftly to relay the message, he leaned further out along the sill, watching for the next move. He didn't have long to wait. From beyond the outer wall a riot of sound crested towards him; anyone used to horses and battle would have identified it, the familiar massing of a cavalry charge just before it engages. Then there was a swirling, a great thrusting against the gates and they splintered apart like rotten twigs. Through the gap a line of horsemen poured, lances ready to thrust and spike.

By the flickering firelight William counted them as they came, riding in pairs, separating at the entrance to circle the courtyard. As they rode they leaned over their saddles to strike at what they thought were sleeping men. No one moved or struck back; and de Gacé's men reined up, puzzled, shouting now among themselves.

They were armed like William's guards with chain-mail hauberks; their helmets were Norman, pointed, with nasal bars; their steeds were heavy footed and stolid. He thought: they're Norman soldiers riding Norman chargers; Normans who have let themselves be hired. He gripped the hilt of the dagger as realization washed over him. Normans, he was thinking, whose loyalty should belong to me. And then, in a great fit of anger: traitors, bought for money.

Death or victory.

He might have shouted it aloud. On all sides it was taken up by those true to him, as now the attackers wheeled and thrust again about the embers of the fire, finding nothing to fight against except sodden clothes and charred wood. Behind their backs, what was left of the gates swung to, shutting them inside, and from the inner roofs a flight of arrows hissed, clattering against their unslung shields and ringing on the paving stones.

Once, twice, thrice the arrows sped, the courtyard was rimmed with steel. Sparks flew. Horses slipped and fell as their riders were cut down. Those who avoided that rain of death collided with each other, raged against their bad luck as they fought now to escape. Mounted themselves, the Falaise soldiers rode out from their hiding-place and swept into that packed confusion to make an end.

Seeing they were in a trap they had thought to make, the attackers steadied. Rallying themselves they began to fight in earnest; proof, if proof were needed, that they too were professionals. Their leader was a massive man mounted on a tall bay horse; he held it backed against a wall, swung with his sword, and shouted hoarsely to his men to give them heart. He had a guttural way of speaking, loud above the ensuing din, different from any Norman speech. William noted it, as he did the man. It made him lean further out to watch, too far perhaps, for he saw how the knight looked up to mark him, one quick glance. Suddenly frightened, William scrambled back, but did not relinquish his place at the attic opening.

Like the master of a ship, William now watched everything beneath him, enthralled despite himself. The swirl of men and horses, the clash of steel on steel excited him; so much so that he almost forgot what the fighting was about. Each time a horse or rider fell a shout went up and he echoed it; each time a friend was cut down he shivered in sympathy. He tallied numbers; saw how, for every one of his guards downed, three of the enemy fell with him. He marked how gradually the cries diminished as men tired, their energy dulled by constant repetition. Only the knight on the bay horse never seemed to tire, even when all about him had drawn aside and the shouting had dwindled to a mutter. A silence followed in which moans, curses and pleas for help could be heard as the Falaise guards swiftly took charge, surrounding the remaining attackers and herding them like sheep.

A sudden scratching beneath the attic roof made William lean out again. Inches beneath his nose the enemy captain was climbing. He must have reached above his head and, with the help of some piece of timber, heaved himself off his horse, a prodigious stretch for a man fully armed. He was mounting rapidly towards the aperture in which he had spotted William. When he saw him again he grinned and, before the boy could draw back, reached out to grab his arm. 'So little master,' he said in that guttural voice, panting with effort, 'I've got you fast.' And, as William tried to struggle away, 'Hold still, or we'll have you flying like a pigeon without wings.'

Even as he spoke he was swinging himself up higher, feeling for purchase against the outer wall of the chamber, one hand clamped like a vice around William, the other, encumbered with its sword, searching for finger holds. One final heave and he was level with the window ledge, could swing himself up to straddle it, letting William dangle head down across him while he flexed his sword arm and levelled his weapon.

'Here's a snug warren,' he sneered. He ducked his head for a quick look inside where Herleve was making ineffectual efforts to reach William. 'Stand back,' he cried, 'or he goes overboard.' And swinging round he shouted down into the courtyard below. 'Parley, parley! In the name of God, a truce!'

He grasped William more tightly. 'And here's our pardon.'

William was too busy fighting for breath to take in the man's words. Each time the knight's grip tightened he swung to and fro, the world seen upside down. When someone below seized brands from the fire, relit them, held them up high to illuminate the building, the glare was dazzling. It made William close his eyes as he swung in giddy circles. There was a sudden hiss, followed by an angry clamour as the enemy leader was revealed with William in his grasp.

By now the man was angled securely across the window ledge, one leg inside, one out, beyond reach of any weapon except an archer's bow, and as he spoke he hauled William up by the hair to use as a shield.

'Freedom for me and my men,' he cried, 'let us pass. Or I cut your little duke's throat and his peasant mother's with him.' And with deliberate effrontery he mimed the action to suit the words, pulling William back against him and pressing the sword against his neck.

If he thought to frighten William into submission he was mistaken. The touch of steel against William's skin had the opposite effect, made his senses suddenly run cold and deliberate. He wouldn't let himself cry, not even when the man tightened his hold again so that his head was jerked back like a lamb's for the killing. He bit his lips tightly together until they bled, so no sound should escape. Although shivering with fear he forced himself to remain still, rigid with determination. Behind his back he worked his fingers to try and clasp Herleve's little dagger. 'Strike hard,' he heard Turold's voice as if speaking in his ear, 'you have but one chance.'

He could hear real voices now inside the room: his mother's pleading; Walter's angry; Turold's arguing for freeing the prisoners; they must all be crowded within the chamber, but he was too high up for them to reach him.

'They dispute like fishwives,' the captain sneered. He pressed with the sword blade. 'Quick,' he cried, 'we don't like being kept waiting.'

They were the last words he spoke. Lithe as an eel, William twisted, struck with the knife, deliberately aiming sideways where he knew there was a weakness in the armour, beneath the armpit where even the best chain-mail did not always fit, as he'd often heard the Falaise men complain. He thrust so hard that the blow jarred his arm numb, from wrist to shoulder. Even so, that alone might not perhaps have been sufficient, for his opponent was strongly built, a bull of a fellow. But as the man's grip suddenly relaxed William swung round and kicked. The unexpected force of his wiry legs caught the man off balance. The mouth opened to yell, the eyes suddenly glazed and the great bulk tottered for a moment on the window-ledge before slowly toppling forwards, dragging William with it.

The man fell heavily, like a tree cut at the bole. William felt the air rush past him. The ground tipped and heaved. He had just time to think, this is what flying is, before his own air rushed out and everything went black inside.

Chapter 4

It might have been a day, an hour, a second, before William opened his eyes to find his mother and friends bending anxiously over him. 'Praise God,' Turold said, crossing himself devoutly, while Herleve, doubled on her knees, showed her thanks as fervently, rubbing his hands between her own and trying to get him to stretch each leg and arm to prove he was all of a piece. Walter, as became an uncle with uncle's status, pretended to cuff him about the head. 'Trying angel's wings,' he joked, 'afore you need them,' then choked at the implication.

Everything around William seemed immensely large, or immensely small, he couldn't decide which. Only gradually as his vision cleared did things come back into proportion. He was lying on a heap of cloaks, obviously placed there where he had fallen, and although he ached in every joint it was equally obvious he wasn't really hurt, just bruised as if he had been whipped or buffeted. 'That's the worst fall I've ever had,' he thought with some satisfaction, 'worse than from any horse.' An observation echoed by his uncle who now began to berate him soundly for his foolishness at falling in the first place. 'For look you,' Walter said, 'somehow, with God's help, you fell on top. If underneath . . .' and he whistled, jerking his thumb to where close beside William a dark heap lay silent as if it slept, its head twisted at an unnatural angle.

William winced and looked away. Suddenly nothing seemed so amusing. And now as he began to sit upright, various other aspects of the attack, which hitherto he had witnessed from a comforting distance, began to reveal themselves in all their vivid reality. First there was blood, real blood, sticky and evil-smelling: he hadn't counted on that. And real men, dead, with arms or legs cruelly hacked off and heads staved in. And horses running wild with empty saddles and reins dangling, or standing with drooping shoulders, as if themselves defeated. His own soldiers were still spry enough, bustling about with extra weapons, but then the victory was theirs and they could be expected to look cheerful. The defeated were huddled in one corner, pale and tense, nothing cheerful in their countenances, their survival to date of small concern, for they still faced death.

'My lords.' It was the captain of the guard who spoke, he who had first become suspicious of the pilgrim. 'My lords, the prisoners are at hand. We await your pleasure.'

He was addressing Turold and Walter but his regard was fixed on William. Again, suddenly and without warning, William realized he was expected to respond, and he didn't know how to. He looked from one expectant face to the other, then in perplexity to Herleve, still on her knees beside him. She made a little motion with her hand, gave an almost imperceptible shake of her head as if to say, 'Be careful.' He almost heard her voice warning him, as she sometimes did when in his play he became too rough.

'Spare them,' he said. The words sounded right, although the actual saying of them made his head ache. 'But first I'd like to know,' he added in a burst of curiosity, 'who they serve, and who was their captain on the bay horse. And,' another thought that surprised him, 'I'll keep the horse.'

The captain nodded his head, too, and strode off, stern-faced. William couldn't decide whether his expression showed pleasure or regret and when he glanced quickly at the men around him their faces were equally neutral. Only his mother gripped his arm as if to say, 'Well done.' And with that he had to be content.

A while passed before he felt strong enough to stand up. When he did it was almost day. He would see all too clearly now. The dead bodies had been dragged into one great pile – at least the bodies of the enemy – and the peasant owners of the farm, released from the cellars, were stripping them hastily prior to burying them. Those few of his men who had died had been wrapped in their cloaks and a priest conjured up from some local church to pray over them. The wounded lay in the barn. At Turold's suggestion William visited them, thanking them as he had been taught, although mere thanks seemed a small return for all their suffering.

'My lord,' the captain of the guard spoke up, 'Here is the bay you asked about.' He ran a knowing hand down its sides, feeling for injury. 'A good mount,' he added.

William looked from the captain to the horse. It towered over them, wicked-eyed, large-hooved, its muscles rippling, a real battle charger, worth a ransom. 'Then you shall have him,' William said on that same impulse which seemed to be governing all his actions. 'Keep him safe for another day. He's yet too big for me.' And when the captain's face was suddenly wreathed in smiles and a cheer broke out from the listening men, he was again surprised that a second time he must have made the right answer.

'A Flemish horse,' Turold said knowingly, and the others nodded in agreement. 'And a Lowlander who rode him, by the looks of him and his manner of speaking. But who the others are, and who had the hiring of them, not one will speak.'

'I think my lord.' the captain said, 'they who planned this evil were clever. These poor devils were hired without understanding the whys and wherefores of what they were to do. All they knew was that they should do as their leader bid them. But I have noted when they speak among themselves they use expressions common to the eastern regions of the dukedom; and one cried out, when he heard of the mercy shown to him, that God be thanked he'd be spared to see his wife again in Huest without a mark on him. Huest's in Évreux country.'

William watched his companions digest the news in silence. Its exact importance somehow escaped him but he knew that Évreux was important. He thought, what did my father do when deputations came to him, and frowned himself, trying to remember.

'Before they go,' he said, 'I'll have them swear themselves loyal to me and my duchy,' And again noted how those around him looked on approvingly as if he had spoken what they themselves wished, without their prompting.

During the rest of the day however things did not go as easily. His head still ached and the adventures of the previous night had left him tired and cranky. If he thought to profit by his cleverness, William was soon cut down to size; even Herleve grew tired of his boasting. 'You had no right to crawl up on that sill,' was all she said. So much for his claim that he was protecting her. Yet he had been: they had given him the dagger, and he had accepted it with that very intent in mind. But, he admitted as they rode along, there had been other things that had equally attracted him, things that even though he couldn't put a name to them made his heart pound and his blood race; things he had felt when he saw the enemy stream through the gates. They had made him clasp the dagger hilt, had made him stand up and shout. Even now, despite all that had happened, the excitement still glowed. But underneath the heady thrill there had also been other feelings, not so pleasant. When he closed his eyes he could still hear that thick voice and feel the squeeze of those muscular arms. The enemy captain had hated him although William had done him no wrong; would have snapped his neck as easily as a twig, would have smiled as he did so! And the look in the wounded men's eyes, even the line of defeated prisoners, revealed another side of war: dejection, shame and fear. The bowed heads and low frightened voices stank of terror: he could smell it on them like carrion. He thought, war's not so bad as long as you win, and that too was a thought for remembering.

But there was one last experience to be known. And that as well would be full of dread mingled with grieving.

As soon as the oath-swearing was done the prisoners had been set free to find their own way back home on foot. Their weapons had been confiscated, as had their horses, to be used now as pack animals; their armour had been divided among the Falaise guards, booty of war for the sharing.

At first light the ducal cortège had set out towards the river ford. The day promised fair, like other days; the river ran its normal course, not too high, not low; the current would be neither swift nor slow, their passage ordinary. They rode in line, William and Herleve in their midst, making no secret now of their intent to cross from Normandy into France as fast as they could. At the river bank the foremost guards reined back, causing those behind to jostle them. A cry broke out, spread, a cry of disbelief and horror. The captain came spurring back, 'Turn round,' he cried, 'shield the sight.' He was too late. William had already seen what he would never forget.

Where the path came down to the ford the trees lined the river banks, making a kind of arch. On the last tree a shape hung. Mud-smeared, its throat cut, it lolled there like a piece of beef, hung from a branch with its royal coat slung round its back, the lilies hacked and stained: all that was left of Hugh the Messenger with his merry laugh and his disregard for danger.

'By God,' swore Turold as they cut the body down, 'had I known . . . I'd have killed them, every one.' The others swore the same. William turned his face away. He did not cry but great shudders shook him from head to toe. This too would be a lesson which would not fade: even in his dreams he would see it, how even the bravest of the brave, the most gallant, the most cheerful, can still hang dead; God has no more pity on them.

Hugh's death long had its effect on him. William knew Hugh had a wife and sons of his own; sometimes he had spoken of them. Half envious, he had listened to stories of their pranks: how one had huddled beneath his father's shield, how another had fallen in a well and clung to an ivy vine until he was rescued; they too had become his friends in the days he had spent in Hugh's company, and he had felt how lucky the boys were still to have a father. Now in his dreams he saw their faces bathed in tears as his had been, and their grief mingled with his own until, when he woke, he was not sure who wept for whom, nor whose father it was who had dangled there, all life and laughter leached out of him. But he never cried out at these nightmares; he learned to hide them as he was learning to hide all his thoughts and feelings.

Once across the river, the route ran straight towards Paris. Here, outside Normandy, they had hoped to travel in better style, had counted on the king's messenger paving the way for them. His death dampened their enthusiasm and, lessening their victory, made it seem almost tawdry. Out of respect they still kept to themselves, sought shelter in the most humble of places and continued to travel in closest secrecy, scarcely giving themselves time to marvel at the things they passed. In this way they circumvented the holy city of Chartres and, swinging east, came directly to the capital. And whereas they had been relying on Hugh to ease their entrance into the city, when they reached it they had to fend for themselves.

Outwardly they made a brave show as they came through the main gates at a trot, heads high, banners flying, as befitting a noble escort, their little duke cantering on his pony in their midst. The people in the streets, accustomed to such martial progresses and thus presumably immune to them, were forced to stop and stare. They noted the child with his bright hair and bright face, were startled by the piercing gaze fixed at some point above their heads, were amused by his horsemanship, his holding himself as if he rode a stallion. If they noted the woman at the rear, they would have passed her over as of no account. Face shrouded in a cloak, head bowed, Herleve was already effacing herself as she had learnt long ago to do in equally hard and bitter times.

Although he stared between his pony's ears, too proud to show his curiosity, nevertheless William was curious, and when he had a chance he stole interested glances at all he passed. Ever since Turold had spoken so animatedly about this city he had wanted to see if the older man told the truth. He noticed first the lines of walls, triple built, and the huge entrances cut in their depths, hung with massive, iron-studded gates where cautious guards peered out before issuing a challenge. In spite of his promise to himself not to be impressed, he marvelled – as who could not – at the height of those walls, the thickness of their stones, the strength of their gates. To think that once the French king had been too afraid to trust to them when Rollo the Viking came a-visiting! The narrow paved streets twisted snake-like round these walls, tempting him with their maze of stalls where all kinds of marvels hung and where people bought, sold and traded in a swirl of tongues. Bolts of silk, daggers, swords, even a coat of ring-mail like the one he had been promised filled one street completely; another narrow lane was hung with caged birds that chirped and sang: all caught his gaze, for a moment in sharp relief like a line of images overshadowed by other pictures, equally vivid. There was a constant hum of sound, of people talking, laughing, arguing. Men at arms clanked along, their swords dragging; mounted men urged horses forward, angling for space where the press of bodies was less thick. Nor did pedestrians immediately leap out of the way as peasants did at home. Pretty girls flounced their skirts and tossed their heads at the soldiers; ladies glided past, eyes modestly downcast, hands pressed about their psalters. Dark cowled monks slid by in twos and threes; black robed priests gossiped; young gallants swaggered. All the while, in the background, bells rang from what might have been a hundred churches, and equally a hundred smells assailed the nose with odours both pleasant and disgusting – the smell of fresh baked gingerbread and roasted goose vying with that of too-old fish and too-fresh sewage.

This teeming life, this noisy, vibrant life, seemed to have no connection with the world as William knew it. And these city folk were as unusual. They served no lord, Turold said, were not peasants to work the land, were neither shepherds nor swineherds or such; rather they were craftsmen who lived by trade. 'Like Grandfather Fulbert,' William thought, although Turold had been too tactful to point that out.

William knew a trader's life was less than a knight's; was nothing compared with a great lord's who controlled many knights and owned many acres of land. And yet, for all that, these Paris houses were made of stone and their inhabitants wore rich clothes, almost as rich as his and just as brightly coloured.

And the source of all that trade, the means by which the traders made their wealth was the mighty river which Turold had described. In truth it did gird the city round like an extra wall. From time to time as William rode along he caught glimpses of it through the trees and stunted bushes which in places lined its banks.

'The Seine is the life force of Paris,' Turold reminded him. 'It is the thread that binds the country. It brings the ships in from the sea. Wherever it goes it carries wealth and power; whoever controls it controls France, for its tributaries spread deep into the land like nettle roots.'

One day, William thought to himself, I shall control it. One day I shall be powerful as a king myself. And the thought cheered him as they rode deeper and deeper into the labyrinth of streets towards a real king's palace.

His sense of confidence did not last long, only long enough to take him to the palace walls. These walls too were thick, and black-encrusted with age. They reminded William of rocks along the seashore where water drips and barnacles grow below the high water mark. There was the same sort of wet smell, but here full of mould without the clean tang of salt to freshen it. As he passed under the first gateway the contrast with the outside light, already fading into dusk and at best fitful in those layers of streets, nevertheless made the blackness inside seem as heavy as iron. The gates themselves had bars as thick as those which hemmed in the dungeons at Falaise. When they clanged shut with an equally hollow ring, William thought, this is what prison is, and panic made him duck, causing his pony to shy and dig in its heels.

That momentary sign of weakness embarrassed him into paralysis. his mouth was dry yet sweat beaded his hair; he was incapable of movement and had not Walter's equally instinctive flinch and an accompanying sheepish grin steadied him, he might have shamed himself by crying. Walter's rueful wink confirmed that his uncle had felt the same sense of constraint. 'We're in for it, no mistake,' that wink said, 'no back stepping. So head high, forward, *mon brave*. Trust to God.'

Gripping his reins tight, thrusting for his stirrups where the pony's jump had unsettled them, William straightened up, acknowledged the wink with a flick of his own eye. Out thrust his chin, as arrogant as his father's had he but known it, and his blue eyes narrowed; he dug in his spurs and pranced into the royal court like a prince of the blood.

The business of arrival was as complicated as Herleve had foreseen. She herself dismounted swiftly, was greeted by some tire-woman, and passed into the corridors out of sight, a slight, bowed figure hidden beneath her enveloping cloak. but from an embrasure high above she paused to watch her son. She saw how he was forced to remain in the saddle without fidgeting. Showing no signs of fatigue as so young a child might well have done, arms crossed on the saddle prow, he listened with the courtesy his father had taught him. Herleve marked how the heralds blew and men clashed to attention and court officials in royal surcoats recited lengthy and incomprehensible greetings. She sighed. It was what she had hoped for. And with Turold at William's side

49

to acknowledge royal favour on his young lord's behalf, and with Walter to act in place of parent, nothing but good could come of this desperate venture. But oh, she thought, that we were all safely back at Falaise and things were as they once were; then we'd have no need of all this ceremony.

She wiped her eyes, passed on into the obscurity she had deliberately chosen, missing William's last gesture of courtesy, an instinctive grasp of protocol, though Walter was to tell her of it later. When at last all were free to dismount, her son escaped from Turold's grasp and although in truth by this time faint with hunger and thirst and having a dire need to relieve himself, nevertheless he went first to his men who were as wearily swinging themselves off their horses.

'My thanks, good sirs,' he said with the little bow that Herleve had taught him. 'And when we are all safe home again, then shall you know my gratitude.'

He left them smiling after him, jesting among themselves at the gravity of his remarks which were more suited to men thrice his size and years. In good humour that their journey was done they raised up a cheer. And that night while they dossed down with the others of their like among the French king's guard, glad of a proper night's lodging at last, they were not slow to boast of their little duke's prowess with a weapon, nor to swear to prophecies that once had been spoken of him. These they but hinted at, cautious where they were and to whom they spoke and not willing to spread rumours blatantly. In that they were wise. Nevertheless the hints were noted. They were recorded and in time were carried to the king. So that later, when they were spoken of again, the effect they had on King Henry was perhaps greater that it should have been, appearing more threatening in the hidden meaning than the actual prophecy itself.

As for the nature of the prophecy, William himself remained ignorant of it, for Herleve would not speak of it, and in Falaise no one boasted of what was common knowledge. Now, by a strange twist of chance, William was to learn of it almost at the same time as the king. And its effect on him was of equal importance although felt in a different fashion.

The way this came about was simple, growing as all revelations should do from natural causes. Because of his youth William was spared the obligatory formal audience that first evening, and allowed to go straight to bed where he promptly fell into a sleep so deep that there was no place for dreaming. He awoke in the middle of the night to find the moonlight pouring on his face through an open aperture, and to hear his uncle's soft snoring by his side. He sat up with a start. His first conscious thought was of Herleve. Since the start of the journey they had never slept apart, and he had been her near constant companion since his father's leaving. Never in his life had he slept without knowing where she was or how he might find her. Now she was closeted somewhere in the depths of this great fortress and he had no idea where to begin his search. Moreover she had warned him not to try, had told him to be brave and do without her. He gritted his teeth and, careful not to wake Walter, slid out of bed.

The chamber was larger than he had ever known, bigger by far than the little room his parents shared at Falaise, so that for a moment he was daunted by the vastness of it. Then he stole to the window and looked out.

The walls gave on to the Seine, straight down. A hundred, two hundred feet below the water gleamed. Overhead swung the harvest moon, as round and full as at Falaise, and on the crenellated battlements on either side he could hear the steady tramp of feet and the muttered challenge and response of the guard, just as at home. Overcome with longing for the familiar he did not stir or speak when Walter came up and put a cloak around him.

Walter did not say anything either, but stood gazing up at the moon as if he saw beyond it all the way back to the Eure. His stocky body was covered with a shirt which smelled not unagreeably of sweat and horse, and when he stretched William felt the slight shiver of cold. It reminded him of Walter's wink as they had passed under the gates. For the first time it occurred to William that he did not really know his uncle well, that until this journey they had seldom had converse together, although he knew of course that his mother favoured her brother and relied upon him. Under cover of the dimness William regarded Walter carefully. It came to him that perhaps if Walter had held back from visiting Falaise this was, by his own choice; that he might sometimes have felt as out of place there as William now felt here. He considered. He knew for example that Walter did not ride well, at least not as gracefully as a knight trained from childhood; yet recently he had seen Walter fight and ride as a true warrior. And there was a feel about him, a sense of honesty that made you want to trust him. He drew a breath, took a chance.

'Do you think,' he said, for it had been troubling him, 'that we do well to be here, so far from Normandy? And do you think they will let me go when we are finished? I do not care for myself, or . . .' he hesitated, was truthful, 'I do care, but I care as much for my mother's sake, and yours and Turold's. We are all Normans. Normandy is where we belong.'

Walter was slow in replying. 'Well nephew,' he said somewhat shyly, 'you know perhaps how I spent my youth, far from men as a rebel and an outcast. My older brother was outlawed with me, and came so to like his outlawed state that I think he preferred it to any other. But I was different. I cared for my village and family, hoped always to take my wife and children back to where I was born. So they say are some fish of the sea, such as eels or great salmon which, although they swim to the world's edge, nevertheless turn and come home again to the very pool and stream where they themselves were spawned. I think, nephew, in your case, it is the same for you. And it is right and proper for you to feel the way you do, and to hold to your right. For God knows my needs are small and I am not Fulbert, your grandfather, to predict what the great should or ought to do in such and such a case. But this I do swear to.'

He leaned forward. 'Long before you were born,' he said, and William noted now his eyes shone, 'an old woman lived in Falaise. Some called her witch and devil-cursed, but though I am a Christian baptized and believe in God, yet once I heard her speak. She spoke in Norse, our former tongue, and her prediction in part was a curse against those of us who had forgotten our old ways and gods. She prophesied thus.'

He hesitated, licked his lips, his voice deepening as if he spoke from memory. 'Out of our peasantry shall a leader come,' he said, 'out of old blood a new Rollo to conquer new lands and make them his.'

William wanted to ask, 'What has this to do with me?' but the question froze on his lips. Something was thudding in his head, louder than that thudding he had felt when he leaned over the sill above the farm courtyard; something hot was running in his blood, so hot it drained the rest of him cold.

'Before you were born,' Walter continued as deliberately, his eyes still shining in the silver light, 'Herleve had a dream. Oh, they say all women do, and when my son was born my wife had dreams. But not like this. Herleve dreamt that from her sprang a great oak tree, greater than any in this land, and from its roots there climbed a child crowned with oak leaves. In his hand he held a sword with which to beat the branches aside. And as he climbed, behold, the tree was turned into a boat as in Viking days, with its striped sails spread, and the oak chaplet on his head glinted with gold, and from many mouths there rang a cry. "Hail to the Conqueror," they said.'

He took William by the shoulder, turned him round. 'My lord,' he said, 'for my sister's sake, for your father's love he showed to me, I am sworn to be your man, albeit as a peasant and one-time outlaw I am accounted nought and without honour to swear or be forsworn. Yet because of that prophecy and dream there need be no oath or swearing between us for we are bound stronger than this world knows, with or without our will. And so, though I am a Christian, my oath, such as it is, is sworn by the ancient gods, by Thor and Woden and the old gods of war that my father still believes in and by whose help we gained Normandy. Under their favour, and with God's Christian grace, I think one day you shall return to Normandy and conquer greater lands than are yet dreamed of.'

And he knelt there in the moonlight and wrapped his strong, workman's hands about William's smaller childlike ones. 'So is it done,' he said. And William felt the power of the moment pass between them; for that moment he stepped out of time. And the light of the moon and the cry of the sea were in his blood and he knew without being told that this oath-swearing stood in higher stead than any other he was obliged to make to any king in any court. And of all the events on the road to Paris and since their arrival here, this last was the most to be remembered.

Nevertheless, because he was brought here to Paris with a special purpose in mind, and because he had no way to turn his back upon the protection of his temporal overlord, when day came and he was brought to do obeisance to the French king, William submitted with grace and with a gravity that again made him seem older than his years. He went through the ritual without mistake, kneeling before the king and uttering the usual words of faith and loyalty. Only when he spoke of the king's part in return, that is, the king's duty to protect the dukedom of Normandy and acknowledge William as its new duke, did he falter for a moment, then steady himself and continue without hesitation to the end, stronger than in the beginning. And when it was done, even though Herleve was not present to give her little nod of approval, both Turold and Walter did so in her stead, letting him know he had acquitted himself with honour.

The court was captivated. King Henry, still pleased with himself at his unexpected chivalry (and not yet having heard of the Normans' boasts), listened to the child's clear words with a smile almost bordering on complacency, as a man might who sees a favourite pet display its favourite trick. And when the child was finished, Henry himself stepped down from the dais where he sat and raised William up. *'Bien fait, mon petit,'* he said, 'spoken well. Your father would be pleased with you.'

He looked William up and down, holding him at arm's length. 'You've grown,' he said, 'since last we met. And is your mother come with you?'

He turned to his other courtiers. 'This young man and his mother did me proud,' he said, 'when I was driven out into Normandy. So do we tender them all honour in their stay with us.'

His courtiers shuffled: those who had not supported him but sided with his queenly mother were ill at ease; those who had gone into exile with him were fawning in their desire to equal his respect. Henry, well aware of the effect of his words, sat back on his throne and enjoyed himself, satisfied he had done his best for his visitors. But that was before he had heard of the prophecy.

Chapter 5

The way the news of the Norman prediction came to the king was round-about, and dubious, in that the teller of it had reasons of his own to lie. Later there were claims that the king had always been suspicious, had heard rumours about a prophecy when he had been in the Norman court, had in fact offered William succour for the very purpose of securing control over him. His excuse of repaying Duke Robert's kindness was seen as a ruse to persuade the young duke's followers, against their better judgement, to trust the king and bring William where Henry could keep his eyes on him. The truth probably lay somewhere between the two. But the actual revelation evolved from what was really a boyish quarrel, blown up from air as such things usually are, and had nothing to do with politics.

The original cause of the dispute stemmed from the notice shown the little duke. While the older courtiers fawned, or pretended to, William was established as a firm favourite. But there were others, mostly younger men and boys, who hid jealously beneath their smiles. Aware of that possibility, at first Turold had judged it wise not to bring William much on view. But sometimes he was forced to do so: when the king commanded, for instance, or when some affair of state would make the little duke's deliberate absence from the great hall where the lords and ladies of France paraded too obvious. At such times William would be instructed to be silent, to smile or bow as Turold gave him sign, to leave all the talking to his councillor. William was more than happy to obey, overwhelmed by the attention. And for his part the only time he was ever at ease in the king's court was when a special feast took place where at the king's summons some minstrel would sing. Then he paid close attention, listening to every word. No one could have known that secretly he was comparing the singer to his mother and remembering how Herleve used to sing for him when they were alone. Herleve's voice was low, sweet, slightly out of tune; his father used to say it reminded him of water flowing over pebbles, or breezes in the high beech trees. To William's ears it was better by far than these famed minstrels who sang of war and fighting and death, although had the time been normal and he still at Falaise stories of such adventures would have thrilled him to the core.

By now the death of Hugh the Messenger had been reported, and while men looked grim at the news of ambush on the royal borders, and wondered aloud at the attackers (for Turold was too wise to hint that Normans were behind the attack or even to admit to a suggestion of unrest in Normandy), the ladies made much of William and marvelled at his part. Which equally in due course had become common knowledge and was greatly misrepresented.

William himself acted modestly to avoid causing offence. Where once he might have enjoyed such fame, now, mindful of his mother's disapproval, he said little, but he could not stop the ladies' talk, and their exaggeration troubled him. He wanted to explain he had not really charged into the fight upon a great bay horse, nor drawn a sword – but to be armed with a little knife and hung upside down now seemed puny by comparison! Even his modesty did not spare him, that too was praised; the ladies flocked to pet him as if he were in truth a Norman wolfling, a cublet without its teeth. And if perhaps their flattery tempted him it was only that their soft voices and winning ways reminded him of his mother and to some extent filled his need for her. The ladies' attention did not please William's contemporaries. They scorned it. Some came to hate him for becoming a favourite and supplanting them. So when a chance arose to cut the interloper down to size they seized it.

Turold had tried to keep William out of sight, kept him penned up indeed as if he were a prisoner. All this William might have borne – if there had been some end to the imprisonment in sight, or if he could have sometimes seen his mother. But despite the king's seemingly gracious mien, Herleve remained firm in her decision to remain aloof from court life. True, using Walter as envoy she often sent messages and gifts to William – new shirts; new hose to replace the ones he tore so frequently – but that was not the same as bringing them herself, and as Yuletide approached, in Falaise a season noted for its mirth and jollity, William felt a great darkness descending on him as if he were being plunged into a hole, like the dark pit of the nights when he lay wakeful, thinking of the past and longing for Herleve's return as he had once longed for his father's.

Turold could not fail to notice William's forlorn state, and out of pity was forced gradually to relax his hold. He told himself such melancholy was not good for a child, remembering William's sad decline after the news of his father's death. 'Take him into the stables and guardrooms,' at last he ordered, 'let him wander there as he will.' And so with Walter for companion and two stout bodyguards, William was finally given the run of the fortress.

As the months passed, came to spring, summer, another autumn and winter, he was at least free to visit his own men, listen to their talk, watch their activities with avid curiosity. He saw how they cared for their mounts, their most valued possessions, how they cleaned and cared for their tack, how they polished and sharpened their weapons. To Turold, these expeditions provided fresh air and exercise, meant William had something to occupy his time, and within the confines of the royal household he was not likely to come to harm. He had no inkling of the treacherous purposes that would be attributed to these moments of freedom when a jealous king heard of them. Or how William's younger rivals might make use of them.

Tiring of his own men's quarters, William took to investigating the royal stables and guardrooms where he became a frequent if critical visitor. 'The French king has more guardsmen than we do in Normandy,' William confided to Walter at the end of one of these unofficial tours, 'but my father kept ours better armed. Imagine!' His eyes grew round. 'Here are rooms full of weapons never cleaned! They are so rust-thick I swear 'twould take two men to lift them.'

He was sitting with Walter in a favourite place, which he had found behind one of the towers, with a clear view of the courtyard so that no one could creep up unawares. Perhaps it was thinking of home that made the two unusually careless, for hitherto they had kept a close watch on their tongues, as Turold had insisted. Or perhaps the wind caught William's words and his high, still-childlike voice carried further than usual. In any event, his comments were louder than was wise.

'And our horses are better groomed,' he went on. 'Look. My father would never have permitted such carelessness.'

He pointed to a large black that was being brought out. Specks of mud still clung to its hooves and its tail was matted. Its owner, a tall, dark-haired boy of near knighting age, swung round and scowled. Then, attempting a display of horsemanship, he leapt on his horse without using the stirrup iron – or tried to. At the crucial moment the horse moved and left him floundering, half on the saddle, half off.

William laughed, his clear child's laugh full of mirth, without malice. 'That's hard to do,' he said. 'But you know, uncle, my father could, with all his armour on. It depends where you put the weight, or so Turold says.' And with a stick he began to draw a picture in the dirt to show Walter what he meant. A shadow fell across the place and he looked up.

The other boy was glowering down at him, his round face flushed with mortification, staining his white skin red. Close to he was not so old as he had first seemed, although much taller and broader than William, and he was angry. 'As your *dukeship* wishes,' he sneered the title, 'perhaps your *dukeship* will demonstrate. If your bodyguard will let you, that is, without doing it for you.'

His scowl took in Walter and the two Falaise guards who had immediately closed the gap between them and their charge and stood at the ready to protect their lord from this angry young man. He stepped back to give them room, perhaps not liking their drawn swords so close, and let his lip curl disdainfully. The flush had faded but left behind angry weals along both cheeks and his black hair had matted down in curls across his head like a bull's.

'Although perhaps I do them wrong,' he continued in the same heavy voice. 'Perhaps your dukeship prefers talk to deeds. Ladies' talk,' he added deliberately, 'but then perhaps your dukeship has not met ladies either before this. Real ladies, I mean.'

William looked from the youth to Walter, perplexed. 'Sir,' he said, beginning to jump up but Walter pulled him down. 'The duke meant no harm,' Walter spoke for him. ''Twas but child's folly.'

The boy laughed, a cold, sneering, laugh. 'Then keep the bastard in the tannery where he belongs,' he said, 'not flaunting himself above his station, aping his betters.'

Brushing himself down so that the mud flaked off on to William, he strode away, bellowed at a groomsman to hold his horse, heaved himself on in bad humour and whipped it from the yard, the blows falling indiscriminately upon man and beast.

'Walter,' William said, low-voiced, 'why did he speak so? And why did you answer him?'

'My lord,' Walter stammered, as if not sure what to say, 'my lord, better not to ask. Keep out of his way. 'Twas not wise to anger him.'

'He angered me.' William's answer was bleak. 'He meant to insult.'

He looked from Walter to his two guardsmen and back. 'He put me in the wrong,' he said. 'And so did you.'

That was the beginning of the quarrel. From such small starts come great conclusions. Henceforth William knew himself disliked. Whenever he now ventured out of his chamber there would be someone loitering in the shadows, not an assassin with a sword to be sure, but a boy, a squire or page of the royal household, armed with a tongue and a ready wit at William's expense. The taunts were made under the breath, not loud enough to hear, a hiss like the wind, but William understood them, and the laughter was sharp. Walter urged him to pay no heed and in the beginning dutifully William obeyed. The sneers stung all the more because he still did not know the cause and was yet unused to them.

One day he found a straw figure by his bed, more than likely placed there by one of the palace servitors. William was too proud to mention it and hid the thing before any could see it. It was a mockery of a figure, a peg doll dressed in skins, mounted on what must be a mule, with a painted wooden scrap meant for a shield and a thick red line scratched across it: the bar sinister of bastardy.

He sat down to think. Until then he had not met unkindness in anyone he knew; but then, he thought, neither had I met any who wished my death until my father died. It suddenly seemed important that he resolve this matter and alone, without the knowledge or help of any of his retinue. And although he understood very well the reasons for Turold's tight control of his movements, nevertheless he resolved to disregard his instructions.

Until now he had been careful not to go anywhere or do anything that his councillor would not approve, but had he chosen he could easily have given his guardsmen the slip, albeit he would have been unlikely to have had a second chance. Now he took the risk. That same afternoon, when Walter was leaning over a table engrossed in mending a sword-belt (for like Fulbert Walter was good with leather and disliked idleness), William gauged the distance to the door. He knew his guards were outside, but they had just dined, would be sleepy in the post-noon sun. He tiptoed to the entrance, listened. In his belt hung the little dagger, his father's gift to his mother which his mother had in turn given to him, and he fingered the hilt as he grasped the iron handle and eased the door open a crack.

As he had thought, the two guards were leaning back against the wall, their spears at rest. He eyed them, eyed the length of the hall. At one end, just before the main staircase, he had spotted a small embrasure which he knew contained another staircase cut into the thickness of the stones at an earlier stage, a curling spiral stair, which he guessed must lead to an inner yard. If he could reach it before he was caught he would have the advantage of quick descent by virtue of his smaller size, and once in the yard there were surely fifty places for a boy to hide.

He looked back, looked out. Walter worked on unperturbed; the guards chatted softly, companionably. With a faint air of guilt, for he did not like to contemplate the disturbance he would cause, he slowly detached from his inner tunic a heap of pebbles gathered over the past few days for this purpose, then with a jerk tossed them across the floor away from the staircase. They rattled along the paving like hailstones.

The guards jumped up, stepped from the door. Swift as a fox he was out through the gap and along the hall before they could stop him. He heard their shout, the thud of their boots, felt the grasp of their hands just before he ducked into the narrow stairwell. Down he went, half on his back, slipping eel-like down the stairs which their spurred feet had more difficulty in coping with. He reached the courtyard as he had hoped, with time to spare; slid into a second narrow archway out of sight, and was gone up more stairs and along a second corridor before he stopped for breath.

He considered then. It seemed to him it did not matter where he went as long as he found what he was looking for before he himself was discovered. And so, pausing now and then to get his bearings right, he moved swiftly by instinct, along and down the many levels of the fortress towards the main courtyard where he was certain the person he was wanting would most likely be found. Or where the boy's friends would be who would send him word.

When he emerged at last where he had planned, the courtyard was more crowded than usual, some formal exodus having just taken place which had brought most of the court to watch. And there by the back wall, sitting on its edge, where by long custom they had established right of occupancy, were the royal squires and pages watching too, a bevy of them, just as he had hoped.

He made no attempt now to conceal himself – had in fact donned his best tunic with the gold embroidery the better to be seen – and clasped the little dagger hilt, hand on hips. That they were surprised to see him he judged by their start and the ripple of interest. He gave a quick look round. No sign yet of Walter and his companions, but there was no time to waste. There might be other Falaise guardsmen in the yard and, God forbid, Turold himself might be in attendance. William straightened his back, threw out his chest and, although his knees were trembling, stepped out with as good a swagger as he could muster to prove he was alone, then melted back into the shadows. Behind him he felt the stir of the crowd as the other boys swarmed after him.

When he was sure of them he stopped and turned to face them, hand still on hip. He had brought them into another empty passageway which led towards the outer battlements. From time to time a soldier passed, intent about his own business. No one here would take notice of a small group of boys.

'Well,' William said, 'I think you have been waiting to tell me a thing. Here I am.'

Despite himself, his voice came out child-bright. As the pack advanced upon him he noticed how tall and big they were, almost men, some dozen of them. But he wouldn't let that trouble him. They would have ringed him round had he not found a wall to back against. He leaned on the stones almost nonchalantly. It was up to them now; he had done his part.

They circled warily, nudging themselves. They were waiting too, he thought, and he waited with them until there was another commotion and their ranks parted to let someone through. As he had expected, it was the horseman.

They called him Guy, crowding round him eagerly to explain. 'My lord Guy . . . my lord . . .' A young man of substance then, of noble birth. His dark hair was sleek today, and his face was pale but round, with small, oval-shaped black eyes and a sharp nose. 'Well, well, indeed,' he said, in the thick voice William remembered, 'on its own the cub comes out.'

He wheeled round on his heel, suddenly tense. 'Alone?' he asked, and when they all swore so, 'That was foolish done,' he said.

He came up close to William. 'What,' he sneered, 'all dressed in its little finery and nowhere to go? No sword three cubits long, no horse of monstrous size? By St Denis I vow the bastard's armed with nothing but a stickpin. So bastard,' he went on, with each word closing the gap between them, 'what have you to say for yourself?'

'Nothing,' William said. 'Or, if you will, only that I did you wrong. 'Twas ill-done to laugh when you fell from your horse. But you have done me worse wrong, as you do so now. And I am come to pardon you. Or, if you prefer, make you ask the pardon.'

The last words came out suddenly, quick, a snarl. They made some of the younger boys shift and whisper among themselves. Even the one they called Guy stopped in his tracks. Then he too began to laugh – not a pleasant laugh – and a streak of dark crimson spread up from his neck.

'By the bones of Christ,' he swore, 'by St Denis, the bastard stings. Whence came that little temper flourish? Not from its father, I'll be bound, perhaps from its dam. They say she whines.'

He grinned. 'They say the dukeling hides behind her skirts,' he said, 'a peasant whore. Run home to her, bastard, she saves your skin. No lord of note will fight with you.'

He wrinkled his nose exaggeratedly, 'You smell too strong of hide.'

He said no more. Head lowered like a ram's, William rushed from the shelter of the wall to catch the older boy around the waist, doubling him up on the floor and knocking the breath out of him. For a moment they lay there together in the dirt, then William heaved himself up first. 'Call me what you want,' he told the motionless figure, 'but who wrongs my mother, by the gods of my forefathers, Dukes of Normandy all, I swear he pays.'

He spoke so fiercely, with such sharp intent, his eyes blazing so blue, that the other boys began to back off in earnest, some urging the others to retreat while there was time; some, with perhaps more grace, calling that it had been ill-done to make mock of the duke, a few perhaps genuinely ashamed of their jeering. Guy rose to his knees, shook his head like a downed bull and lumbered to his feet. 'By God, tanner's get,' he wheezed, ''tis you will pay.'

A dagger appeared in his hand: he threw off the sheath, the point gleamed wickedly. 'Now bastard,' he whispered, 'what was begun at the Eure shall be finished.' And he lunged forward with all his might.

William managed to dodge just in time, felt the knife's edge whistle past his ear. He himself had hold of his little dagger, had raised it in defence, but already he knew it would be of little use against the heavier, longer knife wielded by a heavier, longer reach. But he was quick. He waited, poised ready to jump when the other boy recovered and turned to strike again.

Twice more quickness saved him. And to their credit the other boys gave him space. But he could not keep ducking indefinitely, neither would he use agility to run although there were those who now urged him to. Each time Guy missed, each time he struck at air, the older boy's anger increased, matched in his face by a mounting crimson tide, so that in the end he neither knew what he did nor cared. The third blow caught William on the arm, above the elbow.

William didn't feel the pain at first; what he noticed was the slash in his tunic and his first thought was, 'Poor Herleve, what trouble I cause.' He saw the spill of blood, drops, then a steady flow, with equally detached attention. It was only then he felt the pain, his arm too heavy to lift and a sickness congealing about his chest which surprised him. His legs became slow, fixed to the ground as if he were standing in a bog, as if mud were pulling at his boots as it did in winter-time, and he heard a sound from a great distance as if the other boys were sighing. He closed his eyes for what seemed a long while, then opened them to see his adversary advancing upon him, knife raised for the final thrust and wearing a grin that seemed to spread and fill the universe.

William stood swaying on his feet, braced for that last blow, but it never came. There was instead a swirl of movement, and shouts, 'Ware! Ware, the guards!' And a pulling on his sound arm. A rush of feet, then more shouts from a distance. He felt himself being dragged along at speed between two of the other squires, in and out of corridors. They deposited him none too gently on what looked like a disused stable floor, conversed with each other in low tones, and then disappeared. They must have done, for when he came back to himself he was alone, or so it seemed, and when he dragged himself up against the partition wall the sound of his movements echoed hollowly, as through empty space.

His arm smarted like fire. It burnt, and when he tried to straighten it the catch of dried blood on the cloth made him hold his breath. Sick with it, he sagged down again on the hard stones and considered. It was then he heard a wisp of noise, like a rustle of straw, that sent him at once into full alarm, his head buzzing, his heart jumping in his chest. He cradled his arm, attempted to stand up, and was forced to close his eyes to quell the waves of nausea. When he opened them he found he was looking into a pair of eyes almost as blue as his own, but round, long-lashed, and interested.

'Does it hurt?'

The voice was low but sharp with curiosity of the sort he recognized, and when reluctantly he nodded, 'Don't move,' it said. There was a rustling, a silence, then further rustlings. Almost amused, William wanted to say, 'Where do you think I'll go?' but he hadn't the strength to speak. The rustlings returned and he felt the coolness of fresh water in his mouth, splashed liberally over himself as he drank and drank. When he opened his eyes a third time the bearer of the water was perched opposite him waiting for him to recover.

Once more he was drawn to the eyes, their pale blue luminosity fringed with surprisingly dark lashes. Then the hair, fair like bleached thatch and tied in two thick plaits; then the whole of the curious creature who sat with her skirts rucked up like flower petals. A girl then, of some indeterminate age, with sturdy legs outstretched and sturdy arms bared.

'That's better,' the voice said, 'you don't look so white. At first I thought you'd died.'

He recognized the voice as a girl's now, too: high-pitched yet having a strange timbre to it that made him think of someone, he couldn't imagine who. Remembering his adversary once more he tried to get up but the girl pushed him back. 'It's all right,' she said, as if she guessed what he thought. 'They've gone. They heard the approach of the royal guard and ran. They're cowards at heart, especially Guy. We're quite alone.'

He wanted to ask, 'Where have you come from then?' but his voice seemed to catch in his throat. Yet perhaps eventually he did croak out the words for she said, 'I followed them. I often do – when I can be rid of Beatrice, that is.'

She added impatiently, as if he had questioned her, 'I know when they are planning some mischief, you see. They pride themselves on secrecy but I know better. And I know more about King Henry's court than they do. There's not much I don't know.'

She sounded so confident, so perfectly sure of herself that, despite the constant waves of pain, William was almost amused again. She reminded him of a puppy he had once had, which used to bridle when the larger castle hounds approached, ready to take them on. He leaned back, nursing his arm, and looked at her more carefully. She wasn't very big, perhaps not much older than he was – or perhaps not even as old – but she spoke in such a way that he recognized himself in her. I sound like that, he thought, when I'm not in the least bit sure. It made him like her despite her sharpness. He wasn't used to girls, hardly knew how to address one, but knew enough to gather that he had better keep on this one's good side if he were to make use of her.

'Who is Beatrice?' he heard himself asking.

The answer was a shrug, a twitch of the lips, all in parody of an older woman. 'A Flemish slut,' the girl said, quite definite about that. 'Or so my mother says. But I don't keep her as my maid because of that. I keep her because she is so slow. One of our cows could run faster. It's easy to give her the slip. And we have a pact. Or at least I have made a pact with myself on her behalf. I say nothing of her love affairs and she keeps quiet about my adventurings because she's not able to stop them.'

She sounded so definite he was almost abashed, knowing now

what sluts were, having heard men talk of them, but not certain
that a young girl should, certainly not in the way she did, with
such authority. And yet her directness itself made her sound
younger, almost innocent, especially when she added, 'I can run
very fast when I want to,' as if she were proud of it. 'As fast as
any boy,' she continued. 'And if they'd let me I could ride as
fast. That's why those boys are stupid, claiming I should stay
with the other maids when I don't want to. But I can follow
them; they can't prevent me if they don't know. And I'm careful
to keep quiet about what I do.'

He gaped at her, lost almost in the torrent of words. He wanted
to say, 'I think young maids should stay safely with their mothers
in their mother's bowers,' but some vestige of good sense made
him bite his tongue.

''Tis better to keep quiet about everything,' she was adding,
as if in warning. ''Tis much safer not to speak of anything important unless you have to.'

The warning was not new to him, was what he had already
decided upon. 'Lady,' he said cautiously, trying once more to lift
his arm, 'I thank you for your help. If you could assist me in
getting up . . .'

'Pooh,' she said, not unkindly, 'you're as weak as a kitten. But
if you wait a moment.' There was a tearing noise and when she
spoke again her mouth was full. 'If I bind your arm with my
sleeves,' she said, gripping the cloth between her teeth, 'look,
so, 'twould help.' And when he demurred, ''Tis what my father's
soldiers do when they break an arm, and I think a knife wound's
as bad.'

He felt her fingers busy but not ungentle, and the rustle of
cloth, fine and soft, and then his arm held in place by a kind of
scarf which she proceeded to knot about his neck.

'There,' she said, 'that should hold. And the bleeding's
stopped. You bled like a stuck calf at first.' She went on, still in
the same high, breathless tone, with its low under-ripple, a curious mingling of worldliness with innocence and a sudden unexpected comment of pure worth, 'Guy of Burgundy is vicious.
You shouldn't have crossed him.'

She held out her hand, let him lean upon it. 'What did you
really fight about?' she asked.

Now he was standing the stable seemed to spin in circles as it
had done when the Lowlander captain had hung him upside
down. Out of his giddiness he heard himself repeating, 'Guy of
Burgundy, is that his name? Then, thanks to you, I shall remember it.'

She helped him to the door, step by careful step, he leaning on her more heavily than he meant. When they came out again in the corridor she looked about her, he thought worriedly, and it occurred to him that she was serious about not being seen, on her own behalf as well as his.

'You may leave me here,' he said, with an attempt at confidence he was far from feeling. 'My men will find me soon enough if you will but pass them the word. Tell them it is the Duke of Normandy who requires them, William . . .'

'William the Bastard,' she said, 'son of a tanner's wench!' She dropped his arm. 'The wonder is Guy fought with you at all! I was too far back to hear all that was said but I know Guy of Burgundy swore if he caught you alone he'd have you flogged like a serf. I have heard of you, William the Bastard. Why, they said you withstood a whole army by yourself, but now I don't believe so.'

She regarded him, her look quizzical, perhaps even condemning. 'You're almost as small as I am,' she said, put out.

William was suddenly angry, angrier than he had been all day. With a strength he did not know he still possessed he wrenched himself away and leaned upright against the wall – had he thought about it, very much in the position he had assumed when he had first faced his tormentors.

'Lady, my thanks for your aid,' he said, his tone cold as ice. 'What name shall I give to you?'

Surprised, she answered readily enough, perhaps she even sounded a little ashamed, but she could not prevent the pride creeping in. 'Matilda of Flanders.' And when he did not reply, 'Matilda, daughter of Baldwin, the Count of Flanders, and of Adela, the French princess.'

'Listen then, Matilda of Flanders,' William said. He did not look at her, it took all his strength just to speak. 'And all the other names you bear. Mine is simply said. William. William of Normandy. Do you remember it. For many men shall. And if you think to heap scorn on me,' he added in a sudden slip into boyhood which he was afterwards ashamed of himself, 'not all are called Conqueror as I shall be.'

She gave a little laugh, 'You're testy as a bear,' she said. 'Very well, William of Normandy, I'll do as you ask. But remember, you never saw me, nor I you. As for the bits of my gown, you can keep them as a memento of something that never was.'

She gave a sort of skip and was gone. William let out his breath, sank down again on his heels and hugged his bound arm to his chest to stop the throbbing. 'I hope I never see you again,' he thought, his anger still hot, 'I hope to God we never meet. For if we do, by the Holy Cross 'twill be the worse for you.'

And with his anger to fan the flames, there he remained, until after a while he first heard Walter's voice and then saw his uncle come running towards him.

One piece of advice he did take, despite rather than because of all the scolding, the threatened whipping (which he got when he had recovered), and the entreaties of uncle, councillor, even of Herleve. He never would reveal why he had done what he had done, nor who it was who had caused his injury, nor who had been his rescuer, although the bits of cloth were revealed in daylight as finest silk, proof enough that Matilda of Flanders was who she said she was. In the following days when William lay abed and sickness and infection had their way with him, he kept close counsel as he had trained himself, not even in his feverish mutterings letting a word of the truth escape. But he did keep the scraps of cloth, torn from the sleeves of her gown, and he did mull over the names she had let fall so carefully, remembering also the sound of her voice with its underlacing of pride. And he vowed to himself that one day she would unsay those careless words she had spoken and, at his mercy, would ask forgiveness, which he might or might not bestow as his mood took him.

He kept silence, recovered in silence. Not so his adversary. For when the story spread, as it was bound to do in time, Guy of Burgundy had an excuse prepared. 'For look you, sirs,' he told first the king's guards, and then the king's councillors, and then in turn the king, 'the boy swore he would be king himself. William the Conqueror, he called himself. Ask others, they will swear to it. And if in anger I lashed out at him,' he paused to blink, his dark eyes hooded like a snake's, 'pardon my zeal, good my lords, that his treachery had such effect.'

King Henry listened. William's extreme youth, his condition, his lack of experience in court ways was weighed, as was Guy of Burgundy's age and veracity, or lack of it, for Guy of Burgundy was not known for honesty. In secret, witnesses were called. Some remembered the first day of the quarrel between the two, swearing that William had mocked the older boy and had made invidious comparisons between his Falaise soldiers and the royal house-guard; others, with more justice, vowed he had done so as a child, and like a child had offered amends. Set against this, the earlier boasting of the Falaise guards was now recalled, and suddenly became of great weight; the nature of their prophecy was discussed and enlarged upon to appear to include claim upon the French throne. All was debated by learned men who sought not only devil's work but its more deadly counterpart, treason. At the end, what could be proved or denied, except a boys' escapade which had ended better than it might have done, given the differences of age and strength? Or was it an abortive attempt at treachery by a child already grown older than his years and capable of great subtlety? In any event, the suspicion was sown. And so, caught in trap without escape – for who can answer a charge not made, or deny treachery unless he himself first mentions it? Turold had no other recourse except to withdraw the duke from Paris while yet there was time.

So, earlier than he had intended by far, Turold led the ducal party back again to Normandy, to danger sure and treachery of its own. That the king had not been quite unkind, had promised William new guardians, had offered knighting when he was of age ('If he reaches it,' the king had added in an aside meant to be heard), was more than could be hoped for. And one last thing had been promised, which for better or worse Herleve had requested and received, to her own detriment and for her son's sake.

But they did not tell William of that until he was back in Normandy.

Chapter 6

Many spectators watched the duke's party leave with as much ceremony and outward show as it had displayed on arrival over eighteen months before. Perhaps even greater, it being imperative to the Norman cause that no hint of unease be suggested between duke and overlord, the king's protection now of more value than ever. The young Lady Matilda of Flanders was conspicuous by her absence. This was not by choice. She had planned to be in attendance, had in fact already chosen her place and would have sent the Flemish maid, Beatrice, to reserve it for her. Instead she was seated on a low stool between her father and mother while her mother wrung her hands and her father tried to placate his wife and scratched his head.

The subject of their debate sat still, hands folded. Her plaits were immaculately tied, their tresses woven with flowers; her gown was flower-sprigged, pale blue to accentuate the eyes whose gaze today was fixed demurely on the floor as if what her parents spoke of was no concern of hers, or at least was a topic she knew nothing of.

'Three times,' the poor mother shrieked. She jangled her row of rosary beads. 'Twice your horse, my lord. Or at least she tried. Once a squire's of your court who should be flayed for allowing it; although he swore she gave him the slip and mounted it before he could stop her. And who knows what other mischief before or since, for ever about the court more like a camp follower than my own royal get. And once last year I found her gown in rags as if she purposely tore it. God's mercy, sir, 'tis a creature possessed.'

And the poor lady closed her eyes and began to pray in earnest.

Count Baldwin sighed and gnawed at his thumb ring. He looked from wife to daughter. How could this slip of a maid have power to twist all things into such a fret? Here was his royal wife in a royal mood, like to retire to her bower with such weepings and tears, and such hours of seclusion with chaplains and clerks as to preclude all kind of attention on his part, unless he forced her to admit him. And when finally she did, what moans she'd make, what blame she'd cast, 'Your fault for this, your fault for that,' such as would hardly be worth the trouble! He'd end up as miserable as she was and all because he had sired a lass with spirit, more full of fire than all his sons! Had Matilda only been a son, he thought, he'd have no fears for the future. He sighed again. A man could do worse than such a heir; if only it were not bound up in skirts.

As if she divined his thought, the royal mother jerked open her eyes. 'She's spoilt,' the mother said, her voice now as flat as when her brother, the king, pronounced judgement. 'When she was little, back in Ghent, perhaps it seemed a jest to teach a maid to ride astride like a boy, to show her how to use a bow and knife, to turn her into that unnatural thing, a girl half-boy. But now she is older. Soon of an age to be betrothed or wed, and then how serves all that, I ask you? 'Twill not win her a husband: husbands want wives, not play-mates.'

The almond eyes narrowed, the aristocratic nose quivered. 'And do not argue she's still too young. Girls half her age with half her dower are spoken for every day. I was younger still when I was wed. And we've brought her to court for that very purpose. But who will want her as she is? Who could rule her?'

The count gnawed at his fist again, felt the calluses on his palm, wished for his horse, wished to be anywhere but here, to be taken to task as if he were a fledgling squire with his duties left unfinished. Given a choice he would have been off, would have ridden back to his native land and been well content. But royal wives are more particular.

Perplexed, he tried to remember how old Adela had been on his marrying her, when to have a princess for a bride had been the summit of ambition. Those days did not seem so long ago and yet here he was with a daughter growing up whose future must soon be settled. 'I am loath to let her go,' he wanted to protest, 'I'd miss her,' but sensing his wife's fixed gaze, he closed his mouth with a snap.

Instead he roared at his daughter. 'Hear now, hussy, mend your ways, or it'll be the worse for you. I'll have it beaten into you.'

Matilda's eyes looked up at his. Her plaits swung. Her feet were planted firmly on the ground as if they were fixed to the saddle. Then she lowered her head and smiled. 'Yes, father,' Matilda said.

When she had gone and her mother with her, the father called for wine and sat deep in thought. It was all very well to threaten

Matilda, but he knew from experience it would not work. Neither beatings nor prayers would change her nature. But neither could she long be let to run loose, even if he were to blame for it. He did not fancy having her tamed in a marriage bed – she was still a child – yet, God knows, he thought, better marriage than shame. But it wasn't wantonness that turned her wild. It was, it was . . . He shook his head, not having a word to name her wants, though had she been like his other children and a son, he could readily have listed them.

He twisted the heavy ring he wore as if to admire it. It was old too, older than this royal line from which his wife was descended, had been passed from father to son in strict succession. But the counts of Flanders were not kings, there was a difference. Still, his daughter was not any man's child to be palmed off lightly. He rose with a groan and made his way to his wife's chamber. If he were to win his way back to grace he must appear to give in, although it cut him hard to part so soon with his Matilda.

After her mother had locked her in her room, had taken the key and shut the door, promising food and water only after penitence, Matilda ran to the window embrasure. It was but a moment's work to climb up on its broad ledge, tearing her skirt on the sharp projections. The sky was bright, the sort of February sky that promises cold: had she been at home she would have smelled the snow before it came, but here she was not sure. The city hemmed her round too close, you needed space to be sure of things.

She leaned out as far as she dared, sucked in the air, cold and fresh with its hint of wetness. Down below, beyond the river banks, even the fields in their winter greyness looked inviting. Better than inside these walls. But then anything was better than being shut up here, where the ladies were so proud they walked on clouds and where girls of her own age stared as if she were a monster. They never dared say what they thought, simply whispered in secret, all because her mother was a princess of the blood, and she the niece of a king.

And the boys were no better. Except they had the advantages she lacked: freedom to ride and hunt, freedom to move about, freedom to speak. If I were a boy, Matilda thought with a sudden surge of bitterness, I'd not waste my time in stupid quarrels. I'd be like, like . . . not Guy of Burgundy, for all he swaggers, but a real man. She crossed herself. She was not too young to know that such thoughts were unbecoming to a maid and therefore dangerous. Had not an ancestress of hers had witches burnt for

71

less? Had not another ancestress been herself tortured and tied to a horse's tail? And was it not wickedness to wish to be other than what you were, where God's will had set you? Like her father, she folded her arms and pondered.

Since the day she had followed the mischief-making pages into the corridor she had been expecting trouble. When that incident was discovered, riding horses without permission would pale in comparison. She had often been curious to see what happened when boys fought, but until then had never actually caught them at it. The signs she knew: the sudden hush followed by a rush of air like starlings swirling; the bunching together of pages and squires, playing the innocent, hiding anger, quarrel, in their midst as if nursing a secret. But how they came to fighting, how tempers flared so hot and fast that in a trice weapons would out and blows be struck was new and therefore infinitely more interesting. But although this fight had been the first she'd actually witnessed, she sensed it had been different from the usual scuffles.

She had seen right away that William of Normandy had led them to it. He had meant them to follow him and they had. In that alone surely he had won since it was his intent which had prevailed, not theirs. And then, when Guy of Burgundy had appeared the younger boy had faced up to him, talked him down even when Guy had insulted him, had actually stayed to fight although the rest had urged him to run . . . It wasn't fair, she thought, one against so many, yet he didn't seem to notice. And he never boasted of bravery himself as I've heard Guy boast. Perhaps after all he is as brave as people say he is. It takes courage to confront someone older than yourself; a squire with a dagger honed to kill cannot be an easy opponent. And William himself had been armed only with a little knife and only drew when he had to, not before! Nor did he complain of his wound, for all it must have pained him. Shrewd beyond her years, Matilda thought: if I were a boy and had the right to arms, his is the example I would follow, not that of a bully and a coward.

But she was not a boy, and in her own self she had not been gracious. That too troubled her, although at first, after she had left him, she had been offended. She did not like being spoken to in the way he had spoken. She was used to subservience, not arrogance matched with arrogance, not pride put up against pride. Worse, the young duke had made her feel petty and ashamed and those were sensations new to her. Again she considered. She knew she had angered him and yet she had not really meant to. The difficulty is, she thought, my tongue often goes too fast for my words. It says things of its own accord, without waiting for me to tell it what to say. Guy of Burgundy's insults were enough without my adding more. Yet I did not mean them in the way they sounded. And whereas when William felt he was in the wrong he was ready with apology, he never gave me chance to do the like, or rather, I was too choked with pride to begin.

And if that be so, she thought, half resentful – for she did not like being put in the wrong and, like her tongue, her thoughts could not be curbed, were forever leading her into dangerous realms where she wished them not to go – then in very truth is real penitence required, certainly more due than for riding some stupid squire's horse? Especially since he probably hardly knew how to ride the animal himself and never should have left it standing, reins a-dangle.

She slid down from the window ledge, to her knees and closed her eyes. The floor bit cold. Slowly, with deliberate care, she began to recite her prayers. If at their end she added a particular prayer that William be granted a safe journey and a safe return, well, it too was a thought for hiding. And when she had done and had smoothed her dress, she planted herself firmly on another stool, like a boy would, sturdy legs spread apart under her skirt, and reluctantly picked up her embroidery frame. On her mother's return the Lady Adela should find a model daughter busy at her needlework. Only . . . the needle paused and the coloured thread slackened as she remembered her mother's discourse. Young though she was, she knew enough from Beatrice what marrying meant and the knowledge was distasteful to her. Let my lady mother plan and scheme all she wants, she thought, I'm in no mind to be betrothed, nor wed; certainly not to one of those silly posturing boys who thinks to rule the world and take me for his pastime. But she was not overworried. She had an ally, although her father would not exactly admit it, and that was her protection. And for all my mother's weeping, she thought, for all her nagging, I am safe, as long as my lord father holds steady, God keep him so. But as the needle moved again and the stitches crossed and doubled, it was not of any abstract posturing boy she thought, nor of any abstract marriage. The image that came into her head was of a real boy, about her age, who claimed to be a conqueror in waiting.

Matilda's prayers and thoughts notwithstanding, William rode joyfully out of Paris without a care in the world, and without a backward glance. Weeks had passed while he had been confined to bed and he felt himself pallid, like one of those Norman plants which grows too soon in early spring and gets buried under snow. But he had grown! His legs were longer than they had been and his horse with its thick, cold-weather coat suddenly seemed as small as his previous pony had been. It was frisky though, gave a playful buck or two, kicking out with its heels as if glad to be on the move once more. William sat more firmly in the saddle and gripped tight with his knees. His arm still pained him but had regained its former strength. Herleve had wept when she saw the scar but he was rather pleased with it.

'Like his father,' Herleve had said as she sat by his bed. She did not know he was awake and had heard her. 'Never hanging back.' She had wiped away the tears. ''Twill win all or kill him,' she had said. He had liked the sound of that.

And now they were riding towards Normandy as she had promised, and all those sad lonely hours were finished. He would never tell her what the boys had said, but he had at least avenged her reputation, and that too was something that pleased him. And if at their parting from the court he had surreptitiously looked for the saucy girl who had bedevilled him, it was just as well she hid herself; he'd no real longing to meet her again.

They rode openly this time with the king's outriders for company. King Henry had not been so mean as to deny them that added protection. And they stayed in comfort as became them, no more need for hiding. Their method of travel gratified William. It was not that he had become fastidious about such things, but he knew now what was due a ducal party and wanted nothing mean or tawdry to mar his return that meant so much to him.

Herleve was quiet. She too has come out of hiding now she is beyond the court, he thought, like a flower that has lost the sun and now turns to it. February had been chill, but in a week or so winter surely would be gone. Soon in Norman orchards the apple blossom would be out, the trees smothered in white like clouds. And the grass would turn bright green, starred with daisies and celandines. He wrinkled his nose. *'Ma mie,'* he wanted to say, 'can't you smell the spring?' But he didn't. Knights didn't talk of spring and flowers. And soon he would be a knight. The king had promised him and Turold had said that on his return his real training would begin. It should really have begun earlier; he'd have to work to make up time. He thought, two years ago, say two years to this day, I was a child. My father was still alive and we waited for him. Look how much has happened since. And now we are coming home together Herleve and I, God willing, never to be apart, never to leave Falaise again.

Under cover of his cloak he crossed himself and for a moment his eyes closed as if in prayer. Then joyfully he rode on to re-enter his dukedom.

Herleve was silent because she had too much she wanted to say, and so little time to say it in that she did not know when or where to begin.

The past months had been long and bleak for her, as they had been for her son. Like him she had pined in that city air, and longed for the freshness of the countryside. Perhaps even more than William the restrictions of her new life had hemmed her in. Yet she had herself chosen it and deliberately come to Paris when she could as well have stayed behind. That she had come, that she had kept herself away from William, allowing them to be separated, was all part of a plan she had.

Plan was not quite the right word, for there was nothing contrived or manipulated about her actions. It was more a conviction, growing from something the archbishop had said at their last meeting. His jibe that she lacked powerful family connections to support her son had been reinforced by Fulbert's similar assessment. She was a country girl, lacking the guile of a courtier, lacking the skill and wiles of a lady of rank; nevertheless those remarks stung. She had resolved to obtain power in the only way open to a woman, that is, by asking the king for a new husband.

She had no qualms about such a request, for she did not make it for herself. As long as the man was Norman, of noble birth, and loyal to her son's cause, she cared not who he was. As for the king, her sense that Henry would receive her petition kindly was equally without guile, for she did not see why he should refuse her. Among his subjects he had the right to arrange many marriages, why not one for her?

But there was another reason why she counted on the king's friendship. She remembered Henry only vaguely, on the perimeter of her former existence, an unhappy young man, not much older than she was, who once had himself been in need of protection. True, at that time, all men – young or old, kings or peasants – counted as nothing compared to Robert, but the young prince had certainly been impressed by her. Not being without feminine perception, she had sensed Henry's admiration. Naïvely perhaps, for at heart she was a simple person, she had now decided to rely on that ancient liking, again not for herself, not out of vanity or false pride, simply as a means to the end of helping her son.

She did not relish using the king to achieve her aim, as indeed she would have disliked using anyone. But when she arrived in Paris she had felt justified. It seemed to her that Henry continued to show her marked favour out of good nature itself. The rooms she occupied were worthy of a duchess, as comfortable and well furnished as any rooms in the royal palace, itself not noted at that time for luxury. All she had need of – maids to wait upon her, food and drink, horses to ride – were laid at her disposal. If she had cared to, the king would have had her grace his own table. All these signs of attention embarrassed her even as she welcomed them. Pleading time of mourning, no lie this – in some ways she would forever mourn her dead lover – she had at first declined all the most obvious offers. But she was practical; life must go on. Intense mourning, like other things, like love itself perhaps, must have an end. And when it did, when the wound was no longer raw and time had healed it somewhat, when she could steel herself to put all her former life behind, then she would make her request and be sure of succeeding.

As time had passed without incident, as she in turn had become used to monotony, days spent in prayer and work – on clothes for a growing boy, so that William should look his best – her only pleasure revolving around the little scraps of news that Walter brought, she had begun to hope for reprieve. If William could be happy, if he could remain in Paris under the king's own guidance until he was grown, if affairs in Normandy could settle, then perhaps there would be no need for her to remarry at all. William's escapade, for so she thought of it at first, some boyish bravado which, praise God, had not ended as badly as it might, had brought her out of seclusion. Not only to tend her son, but to accept the reality of their situation. When Turold warned her of the dangers inherent in the incident, when he argued that since affairs had turned out so badly they must return to Normandy as soon as possible, even if Normandy itself still was unsafe, she felt forced to act.

By some good fortune she did not even know the true extent of, she chose a time for asking when the king had not yet given full rein to suspicion, was still in two minds about William and was still disposed to remember her with unsullied sentiment. Her request for a private interview flattered rather than alarmed Henry. And although Herleve herself dressed with care for Robert's sake, to do him and his son credit, certainly not to enhance her own vain opinion of herself, she immediately realized the effect she made on the king as she entered the chamber where he had consented to receive her.

The gown was plain, of soft grey wool, not silk, uncluttered by gold or pearls; her hair was loosely combed, without the adornments a great lady would wear. She wore no jewels about her neck, no rings on her fingers. Flexing them she thought with a sudden sadness how white and smooth they now looked, unlike the brown roughness when Robert had first kissed them. She had supposed Henry might find her greatly changed from what he remembered, older, worn by grief, as she felt herself to be. She had not expected the king's gleam of interest, nor his surge of gallantry, nor his warm embrace, his kiss of greeting upon her lips, which no man but Robert had ever touched.

'Lady,' he had murmured, holding her hand tight in his, 'or rather I believe I should call you Herleve, you have been in hiding too long. What shall I do to bring light back to your lovely eyes? Since my stay in Rouen, I have never forgotten them, or you.'

If she had been her old self she would have laughed at his compliments and teased him for their excess. Now she forced herself to accept them, forced herself to smile, curtsey and listen to him with affected animation as he spoke of that time in Normandy as if it were the summit of his happiness, not the nadir of his misfortunes. It was only when he stopped talking that she was able to force out the words which she had been rehearsing for so long.

'Great king,' she said then, 'for the love you bore my dear Robert, and his for you, I have come to ask you a favour.'

Some instinct stopped her from adding, 'Not for myself, but for my son, to whom you have already shown great mercy.' Instead she said, 'I do not know how to thank you for all your kindnesses. Any we did you pale by comparison. And asking for another is no way to show gratitude, seems mere greed instead. But I do ask, and do beg pardon. I know,' she added as she saw the king's face darken and his lips turn down, 'I am no great lady of fashion, no heiress of lands and property and have no standing of my own. What I am is not for show, yet I do think it is of worth, if it be not unbecoming for me to say so.'

Her air of modesty, her beauty, her simplicity touched the king despite himself. And her air of dignified restraint in her grief. Almost without knowing what he was doing he nodded agreement, and saw her smile again as once, long ago, she had smiled in the courtyard at Rouen. Her trust in him had its effect. Before she left he had granted her her wish, although common sense, had it prevailed, would have led him to deny it. Any gain to her must perforce be a gain also to her son. And it was this news that she had to tell William when the time was ripe.

77

She waited until they had crossed the north-eastern border into Normandy. Then she waited while the days passed in joyful feast and welcoming. Although her heart was heavy, she rejoiced for her son. It was fitting that here in the eastern districts, where his enemies had thought to make a stand, the local knights and commoners should recognize the duke's flag and flock to pay homage, turning the homecoming into a proper ducal progress. And she waited until they were clear of the Seine where it snaked around the city of Rouen. Better to be free of Rouen before voicing her thoughts. But the archbishop sulked in his palace and they neither saw nor heard of him, and his sons too seemed gone without a trace, so much the better.

They even found time to detour from the path and visit Jumièges so they could pray at the famous abbey, rebuilt by William Longsword, its abbot loyal always to the ducal house as the grants of land and charted deeds required, the monks themselves appearing suitably impressed by this fresh mark of favour.

The abbey itself was of ancient foundation, William Longsword had rebuilt on the ruins of the former building destroyed by Vikings. Although Jumièges was famous for its learning and already planning future enlargement, its present moderate size suited Herleve. The monks were especially proud of their orchards, and when she and William walked in the meadows, swathes of cherry blossom lay in drifts just as William had imagined the Norman springs whilst in Paris. The Seine flowed by quickly, its high tide marked by a giant wave or 'bore' that seemed to gather all its force into a wall of water. But today, here in the bend of the river, the sun was hot; on the banks placid cattle browsed among stands of willow herb. Birds were chirruping in the trees that stretched like a green wall on either side; in the fields lambs frolicked; while within the chapel bells rang as if in jubilation. For the first time in months Herleve and William knew the taste of food and drink they recognized: bread that had the flavour of wheat, milk that thickened into cream, cider that smelled of fruit. On all sides, content flourished. Only in Herleve's breast remained a core of ice.

Still she kept silent awhile. And in a sudden descent to childhood, she and her William were free for a couple of days to run upon the river's verge, gather shells and stones, and pick the wild flowers that grew in profusion there.

The morning they were to leave, she led her son out into those meadows of which they had both become so fond. There in the early mist she took his hand, kept it close for a moment against her cheek as if to draw out its warmth. 'My love,' she said. She smiled although her face was tear-stained. 'You are the strings of my heart, you and your father, my life's blood. Even when times change, and we must change with them, that truth remains and you must hold to it. And see, how fortunate we are. For whereas when we left Falaise our very lives were at risk, so now we return in triumph. The king has given you more than we asked, has granted you new guardians to be your guide, has set his seal upon your inheritance. All that we hoped for from this journey has been achieved and, God be praised, we come in peace.'

William nodded sleepily. The pale sun was hidden behind a grey mist, the grass was cool with dew, and he enjoyed hearing his mother's voice, feeling her hand on his.

'And I too have been granted all that I hoped for, and more,' she said, 'although God knows the accepting of it was not easy . . . I have found another husband, William.' She tried a smile. 'Or rather a first husband, although he has been married before. A kind man,' she went on, 'older than I, in need of a wife. The king has taken the arrangements on himself. And he holds lands, has titles – not great ones, to be sure, but for a tanner's daughter a good match.'

She did not add, 'And for a tanner's grandson, a loyal lord to succour you.'

She let go his hand, played with the fallen petals, sifted them through her fingers, watched the colour fade as the sun shone through the greyness, watched the light fade from William's eyes, felt his body stiffen in shock.

'His name is Herluin, viscomte of Conteville,' she went on, talking as if by rote, as if by enumerating facts about this stranger she might conjure him up and make him real. 'Conteville lies north of Falaise. Not so far away – only a day's ride will separate us.' Again she tried to smile. 'When you are big enough to mount that bay horse you took, why, a hop and jump will bring you there.'

William did not reply. The words beat like icy rain on his ears. He heard her say, 'We shall never truly be apart, my son, for as God is my witness you are so much of me as would tear out my soul. And as proof, I give you this as once your father gave it to me.'

She took her gift out from her sleeve where she had hidden it, a gold medallion from St Michael's Mount, which Robert had once visited; the image of the saint was stamped upon it.

'Keep it,' she repeated, 'to remember me by. May it bring you safe to your journey's end, and give God's goodness in full measure.' And she hung it round his neck.

William ducked his head obediently, and felt the metal burn against his skin. The coldness of it made him cringe. He wanted to scream denial. You should have told me, he wanted to accuse, you should have warned me from the start. How dare you keep me in ignorance as if to kill me, merciless as any enemy. Yet his thoughts were small and distant, as when Guy of Burgundy's knife had slashed down. They have won, he thought dully, they have won, we shall never be together again, although who the 'they' were he could not have said. It seemed to him that all the colours in the world were suddenly leached out, the grass became white, the sky white, the cherry trees ghost-white, as if they had bled his blood away, just as that knife cut had done. And a great weariness overcame him and he longed to sleep, but the mighty yawn he gave was to feign indifference. I must not let you know how much I grieve, he thought; I must not torment you with my grief. And so he tried to smile and spoke of other things. Yet never again would he go into an orchard without the scent of trees in blossom making him vomit, so great was his sense of loss. And never in his life again was he to know happiness without anticipating pain, and never could he trust in anyone without expecting ultimate betrayal.

Thus was his return home, and thus his parting with Herleve. Only one last thing she said in self defence. 'Some things do not always seem as they truly are. God does not easily show His face.' He did not reply, but watched in silence until she had crossed through the shallows of the nearby ford and was almost lost in the forests on the other side, grown as small as a child herself. Something about the way Herleve rode, proudly upright, not once turning back, gave William the strength to continue on with Walter and Turold, too proud himself to reveal what turmoil he felt. In turn he mounted and splashed across the ford and went on after his guardians, not towards Falaise as he had supposed but closer to Rouen, to Vaudreuil, so that even his boyhood home was denied to him. And when in later years he finally came back to Falaise, it was as to a place he had never known, all his dreams and longing for it wiped clean away as a slate is wiped. And when he had come to Vaudreuil he took off that medallion of gold and hid it in a coffer under his clothes and only ever wore it once again, in this way trying to come to terms with the past.

Chapter 7

Vaudreuil was not unlike Falaise, though it was not so grand; a Norman castle built of wood and stone, meant for war and soldiering. It was set in a loop of the Seine, and was chosen to house the young duke because of its secureness: its position near the River Seine and the king's lands beyond made any open assault on the castle foolish. Another reason for its safety, stranger perhaps, lay in its very proximity to Rouen. For though it must be supposed William's enemies lay gathered there, that same spring an event had occurred which had changed matters.

While William had remained in Paris the archbishop had kept quiet. He had not approached his great-nephew, or even made contact with him again. Partly, it was said, this was out of pride, because he would not permit William the chance of accusing him openly of complicity in his son's crimes, or let others accuse him on William's behalf. More likely age had begun to take its toll and ill-health was forcing him to retire from active life. He still fulfilled his duties as regent (which, in name, he remained) such as the administration of oaths and issuing of charters and other legalities, but now he seldom ventured from his palace at Rouen and, like all old men whose power has passed, sank from sight and was forgotten. In the spring of 1037 he died, his death rousing little notice, certainly no grief and no official time of mourning. But with him and his son's ambition apparently thwarted, William had no more to fear from Rouen, or so his councillors reasoned.

Two new councillors, new to William that is, took the archbishop's place as regents. They had been old acquaintances of Duke Robert and had been loyal to him. Count Gilbert of Brionne, King Henry's choice, was a relative of William's by an earlier marriage. A large, congenial man, he never visited Vaudreuil without bringing some gift: a tooled gilt belt, a hound puppy with enormous feet, and even a specially made mail-coat such as William's father had once promised him.

Alan, Count of Brittany, third of the name, was another rela-

tive unknown to William. Alan and Duke Robert had been
cousins, for Robert's mother had been Judith of Brittany, whom
he had adored although she had died young. The duke and Count
Alan had not always been friends, had in fact been brought to
terms by the very archbishop Alan now supplanted. But William
learned to like this new relation, liked the way he openly admitted fault in quarrelling with Normandy and to make amends
swore on his honour to help his cousin's son. With two such stout
allies, with Turold and Walter as constant companions, with
Osbern come from Falaise expressly to take up the stewardship
of William's new residence, bringing many of the ducal guard
with him, Vaudreuil should have been the most secure castle in
the duchy.

Should have been – there was the rub. And as long as the
archbishop lived perhaps it was so. As long as the archbishop
lived, despite the frailty of his body, his will held predominance
over his sons, even over Ralph de Gacé, who since his failure at
the Eure had slunk away to nurse his wounds. But it was equally
true that de Gacé's malice had been growing all the while, the
more bitter because it had once been thwarted.

What the archbishop's sons felt on hearing of their father's
death depended on their particular circumstance, according to
how they benefited. The eldest, glad to get Évreux intact, was
more than willing to show filial devotion, to dispense time and
money on a fitting burial, to have alms given and Masses said
for the dead man's soul. The youngest, uncertain of 'his' bishopric which he had always counted on, was in two minds: at first
still hopeful of obtaining it, willing to fawn and show respect if
it were necessary to win him support, but in his heart more
inclined towards Ralph's cause, perhaps more sympathetic to
Ralph now that he himself felt what it was to be disinherited.

'He should have acted sooner and had me confirmed. He
should have had all prepared. He could have stepped down
earlier and had me installed before he died.' The youngest son's
wails heaped fretful condemnation on the poor dead archbishop
for not arranging death more conveniently. 'Brother Richard's
well enough; shut up in Évreux he's no call for complaint, he'll
not venture out of line. But what of me? What of my rights?
Who speaks now on my behalf or has the power to persuade the
Pope to grant me what should be mine?'

Ralph ignored him. The archbishop was dead. The father
whom they had hated and yet grudgingly admired, who alone of
all men could reduce them to stuttering impotency, was now,
praise be to God, the devil's own where he belonged; let him

strike the devil dumb, let him worm his way through hell. In this world they were free of him.

'First things first,' Ralph said. He strode up and down the chamber where they were lodged, in Gacé itself, that village despised and held in scorn because it seemed not big or powerful enough to contain Ralph's ambitions. It lay south of Rouen, which the younger brother had thought to have, and still might have yet, if he, Ralph, put his hand to it; if he, Ralph, did not have better use for it. His mind spun round, grappling with swarms of ideas. First one, then the next threatened to over-whelm him as he tried, for once in his life, to go slowly enough to put all in order before carelessly leaping ahead as his father had always accused him of. He heard his father's sneer at the improbability of it.

But here was a chance, a chance that the archbishop's corpse, laid in state in his church, mourned by his monks and clergy if not by his sons, alone gave. He, Ralph de Gacé, had all within his grasp if he but manoeuvred things right and did not bungle them. 'Take care,' he heard his father say, 'think.'

Thinking was abhorrent to Ralph, thinking took precious time. But he would take the time. 'By God,' he swore, striking the wooden table to make the wine cups dance, ''tis just a question of listing what's of prime import, what second, and so on down in order of significance. So be quiet, brother, and let me con-centrate.'

He leaned over the polished surface where the spilled wine had made pools and drew a finger through them. 'Father is dead,' he said. 'There's our cue. No sense in letting the world know what we do next, that's information to be withheld as long as we're able. Second, Évreux's safe enough, but Rouen's lost. No use crying over spilt milk. Rather concentrate on how to turn loss to advantage.'

The younger brother pouted, grumbled, was silent. Used to his father's dominance he accepted it now in turn from his brother, without lasting resentment. He waited docilely while Ralph de Gacé outlined his plan. A similar one to that Ralph had made before on receiving news of Duke Robert's demise, encompass-ing William's death and his own advancement – but with a vital difference. He did not tell his brother all his thoughts. And then he summoned the other claimants to take part in the division of the duchy.

This meeting was a complicated affair, the organization alone costing many hours of painful contemplation. The place selected was along the coast, both on the way to St Michael's Mount and close enough to Caen to give credence to the excuse of pilgrimage for the dead bishop's soul, which the parties concerned might well have planned to undertake. An isolated tract of sand and low dune, it was perfect for an illicit rendezvous, in neutral territory where none held special influence, where the very openness of the terrain precluded fear of ambuscade, and a small harbour permitted travel by boat if any should prefer. Nor was it too far westward to deter Papia's sons, coming as they did from Envermeu in the east, near Dieppe, but it might possibly be too far from the abbey of St-Ouen in Rouen itself where Nicholas was cloistered for him to attempt the journey. (Of the three other claimants to the duchy this unknown monk, the one who had most legal right, was the one Ralph was most wary of: he almost hoped he would not come at all.) The archbishop himself could not have faulted Ralph's choice, nor bettered it.

The wording of the message, and the choice of messengers to carry it, also cost agonies of thought, for if Ralph de Gacé were suspicious of the other claimants he knew very well that they must be suspicious of him. Like others before him he listed them, but in order of threat rather than claim to succession, so that in every case the message was slightly different, slanted to appeal to the recipient depending on what Ralph knew of the character of each, such as firmness of purpose, or potential usefulness – or possible interference and hindrance . . .

The suggestion that they meet was delicately phrased, sometimes larded with flattery or persuasion as he saw fit, sometimes laced with threat. And afterwards, having selected envoys known for their tract and discretion to persuade each to comply, he sat back, proud of work that even his father must have admired.

But all this took time. It was many months after the archbishop's death that the conspiracy finally found form, the conspiracy upon which all Ralph de Gacé's hopes were now pinned. And he, with only hired mercenaries for company, came to that lonely part of the northern shore where his guests – his unwanted relatives and projected co-conspirators – had consented to have converse with him.

They met in the open. From a viewpoint on the low dunes Ralph saw the first of them wind their way across the estuary – the Envermeu brothers, who would, of course, have preferred land travel, accompanied as they were by their armed guards and retainers, their horses and their laden baggage-trains. Behind him, de Gacé's own troops leaned on their pike ends, counted and noted the comportment of this new force, their arms and equipment, their warlike appearance, even the markings on their shields, for almost all carried some scratched device to distinguish him from his fellows. On seeing the variety and the professional approach of the newcomers, the more cautious of the watchers began to sharpen their own spears. Ralph de Gacé liked that, readiness was what he hired men for.

Careful to ensure that he and his men were seen – for he wanted no fear of ambush to mar this moment – he too leaned forward on his horse.

He recognised Mauger of Envermeu immediately; his cousin had not changed much since more youthful meetings. They were cousins by virtue of their mutual relative, the old Duke Richard II. This duke had been his uncle, brother of the archbishop. And had been the Envermeu brothers' father, as he had been Duke Robert's, by a second marriage. Mauger was accompanied by his younger brother whose qualities were unknown, both of them sons of the same mother, Papia of Envermeu. They rode side by side, almost hand in hand, a filial devotion Ralph had not counted on! His lips closed in a perplexed sneer. No hope there of buying one at the other's expense; take one, take both, that was what their proximity announced.

Their following was long, the estuary traverse slow, they came armed and wary, well provided for by their mother's own inheritance. Yet ready to be tempted by greed, for here they were. Their very presence was itself indicative of an open-minded attitude to conspiracy.

Ralph waited until they were within earshot before having his herald blow the signal. When that trumpet snarl had set the seabirds screaming, he himself rode out to meet them, accompanied by a handful of his guard, coming down the dunes between the tufts of sea grass in a smother of sand before halting just out of bowshot reach.

He raised his hand and spoke loudly, for the wind was strong enough to set the banners crackling, and blew at the horses' tails making them skittish. 'Greetings, cousins both,' he said, 'heartily are you welcome. I bid you dismount, refresh yourselves. My pavilion is waiting.' He motioned behind his back to where a tent was set in a hollow out of the worst of the wind.

The two brothers conferred, but though it was the elder one, Mauger, who spoke, Ralph noted that it was at the younger's insistence, what was his name? – another William, just to confuse the issue. He frowned, listened while Mauger made excuses: they would come no closer; the sand bothered their horses, why did he not join them . . . ?

'So you're a-feared,' Ralph broke in, impatience showing.

'Why not say so? Very well, we'll talk from where we are, although shouting's a nuisance in this wind and I myself am thirsty.'

Mauger frowned in turn at the implied insult; William of Envermeu whispered; a ripple like the wind itself spread through the waiting ranks on both sides causing the more experienced to tighten their grasp upon their weapons. A new arrival was thankfully turned to by each of the three lords as a diversion and the level of tension eased.

The latest comer was a monk, dressed in black, his head cowled. He too came on foot from the direction of the estuary where now some small boats could be seen dancing in the choppy water. They had not been anchored there earlier in the morning so the monk must have chosen a sea passage. He was not without his own attendants, though: a line of them, two by two, preceded by a group who struggled under a large wooden cross. Seeing the waiting horsemen he straightened up, drew back his hood so that the circle of red tonsured hair showed. His black robes billowed as his sandalled feet strode more purposefully along the shore close to the sea, the mournful chanting of the accompanying monks for a moment drowning the noise of the waves and wind. 'By Jesu,' Ralph spoke aloud, ''tis cousin Nicholas. I'd not thought he'd come at all, at least not bring an abbey with him.' And he crossed himself at the prospect of all those listening ears.

Cousin Nicholas, monk of the Monastery of St-Ouen, obviously felt no qualms at the prospect of their meeting, or if he did he may have felt an aura of sanctity protected him. He did not pause but came on until he was well into the open space between Ralph and the two Envermeu brothers. There he motioned to his fellow monks to set up the cross in the sand, after which he approached Ralph de Gacé's horse and put out his hand to pat it, not at all disturbed by the violent snorting of the great beast that left gouts of foam on his black habit.

'Greetings, Ralph de Gacé,' he said. 'I come in God's name, as I have been summoned, although it is not often my order is permitted to travel far from the confines of our church. But these are special times, and momentous happenings are mooted abroad. So I have sought and been granted special dispensation. What you have to say may be said freely to me in the presence of my brothers. We are of one mind and company.'

'Not to what I may say.' It was William of Envermeu who spoke. He suddenly swung himself off his horse and came clanking across the intervening stretch of beach, his spurs dragging in the tufts of grass. On foot he looked even more formidable;

broad of shoulder, bull-necked, his close cropped head jutting out belligerently. 'By God, I've not come this far, nor risked so much, to have all the chroniclers in Normandy write it down in lies.'

He turned and beckoned to Mauger. 'Join me, brother,' he said bluntly, 'I've changed my mind. We'll never come to terms unless we hold private talk. And with God as witness in these monks to ensure there's no planned treachery, we're safe enough, as long as we prevent these holy servants from eavesdropping.'

He addressed the new arrival. 'So you're Monk Nicholas. Well, I'm of your grandfather's second brood. I never knew your father, made duke while I was still a babe-in-arms, and dead and gone before I was much more.'

He turned to Ralph de Gacé. 'But I knew of the bastard's father,' he said, equally blunt. 'And what I've heard makes me like him better, as different from Nicholas's father as chalk from cheese. If his son resembles him, then by God we may yet have our work cut out.'

And as Mauger in turn now dutifully came stumbling after him, he uttered aloud the words that were long to be remembered, loudly enough for all those would-be monkish chroniclers to quote. *'Il est petit, mais il creistra.'*

'Si Dieu plaist, si amendera,' Nicholas intoned, and crossed himself. and behind him his fellow monks also made the sign of the cross.

This dialogue displeased Ralph de Gacé. He sensed things spinning out of his control. First the younger of the Envermeu brothers had challenged him, the oldest grandson; then came this shaven monk, this weakling he could break with one hand, but the rightful heir if direct lineage was counted. 'William may be small,' he said, 'but we're here to ensure he doesn't grow.' And he too swung himself off his horse, took off his helmet and his gauntlets, held out his arms. 'With or without God's help,' he said, and held the three cousins steady with his gaze as he clasped first one hand, then another, and took his measure of them.

On foot the resemblance between the cousins became more marked. All four were of a height, strong of build, with either chin or eye or nose to mark their common Viking ancestry. Most of all, their way of talk was similar, at least in the three who now took charge: William of Envermeu, Nicholas the Monk, and Ralph de Gacé, each contending for dominance. Ambition sat on them all three, almost tangible like a sheen. And their shared ambition's greed. That was the thing they had most in common.

By mutual consent the three lords who had come armed left

their swords and daggers at the foot of Monk Nicholas's cross; commanded their adherents to keep a distance and wait, which they did, cowed perhaps by that half circle of praying monks. By mutual consent the four cousins then withdrew to squat down together in uneasy proximity: the watchful, silent Mauger, the blunt William, the naïve and pious Nicholas, and Ralph, the most experienced in treachery. They accepted food and drink, which Ralph had previously had prepared, from a trembling old servitor, although none touched what was set before him. The time had come to put matters straight; there could be no more subterfuge.

Ralph went to the heart of the issue, no delicacy left in him. 'Give me the duchy,' he said, 'I merit it. When I have it, and I shall have it, with or without your leave, then I will grant you what you want.'

'And if I want the duchy too?'

'It is mine by right.'

William and Nicholas spoke as one: why should Ralph have thought these cousins any less backward in their demands than he was? He eyed them. 'Careful,' he heard his father's voice whisper again.

Carefully then he said, 'Cousin Nicholas, your claim is just, but who will back you?' He gestured to where the monks still crouched. 'They are not armed, these men of God.' As Nicholas opened his mouth in protest: 'Oh, God speaks through them,' Ralph added, 'that I know, but it is swords not words that will win this time. You have grown up a monk. For right or wrong your uncle made you one. Where are your bodyguards, your retainers, your feudal levies to form your army? You do not even know how to draw a sword yourself.'

He leaned forward, his words honey-coated in persuasion. 'St-Ouen has been your home, your shelter, your dukedom. Withdraw your claim and St-Ouen shall be yours for good.'

And, as he saw understanding leap into his cousin's eyes, 'I'll make you abbot of it,' Ralph said.

The monk's struggle was short, the lust for power over things appreciated and familiar contending with the privileges of those unfamiliar and perilous – and when Nicholas said, 'There must be no killing. I'll have no blood,' Ralph knew he had gained one adherent.

He ignored the last remark, turning next to the brothers Envermeu. They'd be more difficult to handle, and were two to his one. They again sat side by side, shoulders touching, Mauger letting sand drain through his fingers but missing nothing, William with his neck and jaw thrust out even further, his eyes dark and demanding. But they're younger than I am, new come to collusion, Ralph told himself, once more measuring them. They act together, I see that; they speak as if of one mind, but the younger is the dominant. Softly now, let's negotiate, he thought.

He spoke to the younger first. 'I grant you are strong,' he said. 'I grant you are rich. But in reality these things will hinder you. For who among your fellow lords will wish you greater than you are to give you the whole of it? I myself would not countenance it, and I already have at my command the greatest part of Normandy. Remember, I still hold the title of "princeps" of the Norman troops. As head of the Norman army, I can call on it. Back me, and I reward you with lands that will cause no envy nor counter-claim. I make you Count of Arques,' he said, dangling the bribe. And to the elder who waited silent but expectant, 'And for you my Lord Mauger, as good a gift: the Archbishopric of Rouen.'

Again he watched hopes leap behind greedy eyes. 'Two for the price of one,' he thought, 'and farewell to my brother's hopes. But in the scale of things that's cheap.'

He took a drink of his wine that they were afraid to touch, spread out his hands, palms up to show they were empty. 'But if you refuse,' he said, 'I move alone. And I move now while the time is ripe. We shall not have a second chance. I know well the castle where the boy is kept,' he added in a lower voice, 'and I have the means to get at him.'

'And in return?'

Ralph laughed. 'Why nothing, cousins,' he said. 'There's the beauty of it. Nothing at all, save your indulgence to let me do what must be done in my own way. And neither knowledge nor blame on your heads. That's a bargain you can't miss.'

It was his masterstroke. No matter that it stabbed his own brother in the back, no matter that he gave away lands and titles and offices that were not his to give, the bribes dangled to good effect. Before the sun had sunk behind the dunes and the evening wind had quieted, the agreement was sealed. To the three who accepted, titles, lands and influence, both temporal and ecclesiastical. All in return for quietude, for acquiesience while Ralph de Gaće alone put his own mortal soul in jeopardy and began his devil's work. *The time is ripe.* And the sin, if sin there were, all on his head: not even a monk could fault that. As Ralph had said, the bargain was cheap.

Except before they parted, William of Envermeu, the new Count of Arques, claimed the satisfaction of having the last word.

He lumbered to his feet, his bull-like neck thrust forward. 'So be it,' he said. 'We accept, and agree to your conditions. Now hear ours. First that there be no trickery. Whether you succeed or not, the bargain stands as struck. And second, you have one chance only.' He held up his finger. 'One only,' he repeated. 'Fail, and we override you and act on our own behalf.'

So that was how the conspiracy was hatched and why it took so long in the making. More than three years were to pass after the archbishop's death before de Gaće's malice was liberated. During that time William had lived in Vaudreuil, growing to young boyhood, at the half-way stage of life: no longer a child, not yet the man he hoped to be. By then he had come to like Vaudreuil well enough. The memory of his former existence, and his years at Falaise with Herleve, his stay in Paris, even the recollection of that strange girl whose insults had so marked him, had begun to recede. He never spoke of Matilda of Flanders, held Matilda in abeyance, as it were, for future reference: but to keep the other things alive sometimes he spoke of them with Walter, relying on his uncle's memory to supplement his own, sensing in his uncle's words Walter's deep and abiding affection for Falaise. And as the castle lacked any softening woman's influence, Osbern's wife being so timid of nature as to avoid even the office of chatelaine, leaving that task to two old serving-dames, he would have been in fair way to grow up as gruff as any hardened soldier if it had not been for these moments of family intimacy with Walter.

Most of all he loved his uncle to talk of Herleve, and what her life had been as a little girl in Fulbert's tannery. Then he would feel comforted that at least Herleve would not have forgotten him, as if speaking of her brought her again within his reach. The story of how she had met his father, and how Duke Robert had fallen in love with her when he had seen her washing clothes near Fulbert's cottage, cheered many lonely hours. And afterwards, he would sometimes hug his uncle in an excess of affection, showering on his uncle all his latent feelings for his mother. But as time had passed these sessions also had gradually diminished, for natural reasons.

During these three years Turold had begun William's training as a knight and it was with Turold now that the young duke found his true occupation. As a commoner Walter had no part in that venture, although sometimes William persuaded his uncle to speak of their adventures on the way to Paris, as comrades-in-arms might do, recalling, and exaggerating, shared dangers.

Yet whenever William came to his uncle with some request, to mend a piece of leather, to stitch a new belt, Walter's good humour never stinted help. Walter was like a pillar, William thought sometimes when he looked at his uncle: he remains in the background, always relied upon. The strangeness of the oath that Walter had sworn, and the belief in William's future greatness were still bonds between them: they had never passed from William's memory.

William had thrown himself wholeheartedly into military discipline, vowing to himself to excel at soldiering and be worthy of the men he would lead. Soon there was little he did not know about arms and horsemanship, although for monkish learning, for writing and reading, he showed small aptitude, and in spite of the priest's patience seldom remembered anything long, those small dark squiggles of quill and ink remaining as mysterious as the sound of Latin and the meaning of its words. One day then, in the spring following his cousins' momentous meeting, he and Turold were practising tilting at the quintain in the water meadows, it seemed for hours. Of all the things William had learned, such as swordsmanship and use of a lance and shield, horsemanship came to him most naturally, as if the skill had been bred into his bones. The horse he rode was a warrior's stallion, battle-wise, and William had already learned to stop it mid-gallop, to wheel and charge again, to mount it by leaping on fully armed as his father could – and Guy of Burgundy could not. Now he was learning to control the reins while hefting a lance, a war spear still too big for him. He held it at a slant while he aimed the point at the quintain, a metal ring hung on a chain from a wooden beam. The object of the exercise was to strike the ring as accurately as a diving falcon, meanwhile avoiding the return swing of the tilting chain. If it hit him William fell off but no one ran to pick him up. He had to scramble up as a real soldier would, an unhorsed knight as vulnerable as a hedgehog on its back. Again and again he had mounted, galloped, lunged, tumbled, until he fell no more, although his body ached and his arms were sore, his rib-cage so stiff it would not bend. Still Turold was not satisfied, having reached a stage where it was not 'expertise' he had to teach but caution and restraint. Finally William had been allowed to rein up, and was resting on his saddle bow, listening with half an ear while Turold chided. 'Lean so far out at the charge and you're dead; 'tis recklessness no experienced knight would resist; a seasoned rider will catch you in the ribs, winkle you from your horse like winkling shells from rock. God's

teeth do you think to grow wings and fly!' And so on and on . . .
until the sight of Steward Osbern's hasty progress towards them
halted the tirade mid-sentence.

Turold and William watched the steward without alarm until he
drew close enough for them to see his expression, close enough to
note that over his fur-lined gown he had belted on his sword,
and that, behind him, issuing from the castle gates, a number of
men came at a trot, spears at the ready. It was not for Osbern's
own protection that the guard was called. Although of high birth
he took little pride in his own rank, and seeing the steward
surrounded by that company was enough to make Turold grasp
for William's bridle to steady him. Meanwhile from the battlements came the sound of running feet, the shouts of men, all the
hubbub and disturbance of a castle put on alert.

'My lord, my lord,' Osbern was panting, his boots slipping on
the churned-up turf; he began speaking to them while still some
distance away. 'Come you within. You are in danger even as we
talk.' And impatient to be gone he hurried up to William and
seized the rein as if he wanted to tug William, horse, Turold and
all, back towards the castle. But William sat like stone, narrowing
his eyes against the sun and trying to still the thudding of his
heart.

It was not until the guards had surrounded him, had begun to
escort him back, Turold and Osbern keeping step with them,
that the older man relaxed sufficiently to ask the questions and
receive the answers that were required.

'Bad news,' Turold stated quietly. He did not have to ask, the
fact was written on Osbern's lined face, grey with sudden anxiety.

'The worst.'

Now that his young master was out of danger, removed from
the meadow where closeness to the forest's edge could have
exposed him to the arrows of hidden assassins, Osbern could
permit himself to respond. 'The worst,' he repeated. 'Messages
from Brittany and Count Brionne's court and from Rouen, each
contending with each, which to tell first.'

He paused, collected himself, and spoke more calmly. 'First
from Rouen, the lesser this, although not unexpected since the
old archbishop's death. Well, the archbishop's usefulness had
passed. But not to us,' he added in a lower voice, 'for he kept
other evil leashed, which else would have struck us down.'

He did not name that evil then but William understood the
meaning. He felt a quickening of his pulse, like a tremor along
the skin.

'Since the archbishop's death it appears that evil has been

waiting, gathering strength like a viper coiled in a nest. Hear this, how now it strikes full force. For three years the archbishopric has been held in abeyance. It goes, not to the youngest son as the old man had planned, but is seized – usurped he would have said – by Mauger, your father's step-brother, Papia's son. The archbishop's eldest son retains Évreax all right, but Papia's spawn take advantage to make their move against the others. Mauger becomes Archbishop of Rouen. God save the mark, 'tis putting a second devil in God's seat. And Mauger's brother becomes Count of Arques.'

He groaned, smote his forehead. 'Whence came his right to a title of that sort, by Jesu, that too smacks of collusion. Why him, when two of the old archbishop's sons are unprovided for? Two rewarded, two not, and the balance shifts. I mistrust such dealings.'

Again Osbern groaned. 'Now for the worst,' he said, 'misfortune comes in droves. God forgive the words I speak. From Brittany, a message that Count Alan is dead, dead in the midst of health, unexpectedly torn from life, one moment breathing, laughing, speaking, the next withered, like a plant plucked by its roots. His people whisper,' he went on, 'that such quick transition speaks of deeds unnatural. They recall the manner of Your Grace's uncle's death, and before him your grandfather – both dead, 'tis claimed, by poisoning.'

By then they had come to the shadow of the castle gates, and there at last Osbern let the bridle loose and stood aside to let William pass.

'And from Brionne a last calamity. Count Gilbert also is dead, God save his soul, that good man cut down where he rode among his own people on his own lands. Murdered.'

The words trailed like a gloomy shadow, as deep as the shadow cast by the gates, beyond which they could see into the sunlit courtyard, already humming with military activity, as solid as those dark bars which once William had felt close about him in Paris.

'Who the murderers?'

William heard Turold speak calmly but his own heart beat loud in his throat as it had long ago when he had suddenly been hauled upside down to feel his head swing through air.

'The archbishop's sons, who else?' Osbern snarled. 'The disgruntled sons, or rather the one with venom left. Some of the assassins lived long enough to give him name, squealing blame to win a few more moments' grace of breath. Ralph de Gacé has made his first strike.'

That name cast its own shadow, deep and jangling to the nerves, like the clanging shut of gates, resonant with threat.

'So he steals from us our most powerful friends. But, praise God, we shall nevertheless not lack for them.'

Osbern suddenly stopped in his tracks, his round honest face contracting with pain. 'My sister, Gunnor, married a Norman duke,' he cried. 'Count Gilbert was a grandson of that same duke. Did either Gilbert or I covet what is the duke's? Praise God,' he repeated, 'there are others loyal in this land who will stick with us. We may grieve for these foul deaths but we will not be destroyed by them. Nor lack for honest messengers and loyal guards, nor faithful allies, whose walls and gates are built to shut our enemies out.'

And with these words of defiance, when all were safely inside the castle, he himself barred the gates, ordering them not to be opened on pain of death.

He spoke too soon. And he spoke wrong. Not all were as loyal as he hoped. Messengers can be bribed, messages delayed or misdelivered or falsified. Guards can be seduced and brought to treachery; friends bought and sold. And gates and walls are only strong if the enemy is locked without, not hidden within. The messengers who came to Vaudreuil brought news of Ralph's immediate strike, a shrewd attack against the young duke's main support, reducing William's power by murder of his guardians. Within the castle itself his secret spies made ready for the final attempt.

The signal could have been easily given, prearranged long ago, perhaps even before William went to Paris. A messenger, especially one from a supposedly friendly court, is granted immunity by courtesy of rank. He needs but a moment to take advantage of immunity to give a sign. The dropping of a stone, the plucking of a leaf, even a supposed scuffle with a castle guard, and the word is passed with never a hint of suspicion on giver or recipient. Steward Osbern, man of the world though he was, was not prepared for it; not for the fact that among the members of the ducal guard infiltrators could have crept, to their disgrace and his shame. Nor that even in William's own household, where Osbern's writ ran, treason lay waiting. Had he known he would have given his honour, nay his life, to prevent it.

Chapter 8

In Vaudreuil that night all was prepared for attack, the sentries set to double watch, the guardroom armed, even the victuals siege-rationed and served as such – to the castle's disgust. Who would willingly eat salt fish and stale biscuit when outside fresh baked bread and roasted meat and good Norman milk and cheese were abundant? The local peasants even went so far as to hammer on the gates to be let in with their wares. 'You may enter if you wish,' Osbern roared, 'but once in you stay. And leave your cattle and your goods at home. We eat what we have, and thank God for it.' And to his nervous wife, 'Hurry woman, and serve the newest wine before my men drag out the old, pretending it will go down more unpalatable.' He did not rest from worrying, and together with Turold he toured the castle, from dungeon to battlement, to ensure all was in order before they retired.

All was. And so outside, nothing stirred except serf and peasant going about their tasks in field and byre. Yet Osbern's nature, his duty, was to anticipate the worst. Even when he inspected the castle watch, as steady a band of troops as he could muster, he was still troubled, some sixth sense perhaps pricking at his thumbs. 'I could wish for Count Alan's men,' he fretted. 'Were they here I'd feel better prepared. Or others from Brionne to supplement the guard. Come the morrow I shall send to Conteville to ask the Lady Herleve for help. She and her new lord will willingly give support.'

He did not mention her name to William, having been careful in all the intervening years never to do so: mainly to shield the boy from his own loss, but also to distance him from her as she had herself desired, lessening the relationship both she and he knew was demeaning in many eyes. But he did warn Walter to prepare to leave for Conteville with the dawn. Walter he could spare for the message he meant to send.

In the chamber where he slept – similar to his father's at Falaise but more simply made, with floors and walls of wood –

William was remembering all that the day had brought. As was his custom he said his prayers, in them remembering his mother, and if sometimes his lady mother and the Mother of God became interwoven and indistinguishable, he meant no sacrilege, only felt something warm and tender in the darkness. This night he especially wished for her. On an impulse which he never afterwards could explain he took from under his treasures the medallion she had given him, and looped the chain around his neck. Saint Michael was said to protect travellers. Perhaps in the days ahead he'd need the saint's protection.

But neither the touch of the medallion, nor his prayers could keep away the other thoughts that rose solid and threatening from the dark, for all he tried to force them down. From the embrasure he could look out over the sleeping meadows and woods. He knew Osbern well enough to know that until this crisis passed he'd be kept inside, no more riding down those forest trails with the wind in his face and the thud of his horse's hooves beating a tattoo and the trumpet signalling the chase. He tried to think of deer with wide branching horns. Or hares, doubling back upon their tracks, fast and cunning. Or boars – why not a boar with fetid breath and small red eyes and glittering tusks . . . ? The great hound that Count Brian had given him thumped its tail in sympathy.

But Count Brian was dead – there came new darkness – and Count Alan also. Two men dead, his friends, his kin. And him responsible for their killing!

All day in the privacy of his thoughts he had grieved for them; now he twisted and turned upon his pallet of straw, bunching it in wads. He knew why both men had served him as they did – to keep him safe to rule Normandy. They wanted a better, fairer, rule than Great-uncle Rouen's. If then they had been killed it was because of him; they had always been at risk because of him, and he not able to lift a finger in their defence.

Great-uncle Rouen he had not grieved for; Great-uncle Rouen had wished him dead – at least his son had. And now Ralph de Gacé was accused of murdering Count Brian, perhaps of murdering Count Alan as well. Where was the justice in Normandy to hold Ralph de Gacé to account if the Holy Church did not? Ralph de Gacé he had not met, had never even seen the man; Great-uncle Rouen he remembered as someone tall and cold and hostile. But the faces of those younger lords came clear to him as if they stood before him and would not go away: Count Brian with his generous laugh, Count Alan slighter, taut like a bowstring. What of the children they left, the sons orphaned, the wives widowed? Who spoke for them?

Merciful God, he prayed, take from me the blame of their passing. For I purposed not their deaths when I held them as my friends. I meant not to bring destruction on those dear to me.

He held his breath so no one should hear him, and listened. A log shifted on the hearth, the flames spluttered. In the outer room he heard Turold's voice and Osbern's answer; he heard Walter's laugh. They were all three of them together but he felt no relief in their nearness. That darker, more cruel thought pressed upon him; he needed to think it through as a man presses on a thorn where it enters the flesh. For it was not only these most recent deaths; there were all the others – even that first one of Hugh the Messenger – that were to his charge. God forgive, he was as bad as any murderer himself. Perhaps I should be like Uncle Nicholas, he thought, and hie me to a monastery and let the dukedom go to waste. But it was too late for that. He knew it as he heard Walter speak, 'We are bound stronger than this world knows, with or without our will.'

And it seemed to him that his father's voice came to him from the past, that voice with its hint of laughter that he could never duplicate of his own volition; now he heard it and marvelled that he could forget. His memory faded into dream, he was once more in Falaise. Beside him, his father leaned upon the battlements and looked down at the cottages underneath. The village spread pale and sleeping in the moonlight; beyond it stretched the mighty woods, beyond again the whole of Normandy. 'There's our charge,' Robert said to him. 'For every peasant has as much right to life as every lord. And as I swear allegiance to my overlord for my title and land, even to the king of France, so am I sworn to them below to protect and succour them.'

'It is a holy trust,' he said, his voice sober now, speaking as much to himself as William, 'handed down from father to son, five generations of Norman dukes. And you the sixth.'

He smiled, bent down and ruffled his son's hair. 'Rollo the Viking, first of the line, won Normandy,' he said. 'Fought for it with fire and blood. Once his, he settled it with farms and villages and towns, made laws. He handed it to us, his sons, to keep intact. If we must fight to preserve it we will. But after fighting comes the peace, so that law and justice may thrive. That's also our task. And though it bring responsibility so great as to burden us, yet such is the will of God that no man may lay aside the load which fate and destiny have placed on him.'

'By birth and breeding you are my son,' the voice said, 'you have no right to drop the burden God gives. Upon us the weight . . .'

William woke with a great start. He sat up, his breath coming in gasps. The fire had died but light streamed faintly through the loophole cut in the thickness of the wall: starlight, moonlight, he could not tell which, but bright enough to pick out the rough-hewn beams, now so familiar, the coffer where his clothes were kept, the narrow opening that led to the privy draining over the castle sides. Opposite it, the door that gave on to the outer room was closed but light streamed under it, too bright for the usual taper. And the sound of voices was loud, louder than it should have been. Although he distinguished those of Osbern and Turold, William instinctively reached under the pillow where *ma mie's* little knife was always kept; when he pulled his tunic on he slipped it into the sleeve, as Walter had taught him, ready to hand. Barefoot he crept to the closed door and looked through the cracks. Beside him his hound growled low.

Osbern and Turold were standing close together, Walter a pace behind them; a table spread with parchment stood between them and a second door which gave on to a main stairway. None had swords belted on, their weapons rested sheathed against the wall. They would have been passing the night as they often did, with discussion of strategy, with charts and calculations of troops and castles and placements of allies. William recognized those charts with their spidery drawings of maps; he had often studied them. Although he could not read, the thin lines of rivers, the circles of castles and the indented coast had fascinated him. It would not be quarrel over charts that had made his companions raise their voices.

Then a movement caught his attention, a flicker where there should have been none. He strained to look. The outer door was open, men were standing there, he could not tell how many but several. He caught a gleam of their drawn weapons, heard Osbern shout again, 'What madness this? We gave no alarm. Where is the watch, where the captain of the guard?'

'Dead.'

A man stepped forward, sword in hand. William knew him, a thin, black-haired man with broken teeth; a quiet man, noted for his swordsmanship. 'Dead. And his fellows with him. The guardroom gate is locked. We hold it until you yield yourselves, and William with you.'

William caught a moment's frantic exchange between his

friends, then chaos erupted. The men at the door charged forward. Osbern met them with his own body, hurled himself against their sword-points valiantly, giving Turold time to snatch a sword and back up against the inner door, while Walter slid through it fast, almost stumbling over William and the dog.

'Quick,' his uncle breathed. He was already dragging at the coffer, straining to heave it against the door, pushing at the bedpost, the wooden legs scraping roughly on the uneven floor. William strained to help him. In the outer room there was a clash of steel, a broken cry, then a heavy fall.

'Treachery,' Walter said. Tears were streaming down his cheeks and blood from his torn nails smeared his palms. In a bound he crossed to the small privy entrance. Behind them came another cry, another shout, the shout of the Norman dukes: William recognized Turold's voice.

'Bid your hound stay.' Walter was pulling at William's arm. 'Through here's our only chance.' He had bent to peer through the wide-mouthed embrasure that gave on to the outer walls, and was unwinding a coil of rope that had never been there before; Osbern must have had it placed there as extra precaution. As in a nightmare William watched Walter measure it, loop one end round a projecting beam of wood and haul tight; felt the other end knotted about his waist and shoulders in a harness.

'Down you go, 'Walter cried, 'no looking back. They're all inside as yet. Turold will hold.'

He suddenly whispered as if stupefied, 'Treachery, and from our own guard. And I not even armed.'

As William still resisted, crying out that they must stand and help, Walter repeated, 'Turold will hold, but afterwards the door will break.' Anguished, he cried. 'Would I choose to leave my friends? But we cannot help them. Turold and Osbern are dead men. They sell their lives to give us time.'

Then, although William clung to the ledge, 'Hold fast,' Walter said and with great strength manhandled William out of the window.

The rope went snaking out under the lip of the battlements. William went with it. He found he was being lowered quickly and not very expertly into a void, much as he remembered from the farmhouse on the way to Paris, the stench of fresh excrement stinging his eyes and nose, the wood splintering into shards which scraped his face and hands raw. The more he clawed to stop or reverse the descent, the more the rope cut at him, the medallion round his neck catching in his eyes as he dangled like a granary sack.

Now the ground was coming up fast, littered with rocks in the shadow of the keep. Overhead the moonlight streamed in fitful shapes. There were snatches of other sounds – screams cut off short, more shouts, the clash of weapons – all proof that the unbelievable had happened, the one thing Osbern for all his care had not counted on. Strangely the realization steadied William. He no longer fought the rope, but reached out for hand- or foothold to take some of the strain. When he was fairly down, he severed the knots that held him with his knife and steadied the rope's end as Walter slid as quickly after him.

Smelling like a sewer, their clothes and skin stained with ordure, they crouched like hares in the rough gorse and grass which lined the sides of the mound on which the castle was built, straining to hear the louder shouts that would warn that their escape route was known. Behind them came another burst of cries, a woman's scream, surely that was Osbern's wife, poor soul, for all her reticence she too paid the ultimate price for her husband's loyalty. The moon, like a lantern, lit up the entrance to the keep but left long shadows on its eastern face. 'Now,' Walter hissed.

He thrust himself face down in the grass, slithering snakelike through it into the shadow. Once there, he stood up for a moment to take stock, then began again to move on all fours towards the forest edge, for all his girth moving so rapidly that William could scarcely keep up with him. The gorse bushes tore at their faces, their hands bled again; Walter didn't pause until they had come squarely under the shelter of the trees where he motioned William to lie still and listen. The noises on the battlement, where some loyal guardsmen survived to keep up the fight, continued to ring out, but of pursuit there was no sign.

'Turold still holds,' Walter said, grimly pleased. He started out once more, running now along the forest's rim, ducking in and out under the branches, William after him. They ran and ran, a weaving course that brought them to the bank of the mill-race which gave its name to the water meadows. Here, below the mill, the race was not wide but fast and deep. Walter plunged in without a word, pulling William after him, thrusting breast-high out into the current until it took hold of them.

The touch of the water was cold; it stung their bruises and burns. When William started to protest he could not swim, brackish water filled his mouth, blocking his nose and almost choking him. 'Lie on your back,' Walter said. 'Let your legs go ahead. Lean on me when you tire; the current carries us.'

He held William's head crooked in his arm and for the first

time let a grim smile form. 'Now the odds are even,' he said. 'The water hides our tracks. If we can but come to where the race joins a river further down, and if from there we can make progress to the Seine, then God gives us a fair chance. So keep close your mouth and pray, while I plan.'

They floated along in silence for a while, then hurriedly he began to tell William what to do if and when the hunt followed them. 'For they'll follow afterwards,' he said. They'll have out horses and hounds to track us down. If your hound lives they'll use him. It's the surest way of catching fugitives.'

He did not explain whence came his knowledge but William knew it was from some personal experience. Nor did he explain what that *afterwards* meant but William understood. *Afterwards*, when Turold is dead. *Afterwards*, if they don't kill your dog; *afterwards*, if there is an *afterwards*.

He told William that if they were separated or he was caught, William must not try to help, must not turn back or hesitate, but go on alone. And where the mill-race entered a first river, the Eure, which William might remember from a previous time when they had crossed it much further south, there would be rough water for sure, but no barrier to one who knew how to navigate it. And beyond this joining point William would find the river split, spilling into large, reed-lined pools where he could hide, all day if need be, until the hunt had cooled. And when he was free to journey on he must go eastwards towards a second river, some four miles beyond, crossing through a marshy plain, always keeping in water if he could since water drowns out scent.

And on reaching this second river, the mighty Seine, he must somehow gain its eastern bank, if necessary going upstream, never down, for down would lead back towards Rouen.

Walter spoke quickly, without mincing his words, and with such conviction, with such quick and certain energy, that William almost had the impression that Walter had it already planned – as might a knight, being a stranger in a castle, previously search out the lie of outer walls and sally ports and battlements.

Nor did William question his uncle's strategem although the name 'Eure' was one he certainly had never forgotten and almost dreaded. He listened intently to his uncle's words, hearing nothing else except the gurgle of the current and the flap of birds disturbed from their roosts, letting himself float through the moonlit night, letting the coolness lave his cuts, washing the fever out of them. And washing out the horror and fear.

Tree branches trailed across the stream, catching at them with their leaves; sometimes the smell of hay rose new and strong from unseen fields. They might have floated on in this strange, insubstantial world, had not a louder sound behind them rent the air with its frightening blast; a trumpet, blown from a distance still, but following fast.

'They come,' Walter had time to say before another danger took hold of them. The race narrowed, the current strengthened as freshlets came tumbling in. Lines of foam and bubbles clung to the rocks which lined the banks and forced man and boy down into a kind of sluice.

It tore William from Walter's grasp, spun him round while he struggled to remember what Walter had said, how to lie on his back, feet first, and go with the current, fending off rocks and avoiding undertows. All in vain. He was tossed like a twig, unable to remember anything. Boulders, smooth as glass, reared up, frothed past; a sudden patch of calm erupted in a line of spray; waves crested white as teeth. Then one final wave, higher than the rest, threw him in the air, plunged and held him under. He came up gasping like a fish, hauled by the collar as his uncle stood on the lower bank to reel him in.

'Well done, my lord,' Walter said. Water streamed from his clothes and hair; he looked more fish than man himself. 'We'll make an outlaw of you yet.' And without giving William a chance to recover his breath, he slid once more into the quieter waters of the Eure.

Strands of green weed floated beneath the surface; in the shallows moonlight gleamed on pebbles. Still holding William, Walter paddled slowly along looking for a perfect hiding place. He found it a half-mile downstream, where a small spit of rock stretched out to trap mounds of driftwood to form a pool. On the outer edge of the rocks, the water was still and deep; dense reed beds fringed the inner. Low bushes and shrubs grew among the sand and gravel between the rocks. Together with the debris this afforded additional shelter but still allowed clear views of the main river banks in both directions. And here they were safe to drag themselves out and rest for a moment, and when the sun came up, to warm themselves.

There was no further sound of the hunt. As time passed they began to believe that the pursuit must be concentrated around the forest in the vicinity of the castle, as Walter hoped. But just in case, Walter took William's knife to search for hollow reeds which he cut and peeled for use as breathing tubes if they had to dive beneath the surface to hide again.

William lay on the rocks with eyes closed, naked in the sun, for he had taken off his tunic, wrung it out and spread it on a bush to dry. His skin felt wrinkled like overwashed fruit, his mind was blank. Behind his closed eyelids lights danced. He was too tired to move. Too tired to eat. Yet when Walter came back with berries and plants he sat up, suddenly ravenous.

The breakfast was meagre, the weeds bitter or pungent and strange to the taste. But the berries were sweet and the sun hot. For the first time since their flight William dared think of those whom they had left behind. He was just about to speak when a sudden rustling on the bank upstream alerted them to another's presence.

A horseman stood there, for a moment outlined in the sunlight; William could see the gold leopards of the crest; beside him two hounds sniffed. The another horseman came rearing up beside the first, together they conferred before turning as if to make their way along the bank towards the rock spit.

'Jesu,' Walter breathed. 'I guessed wrong.' At his nod, William seized his tunic and, under the shelter of the bushes, slid along the outer logs into the depths of the river. Beside him, sleek as an otter, Walter moved without a ripple. Clasping William by the waist, he drew him down; together they sank down to sit upon the river bed, let the green sun-shot water close above their heads, and waited. Floating among the debris like two innocent air bubbles were the two hollow stalks upon which their lives now depended.

The riders were weary, and in ill-humour. While the rest of their companions had taken easier routes through woods away from the Eure, they had been detailed to follow it. Theirs had been the harder ride, and nothing for their pains either; no sniff of scent, no trace, no likelihood of finding any, for certainly their quarry could not have swum this far. Yet still they persisted. Their master had paid them well, they owed him thoroughness. But they themselves were hot and tired and in bad temper.

'We should have spared his hound,' the second horseman was grumbling, a young squire in the ducal court, son of a minor lord, turned by some bribe. 'Alive, at least it'd have given lead to the boy's track. And it was a noble beast. Did you see how it leapt at us when we broke down the door?'

The first, the same thin dark guardsman of the main attack, trained by Osbern himself to be thorough, grunted. 'And made us waste more time,' he said sarcastically. ''Tis all of a piece. Who would have thought Osbern to have sacrificed life so readily, old Turold to have resisted so long, and the peasant to have got the bastard down the wall? Even the forest to have hidden them so well? I tell you, comrade, 'tisn't natural. And for our pains what shall we get? Curses and blows, if that, and wet boots into the bargain. I'd set my heart on gold.'

He stretched and yawned, showing his shattered teeth, for all his riding spry in the saddle, one of Ralph de Gacé's 'spies' who had been long sent to infiltrate the ducal guard and who at last had been called on to play the part for which he originally had been bought. And who now saw reward fast eluding him. Gold was what he wanted: money to buy him a tavern in Honfleur and a wench for company.

'Call off the dogs,' he commanded the younger squire. 'Tie them up before they stray. Unfasten your saddle bag, then fetch water. We'll mix it with the wine to stretch it further. And when we've eaten – then, by God, we'll just hunt on. They can't have vanished.' He shouted to the other's retreating back, 'And water for my horse as well; he needs it.'

The younger man did not reply, perhaps not hearing over the tumble of the mill-race where it spilled into the river. In any case, he was too busy with dogs and saddle bags and his own horse to see to everything at once. The older grunted again and urged his horse down the path, its hooves slipping on the stones which poked up through the grass. He let it crash among the reed beds and drink its fill, its big feet muddying the water until a strange glittering caught his eye; a shiny object lay in a small spit of rock where some low bushes grew.

He was tired but curious. Dismounting, treading carefully with his spurred feet among the reeds, he made his way out through the bushes until he came on to the outer rim of the rock spit, where logs brought down by winter storms were stacked and where the water eddied past rocks flat, like beached whales. The shining thing was small but it glittered brightly in the sun, and as he bent to pick it up the gold image of St Michael stared back at him, lying where it had fallen from William's neck when he had removed his tunic.

The guardsman started up, looked around him, looked back towards where his companion now sat in the shade beneath a tree. Here the rocks were shimmering also with heat, but wasn't that a trace of wet, there on one side, and weren't those stalks and pits of berries, fallen where none were growing? An animal perhaps; but animals don't wear gold.

He opened his mouth to shout, thought better of it, loosened his sword, walked with firm and certain step towards the water's edge, and looked down into the depths.

The swirl of light and water bothered him; he shaded his eyes as a man who tries to see a fish; two shapes like shadows there on the bottom, weren't there two? He leaned further out, his smile of satisfaction reflected for a moment on the surface. Like a trout that leaps for flies, Walter broke the water in a swirl, caught the man about the knees, toppling him headfirst, then dragged him under.

He fell ponderously, with one great splash sinking without trace, the weight of his helmet, armour, sword-belt and sword anchoring him upside down. Walter never let go his hold, struck under the arm with William's knife until the water grew red. And when the thrashing had ceased, and no more bubbles formed, when the shape lay rigid like a piece of piping, Walter rose again from the river bed, crept out among the bushes, hugging the ground without causing a single stir. But this time he was armed with a sword.

Such care was unnecessary. Seated unsuspecting against a tree, back to the river, corslet and helmet put aside, his sword-belt dangling, the second squire had heard nothing above the sound of the mill-race; he was too busy with goat cheese and oat cakes to know what struck him. One swift leap, one thrust, and Walter had taken possession of a second sword and a second horse all before William could join him.

'Now, nephew,' he said as William came up, 'we have matched them. Throw this fellow to join the other, and we'll ride off, no one the wiser. And this time when we leave,' he struggled with the sword-belt to tug it free, 'we'll be armed like men.'

Walter could not keep the triumph from his voice. It came out almost without his knowing, the triumph of a peasant who bests those who have mastery over him. And hearing it but not yet knowing it, William shared in his jubilation.

Hastily they anchored the bodies beneath the logs where drift and sand would hold them, let water and weed lap them round as secure as lead. Even had William missed the gold medallion he would never have thought to look for it in that iron clasp. As best he could, Walter armed himself in the young squire's armour, for it would not fit William and in truth Walter was too short and wide for it. Binding the leopard flag beneath his shirt, William girded on a sword. Both he and his uncle took up the horse bridles, mounted and rode on through the marshes towards the Seine.

The land sank into bog, and became even more thickly spread with rushes; the hot sun beat down and flies and mosquitoes buzzed, driving the men and their horses wild; and as Walter had described, the River Eure spread and coiled. They could not even be sure which was the main water-course, but when they came to the Seine they knew it by the wide shimmering expanse that suddenly spread before them.

Again, by luck, avoiding the jetty where a ferry boat poled back and forth, they rounded a great bend where a narrow stretch of sand, shaded by low-hanging willows, edged the river. 'We cross now,' Walter said after a moment's thought. 'No use to wait.' He urged his horse into the water; when the current took them it began to swim. As if used to this method of travel, he stuck his feet out straight, leaned back on the saddle and smiled over his shoulder at William who still hesitated on the bank. And encouraged by that smile William too gingerly entered the Seine and let his horse carry him to the other side. On the eastern back the great Forest of Lyon covered their tracks and hid them.

When, days later, the rest of Ralph de Gacé's men came to where the mill-race entered the Eure, they found the hounds tied to a tree and mad for hunger. But of their two comrades who should have been waiting, and their horses, there was no trace except a few hoof marks already old and fading.

Meanwhile in his little stronghold of Gacé, Ralph sent order after order to search and find, gnawed his knuckles with chagrin, and cursed God that for all his efforts William again had escaped him. *The time is ripe*, de Gacé thought. He had made his bid with all the cunning of which he was capable. If he had failed he would never get a second chance. William of Arques would make sure of that, and he, Ralph, would be finished. It was a sobering notion.

Chapter 9

All through the day and part of the night the fugitives rode through the forest, Walter in the lead. William was not sure where they were going but guessed Walter was still trying to keep parallel to the winding river. Walter himself moved confidently, as if this green and dim undergrowth was as familiar to him as the green underwaters of the Eure. Perhaps it was. In his youth he would have known many such wanderings. Whenever they came to any path, he made them dismount, crossed first to make sure no one was about, then beckoned to his nephew. It was only when the moon began to wane that he gave the word to halt. 'We rest now till dawn,' he said, 'then we go on again. For they'll not tire either, and we must keep ahead of them.'

Walter dismounted, throwing his weight awkwardly against his horse. But riding did not weary William; William could have ridden day and night. It was the thought of resting which bothered him. He did not want the darkness to bring sleep. In sleep there would be too many ghosts.

Walter had already tethered his horse under a large oak whose branches gave added cover and was searching for bracken stalks to use for bedding. He looked at William, head on one side as was his sister's habit. 'Courage, *mon brave*,' he said as once before, as if he guessed what William felt. 'So far, praise God, they have not laid their hands on you. Oh, I know the cost has been great,' he went on, standing still. He spread his hands. 'God hears me, only He can judge how great, to lose at once so many dear, true men. When shall we see their like again?'

He said, 'And I to run and leave them! Nephew, I do not boast but never in my life have I failed a comrade. And I do not blaspheme to say God takes that sin upon His own conscience. Yet they themselves would have wished it so. And therein lies comfort. That it falls to me alone to keep you safe is proof of their trust.'

He was silent then, but after a while he sighed, and looked critically at William, who had followed his example – tying his horse and feeding it from a saddle bag knotted on the cruppers. 'Fresh as a daisy,' he said, 'and I as stiff as an old rake. How to hide you? On horseback you are even more yourself. Can't you sit askew, all of a lump? Or dangle your legs like a plough boy?'

He laughed suddenly. 'Who am I to teach you horsemanship?' he said.

While they ate of the remaining oaten cakes he took up a twig and began to scratch on the earth, trying to recreate from memory Osbern's charts, plotting routes, assessing distances. There was no sound, only night-jars cried and once an owl hooted in the distance. The air was warm, laced with the scent of fresh-cut grass and bracken which they had gathered for a bed; they might have been on a hunting expedition rather than being hunted themselves.

Finally Walter put the stick aside and with his boot rubbed out the marks. 'We've gone too far east,' he said ruefully, 'although 'tis true we had little choice. And the loops of the river are confusing. This way brings us to the lands of the French king.'

When William cried, 'I'll have no more dealings with him!' Walter replied, 'I am at one with you. But here's a difficulty. If we are to reach Conteville, as I think best, we must reverse direction and recross the Seine.'

He stopped, waiting for William's response. And for his part William was all for riding openly and fast towards Conteville, trusting to luck; who would prevent them as they now seemed: two men armed and dangerous? 'The whole world,' Walter said grimly. 'Every bridge, every ferry, every ford between here and Conteville will be watched. Not a road or path but they'll be blocked, not a mounted man or boy but they'll be questioned. And even if we got through, how could we avoid recapture when we reached there; it'll be the first place they'll wait for us?'

Worry creased his forehead. He rubbed his hands wearily across his eyes. Responsibility also weighs on him, William thought. Suddenly the forest seemed to close about them threateningly, like that racing river current.

'It seems to me,' Walter said, poking at the ground with his stick, 'the only way to survive is once more to disappear from sight. I admit we needed horses for immediate escape,' he continued, as if arguing with himself, 'there's none better than those of your stable, trained to go unfalteringly for days. And true, in these dangerous times armed men ride safer than those unarmed. But to my mind, William, we will never be safe in this guise. These well-bred creatures, this coat of mail, these very swords, are too fine: they mark us who we are.'

Again he gave William an anxious glance. 'My suggestion is we dress like serfs,' he said, 'live with them until a reasonable time has passed and we are free to make our way home.'

'Peasants will not sell you as other men have done,' he added. 'Among them, we sink like stones without a trace. But we must act and be like them. You'll find no fine lords in their ranks. 'Tis lordship which has put them where they are and made them serfs in the first place.'

He flushed but went on, stoutly honest even in this. 'Believe me,' he said. 'I know the peasant world; I have not lost touch. I mean no disrespect when I insist that just as the Norman noble holds the serf as dirt under his feet, so do the peasants distrust the lords who keep them so bemired. They would not accept you as you are; but they will accept us as refugees from noble justice, whatever that means.' A note of bitterness had crept into his voice; he halted, tried to excuse it.

'Oh, I do not blame your poor father,' he said. 'Under him the laws were just. But he has been dead long enough for harsher rule to return once more.'

He made a gesture, taking in the fire, the grassy beds, the thick soldiers' cloaks spread over them. 'Imagine this in winter,' he said. 'Imagine how the poor people live, whose only means of livelihood is the cultivating of your lands, or the harvesting of your grain, or rearing of your pigs and cows. And whose only crime is trespass in your forests for food and fuel to keep them and their families alive.'

He eyed his nephew. 'Did you know a man can lose a hand, an eye, an arm, for killing deer without your leave?' he said. 'Or that a begger who starves and steals a loaf of bread must hang for it. Or that a cripple who does not move fast will be trampled under your guardsman's horse and no one think twice of it?

'I swear, sometimes in Normandy it takes but a batting of an eyelid to damn a man. And those who run before the law seldom come home again although they may long for it as I did.'

He was silent then as if he feared he had spoken out of place. But after a while he added, 'You should pity the poor who suffer under such a heavy load. For you will enter in their brotherhood just for a while; theirs is a lifelong servitude. Yet I can see that living as a peasant may be difficult for you. You must change your nature, while I return to my true self.'

William had never heard him speak so vehemently nor defend his peasant background so passionately. He knew a little of Walter's former life, but not much, for Walter had always been circumspect. What he did know made him suspect that in his youth Walter had been guilty of some crime greater than poaching deer or game. Some insurrection perhaps, some peasant revolt or rebellion had sent him into banishment, which William's father for unknown reasons had excused. And although he was fond of his uncle and knew him to be brave and honourable it was true that compared with other men, Turold or Osbern for example, Walter had always seemed the lesser, somehow of smaller consequence. But today he had seen another side of his uncle, seen him as a man who could disappear into the woodlands like a shadow, who like some wild animal moved instinctively through a natural environment where he was at ease as his nephew was not.

He looked at Walter carefully. His uncle's thinning fair hair was ruffled, the moonlight peaked his face, turned his nose sharp and pointed; his very ears seemed pricked, as if he were listening while he and William talked. William thought: I have often heard Walter regret his years of banishment and openly confess his happiness at returning to Falaise. But today in the forest, picking his way through danger, Walter was like a deer that steals through the underbrush. Today shows another side of him, he thought, a Walter who is in his element, revealing skills I never knew he had.

William knew that what his uncle proposed made good sense, although at first it went against his own instincts. He found it difficult to explain his feelings without giving offence. It was not that since his time in Paris he had become ashamed of his half-lowly birth, though the taunts he had received there, the insults, had bitten deep. Nor was it that he had become too proud, used to being treated like a duke and to having others defer to him – although in part that was also true. There were more complicated thoughts which, like many others, were impossible to put into words, bound up as they were with that new idea of *responsibility*.

It had occurred to him that if his uncle had voluntarily entered exile again the only reason was to be of service to his nephew. And once more he felt the guilt of accepting Walter's sacrifice, if 'guilt' and 'sacrifice' were not too strong. Walter's sacrifice differed from that of Osbern's and Turold's and his other councillors', to be sure, for they had given their lives; but in its own way it was as great. And just as in his dream he had known that if he himself did not hold fast to his noble part he would be betraying his father's trust, so now he feared that if he gave it up in real life he would be betraying his own birthright. And he would become a person torn in half, neither one thing nor the other, a true half breed, open to all men's contempt because he fitted no man.

In truth these were complicated ideas that needed long and hard sifting. So William remained silent and while they rested let Walter explain how their new role would help them in their journeying. They would become tinkers, he said, never staying in one place long, working for their keep and then moving on. When they travelled they would go by instinct far from the ordinary roads, like birds using landmarks such as trees and rocks and river beds. Walter had no special route in mind and planned to find hiding places within the wilder reaches of the duchy, only turning west towards Conteville when the hunt had cooled – however long that took, mayhap months.

But first they must rid themselves of these rich accoutrements and find the means to recross the Seine; these were their immediate concerns. Once William, by his silence, had given consent, Walter warmed to the task. 'Within the forest there are men who owe allegiance to no one,' he said. 'Charcoal-burners, woodcutters and their like. And on the forest edges, towards the river marshes, live thatchers, basket-weavers and such, who work with withies and reeds. In a sense all these are free to help us or not as they alone see fit. They'll help.'

For the second time he permitted himself a grin. 'Two fine horses,' he said, 'weapons, a chain-mail coat, all in exchange for ragged cottes and a river passage: there's a temptation they'll not refuse.' And when William again looked dubious, 'Nor will they betray us. If for nothing else, out of fear of forfeiting the prize, more than a lifetime of dreaming might get them.'

The next morning they rode on, this time deliberately close to the forest tracks although not actually using them. It soon became clear that Walter was searching for something, or someone. When the sound of chopping filtered through the trees he left William with the horses and armour, went on himself by foot, promising to be quick. Perhaps he was, nevertheless the waiting dragged. The forest that before had seemed safe was suddenly full of noise as if every bush held a trooper; every rustle heralded an armed assassin. Soon William found he was sweating with fear. When Walter returned, laden with food and a bundle of dirty clothing, William was so relieved to see a friendly face that he omitted to ask for details of the exchange.

Walter himself was in high humour. 'All arranged,' he said. 'We leave the horses tethered, no questions asked. They'll be up for sale at the next horse fair, again no questions asked, so altered in colour and markings not even their original riders

111

would recognize them. And God favours us. In a few days' time, on the western bank of the Seine, all the horse-traders and pedlars in the world will be making for St Leufroy Fair, and we along with them.'

He smiled, flexed his fist. 'I was trained as a leather-worker,' he said. 'Like my father I make good straps and belts. Why else should I come to St Leufroy if not to peddle my wares? Tonight we lie low; tomorrow we join a group of fellow workers I've had word of, and cross the river with them under our enemies' very noses.'

He made it sound simple, as if it were something he had arranged a score of times. Perhaps he had. When he and William finally clambered out of the small coracle, having been poled across at dawn by a grumpy ferryman, there was nothing to distinguish them from a load of similarly dressed commoners whose whole intent was to reach the village in time for the fair. Nor did Ralph de Gacé's men posted on the western side – still engaged in an intensive search for the missing heir – give them a second glance, failing to identify the young duke in the grubby apprentice who bent his head and followed his master obediently on foot. Yet every horseman who passed was stopped and carefully scrutinized.

The fair itself they bypassed, to Walter's regret and perhaps even to William's. When well clear of the river guards they slipped off into the woods. Thereafter, as Walter had intended, they kept to places far from any known routes, deep in the forest lands, a game of hide-and-seek at which he excelled. They still did not go straight towards Conteville, but detoured south, taking their time. And after that first occasion, when William had felt that he must be known, when he was terrified his very fear would attract the guards as if it shouted out to them, gradually he too came to play his part with zeal, revelling in the freedom of the vagabond life. If sometimes he felt the lack of security or missed the comradeship of his own kind, he comforted himself with the thought that even in his own world he had often been alone. If at nights he tossed and turned, dreaming of Herleve, this was a loss he had long endured. And if sometimes in nightmares he remembered the manner of their flight so vividly that he woke, drenched with fear, the very air rank with it, so also did the desire for revenge burn in him.

The thought of how one day, to the confusion of his detractors and the defeat of his enemies, he would assume his noble self and return in triumph was a comfort in those bleak and lonely hours. But of all the taunts he recalled, it was those words spoken

– almost it might seem in amaze – by that fair-haired, proud-voiced little maid so many years ago, which rankled most. 'William the Bastard,' she had called him, as if he had no other name. And so had Guy of Burgundy taunted him for a low-born serf. One day, he vowed to himself, those taunts shall recoil on the ones who first uttered them; they shall pay for their temerity. And she who was so proud shall acknowledge me as her lord.

And childlike he revelled in the idea of how she might grovel before him and how he, at last, in Christian magnanimity, might raise her up and give her the kiss of peace. Yet at other times the memory of her was tinged with other thoughts, less belligerent, and he wondered often where she was, what she did, and whether she ever thought of him.

But when the rains came hard and the cold winds blew, just as Walter had predicted, and food was scarce or wanting, who could blame his bitterness as he crouched under a tree bole or hedge and remembered. For now in truth fate had made him no better than a villein, nay worse, since even villeins for the most part had a fixed roof over their heads.

Far off in Flanders, Matilda in truth might be said to be much better housed and fed than William, but he misjudged her to think she would scorn rather than pity him. She herself may never have experienced anything but security, might have found William's sufferings beyond her imagining, so far was her life removed from violence and danger (her few childish mishaps being truly of her own making and by comparison scarce worth the mention); yet when news of the conspiracy in Normandy spread to her father's court, Matilda felt nothing but sympathy for the young duke. And curiosity, that mischievous fault which had already caused her so much trouble.

Although it was over three years now since she had last seen William, she remembered him well. His air of future greatness still remained with her, not like the bragging of other boys, nor the swaggering of her brothers, all froth and wind. Rather, his had been a firm reliance on himself that brooked no interference, a belief in divine providence, of the sort she had decided that priests have. How could such assurance come to so miserable an end?

She did not like to ask her mother for details of William's misfortunes, having become secretive about her own feelings in the years since Paris. But she did ask Beatrice. Albeit she professed to despise Beatrice's intelligence, or rather the apparent lack of it, as she had grown, so her trust in her maid's common sense had increased. The slow Beatrice who could run no faster than a cow was quicker to guess at truth than a princess mother. The Princess Adela had only heard of the torn gown, Beatrice had seen and discreetly concealed it. And the bloodstains on the skirt. Beatrice might even have guessed whose blood it was. Rumours of the young duke's mysterious 'illness' had proliferated, yet Beatrice had never questioned her.

'Is it true then,' she said to her maid one day, soon after the first news of Norman unrest, 'that all men boast?' She twisted in her chair, playing with a looking-glass as Beatrice brushed her hair. The chair itself was tapestry-lined, as were the walls; the glass was silver-backed. The scent of cut flowers among the rushes on the floor was strong. She curled her toes in her pointed shoes and, remembering William's plight, felt guiltily grateful for the chamber's warmth. Without waiting for a reply she hurried on, 'And suppose, for example, a man should claim that he was born to greatness, that there were portents noted and witnesses sworn to that prophecy, would that still be boasting?'

She had begun with a generality before moving to the particular and she said 'men' to throw Beatrice off the scent, but Beatrice was again too quick for her.

'Very true, my lady love, my dove, my darling,' Beatrice cooed, smoothing Maltida's tresses with one hand. 'Men are but babes, needing constant attention. I remember how Gaston first courted me. He swore he had been on pilgrimage to the Holy Land and there had fought great monsters for my sake. All lies. But if you are speaking of that child Duke of Normandy, who claimed more land and titles than any king since Charlemagne . . . Why lady love, even the first of his promised greatnesses is lost, for his own family has spurned him, and even murdered him according to some.'

She crossed herself, her hands making swishing motions across her ample bosom. 'Why speak of him at all?' she said. 'Normandy is far away and has nothing to interest us.'

'Perhaps.' Matilda pursed her lips. 'Perhaps not.' She looked sideways at Beatrice. 'It might have,' she said, 'if I were to marry him.'

For once Beatrice did not look shocked, did not say as she always did when there was talk of marriage, 'As shall please your noble father and his lady wife.' She put down the brush and stared at Matilda. Her round face, usually so rosy-cheeked, grew pale, and her robin-egg-blue eyes narrowed. 'I know nothing of portents,' she said at last, 'and less of Normandy, where they say pagans live without fear or care of God. But this I will swear to. Marriage is not something to be lightly thought of. Without affection betwixt man and wife no marriage ever holds good, and without lusting no man ever remains faithful, no matter how much he boasts, or how high-born is his wife. But that is all I do know.'

She picked up the brush again, began to braid Matilda's plaits. And when Matilda continued to probe: 'Ask your noble father or his lady wife,' she repeated sharply, as if cross with herself. 'They can best advise you.'

Matilda was intrigued. She did not know why she had mentioned marriage, that had just slipped out. In fact since her return from Paris, although her mother spoke of the subject often, the possibility of an actual marriage had never really been broached again. She sensed she had her father to thank for that. Yet she also recognized instinctively the truth of Beatrice's casual remark, 'As shall please your noble father.' When Count Baldwin finally decided, Matilda knew she would have little say in the matter. Yet the thought of marriage, which in many ways was distasteful, did not seem so bad when it was she herself who introduced it.

Dismissing Beatrice she sat a while and thought. Her mother's assertion that girls her age were married every day had never troubled her before. Now she stole a quick glance at herself in the glass she still held. Yes, she did look older, this new style of dressing her hair made her face appear more slender and her neck longer. It was only her lack of height that made her seem still a child. And had William changed at all, was he as arrogant as ever? What would happen to him? Her curiosity concerning William's fate was rekindled. After all, it would be foolish to think of marrying someone who no longer existed, if he had indeed been murdered. But that thought too she beat down. As Beatrice said, the concept of marrying was too important to be treated lightly. And William deserved better than a foolish jest.

After a while she stood up and went to find her father in the mews where the hawks were kept. He was inspecting his newest purchase, a peregrine falcon of prodigious speed and strength. Matilda looked at Baldwin with new awareness. He was perhaps more ponderous in person than before but otherwise little different from the father who had always protected her, and in a rush of gratitude she came up and stood beside him, her head not quite touching his shoulder, her hand confidently placed in his.

The last few years had not changed Count Baldwin's favour, and Matilda's freedom to approach him was but one small sign of the bond between them. As was their common interest in

115

hunting. After she had admired the hawk, noted its sharp talons and its curved beak, its yellow eyes and its smooth plumage, she put her question. With her father she would be direct. It had always been better so. And she knew Count Baldwin well enough to guess he would be amused by her apparent interest in politics.

'My lord father,' she asked him bluntly, 'do you think William of Normandy is dead?'

Count Baldwin took one further look at the falcon on its perch before he answered her. 'Perhaps,' he said at last. 'The Normans are a wild race, snarling like wolves among themselves. But when I first saw him I said he'd the look of a survivor. I hope he does survive.'

When, echoing Beatrice she asked why – wasn't Normandy far away from Flanders, of no interest to them – at first he turned her question aside. 'These are not things for your pretty head,' he said. But Matilda insisted.

'Think of it this way then,' he said. 'Normandy is one of the biggest dukedoms in the kingdom. Is it to be thrown like a cabbage this way and that? Such misconduct sets an evil example. How shall we manage, who have estates of similar value, when our time comes?'

The very idea of Flanders being torn apart frightened Matilda. She felt the hairs on the nape of the neck stiffen. 'You mean,' she burst out, 'someone might try to take your lands away? Or if, forgive me father, you should die before my brother is full-grown, enemies would kill him to inherit?'

Baldwin frowned, not liking that idea. Then he laughed and pinched her cheek. 'My vassals honour me,' he said with another little laugh, 'I keep them controlled. But if your brother were under age, or if his birth were suspect, if there were no strong king to act on his behalf, why yes, such things could happen. And alas, we do not have a strong king these days,' he added, more softly now, almost to himself, for the theme of the king's lack of skill in leadership was a constant source of complaint, making for troubled conflict between Baldwin and the Princess Adela who naturally enough favoured her brother.

'Treachery is always a danger,' the count continued soberly. 'That and conspiracy are the greatest threats. To prevent which, we great nobles need to succour each other in adversity. Otherwise we may all be lost.'

'And will you help the duke?'

Again Count Baldwin laughed. 'You ask too much,' he teased. 'Are you his ambassador? I cannot answer you. In the first place I do not know where he is, or if he be dead or alive. In the second I do not know who would be his successor. And in the third, as you have said, Normandy is far away. I would need some other pressing reason to motivate real interference. We do not play at war, child. Alliances must be carefully weighed, advantage and disadvantage calculated.'

He tapped her cheek again. 'Nor is it fitting for young maids to question their father's policy,' he added, and this time he was not laughing. 'Go your ways. When or if the time comes I make my own decision without your help or advice.'

It was as close as he would come to rebuke. Again Matilda felt disappointed. It was not only that no one could assure her of William's fate, but that her own personal interest seemed not to count, seemed doomed to be put aside. But as the reports continued to proliferate, of de Gacé's conspiracy, of its possible failure and the young duke's possible escape, like her father she began to believe that William was bound to survive. And if he survived then perhaps they might meet again. And then, who knew what might happen. Beatrice's words she buried until such time.

Matilda's belief, though, so far away, so insubstantial, could have no effect on William's life. Yet perhaps in some obscure fashion it might balance the scales so weighted against him. Perhaps her prayers, like those of Herleve's at Conteville, reached up to Heaven. They say that prayers are like a ladder stretching to the very feet of God. The lower William fell, the higher Matilda wished him. Wishing will not change history. But it could be that in his lowly disguise William might have had some inkling of the trust put in him that one day he would mount on high again.

Meanwhile he and Walter continued their roving existence, everyday sinking deeper like the stones Walter had likened them to. Within the forest confines the few hamlets they now came across were so remote as to seem like animal lairs, belonging to no known lord, knowing no allegiance. Could they even be termed hamlets, being rather scatterings of huts set at random round open places which were kept tilled where possible, or left rough for grazing. The men who lived in them were rough too, coarsened by their own misfortunes, yet in their way just. Without interest or curiosity, too bowed under to have time for these, they neither welcomed nor refused strangers, accepted Walter grudgingly (for Walter's skill was of use to them), and took William on sufferance as an apprentice. William in turn learned something of the art of leather-work, and nothing to be ashamed of in that. If both he and his uncle were presumed on the run before the law, well, that too was no cause for shame, outlaws being common in these isolated parts and in many ways kinder to fellow unfortunates than their more lawful counterparts.

At Walter's insistence, William kept clear of all human contact, pretending some incapacity which made him shy of speech, but from a distance he observed. His observations were to last him a lifetime. He liked the way the women bore and raised their children, nay, he sometimes envied those infants, secure at least in their mother's love. He saw that the men were fiercely loyal to their own kind, yet when they quarrelled fought with a wild abandon, almost as if some traces of their Viking ancestry still lingered. He found much to admire and also much to pity in those who, knowing no just lord, were therefore at every lord's mercy. It seemed to him a waste that all the energy which in normal times would have made of someone a good husbandman or carpenter or such, was here dissipated by the sheer effort of living. 'When I am truly duke,' he thought, 'here's room for change.' As with everything in his life now he kept that thought held in reserve, tucked away out of sight to be used when chance gave the opportunity.

But as time passed without incident and days merged into weeks and months, William became restless. His youth and inexperience hampered him; never before had he felt so helpless. At times he even suspected Walter of dawdling deliberately. Perhaps Walter was enjoying his return to the wilderness more than he liked to admit! Worse, for the first time William began to calculate the effects of his disappearance on his friends. The violation of the young duke's quarters, even to murder in the duke's own chamber, were not ordinary crimes, could not be forever hid. Surely by now Herleve would have heard of them; thoughts of Herleve's grief at his fate preyed on his mind.

And suppose, as a last desperate ploy, the murderer pretended William were dead. Then Ralph de Gacé might reverse the whole affair, proclaim Osbern and Turold assassins cut down in their foul deed by honest men hired for that very protection by himself. Then even Walter might be accused of treachery, might be said to be fleeing for his own life. And instead of being praised, all three of William's friends would be branded for their infamy. And whether true or not, what difference would it make if the duchy believed its duke were dead. Ralph de Gacé was next in line. Someone must inherit.

But what sort of inheritance, William thought again, when even murderers appear to thrive and God turns a blind eye on their sins! Like the serfs he had come to pity he realized he had also become an outcast without recourse. There was in truth no justice, unless there was a just duke. Somehow, soon, he thought, I must appear again, alive and well, to impress the Norman lords that I am still the heir, ready to assume control and take over the guidance of the duchy. But how to achieve it – the lack of any real possibility became harder to bear than all the other hardships.

In this dilemma he found he could no longer rely on his uncle. These matters were outside Walter's competence. As an outcast Walter could survive but not plan matters of diplomatic policy. In principle he might have understood what William wanted but it was not something that he himself had considered and it was beyond him to achieve. When asked he could only shake his head as if berating himself at his own stupidity. 'We need Fulbert's advice,' was all he said, at these moments beginning to appear most like his father whose own life had soured because of errors he had once made. In these moods Walter too turned dour and grave, and gradually William learned to hesitate before confiding in him, not liking to seem ungrateful or over-burdening.

When chance finally gave William a way out, he therefore kept it to himself, for the first time in his life using subterfuge to control his own actions (although it was only later that he was able to view events clearly). At the time it seemed to him as if some force greater than himself had taken over, that he was drawn inexorably along and could no more have resisted than he could have withstood the force of the mill-race's current.

The chance was unexpected, coming perhaps from God – or perhaps, like everything else, arising from the very conditions which now surrounded him and his uncle. He and Walter had finally arrived within the confines of the Forest of Écouves. It covered a vast tract of land to the south of the cathedral city of Sées, still half a country away from their destination of Conteville which Walter was still chary of approaching. The hamlet where they took shelter was more miserable than most, its small scattering of fields untended, its people too disheartened to have any care for them. He and his uncle had bedded down in a tumbledown goat pen, the goats that once had inhabited it long gone – as had the sheep and cattle – to pay the extra taxes demanded by the local lord, the Bishop of Sées.

The time was harvest but the rains had been heavy and storms had flattened the corn. Famine threatened. There was not food enough for the villagers, certainly none for wandering strangers. What grain survived went to swell the bishop's granaries.

It might have seemed incredible that men as poor as these

would have any energy left to join in rebellion. But desperate men seek desperate remedies. When they heard of other peasant uprisings, centred round that city whose bishop had been so greedy, encouraged by the example of their fellows, they too agreed to take part and began to arm themselves although not with the speed that William was used to, needing time for discussion and thought as if they were in a council chamber.

That serfs could become a fighting force, albeit an illegal one, was something that had never occurred to William. Part of him still sided with the nobles they revolted against; if asked at first he would have been appalled at the peasants' impudence. But he was sympathetic to their cause and knew from first-hand experience how they had been ill-used. Although it went against his instincts and training to see serfs armed, used as he was to specialized forces, formed of knights on horseback, he soon realized that in the right hands home-forged weapons were as formidable as swords. Of the peasants' personal courage he had no doubt: could it be harnessed to good account? And could he himself make use of it?

In any case here was his chance! Although true to his promise he had kept to himself, now in this nameless group of hovels, among these wretched serfs, he would find the men to lead.

While he waited for the village to prepare itself, William befriended one of the leaders of the revolt and, again in secret, had himself taught how to fight using one of these homely weapons. Nor did he reveal his plan to Walter. Walter would tell him he was a fool. Better than anyone Walter knew the risks of peasant revolt, and its aftermath. Instead he waited until the last moment when the peasants were ready to start their march.

The name of his new aquaintance was Golet, like William and Walter an itinerant worker from the district near Bayeux. A few years older than William, Golet had a reputation for cheerfulness despite the troubled times. He was a broad-backed fellow with a mop of auburn hair and a face scarred in some personal brawl that had caused his original flight from Bayeux. Although he spoke French his speech was laced with Norse which he said was his language of choice, and when William raised the possibility of insurrection he produced a Norse weapon the like of which William had never seen before. Golet kept his most prized possession in a bundle he always wore on his back. It was not a homemade weapon, but an axe of giant proportions. He proceeded to swing it above his head, standing with both feet apart and hefting it with both hands so that it swished through the air, a prodigious feat of strength – William lacked the strength even to lift it waist-high above the ground.

Golet explained that it was not for everyday use but was a special war axe that had belonged to his grandfather's kin. Unwrapped, it glittered in the sun, its blade carved with Norse runes and signs from an earlier age. 'Commoners are forbidden weapons of any sort,' he said. 'Yet with an axe like this a man can pin another against a door, or cut his head off with a stroke. Or use its blade to flay flesh, deft as women with needle and thread. Even great lords duck their heads when they see it coming. 'Tis a great leveller!' he grinned.

Golet proved a good teacher, patient and thorough, finding William a lighter and smaller axe, showing him how to grip the shaft and plant his feet, how to use his bodyweight to swirl and twist. And for the next few days he and William practised in secret whenever William could find excuse or subterfuge for being free of his uncle's company.

'You'll do well, lad,' Golet said once, when William stopped, out of breath. They had come aside into a little dell, surrounded by young oaks, now scarred and slashed with William's strokes. 'But, by God, I'd not take your life upon my soul to put you in the forefront of a battlefield.'

He smiled, showing white, uneven teeth. 'Surely some great wrong drives you, so young,' he said, 'to have you want to accompany us. Myself,' he shrugged, 'I've little left to lose, since at one stroke I killed my wife and her lover both, lying in adultery; but you've the world to win. You're no age at all, my fine young cockerel. Save your crowing for another day.'

It was the first time Golet had spoken of himself and the closest he had come to curiosity concerning William. Albeit lightly done, a hint only, William was aware of it, and he felt himself close off from his friend. And from the regard Golet cast at him he knew the youth sensed he had overreached courtesy.

Golet jumped up and shook himself. They had collapsed upon the grass, their axes lying beside them. Now Golet lifted up his and twirled it round his head. 'Who am I to ask?' he said as much to himself. 'Your uncle – Walter's his name isn't it? – uncle or master, or whatever he is, has you to care about and I've no one but myself. So lay on, young sir, with all your strength and see if you can cut off Golet's head.'

He spoke half in jest, stood in the fighting stance, both hands tightly locked round the handle of his axe. William stood up more slowly. Until this moment, he and Golet had never actually matched each other, their efforts had been against things inanimate such as stumps of trees or blocks of wood. And except for

121

that one desperate struggle with Guy of Burgundy, William had never really fought any living soul, although all his knightly training had been towards that end. He hesitated, bit his lip. It was not that he feared for himself, that thought never crossed his mind, but that he liked Golet and did not want to hurt him.

Golet watched him. In the few weeks he had known the lad, William had shot up like a weed, all skin and bone and long of leg, like a half-grown colt, yet strangely self-contained, as if he kept all kinds of secrets stamped down tight. You get to know a person when you fight with him and Golet suspected William was not all he seemed. He sometimes appeared a child, sometimes not, but it was his air of command which intrigued the older boy, himself more thoughtful than most because of his own past experience. True, William revealed himself only when he forgot, and then but fitfully; that made him even more interesting. Golet had felt a kind of bond with William; that and his piqued curiosity had been the reasons for his tutorship, something he would not normally have offered, axe-masters being a special closed fraternity. But there had been a third thing which he sensed in William, which he, Golet, did not have, a sense of dedication that made the boy strange and remote, a devotion to some cause that had no name yet which seemed to dominate his mind and of which he never let go, no matter how deep it was kept concealed. It was a kind of tenacity of spirit that Golet had never encountered before and it both drew and repelled him.

He twirled the axe again, confident he could keep William at bay and out of harm. 'Lay on,' he said. And as William came at him, 'Not too close to give me cut, not too far back to give me swing: middle ground, middle ground.'

He had no chance to say anything else for William had closed with him. The axe shafts clashed, the handles caught. The two figures bent and strained. When they stepped back both were drenched with sweat, panting for breath. They swung again. And again. In the end it was Golet who broke.

He jumped aside, cast his axe down. 'By Thor,' he said, startled out of Christian speech, 'I spoke in jest. Peace, else we both be mown like a field of barley wheat.' He tried to smile, wiped the sweat off. 'I thought you took me for your enemy,' he said.

For a moment William looked at him as if he did not hear what he said. William's eyes had glazed, narrowed with concentration. Every muscle in his body ached yet he had got into the rhythm of his swing and could have kept on until he dropped. Then gradually he came back to himself. He drew a deep breath, let the axehead fall, wiped his own forehead.

'Not so,' he said. 'Pardon me. I know you are a friend. But when I do meet my enemies, neither by Thor nor any other god will I spare them.'

They looked at each other. There was a silence. The only sounds in the glen were natural ones, of wind in leaves, and flies, and the late honeybees busy in the clover. Golet dropped to his knees. 'Who are you, lord?' he whispered. 'For I swear that never in my life have I met your like. But if Golet, the killer of all he loved most dear can be held to have word left to give, I give it now. I am your man. And here's my hand.'

He held it out, a broad workman's hand. And William took it within the two of his as once he had taken Walter's. That was the second oath-taking he remembered, of more worth than any more formally sworn.

That same night he revealed to Walter what had happened, but not all, for he was old enough now to keep his own counsel, and told him what he planned. It was enough to make Walter leap to his feet in panic.

'Hold fast,' William told him, catching his uncle's arm. 'No harm done. But Uncle, it seems to me if we are ever to reveal ourselves here's the time. And see how we kill two birds with one stone. If I am to show I'm alive let it at least be when armed and ready. And of all the causes worth fighting for, I'd rather lead a peasant one.'

He smiled at his uncle's discomfiture. ''Tis time we came back from the dead,' William said, suddenly sounding older than his years, 'before the world takes us as dead for ever. And I know you well enough by now to guess where your true sympathies lie. So remember who they fight against, Uncle, and what wrongs have been done to them and me. They claim the Bishop of Sées once promised them protection. Let us ensure he keeps his word.'

Walter heard him, knew the folly, knew the chance, held one balanced against the other in dreadful indecision. When he heard that note in William's voice he knew he was by-passed. It was not his nephew, his sister's child, who spoke, but a scion of nobility, an heir apparent. If in the intervening months sometimes he had forgotten that fact, William obviously never had.

He was too just a man to resent being set aside; he was too proud to mention it. And in his heart he may have felt relief that at last a heavy responsibility was being lifted – he was not the one to train and equip a duke for the life he must lead. Instead he spoke of William's practising, of which he was proud, despite his misgivings.

'So did your ancestors and mine fight,' he said, 'and yet, William, of all the axemen I have known, none can compare with your own grandfather, Fulbert of Falaise. In his day his renown was great. How shall I discredit your new skill; it also is your birthright.'

William's eyes danced. Clad in his dirty homespun tunic and hose, his hair uncut, dishevelled, he never looked more a lord than he did now. His enthusiasm was infectious. He gazed at his uncle, standing almost head tall to him. 'Then come with me,' he said, 'and prove to our enemies, and theirs, that I also breathe and fight like my kin.'

'Well . . .' Walter hesitated, and in that hesitation was lost. When the shabby little band of serfs at last began their march towards the city gates he and William rode with them.

As to where the horses had come from, no one hazarded an opinion. Walter had appeared with them one day, shabby beasts, but not totally useless. That he also brought with him coats of mail and broad Norman swords was also proof he had not lost his skill at bargaining. Nor did anyone hazard a guess as to why William should not lead the company. Once in the saddle it seemed his prerogative, despite his youth, and he assumed the position willingly. And he had armed himself with an axe. If it was his uncle who rode by his right hand, it was Golet who ran at his stirrup iron as his close companion.

Mounted men gave unlooked-for authenticity to the small army, added strength to the insurgents; and who were they to challenge good fortune? When they joined their fellows before the city gates, the other commoners as readily closed ranks behind these self-appointed leaders.

Seated on a horse for the first time in months, William gripped the saddle fiercely and looked round him. On either side the peasants surged, armed with their old axes and their round Viking shields, some not armed at all but carrying staves or scythes. It was not the sort of army he had envisaged when he lay awake at nights dreaming of his return. But it would suffice for a beginning. He wore his helmet down; the mail coat fitted his shoulders better than when he had last tried one one, no longer flapping below his knees. Not waiting for Walter's nod, he spurred forward, axe at the ready. From beneath his belt he drew out the tattered banner that he had kept hidden all this while and let its leopards flutter. The Norman cry, not heard for so long, burst from his young throat and echoed in the air like a clarion. '*Dix aie, Dix aie.*' The very walls rang with it. And all about him his peasant followers drew back in amazement.

Chapter 10

Sées was a fair-sized city on the River Orne, a walled city, proud of its new cathedral built on the ruins of an older one destroyed at the end of the last century. Within the city its bishop, Yves de Bellême was waiting. He knew of the rebels' coming, had anticipated it, had in fact already offered compromise. He was a man of a young middle age, of nervous disposition, and belonging to an older school of ecclesiastics who had been made bishops in their early youth. Had he not been timid as a child he might well have stayed in the outside world, might have married an heiress and had his own castle to defend, for he claimed kinship with the noble family of Bellême with whom most of his interests lay. In his mind there was no confusion about the cause of the rebellion. Inside his barns and granaries were sacks and stores enough to keep a thousand men, his cathedral housed a treasury dating back to St Latuin's day and was stuffed with holy relics. He was willing to give all up, if need be, barter all to save himself – but only if he had to. Such was the bargain he had made with himself, such was his vague promise of 'help' when the rebellion had first threatened. But he was young enough to remember his upbringing in a noble keep, knew the value of his worth and at heart scorned the rabble who challenged it.

He had already called on Bellême to his south and Domfront to his west to give him additional aid, had immediately dispatched his first messengers to these castles when the early rumblings of the insurgence had first reached him. One of his parish priests, a kindly soul with little sense, had inadvertently put him on guard. Out of concern for his flock and anxious that no harm come to them, this priest had been full of the threatened rising, had actually condoned it, had approached the bishop for advice. At his request Bishop Yves had received a deputation, had listened, outwardly impressed, inwardly calculating. When the priest on his parishioners' behalf spoke of hardship, disease, starvation, he had nodded in agreement and promised Masses for salvation of souls in distress. Not a word was said on either side of any realistic aid, but the awareness of those full granaries, those treasure chests, must have been present in all the men's thoughts. And as the weeks had passed and no show of force materialized, either from the rebel force or his expected allies, the bishop had begun to hope that the threat would subside without his having to be parted from his riches. And here, God save him, this very day – the support he had requested had not arrived – the serfs were banging on his gates and threatening to tear them down if he did not let them in. As yet there was no open mention of his sacks of grain or his ecclesiastical gold, but why else should they come demanding entrance to the city?

The report that there were horsemen in the throng – horsemen leading the rabble, armed knights – was an unwelcome surprise. What knight would so betray himself as to consort with commoners? Unbelieving, he went to see this phenomenon for himself, girding up his bishop's robes and scrambling on to the gatehouse walls like a soldier trained (which was true at least for his boyhood).

He saw the mob. With practised eye he noted its ungainly size, its straggled look, its piecemeal armaments. With professional skill he judged its strength and found it wanting. Much relieved he then turned his attention to the armed men: only two of them, a nothing. The glimpse of the gold leopards running made his heart thud, but it was not until he heard that Norman shout that apprehension turned to certainty.

He had heard the cry once before, when the grandfather of the present duke had lain siege to his own father's castle. He himself had been but a child but it had struck terror in his soul even so.

'Who speaks?' he cried. 'Who comes in the duke's name? Who dares utter it?'

Forgetting the danger he leaned over the tower and shouted out, 'Who are you, to take upon yourself the duke's authority?'

He saw a youth with long hair and flashing eyes astride a horse, a youth between child and man, not yet grown into his height, who managed axe and shield with expert skill, who wheeled his horse round to answer him. He felt he was looking down at Duke Robert himself, dead and gone, or the very ghost of him!

The bishop sank back and clutched his breast where the cross of office hung. Fear leaked out of him. 'As God is my witness,' he choked, 'I made no false promises. Let them have grain and crops and all, but spare me that sight.'

And when his mercenaries bent over him, concerned that he

must have been stricken with some fit, he croaked out again, 'Who is that boy?'

He grasped the stones and made to rise; his legs buckled under him. There was no response but he did not need one. He knew without being told that this was no ghost but flesh and blood, Duke Robert's son, back from whatever place his enemies, or friends, had hidden him. And between the house of Bellême and the dukes of Normandy was hatred implacable, although Bellême in part owed fealty to the Normans for their lands. Why me? he thought, oh God, why did he choose to reveal himself here to me, and make me party to his quarrel? I've troubles enough of my own. He turned his face to the wall and refused to speak.

Confused, the bishop's soldiers waited for orders which never came: to open the gates or keep them closed, to fight on or capitulate. The bishop lay with open eyes and kept his mouth shut. Finally in exasperation they carried him in a litter to his room and dumped him there unceremoniously beside a crucifix at which he gazed with unblinking stare. Let him ask God for help; the soldiers must do what best they could. And so the gates remained shut up tight.

'Break them,' William said.

The rebels took heart, raised up a shout of their own. They rushed en masse towards the walls, dragging behind them blocks of wood, the tree trunks and staves they had carried for this very purpose. Paying no heed to the arrows which whizzed overhead, they strained to force the oaken planks and iron bolts that strengthened the city gates. Again and again they bent their backs, bore in, were repulsed, until William, leaping from his horse himself directed their labours. One last effort and the oak buckled and splintered. Up on the walls the archers threw down their bows, the pikemen their pikes, and all began the scramble for safety as the insurgents poured through the gap.

William remounted in the way he knew best, leaping for the saddle. His face was flushed, he had cast his helmet off, his hair blew wild in the wind like a real Viking's. With Walter close beside him he was first through the opening, his horse's hooves beating across the cobbled stones and down the empty streets. Behind him surged the peasant horde, swelled soon by the bishop's own citizens, clamouring for their own rights.

The peasants found the grain and dragged it out, the harvest hoardings of years; they found the bishop's stables and ransacked them, taking the bishop's horses for their own and mounting them, with much laughter at their ineptitude. As the Orme flows

127

past a rock so they flowed past the many stone buildings and houses, dividing and rejoining to spread through the city. All this they did with William's approval, although he took no part in their looting, reined back and let them proceed without him. Stampeding through the market place they emptied it of goods, pulled frightened stallkeepers from their hiding places before they tore down the stalls. And when they came into the central square where the new cathedral loomed, dark of wood, squat of build, doors closed, they forced its doors open although the frightened priests within tried to hold tight to the bolts, and clattered their new mounts inside to empty the cathedral treasury.

This was sacrilege. When William strove to stop them, thrusting himself among them, his horse rearing, they paid him no heed, but continued with their pillaging, blithe as birds.

In his palace quarters Bishop Yves heard the shouts, and realized what lay behind the commotion. It roused him from his apathy and restored him to his warlike self, son of lords and trained as such. He raised himself on one elbow, gave the order that his mercenary captains had been waiting for. It was not what they expected.

'Fire the city,' was the bishop's command. And when his captains hesitated, 'Fire it, I say,' he screamed. 'By God, I'll foul my own nest afore they get it. And be damned to the consequence.'

Once more confused his soldiers conferred, shrugged and obeyed. It was not their city, they had little to lose. Having set torch to the buildings in the centre, those who could withdrew from the battle which their master had lost, anxious now only to protect themselves.

The buildings were wooden, the cathedral wooden-roofed, its walls wooden-framed. And a strong wind blew causing the flames to spread even to that new cathedral of which the bishop was so proud. He gave no other orders, but lay back with the fixed stubborn look of a man driven into folly until his palace servants, forced to flee the flames themselves, again carried him to safety.

Success by then had the villagers in its grip; already some had found the wine cellars and were breaking out the casks. Others had thrown their weapons aside and were rushing to enter buildings, not to halt the conflagration, rather to loot and steal before their booty burned. In one of them a woman cried out and men laughed. Only as the flames and smoke rose up, turning noonday sky dark, did they come to their senses.

''Tis done,' they cried to each other then, ignoring William. 'No water can halt this fire; escape while we can.' Turning their back on him they began to stream haphazardly towards the city gates that had cost them so much effort, laden with their ill-gotten gains, leaving their erstwhile allies, the city folk, to deal with this new calamity. And they, suddenly realizing what their excesses had wrought, now turned to despair, their support for the peasants, previously so full of self-righteous joy, in an instant reverted to wrath. The air was filled with angry cries for retribution.

William scarcely heard them. He was watching the swirling smoke, the running figures. He knew he should call them back as he had been trained to, have them regroup and retire in order, not scatter headlong in senseless flight. 'They will not listen,' Walter said grimly at his side. 'And as the city burns so will anger grow among the citizens who for a time seemed so friendly. When the bishop's men return – for he'll have them back – there will be more lootings and draggings forth, more rape in revenge. And after that, the killings. It is always so.'

William struggled against his uncle's words. His first battle lost because he could not control the men under his command. He felt tears of regret seer his eyes.

Seeing his emotion Walter spoke more calmly. 'Listen nephew,' he said, 'I speak from hard experience. My sympathies are with the common folk. Who else should I support? But there is nothing more we can do for them. They have dragged up from some depths energy they never knew they had and once it is gone so are they finished. They must go their own way now as their destiny takes them. And if we stay they will destroy us too, for after destruction of this sort must come a reckoning as absolute.'

He caught hold of William's arm, made to urge his horse forward. 'Believe me also, my lord, when I say this. Your own future, whatever it is, does not end here among poor souls set on their own ruin.'

He held William in a gaze so hard that finally William was forced to acquiesce. Unwillingly he too reined back, let the rabble go on. At Walter's insistence he closed his eyes and heart. He could not fault his uncle but he could the reason for that disaster; its cause lay locked in his mind for another time. Together he and Walter clattered back through the gates, left swinging on their broken hinges and now, completely deserted. Only Golet spied him, ran after him. 'I follow you,' he cried.

'Then meet me at Conteville,' William told him, 'for hither I make my way as fast as is possible. If you arrive before me ask for Herleve, tell her I am coming.'

He raised his arm in salute, and spurred back down the track to the forest. And when they could no longer see the city, only the plumes of smoke which hung low over the trees, he turned to Walter and said in a voice that was hard with defiance. 'My chance has come. It is past time it did.'

And for that Walter had no argument. But he knew without being told that this would be the last time he and William would ride together. William had outgrown his tutelage.

They rode warily away from Sées, under cover, anticipating trouble yet hoping to avoid it. To their surprise they met no one, even minor paths were significantly empty, the threat of a rabble on the move keeping all men burrowed safe, even the lords of Bellême. Bishop Yves could whistle to his relatives for help, it would be long in coming. As they went along William's mind was filled with memories, with images both sharp and blurred. He saw the villagers' elation as the gates fell, he felt his own elation. Yet among all those people, were there any he had wished to kill? The bishop's mercenaries had fled, and he had no quarrel with the ordinary townsfolk. And why should the bishop fire his own city? He did not ask, but Walter surprised him by speaking of it.

'I was not trained as a soldier,' Walter said. 'You know yourself how much I lack in training. Nephew, I have seen men laugh at the way I ride, a jumped-up serf imitating his betters. But this much I do know. Pillage and burning, aye, and murder, are part of a soldier's life, be he serf or lord.'

Seeing William's disappointment Walter hid his own discomfiture, and went on in his kindly way, 'Yet I have heard Fulbert speak of a place called England where men-at-arms are raised from among the common folk, are trained and made part of the army. Fulbert called such levies the fyrd, I think, or some such name in their tongue.'

When William pressed him he explained, 'They serve for a while and after a certain time have the right to return home again. A custom having much to recommend it. For not only are ordinary people permitted weapons to defend themselves, they are taught restraint, and that is to everyone's advantage.'

William knew his uncle well enough by now to see that Walter was attempting to console him. And remembering Walter's own background, he felt sorry for him. Perhaps, if Walter had had only himself to think of, he would not have left his comrades; what had Walter once said? That he never failed anyone. He therefore let Walter talk on; there was comfort in conversation. And, more shyly now – for his uncle was not one to pretend to more influence than he had – Walter explained how in Duke Robert's day Englishmen had sought refuge in the duke's court. 'You would be too young to remember them,' he told William, warming to the subject, 'but they were princes of the blood, escaping from the Danes, in the English language called the "athelings", Edward and Alfred. And Fulbert claimed the fyrd was used with success against those same Danes when they first came a-raiding.'

He continued to speak of the English whom he said William's father admired, and of how the princes' father had been forced to flee his kingdom and how their mother, Emma, had married the Danish king who had supplanted him. 'Emma was your great-aunt,' he said, 'sister to your father's father. Her sons were half-Norman, so your father supported them, and would have planned an invasion to defeat the Danes on their behalf. But again, when you were still too young to know it, the older of them, Alfred, returned alone to England to try to win his kingdom back. He was betrayed by one of his lords, Earl Godwin by name. This earl delivered the prince to the Danes, who took him on to their ships and blinded him, so brutally that he died.'

He sighed and wiped his eyes. 'In all lands,' he said, 'there is misery and treachery. God knows why men are so wicked. To my way of thinking, Nephew, perhaps are most lords so made, and the likes of our poor dead companions at Vaudreuil a rarity. Although these peasants here did not meet with your high standards, do not hold it against them. Remember that they did not of their own desire betray you. And if I have failed you in any way, 'twas not of my own will or intent. But I believe that only when all men are free to stand on their own and swear for good or right will there truly be justice anywhere.'

It was William's turn to offer comfort. But his uncle's words remained with him, these stories of English treachery wound themselves into his memories of his "lost" battle, so that thereafter, even though the details blurred, he never forgot the name of the English peasant army which was trained to be a fighting force. Nor did he forget the story of that prince's betrayal, similar to the betrayal he himself had known. It touched him with sympathy much as his father had showed, made him feel a closeness to his father.

But most of all it seemed to him that Walter was right in saying that wherever one turned there was treachery and destruction and no way to be rid of it unless men were free. When I am such again, he thought, things shall be different.

Here, as with other of his prayers to God, Heaven made no

response; there was no way to know God's mind.

The early autumn nights surrounded William and Walter, the first frosts thick on grass and hedge, whitening the last of the wild plants and touching the trees with silver. Whenever they came to a clearing in the woods they could still see the dark smoke against the silver grey of sky where a great harvest moon hung low over the horizon. Beyond, the plateau of Normandy stretched ahead just as William remembered it, mile after mile, unrolling east and west, south and north, cut where little rivers drained down from its heights. Again William thought, 'This should be mine, to do with as I wish.' But it was so much larger than he had remembered, so much of it unknown, so much hostile perhaps, it came to him how large the task was that he had set himself, so large perhaps that it might be beyond his encompassing.

After leaving the region around Sées, they travelled north quickly, always under cover, bypassing Falaise for fear of what they might find there, even Walter urging them onward. Throughout their ride they saw no one, were challenged by no one. When finally they came to the cluster of huts that marked the village of Conteville, William almost cried aloud, he had so longed for it that now it seemed unreal.

Conteville was much smaller than Falaise and was surrounded by flat, open fields, meant for farming. The castle was set upon a mound of earth, with a ribbon of moat around its base. From the shelter of a distant copse William could distinguish its square outline and, when the clouds parted, sometimes espy the dark silhouettes of men passing and repassing along the upper walls.

'The count keeps good watch,' Walter said, 'so, for the last time, shall we.' He dismounted to lead his horse more quietly making a quick flanking move to reconnoitre. All was still; no besiegers, no ambushers. But the castle appeared to be on siege alert, expecting trouble, although more than a year had passed since the treachery in Vaudreuil. Viscount Herluin was presumably being cautious, taking no chances.

William pursed his lips. There was no room in his thoughts for the viscount. He had ridden away from Sées in a dark mood which distance had not lifted, but now he was overcome by a sudden great joy, an exultation of the spirit. He would be himself again, no more subterfuge. He would see Herleve, boast a little of his adventures, have her chide and spoil him as she used to do. He was not too old for spoiling. For a time he would be among friends, might lay down this burden that he had assumed.

And the tale of his escapades would spread, give heart to his followers and show his enemies – Ralph de Gacé, even his belittlers in Paris – what they faced. He wanted to stand up in the saddle, spread his arms and shout, 'Here I am; take me if you can.'

He kept his excitement in check, waited until Walter had made his tour of inspection, and rode again with his uncle out of the woods and along a causeway towards that dark outline. When Walter's horse stumbled on the uneven paving stones, dogs barked and a voice cried challenge. Torches flared, lighting up the walls.

'Who steals upon us under cover of night?' a sentry shouted, full of fearful suspicion. He held the torch out so the thick wax dripped, and beside him his fellows raised their bows with the arrows notched.

'Travellers who come in peace.' William's young voice was eager. 'Tell the Lady Herleve we would have word with her.'

There was a bustle at that, more lights, a wait while men went running. From where they stood in the dip of the lower bank they could hear feet clattering down the inner steps leading to the guardroom with the keep built over it. Walter fidgeted. 'Better we asked first for the viscount,' he whispered, but William scarcely heard. After a while there was another stir, and a woman's voice rang out, for all its softness, high and quick with fear, or excitement.

They watched while more torches spanned the walls. Hurrying figures passed each loophole, a woman among them. She came with swift step along the outer bastions, shielding her eyes from the flares as she leaned over the battlements. Her head was covered by a cloak but beneath it her unbraided hair hung in ringlets and her arms below the woollen folds were blue with cold as she braced them on the parapet. As the others had done she called out, 'Who is there?', but from the tremulous expectation in her voice they knew she knew or hoped she knew. When William answered she gave a great cry and buried her face in her hands as if to hide her emotion.

She was still leaning against the battlements as the gates began to creak and soldiers issued forth, well-armed and ready in case of some mishap. Serfs ran to light the way for the guests who arrived so unexpectedly. William watched them. 'But a few days ago I was like you,' he thought. 'I know how you live and speak and think as well as you do yourselves.' But when he came into the inner bailey and prepared to dismount he forgot all of this.

Herleve was running down the steps, looking as light as thistledown. Her feet were bare and under her cloak her nightrail fluttered, but the glow in her eyes matched her son's.

'Praise God,' she was saying, between laughter and tears, 'Praise God, oh, my dear son. God answers all my prayers. Come in; and come in, dear brother, and be welcome.' She grasped William's hand in both of hers as if to draw him along by force. A third stir at the guardroom door stopped her short. She started, turned her head on its slender neck and cried quickly to the cloaked figure who stood on the steps, 'Here is William, my lord. Safe, as I always said.' And to her son, 'And here is Herluin himself to give you greeting.'

The vicomte of Conteville was not old, not young, but of middle age and middle height, his chest barrel-shaped, his legs bowed with constant riding, his cropped brown hair speckled grey. He stood his ground while Herleve brought William up to him, then inclined his head in a brusque gesture of deference. 'You are right welcome, my lord duke,' he said, his voice brusque too, even-toned, not over-inviting. 'You come at a late hour, but you have come to set your mother's mind at rest. She has so fretted for your safety that if tears could have brought you back you'd have floated hither.'

The look Herluin cast at Herleve contained a mixture of exasperation and affection, but neither in voice nor look did he show much affection for his young overlord; rather, exasperation showed, as if he, like the Bishop of Sées, wished that William had chosen any other place to make his reappearance.

Somewhat chastened by the coolness of this reception, William followed him inside the guardroom and up the stairs of the main donjon. Like its master it was of middling age, showing signs of having been rebuilt some years before, perhaps over an older fortification of Roman or Celtic design. The main hall was small, log-framed, its walls dark with smoke, encrusted with it from an open fire that burned on a central hearth. Around the fire were arranged the bedding rolls of the household who thus slept in close proximity to their lord, to be protected and protect.

Three or four of them now bestirred themselves to replenish the flames with logs, doing menial service out of fond familiarity, while the seneschal, an old man with grey beard and moustache cut in Viking fashion, ordered bread and meat and wine, again without formality – a small compact household this, accustomed to each other and not standing much on ceremony. 'Sit you down and eat,' he told William in the same familiar fashion. He pointed to a stool beside the hearth. 'You've a hungry look. A few good meals beneath your belt, you'd be the better for it.'

At a nod from the viscount he withdrew to a distant corner, taking the others with him. Wrapped in their cloaks, they lay down stoically to sleep for the remainder of the watch, what was left of it, leaving the central space clear for the visitors.

Herleve had run up a flight of wooden steps that led to the women's bower where she and her husband presumably had been asleep. Presently she reappeared, dressed in a blue gown that complemented her fair hair and the colour of her grey eyes. William ate, drank, watched her beneath eyelids heavy with fatigue. He thought she had never looked so beautiful, nor so happy. He could not tell how much of her content came from seeing him, and that thought also disconcerted him, although he tried to hide it.

She sat beside her husband, opposite William and Walter, and never took her gaze from either as if she feared they would vanish if she did. She looks no different, William thought, but how can she compare this old-fashioned castle and its old-fashioned ways with her previous life in my father's court; how can she bear to? It came to him how much her life too must have changed and he felt another pang that even in her thoughts, even in her fears, he might at times have been displaced by events and people he knew nothing of.

While the visitors ate and drank Viscount Herluin stayed quietly in the background, ensuring that they were properly served, himself pouring the wine as was correct in the company of overlord. Only when they were done did he start to pace about, hands clasped behind his back as if debating how to express himself.

'My lord,' he began, his voice still well under control, 'I repeat, you are welcome. We have been looking for you ever since your flight from Vaudreuil, as we heard of it from de Gacé's men who came swift-footed in search. They have but recently removed themselves. Until then we were under siege.' He added dryly, 'Albeit they denied the charge and preferred another term, saying they but waited to greet you. But to my mind 'tis a strange sort of greeting that bars me from my own meadow lands and burns my harvest and crops and puts a stop to the hunting season.'

There was a silence. Herleve looked down, not meeting their glance yet showing tension in the very set of her head. It was not that she doubted her lord, William thought, nor found fault with his conclusions. He himself believed every word the viscount said, the viscount's honesty was self-evident. But perhaps she wished her husband were more diplomatic in his speaking.

Viscount Herluin was continuing in the same even voice, neither exaggerating the situation nor diminishing its dangers. 'My father's father held his lands of your great grandsire, lord, and thus I hold them of you. And will so continue, at your bidding. What I can do I have done, and willingly. But you must know that the situation here in Normandy has deteriorated since you went into hiding.'

There was no rebuke behind his words, although there might justifiably have been. William, who had felt his hackles rise at that word 'hiding', listened with growing exasperation as the count went on to say what was in his heart without concealing anything. 'Violence has become the fashion,' he said. 'Families shed blood as if they tip out dirty water. The houses of Bellême, of Tosny, of Montfort, to name a few, have taken to pillage and rapine, have systematically destroyed the land of more peaceful neighbours, to be as wantonly attacked in return. By Jesu, I swear vengeance breeds in them like maggots.'

William jumped up, kicking a footstool aside. He swore violently. 'Before God,' he said, 'I had not thought things so bad. And yet my lord viscount,' for it seemed to him that he had to defend himself, 'Walter and I have not been idle. And it is, after all, my duchy, that is so abused.'

And before Walter could stop him, which by winks and tugs and pulling of the arm he tried to do, William poured out the story of the attack on Sées, whose archbishop belonged to one of those noble families. It did not exactly come out the way he had intended, seemed to turn more into a litany of his own prowess rather than a confirmation of Herluin's observations. The viscount raised his eyebrows. Compared with what he'd experienced, William's account must have seemed almost childish. And William, once more subsiding, felt he had been misunderstood. It isn't anything I've done or not done that matters, he wanted to protest; it's the plight of the people of my land. No matter which great lord's to blame, when nobles quarrel like wild cats the peasants suffer; I've witnessed it at first-hand, closer than you've ever done.

Morosely he watched now while Walter tried to ease the tension between step-son and step-father, between master and vassal, without presuming on his role of uncle, or his even newer role as brother-in-law. 'There's no call for me to speak,' Walter said, in his familiar homely way, 'except to add, my lord Herluin, that we would have come home sooner had we been able. For greatly did the duke long for it. That we were kept so far away from the duke's friend and family,' here he smiled at his sister, 'is proof itself of the virulence of the times.'

Herluin gave a snort that might have been of satisfaction. He stood before them without pretence, in his own way a just man, a Norman lord of the old style whom Walter had despaired of finding, forthright and just, as dependable as he was sturdy, reliable in his own keep and true to his bond. 'Just so,' he said. 'And daily new factions rise. Although Ralph de Gacé still retains control of the ducal forces, his place in council is usurped by others of his family. His bolt is shot, no fear of that, but in his stead Count William of Arques has been deeding land and passing laws as if he were in truth charged with ducal authority. In fact it was this same new count, who, vaunting his honours, had the siege here called off, not Ralph himself.

'Through no goodwill to us,' he added in his dry way. 'At least not goodwill as I take the word. He hopes, I believe, to lure you here. Then, having you fast, he will strike at us to force us to surrender you.'

Now he too sounded angry. He frowned. It was clear this was a possibility that he had long mulled over. He was too proud to insist on his loyalty in such a case but he did add, 'Faced with such brutal and unnatural deeds who are we ordinary men to withstand them? You see me as I am,' he said. 'I do not withhold anything from your lordship's knowledge. But Conteville is small. I am not master of vast estates, nor do I command an army. I repeat, what I can I do. But I am not capable of miracle. And I have concerns of my own that absorb my care.

'I am not so free to waste my patrimony as once I was,' he said, 'not with my own heir to provide for.'

'Heir!' The word broke out from Walter who had been listening quietly. He now stood up and looked down at Herleve, and as if on cue from the women's bower there came a squall like a raven's: a baby's cry.

The viscount's expression softened, he made a dismissive gesture, but his eyes shone. 'There,' he said to Herleve, 'it lets itself be heard. Go then, have them fetch your son forth and show him off as you are longing to do. Myself,' he grimaced, 'I had forgot that babes demand so much as to command their mother's whole attention.'

It was the only lie he spoke. When the nurses brought the child out he took it up in his arms, unwrapped the swaddling clothes, himself displayed the infant, proud as any peacock. 'Behold, my lord,' he said, as if it were the most important thing in the world, 'your step-brother.'

William looked at the creature. It was already several months

137

old, red-faced and hungry, its eyes screwed up, its face wrinkled. Was I ever like that, he thought, and then resentfully, a step-brother, to take my mother and fill her thoughts; to grow to be a challenge like William of Arques, who was step-brother to my father. Those two thoughts grew and drowned out any other.

He listened with only half an ear while they talked on, his uncle asking questions in William's place, the viscount replying. He knew he should join in, should assert himself on his own behalf, should probe with questions, respond with answers, to prove himself worthy of the viscount's regard, but all his attention was fixed on his mother with her child.

Herleve did not give the babe suck as he had feared, used now to the ways of peasant folk who nursed their offspring them-selves. Instead she cradled it, covering it with her mantle folds. The baby lay quiet. Long eyelashes fanned its cheeks; its face was pale like wax, its finger tips were hooked around the corner of its covering, like claws. William knew he should not hate it as he did. He felt his mother's gaze still fixed on him, full of sympathy, and he was ashamed. But he would not return her look, and sulkily kept his eyes fixed on the stone slabs of the floor as if all of interest lay there.

Viscount Herluin was continuing his tale of woe; every day it seemed another disaster struck. New castles sprouted like weeds he said, manned by upstart lords who used them to wage war upon their neighbours. Among the established lords old castel-lans ignored oaths of fealty to the duke and usurped power on their own behalf. Lands were seized, homes and villages razed, laws and customs changed to the advantage of the council in Rouen, where the new archbishop Mauger ruled in conjunction with his brother, that same William of Arques, one as bad as the other.

At his story's end, 'I repeat,' he said, 'I can hold my own. But not against all of Normandy. And that, my lord duke, I think even you can appreciate.' His look at William was hard, the unblinking stare of a man who takes stock of what he sees and judges it accordingly.

After a while he went on, 'And so, my lord, my advice is this. Go you again to the king. For only out of Normandy will you find the strength to deal with your enemies.

When William still made no response, he spoke again, 'I hear King Henry offered you a knighting once. You are almost of an age to ask for it. And when he has dubbed you knight you may ask him also for a wife.'

' 'Tis almost time for both,' he added. 'By size at least you are a man.'

Again he spoke simply, without satire, but the words stung William.

'Man or not,' William countered quickly, 'there is no woman that I trust.' His voice was taut. He felt himself bristle like someone who expects insult. 'And I fight my own battles, without help if I must. Certainly without the help of a French king who is no friend of mine.' He heard his voice made petty by his jealousy and was filled with disgust.

The men laughed; Walter indulgently although he wore his worried frown, the viscount scornfully, as if he had expected nothing more. Callow, his laugh said, green without sense. Just as I feared.

Under cover of their laughter Herleve leaned forward, her eyes sad. She did not take William's hand as she had previously done; she seemed to sense his withdrawal. 'The king is not all bad,' she said, 'rather he is weak as whey. But he will not be forsworn, that I know. What he promised he will keep. But consider, William, how much time has passed since you and I journeyed together to his court. You were then a little boy; now, as I see for myself, you are almost grown. So will the king receive you as a friend.'

She added in a lower voice, 'I know what grievous loss you have had, and what deep suffering. And I pray to God that soon your enemies will be overcome and you will deal with them as you ought. And as I think God means you to.

'I know you do not see it so,' she said, her voice a whisper in his ear as she used to whisper to him on nights when they slept together, 'but I pray one day you will do so, that out of loss some good can come, even for us both. Herluin makes me a good husband,' she said, 'and Conteville pleases me. I could wish such happiness for you.'

She held her head on one side in that birdlike, trusting way William remembered. 'I would wish the world for you,' she said. 'You are my first son, your place is secure. And when you were born they told me that with your fists – although they were not much bigger than this child's here – you seized the rushes on the birthing floor and held on so tight there was no way to prise them loose. "That is a sign," the midwife said, "look, my dear, he grasps at life. So will he grasp throughout his years, holding all that he achieves, tenacious as ivy on a wall."

'And so I think you are destined to succeed,' Herleve went on 'but to my mind, William, success is of little worth if it comes not with the blessing of God. And of all the things a man may have – a contented life, a happy home, a wife to cherish him, children to rear – these are first and foremost blessed by God.'

When after some while he did not respond, she stood up and bore the sleeping child away. And all William's hopes and dreams died unsaid, leaving nothing in their place but a sour taste in the mouth.

Yet later, when the firelight flickered low and the hall dimmed, and all the sleeping sounds of a world at harmony with itself surrounded him, William felt his hatred sink. He did not sleep, perhaps too tired for sleep, although the bed the viscount had had made up was the most comfortable he had known in months, albeit straw-made and on the ground.

Beside him Walter snored. He observed his uncle affectionately. He knew how much care had weighed on Walter, how much more he would still accept if William allowed. He thought of Herleve and how he must have grieved her. And he thought of the viscount who in his way also had been loyal and whom he had not even thanked; who had looked tonight for signs of leadership, and been sadly disappointed. Gradually as anger waned he admitted his fault and accepted blame.

Ever since coming to Sées, he thought, I have run amok, caring only for myself, seeing things only through my eyes. That is indulgence; the times do not permit me such weaknesses. Nor have I done justice to my uncle to strain his loyalty so far and bring him into such jeopardy. Carelessly have I broken the trust between us, although he would not say so. And now I have offended those upon whom I should most rely.

Angrily he berated himself, steeling himself to it. It was too late to change the first impression he had given but perhaps in the morning he would rectify the fault.

And one last thing. Reluctantly he admitted too that all his childish yearnings were simply that: childish dreams with which he could no longer deceive himself. His childhood was really done. Even in his mother's house, even in her husband's charge, he must rely no more upon her loving protection. Henceforth he must stand up for himself. Those words he had spoken in such boastful wise were the ones he should have said in all sincerity, albeit with more modesty. And plain-speaking or wishing, what was the use if he could not live up to the promise of his words.

The next morning at first light he sought the viscount out and spoke to him formally. 'My lord,' he said, 'last night you told us of your efforts on our behalf but we answered without thanks in surly fashion, out of some crooked thought of our own not worth the repeating. And you gave us good advice. We should be foolish to ignore it. All we ask of you now is an escort to keep us company. We go to Paris to claim our rights, as mayhap we should have earlier done.'

And to Walter who would willingly have accompanied him he said, 'Good my uncle, you also have done enough. Go back home to your own wife and children as I know you wish to do. Tell my people in Falaise to wait for me, for I am coming.'

He put his arms about Walter, that stocky figure as dear to him as any he had known. And he felt his uncle's spirit as solid as the flesh beneath the shabby clothes.

Already in this past week it seemed William had grown for now he topped his uncle by a finger breadth. And if in similar fashion he had outgrown Walter's loving care, like every child who moves on and away from its first nurturing, he should show always his respect and gratitude.

'Without you, Uncle,' he began, 'I should be dead at Vaudreuil.'

Emotion choked him. Stay with me, he wanted to countermand himself, I cannot do without you. But like that child who moves on and away he knew he had no right to ask.

He went to Herleve and on his knees he kissed her hand. 'As I once was, so keep Herluin's son. For your sake as much as his own I shall not forget him. *Remember me.*'

She laid her hands upon his bowed head with its thatch of darkening hair, and though the tears crept down her cheeks she smiled. 'Day and night,' she promised him.

Chapter 11

It was several months later, in the spring, when William finally quitted Conteville. He rode with a scant dozen of Conteville guards, all he would accept from his step-father, and took only the peasant, Golet, to keep him company. Golet was perhaps a strange addition to the ducal party. He had appeared at Conteville one evening, footsore and weary, yet with his humour still intact. 'By the Mass,' he was supposed to have sworn at the guards who let him in, 'had I known how far Conteville was I might have gone to Jerusalem.'

Setting down his axe which he still wore strapped on his back, he had stretched himself. 'But if this be the gate to Paradise,' he said, obviously pleased with what he saw, 'then Golet from Bayeux has struck gold.' He suddenly shouted in his strange accent, 'By the gods of war I smell blood. Tell William the Conqueror I am here.'

The Conteville guards had not been impressed by him, had urged their count, and through him their duke, to send the insolent beggar packing. William had laughed. 'He is an honest soul,' he said and, taking Herleve to have her look, let her judge for herself. When the time had come to leave, Golet and she were such firm friends that Golet had begged Herleve herself to speak for him. 'For look you, lady,' he had said, 'our lord travels and lives now as a duke. Things serious and grave will be his lot, and nobles and kings his close companions. But I who am serf-born do not have my nose in the air, can see where to put each foot, and will keep him anchored to the ground. I shall be his jester and make him laugh. Besides,' he gave a rueful laugh, 'I am oath-tied to him. Like a swan which has one mate I cannot settle far from him.'

The thought of the solid Golet as a swan had set Herleve laughing too. And indeed it made William smile even in the midst of such important preparations. The joke had its effect though, and Golet his way. And willingly did he assume his role as company jester.

The William of Normandy who rode in through the Paris gates on a bright May day was not the same William who had come before; though the arrogance was there, as distinctive as that tattered flag that he had his outriders carry before him. If on the contrary he remembered that in Viscount Herluin's eyes he was still untried, unfleshed, a 'green' lordling, as unfit for bargaining at court as leading men in battle, these weaknesses only increased his arrogance. And at least the blatancy of his arrival had this for credit – King Henry could not help but hear of it. And whether the king would or no, out of courtesy alone he was obliged to receive the young duke and listen to his requests.

The first was for a knighting as Herluin had advised. It was easily taken care of. 'You are yet young,' King Henry said in an off-hand way that hid his inner thoughts, 'and like your father you top me by a head. But if you kneel at my command I may yet have you in reach.'

Some of his courtiers laughed, but those in his confidence did not, neither did William, some intuition putting him on his guard to hidden meaning. 'As for a wife, you are too young to take your pick. The ladies will not have you.'

A sally that again brought a laugh not exactly to William's liking. He flushed, bowed abruptly, and withdrew in stiff fashion, knowing the king had bettered him. All his old dislike of the court surfaced. If among the crowding courtiers he did not see Guy of Burgundy's jeering face, so much the better. He no longer feared Guy of Burgundy and yet he did not want to meet him. That the king was hostile was evident, but since he still did not know the cause he also did not know how to allay the royal dislike. Nor was he certain that he wanted to, his own former suspicions of the king's insincerity newly reinforced in spite of Herleve's too-generous protestations to the contrary.

Having no one now to lean on, no one of rank to turn to in this lordly world, William came to rely on Golet's judgement. Or rather, since it often echoed his, to turn to him for confirmation of his views and opinions. 'My lord,' Golet said one day, his nose twitching. 'I feel unrest here, a tossing by many streams, all tugging this way and that, all full of deep and deadly currents.'

He sniffed. 'If this is how the great live,' he said, 'give me peace in a hovel. Myself, I'd lie low a while,' he added. 'For albeit I know naught of kings, a weak man is like a reed, swayed this way and that by whatever next moves him. And such a man, having baited once, will wait for response before he baits again, the more to enjoy it. That's human nature.'

He spoke familiarly, as does a friend without thought of

offence, and to his credit William took none. He sensed too that it was the king's weakness that turned the court into a quagmire where dissatisfaction bred. And just as Golet's analogy made for uneasy if shrewd comparison of their present situation with that in the marshes of the Eure, so William knew he could as easily lose his way among these treacherous courtly windings. He therefore held his breath and sank down to wait; what he had learned from Walter's cunning in the wilds standing him in good stead in this seat of civilization. He spoke no more about knighthood. He made no complaints about the treachery of his Norman lords and no comment, yea or nay, to the stories that followed his arrival. He certainly gave no further hint that he had ever contemplated wanting military help (although that might have been considered by many the main reason for his visit), and in no way gave the king cause to fault him. Instead he followed Golet's suggestion to hold himself apart, living as an outsider to courtly ways, spending his days much as he had done in the forest hamlets. This reticence earned him a reputation for sullenness, his critics calling him a rustic oaf tainted by low breeding. Ironically the sneers at least had the advantage of making the king less jealous. But being young and close to manhood William suffered the more he kept tight hold upon his feelings, the more he was cut off from the role he had expected to follow. And as he was young, the more removed he became from the ladies the king had mocked would not accept him.

The king may have meant to mock William; certainly he did not intend praise. The old legend of William's birth still rankled. The king's double meaning was intended to prick and put William out of humour, was calculated to warn his courtiers not to take William to their hearts. But he also let jealousy cloud his judgement. William was no longer the child whom the ladies had made a pet of, now to be put aside and ignored. He had survived, had grown. In his surcoat, belted with his sword – for so he appeared, eschewing the more elegant furred gowns favoured by the French – he looked as dangerous as rumour once had whispered. And he was young, and handsome. Tall for his years he moved in that cumbersome mail coat with an easy grace, almost like a leopard taken from his ducal banner. There were many maids who might take a fancy to him. Illegitimate or not, dangerous or not, young as he was, William was bound to set the dovecotes cooing!

Golet had been quick to point out this other fallacy in the king's malice. 'For to my mind,' said he, 'any man, duke or not, can surely have women if he wants. Your soldiers do, why then not you? Tis only Golet who has lost his taste and no longer lusts for them.' He sighed and rolled his eyes giving the lie to his implication. Yet of all the men whom William could have chosen, Golet was best suited to tutor him on this subject, a man who had killed for passion and been ruined by it.

William was unused to girls. In his world so far there had been no place for them. Now from a vantage point in the main yard, close to the stables within reach of his men and horses, where as a child he used to sit with Walter, Golet helped William understand some of these feminine mysteries. The ladies' heightened laughter, for example. Golet claimed that this and their exaggerated speech – their habit of talking loudly without looking at anyone – were little tricks which in fact showed that they were aware of those around them. Even the set of their heads and shoulders, the tossing of their hair, were displays meant to impress rather than mock, 'Like birds at nesting time,' Golet said, 'although in birds 'tis the males who strut and preen not dowdy hen pheasants.' But although William now saw many women of all ages and types, and, of those, many who were beautiful, not one approached Herleve for manners or looks. To his mind they also were mired by the court and its ways, were haughty or deceitful or sly, without attraction.

Yet in his lonely hours he began to ponder what having a woman might mean.

He remembered what Herleve had said but, half shamefully, he remembered more how she had looked at Count Herluin, how she had gone up the steps to the bower, how her husband had shortly followed after. It was what might have happened after, up there in the private dark, that began to engross him. He began to look for one person, the girl who had once so thoroughly slighted him, but the more he searched, the more he found her conspicuous by her absence. He did not even know why it was she he was looking for until he suddenly saw her, early one morning, half hidden among a bevy of other maidens, all of whom were so much taller than her that she seemed half their age. In spite of her size he noted at once how the others deferred to her, both in speech and action giving way to her as if she were their superior. She was still surprisingly small, almost diminutive, was dressed in finest silk, the harum scarum child he remembered quite lost in this young damsel of fashion, with her hair braided flat over her ears and her little person framed by a fur-edged gown (which was so voluminous he felt she was completely diminished by it). He remembered who she had said she was and his mouth curled. Granddaughter of a king wasn't it, daughter of a princess, niece of the present king who was himself the cause of William's predicament. Well, I am great-nephew to an English queen, he thought, and if her father is a count, I am son of a duke, and a duke myself into the bargain.

Matilda of Flanders had reached Paris only the night before and had risen early. The ride from Lille had been long and wet; as on previous occasions she had preferred horseback to being boxed up in an oxen wagon with its ill-shaped wheels lurching at every rut. Now while her father chatted with the royal grooms and discussed the merits of his own stock, and her mother attended Mass and prayed God for patience with her daughter (and afterwards gossiped with the older women in the queen's chambers, gossip which, being Russian and knowing little French, poor Queen Anna of Kiev was unable to suppress), Matilda had escaped. For the moment she was free to wander without restraint, to glean real news as best she knew how, and to accept the homage of her contemporaries amongst whom – despite her infrequent appearances in Paris – by virtue of her position she was held in high esteem. But she was also an enigma to those contemporaries; and although the ladies of the court fawned on her in public, she knew that in secret they felt very differently towards her.

There was a simple reason. All those grand relationships that irked William, all her father's vast lands and fortunes had not yet given her a husband or any hint of one! Unmarried, unbetrothed and, what was worse, oblivious of the disgrace, for all her mother's trying. Matilda must have caused the Princess Adela many anguished prayers.

Yet Matilda did not really suffer from a lack of suitors; her mother had a list of them longer than a saint's coffin. Matilda's unmarried state was apparently of her own choosing. It was Matilda's own decided opinions, her reputed caustic tongue, even her father's good-natured deference to her wishes which counteracted all Princess Adela's efforts. And it was Matilda's seeming indifference to any nuptial arrangements that caused her contemporaries most envy, although they hid it beneath their fawning. They did not even realize that she herself would have preferred their open hatred. That, at least, would be honest.

Matilda herself seemed unaware of her failings. As she had when she was a child she went her own way, refusing to argue with her mother, seldom confiding in anyone, certainly never taking any of these other young ladies into close friendship. She never spoke of her suitors or lack of them, certainly never discussed their failings or virtues, never giggled or sighed in secret with chosen confidantes. Her reputation for aloofness did not bother her. She preferred to be thought cold and aloof; it gave her clarity of vision. No wonder the other ladies did not know what to make of her!

Being so recently arrived, Matilda did not yet know of William's return, though she would soon have heard of it, it being one of the court's main interests, at once mysterious and aggravating. And in truth, although she would have been the last to admit it, one of the reasons for her presence at that time was her own continuing and unsatisfied curiosity over William's fate. That this morning he should suddenly emerge from a throng of people, should stand in front of her and speak to her directly, was as unnerving as if a ghost from her ancestral tomb had risen up from the past. That his first words were not at all calculated to please any lady, especially one of her own strong nature, only added to her discomfort.

William might have realized all this before he approached her but he didn't. Nor did he ask Golet for advice, simply remembered nothing except her former disdain, spoke hotly what was in his heart, as disastrous in his first approach to a lady as in his asking favour of the king. Bidding Golet stay where he was (his first mistake), William unwrapped his long legs from the wall against which he and Golet had been lounging and began his calculated stroll towards the group, again not a wise manoeuvre. He might have expected better luck had he approached his quarry when she was alone. He ignored the other demoiselles to their chagrin (a third mistake) and addressed Matilda directly.

'So, mistress, we meet again on equal terms, although once you dared me not to. I have been searching for you, you're hard to find among the crowds.'

If the suddenness of William's approach and his method of speaking startled Matilda, if the words were abrupt and thrown down like a gauntlet, it was the actual fact of his presence that stilled Matilda's immediate response. She had no difficulty in recognizing him, for all that he was greatly altered: tall and broad-shouldered now, his hair still thick but longer and darker. The expression in his eyes had not changed, nor the intensity in them; that was how he had looked when he had originally faced his boyhood tormentors. By the Mass, she wanted to cry, where have you sprung from, what brings you here, where have you been, what has become of you? Like a child she wanted to pour out all the questions she had been saving up as if it were but yesterday when they had last met. Instead, his choice of phrase, which suggested that there had already been some recent clandestine meeting 'twixt the two of them, made her curse his indiscretion. Outwardly remaining calm, inwardly she writhed to think how her companions would crow at her and come to wrong conclusions.

She took one glance, looked away. Nor had she ever forgotten the way he had returned her childish ill-manners with elaborate courtesy, deliberately making her suffer guilt for it. She would not show guilt again, rather answer challenge with like challenge.

Of all the things he'd said or hinted, his remark about her being hard to find was the one that most rankled. In her annoyance she took it as some reference to her small stature, about which she was most sensitive. Rearing herself up to her full height she said in a commanding voice, 'What fellow is that which accosts me?' And when her companions whispered, unconsciously closing ranks around her and looking over their shoulders at William, she added loud enough for him to hear, 'The Bastard. I thought him dead.'

Her choice of expression was deliberately chosen. If he were to offend her she would offend him back, Matilda having grown as little in tact as she had in stature! Too late she bit her lip and her cheeks flushed with mortification. Other words formed on her tongue. 'Hold, I did not mean that,' she wanted to cry, 'I've news for you.'

She would have been speaking to his back. William had spun on his heel and strode away without a word, head high, sword clanking, offence written in every step.

'Now by the Rood,' Matilda thought dejectedly, 'here's a fresh fault. Rather than making him angry, I should have been trying to appease him for my father's sake.'

She rounded on her companions, berating their stupidity. Why had they not straightaway told her he was here; what was their reason? She herself had never seen the duke before, but if he chose to speak to her she had the right to know of him. Remarks of the sort that if examined carefully, would have revealed her turbulence of spirit. When, hiding their suspicions at her unexpected outburst, the other ladies answered with the truth as they saw it, Matilda felt her anger fade as quickly as it had grown, to be replaced by fresh suspicions of her own.

No one knew why he had left his dukedom, they said. After his first audience with the king he came no more in the king's presence but hung on the outskirts with his men, confiding only in his jester, as friendly with him as if with a devil's familiar.

Matilda listened in unaccustomed silence. 'Still an outcast,' she thought. Time had not softened her but for this boy, as she still

149

thought of him, the fellow feeling had never diminished. She felt she had almost been tricked into answering him as she did; the last thing she had wanted was to injure him. Careful not to let her true thoughts show since she prided herself on self-control, arms entwined with one of the ladies, a gesture she abhorred, she let herself be led away without a backwards glance. She knew exactly where, close to his familiar jester, William would assume his usual posture: arms folded, leaning against the wall, keeping to himself; a bear chained to a stake, sharpening his claws. The thing she knew, or rather had wormed from her father, the reason for her father's visit, gnawed at her: that would be worth the telling if she could get William's attention.

Most of the remainder of the day she worried at the possibility and how to achieve it. While like a dutiful daughter she remained beside her mother, busy with her tapestry, ideas of how and when flashed through her brain, were explored and rejected. Head kept low as was her fashion when deep in thought, she let her needle flash in and out, following the twistings of the green and blue threads. She was fond of embroidery, it helped her think, the only feminine pursuit she had ever liked or was any good at. The knowledge she had coaxed from her father on their ride to Paris burned in her, the more that she remembered her first encounter with William and the cause of his boyish fight.

When twilight came and she knew that the outer yard would be almost empty, pleading weariness she went alone into the solar where her mother and she were lodged as honoured visitors. Quickly wrapping herself in a heavy cloak to hide her face, and carrying her psalter, she slipped down a winding stair similar to the one that William once had used. Her breath coming short with haste, she stole along the winding passages until she came into the open. And there she paused in the coolness of the night to wrestle with her conscience.

She was not a child now to wander mischievously at will, and what she was about to do might be misconstrued, would smear her family name if the world learned of it. If her mother heard 'twould be her death! As when she was a child, the clash of disobedience and excitement made Matilda's blood race.

It was the time of day when few courtiers were about, certainly none of the ladies. They were attending Mass as she should have been. Holding her psalm book well to the fore, she ventured out into the yard, crossed it at a run and came to the stables. There she paused. The familiar bustle calmed her down and for a moment she enjoyed the sight, wishing for the hundreth time she were a man herself and able to take part.

The great horses were being led in. There was the soft sound of swishing tails, of water carried in leather pails, of equine munchings. Men with straw between their teeth curried the chargers' shining flanks. Although many lords left this work to their serfs and squires she soon spotted William, faithfully adhering to his training. Her father would approve, she thought; she had often heard Count Baldwin say no man, not even a lord, should go to bed without first bedding down his mount; that no knight worthy of the name should be uncaring of the horse that carried him.

She watched approvingly. She noted how William groomed and fed his horse, hung the harness carefully in place and cleaned the saddle. Little better dressed than his men, in shirt and cotte – although the shirt was of fine linen make – he was at ease in these stables, in this like her father. She noted too how he and his jester, Golet, talked; familiar men's talk that she had always envied, Golet perched upon the stable railing while William worked. Yet Golet was not a member of the ducal guard, was a mere peasant, or so rumour said, no fitting companion for a would-be duke. And William's escort came from Conteville, his step-father's men; in some way his own men had failed him, although no one knew exactly how. Yet with them too William spoke and acted like old friends. She wondered what disasters had befallen him to have him in public keep such tight hold upon his thoughts and yet here in private joke and laugh so readily. But when the work was done and all his men gone, and he took up his sword belt, strapped it on and turned to leave, then she saw the shuttered look come down again as if he closed up tight all that he really thought and felt.

She slid out of the shadows before him.

His right hand snaked towards his hip where a dagger hung; the left shot towards her throat. It was the look on his face that Matilda would never forget: surprise, turned to anger, turned to steel resolve. His hold tightened; her head shook until the cloak covering fell off, the priceless psalter tumbled to the ground, but she managed to squeak out, ''Tis Matilda, Matilda of Flanders,' before the air went right out of her.

When she regained her breath she was lying propped against a wall, in a corner of an empty stall where presumably she had been dragged, and William was standing over her, trying to control himself, panting too to take in breath as if he had run a league. After a moment she heard him say, 'So are the tables turned, you in my place, I in yours. But I thought that day when 'twas the other way round was meant to be forgot. As was your

151

name. Or so your highness instructed.'

The irony was back in his voice, and the stiffness that expects insult and braces itself. Holding her throat where his grip had bruised Matilda heard her own voice croak, 'God's wounds but now you're grown you treat a lady rough.'

He did not laugh. She heard his boots crunch over the straw, heard the bucket tip. Presently he returned with water, presumably to give her a drink. Her throat still hurt but she would not let him know. She sat up, pushed his hand away so that the dipper spilled, straightened her gown which was soaked. 'Oaf,' she scolded, 'you've ruined it.'

This time he laughed, mockingly, 'Ever a lady's main concern,' he said. 'You have changed after all. For you have become more dainty and I less so. Pardon me that I am so coarse. But assassins appear in many shapes, and I've become used to them.' Again the steel look.

'So what brings your ladyship a second time spying into men's concerns?' He dropped her psalm book in her lap. 'Holy matters, perhaps, or perhaps ones less spiritual, if your fancy's set on stable boys.'

Again the irony. Be careful, she thought, he means to rile. Carefully she said, 'Not stable boys, nor any man. The news I brought was for a duke, if he showed himself worthy of being so called.'

He ignored the insult. 'What news?' he said. And when she didn't answer, still fingering the bruises on her throat, 'What news, or must I once more shake it out of you?'

Something about the size of him, the hint of menace in his posture, the hint of menace in his tone, made Matilda wary. 'Listen then,' she told him. 'We've heard your dukedom's under attack.' She swallowed. 'They say that only a scant few of your lords keep faith, that while the rest default your own kin, such as the Count of Arques, seek your death. And all because your uncle spirited you away so no one knew where you were. While you were lost your dukedom's gone to ruin.'

He stood back, no longer laughing. 'And that is news?' he said at last. 'Lady, I have lived it through, it is no news to me.'

'But this is.' She couldn't resist a note of triumph. 'It is the reason for my father's coming. To warn the king. Although had perhaps he known of you he would have told you too. You can't have heard of it, no one has.'

His impassive expression could have meant he was impassive, could have meant he did not care. 'As Arques displaced Ralph de Gacé, so he himself is displaced,' she said. 'Guess who next inherits lands in Normandy and grows to power. Guess who next intends to lay claim to it all.'

Still silence. He'll never ask, she thought, pride won't let him. 'An old enemy,' she went on. 'If I tell you his name, you'll remember him.' She took a breath, 'Guy of Burgundy.'

Suddenly her own petty sense of triumph faded. 'Guy's not changed,' she said, trying to recall her father's words, 'no different from when he was a boy. The man's a bully and a coward, and so puffed up with new conceit he vaunts himself like an emperor.

'But he is dangerous,' she added, remembering, 'making his base along the Risle and the Seine. By the death of Count Gilbert he gets Brionne.'

If she had stabbed William he could not have paled more. She felt the shock momentarily go through him. But when William spoke at last it was in his former ironic way.

'So speaks the messenger of doom,' he said. 'Lady, indeed you bring me news. So bear you mine back. As you know Guy of Burgundy, tell him he can claim all he likes but first he must get it. As for Count Gilbert's lands . . . Count Gilbert of Brionne was my friend and brutally was he murdered on my account.'

It was her turn to falter. She fingered the wet folds of her gown and shuffled her feet. 'That I didn't know,' she admitted, then, placatingly, 'nor do I "know" Guy of Burgundy any longer, except by repute. But my father, the Count of Flanders, does. That's why he's here. My father fears the king may favour Guy of Burgundy.' She added, repeating what her father had told her, 'Although he shouldn't, not to strengthen Burgundy to Flemish despite.'

The inference that it was Flemish matters that concerned her, that the king might grant Normandy to whom he liked as long as Flemish needs were served, hung in the air, unspoken.

The two stared at each other in the dim light, dislike welling beneath the surface. Yet there was something more than dislike, something almost tangible, as if each were looking at a mirrored self with all the strengths and weaknesses exposed.

William stirred first. 'You do a service greater than you realize,' he said formally. 'We should thank you for your message. We—'

Whatever he might have added was overriden. There was another scuffling noise at the entrance, louder than that Matilda had made, the clank of steel, a tinder scratch, not the stealthy sounds of assassins but rather of men who wished to make their presence known. A torch flared.

153

'So here you are, my lord duke,' Count Baldwin boomed in his hearty way. 'I trusted to finding you. And hither your men directed me. What better place for men to talk, say I, than stable or hunting field – if my wife'd let me.'

His laugh was hearty too, unforced. Matilda guessed even his squires would be smiling. The count's easy nature was well known, as was the Countess Adela's 'tyranny'. Feeling William's momentary relaxation, frantically Matilda pulled at his sleeve and sank back in the corner out of reach of the flickering light. It was bad luck that her father should have arrived at such an inappropriate moment. For an instant she felt discovery hang in the balance.

But she had guessed right about one thing. No more than she would William want the count to learn of her visit, partly because he also might be compromised, partly because although he might not approve of her, Matilda of her own volition had come first with forewarning.

Now, praise God, William remained solidly placed in the centre of the stall so that he blocked the newcomers' view. He let Count Baldwin continue his rambling discourse until she had squeezed beneath the manger where she was out of sight. Only then did he move forward, firmly pulling the stall door behind him and almost pushing the torch-bearer out of his way.

'I do not remember that you and I know each other, my lord,' she heard William say, abruptly breaking through the count's patter. 'I have only once met a lowlander, and he tried to kill me. So if I seem short of courtesy, perhaps I may be excused.'

It was a bleak beginning. My father will be undone, Matilda thought. But although what William went on to say was equally bleak, his tone now had warmth to it as if he mocked himself. 'We are glad to see you, my lord count. Although what the reason is for this talking I can but guess at. If there be a reason that is.'

The count was silenced. The encounter was taking a turn he had not anticipated. Matilda guessed how his eyes would squint with effort and his large mouth pout as it did when he was thwarted, like a larger masculine version of herself. She almost giggled.

'Your grace speaks in riddles,' the count brought out at last, formal too in turn. 'But I am come to help not harm.' He waved his men away out of earshot, leaned back beside William, certainly more at home in these surroundings than he ever was in courtly ones. 'Although what I speak will not be welcome. But as I am the first to learn of it in all its ugliness so I put to you as it is your right to know. Although had I not found you here I would have told the king instead. And shall tell after this,' he hastened, 'for he too has a right to knowledge when treachery rears in any part of his kingdom.'

In measured tones he repeated what Matilda herself had said, not changing anything except to give the names of all of Guy of Burgundy's new acquisitions, in particular those along the Seine, including Vernon, a valuable fortress, as well as Brionne. He explained too what was new to Matilda; how he had come upon the information, imparted to him in secret by certain of his allies along the Burgundian northern boundary. And as before when Matilda had spoken it was mention of Brionne which broke William's reserve.

'No pretence, no falsity in Guy's original claim,' Count Baldwin went on, eager to regain control of the situation. 'Guy of Burgundy has right to lands in Normandy by succession. Not by descent masculine 'tis true, but through the line feminine. His mother was Adeliza, said to be daughter of your grandfather. Or so his followers now maintain. But on the basis of that relationship will he argue that all of Normandy is his.'

In her hiding place, Matilda felt the shock of affront. Guy of Burgundy to be descended from the same family he had so reviled! His hypocrisy made her angry on William's behalf.

'If that be so,' William's tone was haughty; he almost drawled the words, 'why then, my lord count, is Normandy a-swarm with claimants, like a hive of bees? It is mine.' The snarl was genuine, a leopard's snarl. 'Let those who side against me be warned. With or without the king, God has given me Normandy to keep.'

'Just so, just so.' Count Baldwin was soothing. 'We understand. Not for a second would we underestimate your determination. And right glad am I to hear of it. For though I came to Paris of my own accord, your presence, albeit unexpected, is especially welcome. For it occurs to me, my lord duke, that our position is somewhat similar. And that is what I would really like to talk about.'

Matilda heard him settle himself against the stable walls, his voice low yet confiding. He spoke first of his sons and his fears for them, his fears of the king's capriciousness, things he had complained of before. But when he came to the main content she was surprised at his clarity of purpose. She had not thought her father had so much knowledge in him. And from the set of William's shoulders she could tell he was listening as intently as she was.

'I myself could not countenance false claim,' the count was

saying. 'I know who is true duke. But I do admit that an unsettled Normandy swings all adrift. For although Flanders is far from Normandy, unrest in one can foster unrest in the other. And in northern France these two states, both great, hold the balance of power. If the king gives Guy of Burgundy support, that balance will be tipped in Burgundian favour instead. Now Burgundy is my close neighbour and I do not like to see Burgundian interest thrive. As it grows so do I wane. Like you, I also am endangered by this Guy of Burgundy.'

He continued hastily, alarmed perhaps by William's expression. 'I do not accuse the king of offering Guy military support, although Guy himself may ask for it. At the most I suspect the granting of free passage across the royal lands, and a closing of the royal eyes to what is right and proper. Of themselves nothing serious. But to my mind such lack of royal care for rightful inheritance is deadly.'

He added, even more solemnly, 'Nor do I myself speak treacherously. What I say to you I shall repeat the same to King Henry, no more, no less. But if the king cannot be trusted, and the balance is lost, the time may come when I too shall need allies I can rely upon. As no doubt do you,' he added delicately, 'allies who will not be bought and sold, but who stand firm, upon fixed commitment, arranged well in advance.'

He paused to let the arguments sink in. 'You yourself are young, if your grace will pardon me,' he went on, 'and young men do not always look ahead as we old stalwarts do, whose future is already closing round us, curtailed by age and death. But I would be glad to offer my services at your grace's behest, if, of course, certain formalities were agreed to first.'

Matilda was impressed. She had no idea her father could be so shrewd, in fact she almost clapped her hands. Yet his cunning was typical of him, being in a way guileless; a clever adversary would soon see through it. Was William that clever? She craned forward to hear his response.

'Just so,' said William gravely, without a sign of sarcasm although she was sure that he meant to be sarcastic. 'As your lordship points out, Normandy and Flanders have so much in common that it would go against nature for them not to be friends. Their mutual interest in fact is so strong that had your lordship not come to me, of a certainty I should have approached you. For you are right. I need allies as does a man who is surrounded by a storm, about to be swept away. But I would have more than friendship.'

He straightened his shoulders, stood even taller, overshadowing the count. 'I ask your lordship for his daughter in marriage,' he said. 'Then should we be bound by the strongest ties.'

Matilda sank back again. Jesu, she thought, how dare he! How dare he, knowing I am listening! For a moment she contemplated revealing herself: that would make him look foolish. And as the count in turn hesitated; how dare my father allow him to barter for me as if I were horse-flesh, she thought, as furious with him as with William. But there was nothing she could say or do for the moment, simply bite her anger down and continue to listen while the count rephrased his wish to be of service without committing himself to any decision, and William reiterated his desire to be 'more than friends'.

The two men parted with the understanding of a second meeting; the count still largely gracious, the young duke suave and graceful; both still angling for position. The count's tone suggested satisfaction laced with some confusion; the duke's response being perhaps too subtle for his taste. The duke showed himself more enigmatic, not willing to reveal how deep the blow he had been struck. Yet he parted not without some satisfaction of his own, as his hearty farewells suggested. But when Count Baldwin had withdrawn, taking his squires and torch with him Matilda rose up from the stall, her hair plastered with straw and her dress blotched with dust, her face stained with it. 'Scum,' she cried, 'the pair of you.'

Chapter 12

'Scum,' Matilda spat, stamping her feet. Tears of frustration clouded her blue eyes. 'Curs, swine, whoresons.'

'All at once?' William said. He laughed, his own eyes shining. 'Then the devil himself couldn't better us. You've missed out "bastard", lady, what makes you so kind? But if insults haven't clogged your wits, tell me who bade you come? And why?'

And as she began to argue denial, 'No lies,' he said. 'A child could see through your father's ploys. Well, if he wants something from me, that's a game two can play.'

'You'll not have me,' she said.

William grew thoughtful. 'Perhaps,' he said. 'That's for your father to decide.'

His echo of what she knew very well irritated her afresh. She drew herself upright, although the wisps of straw and the bedraggled gown did not suit such haughtiness. 'He'll hearken to me,' she said, trying to convince herself. 'And I'd not have you, not if you were the last man on earth.'

'You may have to wait that long,' he said. 'I don't see other suitors clamouring at your gates.'

The shrewd retort broke down her final guard. 'There is,' she lied, 'at least one I like.'

'And who is this paragon?'

'Gerbod.' She stuttered over the name. 'And he's . . .'

'A Dane?' Once more William interrupted her, 'Then you marry into heathen land. For if the Danes hate Saxons, think how they hate little Christian maids. They eat them,' he added with inspired invention that again made his eyes shine.

'Or Flemish perhaps,' he went on, enjoying himself, 'stolid as a bull and as clumsy? Or French, wound up with graces and airs? But such a name, "Gerbod". God's wounds, I'd rather be called Bastard myself.'

'Twice have you used that term,' she cried, 'not I. But add tanner to it, and you say all. I'd not marry beneath me so far.'

'Ha,' he said. He leaned back against the stall as her father

159

had done, as if prepared to stay all night. 'That's more like truth. Let's take the first. Bastard, you claim, as if it were a term of disgrace, as if the disgrace falls hard on me, who am blameless in every way of my birth. Nor was my begetting by my design. But listen now to what I say, for I shall not say it twice.'

He leaned forward towards her, so close she felt his breath on her cheek. She could see the glint of his teeth as he spoke through them. 'My father was a Norman duke. He chose for my mother, Herleve, who still lives. When you meet her, the wife of the Viscount of Conteville, treat her with respect, for of her own will she took my father first of men, to love and honour him. As did he her. And had not death struck him down still in his youth, he would have come back to sanctify a union already handfast, as sacred as if it were church-made in the eyes of God. As for tanners, mistress, I have lived with the poor and desolate. Among them a tanner earns just respect, his craft is praised. And I know of a tanner whose skills are such that he can take a paring knife and cut through skin without a flaw, or slide it butter-smooth through flesh, so smooth the victim never feels it go in till it pours his life's blood out.

'As I may yet show you,' he said, closer still, speaking softly, a whisper of threat, a mere thread of it. 'We are alone. And no one knows that you are here.'

She backed away, feeling for footing against the wall, until the corner stopped her retreat. 'God's mercy,' she heard herself say, 'I meant no harm.'

'Nor I you.' He straightened up. 'Nor I you,' he repeated, 'for all that you think otherwise. Well now, we've reached an impasse. If no one knows you've come, presumably you were not sent. But if you were not sent, that still does not answer why you came.'

He stood looking down at her, the expression on his face hard to read. 'Not out of love for me I swear,' he continued softly, 'but nevertheless out of some sort of love. Self-love perhaps, a child playing at intrigue without thought of consequence.'

His anger had evaporated; he sounded disillusioned rather than angry, as if he set her down for nought. It made her want to tell the truth.

'I felt sorry for you,' she said.

She saw his eyes darken, not with rage or threat but with something else that she could not put a name to. It frightened her more than anything so far, so much so she closed her own eyes.

When she opened them, his were hooded, the shuttered look had come down. 'Run home,' he said. He stood aside. 'Play no more. I'll not have my wife play at games with me.'

She drew her cloak about her and strode past, head high. At the stable door she turned back for one last gesture of defiance. 'Nor shall I ever be your wife,' she cried, 'not for threats, not for love.'

He did not answer her.

When she had regained the safety of the main yard, Matilda forced herself to stop so she could pull out the straw in her hair and hide the scratches on her arms. Rewinding the cloak about her ruined gown she swept towards the solar door. Luck favoured her. She was able to slip in without being seen. Not calling for her maid, the most recent successor to Beatrice, she slid on to the pallet bed where she lay with the covers drawn, pleading an aching in her head when her mother found her there.

She did not lie. By turns her thoughts took different shapes to tease and torment her. Sometimes blame fell full force upon her father, whom until then she had always counted on to see her way of things. Now she was not sure he would. Useless to console herself with the thought he had not agreed, that he had only considered; to her mind even by consideration he betrayed. And whatever had prompted William to ask for her in such a way? He cared no more for her than she for him. It was God's judgement on them both, she thought, a punishment for that encounter so many years ago. As for that Gerbod, what stupidity had made her speak of him? She had plucked his name at random, a man her mother once had mentioned. She had never heard more of him, never met him, never more considered him. The fact was that no man who captured her interest for more than a fleeting second, except for William himself. But if she had often thought of him, it was not in the way anyone else would ever understand, not as a lover, not, Heaven forbid, as a husband, but like a private talisman, whose fate was somehow linked with hers. Well then, fate had done her ill now that William had destroyed that secret regard and openly linked their names in her father's mind. She hated William afresh for it.

Matilda balled her fists, forcing herself to remain still. Meekly she drank of the herbs her mother brought, although they nauseated her. The windings of her thinking took her down strange byways. It was not the hate itself, but the objects of it that were the misfortune: her scorn was heaped now upon the only two

161

men she'd ever had any time for. Her father she could deal with; she knew how to punish him. It was the other who would be more difficult.

'I imagined him still a boy,' she soothed herself, 'and so he is a stripling aping his superiors.' Yet neither was that completely true. There had been a shrewdness in his dealings with her father that ought to be admired. Nor had it been completely true that pity alone had driven her to go to him. Self-love, he'd said. If by that he meant indulgence, if by play he meant playing with fire, she was guilty on both counts. 'But I'll not admit it,' she thought. 'I'll not give his insolence that satisfaction. And God forgive my father that he bargains with me, for I'll not.'

Poor Matilda. She knew as little about courtship as her suitor. Pride was what fuelled her soul. When it burnt out it left but ash. As for Count Baldwin, he too kept apart, pleading indisposition, a rheum taken on the bleak lowland borders during his ride here. Absenting himself next day from court and the king's presence he remained in his personal chambers, his by right as a member of the royal household, going over the events of the night before, counting the benefits he thought he had gained and puzzling over the issues he felt had slid away from him.

William's unlooked-for emergence from obscurity was obviously of chief importance. Hearing of it on his arrival, he had grasped its use to him, even if it had meant a secret meeting in the dark. The only clandestine meetings he had known before were for personal pleasures, without his wife's knowledge of course. If the king ever heard of this one he might condemn it as treachery! But Baldwin was no traitor. It was true that what he had told William he would tell the king in the same words, without mincing them. It was just that Baldwin was no longer as dependent upon royal favour as he had been in his youth and his growing exasperation with the king's vacillations had led him to come to Paris in the first place.

William's actual presence would not radically affect Baldwin's complaints to the king but it would strengthen the way of lodging them, to the count's own advantage. Even Henry might be shamed to admit in public that he would not help a rightful duke. Drumming with his fingers, Baldwin numbered the advantages he had gained. One, by confiding first to William, Baldwin had assured that William would be in his debt and thus be beholden to him. Two, and equally important, the offer of Flemish help had been subtly linked in William's mind with return offers – not only with intangible gratitude, but with things more practical. Grants of land, wool trading benefits, fishing rights, these were the returns Baldwin had in mind – all in all a goodly result, all in all to Baldwin's benefit. But the third advantage from the meeting was most important. By confronting William alone man to man, he had had the chance to gauge William's reaction. As he had always thought, the lad was worth the backing – like his father. Robert had been called Magnificent. Perhaps William would be a conqueror.

Three gains then. Against them, two setbacks. What if despite all Baldwin's hopes the king supported Guy of Burgundy – Baldwin shied from the thought of his men arrayed against his sovereign's. And then there was the problem of Matilda. That most of all grated and left a chilling discord. He had not expected to have his daughter turned into part of the bargain.

The reason for Matilda being in Paris at this time was entirely due to the count. Glad of her company he had asked her to ride with him. His wife, looking for escape from the flatness, real and social, of her lowland life, had only at the last moment joined the party, to the chagrin of daughter and father both. Baldwin and his daughter still understood each other well, had planned to make of this journey a pleasant interlude. The Lady Adela, unaware of their previous arrangement, had demanded Matilda's presence as if a mother's right, ever more dissatisfied with her daughter's single state, and seeking constant opportunity to find her a husband.

It was not that Baldwin faulted his wife's efforts, but he did her nagging insistence. Besides it seemed to him that Matilda was not resistant to the idea of marriage; it was only that her parents had not yet found anyone she liked. Useless then for the Princess Adela to maintain that liking played no part in marital agreements. Matilda simply nodded agreement and continued on her own way, dismissive of every man she met. It occurred to Count Baldwin now that the only man she had ever shown any interest in was this very William. He gnawed his thumb, sadly perplexed. But he knew, and Matilda knew, that if he insisted she must follow his wishes whether she wanted to or not. Only, he could not quite decide whether this potential alliance with Normandy was worth such sacrifice.

Left alone in the stable, William continued to keep his position against the wall, arms locked across his chest. Beneath his unperturbed exterior his thoughts swirled. He too was angry, but not only with Matilda. He was angry with himself. The news revealed, for different reasons, by both father and daughter, was another bitter blow; his dukedom was constantly buffeted, quartered like a piece of meat. Who would get the lion's share? It meant he must speak out, that the king's aid was of even greater import then ever, and needed before the king was tempted to help Guy of Burgundy as Count Baldwin feared. King Henry knew Guy of Burgundy, had sided with him once; why should he not do so again? Guy of Burgundy was a greater threat than any Norman lord; his very name spoke of power, Burgundy itself being a great state to be reckoned with. And how had he really acquired those Norman lands? By whose leave? And to succeed to what Count Gilbert had lost – William ground his teeth. God surely turned His back to allow such impiety.

Then there were the personal affronts caused by the count and his wayward daughter. To be manipulated by the father, pitied by the girl; by the pax, William thought, they must take me for a fool! That the count had tried to use him to Baldwin's own benefit he understood very well. On the other hand, Baldwin's offer of help in return would be of enormous worth, worth the blow to William's pride But then, to top it all, to have asked for the girl and put himself in Count Baldwin's thrall only to have her refuse! God's wounds, he swore again to himself, what mad impulse had made him ask? To torment her, perhaps, to pay back her father's condescension; to prove to Herluin and the king, perhaps even to show Herleve that he was capable of having a wife? And to what end? To drive Matilda into hate of him and worse, unwittingly to reveal some of his maudlin innermost thoughts – he groaned in self-derision. But the worst thing of all was to have used his wooing as an excuse, to have defended himself with it: how inept and awkward he seemed!

Shamefaced he accepted his inadequacies. A man should know something of girls before he tried to woo them. A man who had never known a wench, a novice who'd never tumbled with one in bed, never taken one by force – as he knew his men did – would have no luck with them. And of all the women he might have had this was the last he should have thought of, not even fully a woman yet, and by the looks of her never to grow into one! And such a tongue, such quick wits, such pride – 'twould be the devil's work to tame her. Yet for all that some force had surely inspired his words; they had formed seemingly without his intention. So, how to extricate himself from a position in which humiliation threatened on all sides?

On a second impulse he sought out Golet; Golet had been a married man, if not with great success; Golet could advise him on these intimate matters. His questions however seemed to puzzle Golet who knew better than to query his young master. Nor, despite his favour with the duke, would Golet venture advice on such a delicate problem. What did he say, with a half laugh, was itself a riddle. 'Well, my lord, all men make their way as their natures allow them. And to my mind that be true of love affairs as with other matters. Now as you know, although I was married, little luck I had of it. But I heard a story that may answer you.'

He waited until William settled down before the fire with a goblet of wine (for at William's command he had come into the chamber where William slept to do his master squire service).

'Once there was a knight,' he began, 'who had a wife. One day they dined beside a river. "Sit back, wife," he told her. "The water runs fast and the bank is weak." At every word she moved her chair closer to the edge. The bank gave way, she screamed, fell in and disappeared into the torrent. At once the servants hauled out a boat and began to search for her. No trace of her could they find until, exasperated, the knight himself took up the oars and began to row in the other direction.

' "My lord, my lord," his servants cried, wringing of their hands and pointing, "the water floweth this way, downward."

' "Aye so," replied their lord, "but such is my wife, she goes always against the current. And so then must I. For if I said to her as you have said, out of stubbornness would she do the contrary." '

Golet stretched his arms as if rowing. 'And so I repeat, my lord duke,' he said, 'if any man would better woman he must go to the opposite of common sense. But,' he winked disarmingly, 'to test the water's heat no use to ask another. A man must try it for himself. And that's the best advice I'll give you.'

More than that he would not say, but his comments gave William good counsel. The following day he bathed, had Golet trim his hair and shave him, although the knife edge cut along a chin that was still almost hairless. Dressed in his finest gown, given him by Herleve (for she would not have let her son go unsuitably provided even if she took the clothes from Herluin's back), he belted on his father's dagger and, swaggering a little in defiance, he came openly into the king's presence. But except for the usual courtesies he did not speak to him; nor did he approach the Count of Flanders. He made certain the count's daughter knew she was ignored, talking only with maids within her hearing, and turning his back on her near presence. And when with a toss of her braids she moved away, sure enough, shortly afterwards, he would appear again close by her, his shoulders firmly set against her.

The court ladies noticed this, as he meant them to. Not the Lady Matilda's behaviour, for her whims were notorious, but William's sudden affability. It charmed them. By nightfall the only subject of conversation was the young duke's apparent ease of manner, as if, said someone knowingly, a weight had lifted. Conversely Matilda became more irritable. Several times she bit her tongue to choke back a sarcasm. Her father was equally bemused, not certain what to do. The lad's coltish behaviour troubled him. What if William played him false and went to the king with the story of their encounter. True, he consoled himself again, no words of treachery had ever been spoken or hinted at. Nor meant; the meeting had been sought in all innocence. But the king's fear of private meetings was well known, and even if there were no real cause his goodwill could be quickly lost. Meanwhile King Henry himself, sure that William would once more broach the two matters which were dear to his heart and which had supposedly brought him to Paris, waited in vain for William to come a-begging.

Several more days passed in this silent tussle, the king on edge, the count troubled, the lady furious. All three expected another secret message, but there was only silence. William spent his time either in converse with his own men (who at his behest had been scouting out information), or in the company of other females. He used Golet to find out what previously he had not known: the king's long-standing suspicion of him and Guy of Burgundy's part in it. He learned also something of Count Baldwin's own position. It bore out what the count had said. So far so good. Only on the question of Matilda did Golet shake his head, not willing to pass censor on a lady whom his lord might have his eyes on. Golet's discretion told him as much as if he had poured out all his findings, for as William had guessed not many men had time for her, and as many ladies would willingly have slandered her for all their pretended liking.

As for the ladies, female company was not hard to find, for all that he was a novice. Wisely, he avoided all within the palace; noble or base they were tarred with the same ambitious brush. But there was a fresh-faced peasant girl who brought milk from the fields outside the city and who had smiled at him as she poured it out. He felt at ease with her. Her dress was not so dirty that she smelt, and when he asked she deloused her hair so that it waved fine like spun flax. Nor did she come unwillingly, but was too shy to ask for anything except his favour. Like him she was a virgin. They learned together. And if it could not be said exactly that he used her to prove himself – for he found pleasure in her company as he did not in this royal conclave, and being with her reminded him of the best parts of his wanderings, and perhaps also of the best parts of himself – nevertheless in a way he did use her, to his own regret and hers.

Days, a week, passed then, as William continued his own dangerous three-way game. But he dared not delay too long. This new threat to his dukedom must soon be known; the count could not hold it in for ever. Nor would Baldwin willingly relinquish the benefit from the telling. And even King Henry could not ignore the disintegration of one of his largest regions, must act one way or another. It behoved William to settle with the count first.

All this William added up, balanced and weighed, in a manner old Osbern would have approved. And, sensing Golet could not help him in this diplomatic foray, he decided to follow Count Baldwin's example, that is to speak openly without guile, as if hiding nothing. He knew he was young to come to intrigue, but if he were ever to get what he wanted, now was the time to attempt it. Yet never had he felt so bogged down in courtly deception as when he tried now to use it.

He did not ask Count Baldwin for an audience privately, as he might and should have done. Instead he strode up openly to Baldwin when the count was preparing to ride out in the woods beyond the city. It was a fair day, the sort that makes men's spirits leap at the sound of hounds and horns. Like the older man, William was dressed for hunting in leather jerkin and leggings, garments that became his youthful figure better than Baldwin's portly form. 'Good day to you, my lord count,' he said in the affable manner he had been practising. 'I have been seeking an opportunity to talk again on the subject we last spoke of.'

His manner and tone were discreet; no one could overhear him; he stood respectfully at the stirrup iron to help the count mount, nothing suspicious in any of that. But as far as the count was concerned, he could not have chosen a worse time and place.

Baldwin's face grew red with vexed embarrassment. He fidgeted with the bridle and mumbled reply, eager to be off, all his energy and purpose concentrated on the hunt ahead, as William had supposed. 'With your lordship's leave, then,' William said, polite as a prelate, 'I will accompany you.'

He made a gesture; one of his men ran forward with his horse, he swung himself up gracefully beside the older man, the whole thing deliberately timed. The count could not refuse his company. As they moved off together, Matilda, caught behind them in a bevy of other riders, cursed her own ill-fortune even as she admired William's audacity.

Surrounded as she was by ladies whose horsemanship in every way was inferior to hers, she could not fight her way out of the press, and in any case the horse she rode side-saddle was no match for the men's greater mounts. She watched the duke and her father break into a canter as they passed out through the gateway, following the line of huntsmen towards the south banks of the Seine. She knew, as surely as if she had overheard, what William would be asking, no, demanding – and what her father would reply.

She had not told her father why she was so angry with him, but she had left him in no doubt of that anger. Suddenly he was cut off from her company. No longer did she join him in all the pursuits which she had loved as much as he, and which indulgently he had permitted as if she were a boy. His visits to the royal mews, his tours of the royal stables, even this hunting expedition, were all undertaken by him on his own without her presence. The count, used to her moods and in fact a little afeared of them, might have regretted her absence and been disappointed by it, but would have been stunned to know of the real reason for it.

Matilda's own pleasure in the hunt drained away; she rode by instinct, all her attention riveted upon those distant figures who, when they came to the fringe of the forest, disappeared and were lost among the many paths which spread in all directions. Away in the trees the horns rang out with the first sighting of a deer, so loud that the trees seemed to shake with it, sending showers of yellow flowers flying. Under their canopy, by mutual agreement, William and the count drew aside to let the main body of the hunt pass by. When the last of the horses had skitted past, their hooves rustling in the old heaps of fallen leaves, William turned in his saddle to face the count.

'I regret my lord,' he said, 'to curtail your pleasure. And indeed I curtail my own. It is long since I had the freedom to hunt in my own forests, although I have come to know them better than any huntsman, having been forced to live within their confines like an outlaw.'

His gaze at the count was direct, his speech direct. He had thought out carefully what he meant to say. 'I have considered what your lordship told me,' William said. He let the reins dangle through his hands so his horse could bend its head to crop the meagre grass. 'In these new troubles I can do with allies. If therefore you would help I would ask of you two things. First,

168

that you tell the king what you know of this Guy of Burgundy –
tonight, when I am in the king's presence – so that I may lay to
rest the residue of an old misunderstanding between the king
and me. For only when the king's mind is clear will he follow
his obligations.'

He spoke disingenuously, without attempt at concealment, and
his address impressed the count. Baldwin too allowed his horse
to graze and drew off his heavy gauntlets. 'You speak forthrightly, my young sir,' he said, with a heavy attempt at humour,
'and I welcome it. For my part, as you know, I have no secrets
from my king, nor wish for any. But I would also be of service
to you. Your first wish is easily granted. And the second?'

Again William faced him. 'I repeat I need allies. But, to be
fair, allies who lend arms and men deserve recompense. These
are promises for a future, since at his moment I do not even
have firm hold on lands that are mine own. What I can offer
instead is a marriage alliance.

'And so I reiterate my previous request,' he went on in the
same easy manner, 'to marry with your daughter. I do not think
that all the advantages will be on my side. For in Normandy you
too will have the staunch support that you yourself said you
wanted, doubly secured by your daughter's presence. And Normandy is large, powerful, a force to reckon with when it is tamed.
And tame it I shall,' he added. 'Here is my hand on it.'

'You argue well,' Count Baldwin looked harassed. 'And if the
king agrees – for after all, being underage, you are still as ward
to him – and if her mother gives approval, I too am nothing
loath. But she is young, my daughter, and . . .' He fumbled for
the right expression and looked relieved when William supplied
it. 'Headstrong, just so, headstrong, and although I regret to
admit it, stubborn and spoiled.'

When William laughed, anxious to correct a possibly unfortunate impression he added, 'That is to say, not exactly these
things, or not to great degree, but difficult to handle. Like a
young filly,' he went on, wiping his forehead, on safer ground
with horses than maidens, 'not yet broken to bit and saddle, full
of spirit. And yet my lord, well-born, well connected and,
although I say so who should not, dear to me. I'd not give her
haphazard to any casual acquaintance.' Now his own gaze was
hard. 'Nor bargain with her future to my own furtherance but
not hers,' he said.

William bowed his head to hide the smile that crossed his face.
His lips twitched. For a moment he was again tempted to tell the
count just what he knew of his daughter. Headstrong, stubborn,

spoiled and difficult, he thought. Add vain and proud and you've summed her up. Yet dear to him he says. I wonder what he values her for?

'So should I esteem her,' he said, taking his cue from the anxious father. He drew up the reins. 'And so are we agreed. You shall seek out the king in my presence, tonight as I give the word. And I shall seek out the lady.' He bent to check his straps and stirrups, once more hiding the twitching of his mouth. 'With your leave I'll address her myself before you do, so that she may tell you without prejudice what she thinks.'

Another burst of horns was music to the count's ears. 'Heartily, heartily,' he said, his enthusiasm for the chase making him careless, 'ride on, my lord duke. I follow you.'

It was not to occur to Baldwin until later, too late, that instead of taking the initiative as he had meant, in every way he had followed the young duke's lead, even to allowing William to dictate the conditions of their bargain and the timing of it.

That evening, as the count had promised, he came to his sovereign after the meal was ended. The cloths were drawn from the tables, the tapers lit, the room cleared for music, all new niceties that the count's lady wife envied and he himself despised. He spoke calmly, a man to be listened to, all that he had told William and all his own fears for Flanders if its Burgundian neighbours grew too powerful, excluding of course his distrust of the king and his own offer to William. When he mentioned Guy of Burgundy he saw how the king's face darkened and how his eyelids fluttered as they did when Henry was confused. It was then, at a nod from William, that he moved aside to let the young duke step forward, as was correct since it was his duchy that was under threat.

'My lord king,' William's voice ran out proudly, 'you have heard the Count of Flanders' fears for the safety of his possessions. Now hear mine. This new pretender, this Guy of Burgundy, has hated me since childhood, has mocked me with being base-born, has used a boyhood quarrel to blacken my name. And you, my king, know in your heart that his malice was such that he tried to drive us apart. We see full well at last to what ends his malice leads him, that he should threaten a duchy for which I alone have done you obeisance. Therefore, with just right, I ask you now as my liege-lord to support me in burying my enemies under.'

He spoke so well, he looked so much at ease that he made the king's hesitation seem furtive. There was a murmur of approval for his speech, even a little clapping of hands, and the king, caught off-guard by these signs of approval, had no option but to nod agreement.

William pressed home his advantage. 'When I first arrived,' he said, 'I asked for a knighting. I still ask for it. But as for a wife you, my liege, told me, wisely I think, to wait until I was older until I took one. Now you will understand that as my own birth had been marred by lack of legal marriage, so I would wish that my heirs be rightfully recognized. And with my duchy under siege, legitimate heirs ought not be long in coming to strengthen my position. A marriage to a wife of good standing is then of paramount importance.'

He paused, took a breath.

'But it could wait,' he said persuasively, 'if it were only planned. A betrothal is not marriage, and children half my age are betrothed every day. I ask then for betrothal, as your royalty permits.'

Once more the king looked about him helplessly. But even his own councillors were impressed at the youth's argument and whispered among themselves, pulling their beards gravely in agreement. The king gripped the arms of his throne for leverage and stood up. Faced with such united assent he could not refuse. 'So be it,' he said. 'Ride back to your duchy and make a reckoning. Render us the numbers of your own support, we supply the rest. And if the lady be suitable, take her, with our blessing.'

He could say no less, a far cry from his earlier contempt, as both he and William knew. Although King Henry smiled at the court's pleasure as if he had both planned and granted this outcome, underneath he seethed with resentment that this young lordling had so outwitted him. And like Baldwin, it was not until later, again too late, that he realized he had not even asked who the lady was.

The other person who felt neither pleasure nor gratification at the close of this encounter was Matilda. She knew William would not have spoken as he did unless he had her father's leave, and although she might have felt gratitude for not being named openly, she disliked the idea that William dared speak at all. That he wanted a wife merely to improve his own chances proved he was what she suspected, a would-be adventurer, a brigand. Yet that was what maids were used for, so her mother had often told her. A maid was only a pawn in the games men played of alliance and influence; a maid had only one function – to be a wife and mother.

But, here came another 'but' to enlarge the matter. Poor Beatrice, who so many years ago had been supplanted by someone more suitable, she had not had lovers simply to beget children. Beatrice had known some power that had made men her servants rather than the other way round. Now, almost grown, Matilda had only a vague recollection of the maid she used to cajole and threaten into compliance, but it seemed to her, for all that the countess had called her a slut, Beatrice's loving nature and her loving ways with men must have left some mark on her mistress.

'I don't know what I want from a suitor,' Matilda admitted to herself as if she were speaking once more to Beatrice. 'Rank, possessions, prestige, these come as natural I suppose. But there should be something more, I feel it in my bones; for certain sure something more than barter and usury to grace a marriage bed.'

She strained to hear Beatrice's reply. What was it Beatrice had called it, the lesson she had tried to instil into her mistress? Matilda had never forgotten the words: 'affection and lust'. Affection Matilda recognized. Affection was common to all humans, they felt it for each other, for parents, children, animals. Her father's 'affection' for his stallions and his hawks was without question. But 'lusting' was different, she had no real knowledge of that, although she knew its general meaning better now than she had as a child. How did lust differ from ordinary mating? How did a maid learn enough about lusting to recognize it in another? How did one dare find out?

She guessed that either her father or mother would approach her after this public declaration, and she braced herself for long hours of argument and tears. She did not expect William to plead for himself, that was quite contrary to the rules of courtship, and put a different aspect to things. That William was capable of it she did not doubt; it was her own ability to withstand him that troubled her.

William came to her in the herb garden where she had hidden herself with her companions. The day was mild, the garden walled, the herbs bloomed in profusion. Here she had felt safe. Once more William ignored the other ladies, left them in no doubt about his intentions and, equally commanding, ignored her protests, violating anew her sense of herself.

'Walk with me, lady,' he said. He spoke grandly, he walked grandly, every inch a duke, and she knew the other ladies watched her enviously. The fact that she suspected his was an act to hide his misgivings served to revive all her own but, unable to avoid him and having no place to run without causing greater scandal, she was forced to comply.

They made an ungainly pair, she thought, as they strolled

together along the cobbled path, their shadows before them pale in the sun: his broad and tall and hers thin and short, a giant and a dwarf. She flushed with humiliation. He did not speak until they had completed a circuit of the garden: to make more mock of me, she thought, putting me on display for the others to laugh at. It did not occur to her that in fact he was knitting up his courage.

What he did say when he spoke surprised her anew. 'I do not flatter myself,' he said, 'that you have changed your opinion. But you may, given time to reconsider.'

He stopped and looked down at her. She had not noticed before quite how tall he was nor how blue his eyes, nor how when he smiled at her his cheeks creased. 'When we first met,' William said, 'and as a child you helped me, I told you my name and title. Well, I was a child too and spoke rashly. Yet in the years that have passed I have not lost either, although violently have violent men tried to rip them from me. I shall be duke hereafter,' he said, 'and make you duchess, if you will have it so.'

He said more vehemently, 'Do I not have legs, arms, a head, like any other man? Where is the stain that you say my birth leaves on me?' He thought of the milkmaid, her gentle caresses, her tears, and hardened his heart against her. 'And I do not boast when I say that I know how to please women, which is more than many of your fine lords do.'

To Matilda's chagrin, tears of anger pricked her eyes. She too thought of the tales they whispered now, of the peasant girls, and tightened her resolve. Abruptly she turned on him, said, 'I'll not use my name to improve your line. Nor be wed to breed you sons.'

He laughed. 'Fairly spoke,' he said. 'Neither would I. But I think, if we were wed, sons would come all the same.'

She looked away, her face flooded with embarrassment, pursed up her lips. Behind her back she could hear her companions' whisperings. The words 'base-born, base-born' seemed to linger in the air like the sigh of the wind.

She said primly, 'For certain children would not come before marriage, to be a shame and a reproach.'

'There speaks a kind spirit,' he told her gravely – she couldn't tell if he mocked – 'always to think of others. But is not to bear another's shame a most Christian virtue?'

Then as she turned once more to protest, 'Nay, I speak in earnest,' he said. 'For I think, after all, you do have a kind heart. On the outside it may be that you are all prickle,' he went on, pointing to some thistles that grew in a sheltered patch. 'Like them you hide your softness to appear the more fierce. Well, I can accept that.'

This time his smile was without mockery. 'It is no different from what many men do,' he said, 'or what I do myself.'

No one she knew ever spoke like that. Her mother's caution, Beatrice's half forgotten stories, had not prepared her for this. She wanted to tell him so, she wanted to tell him to leave, she wanted to keep on listening.

'Twice have you been my rescuer,' he said, 'this second time more than you know. And if in truth it was for kindness, God forgive me, I need not refuse pity out of pride.'

He took her hand. 'I take my leave,' he said. 'As the king suggests I return home to gather troops so that we can act together. But Normandy is large. My vassals are not easily controlled. It will not be simply done to hold them. But what costs me time gives you a reprieve for a while. Unless you now have a firm answer.'

She felt his quick look but she would not return it. Stubbornly she set her mouth, pouting like her father. I'll not be tricked, she thought, I'll not respond either way, although he wants me to.

If William was disappointed by her lack of reply he did not show it. But neither did he take her silence for refusal. 'Keep quiet if you wish,' was all he said. He shrugged. 'Although I deem it churlish. But as you are young, and I am young, we can afford to wait. Until I come for you, know I remember you, Matilda of Flanders. I have chosen you.'

He bent his head. 'And let that be your comfort,' he whispered. And smiled a last time, the mocking smile that she was beginning to distrust.

Chapter 13

The knighting took place eventually although the king dallied, claiming so great an event needed preparation. It was an impressive ceremony, during which William knelt before the king, perhaps not as submissively as the king might have wished. 'Girded about with his sword, gleaming under his buckler,' as a witness was afterwards to record – the added words, 'and menacing under his helmet' suggested the story of a prophesy which still lingered. The final accolade was a mere tap, although seeing William on his knees may have tempted King Henry to smite harder! Following this, the preparations for departure were also dawdled through, and William's hope of a speedy leave were thus frustrated. Probably Henry could not decide which he minded most: a William here at court where he could keep an eye on him, or a William loose in Normandy where no one knew what he would be doing. And indeed, William at first was all cock-a-hoop. With his escort increased by a token addition from the royal guard, with promises of further royal support, with a coalition with the Count of Flanders in the making, and the possibility of marriage, the young duke's complacency might have been excused: this was no bad achievement for a beginner in diplomacy.

In fact he had less reason for rejoicing than he anticipated. Firstly the king was weasel-sly. Faced with the prospect of anarchy in Normandy, he did honour his commitment there, within months attacking both the fortress of Tillières on the Arve and the town of Argentan on the Orne where several disloyal barons were installed. But these were only minor places, and the attacks – like his offer of guardsmen – only token. The king's retaking of two rebel strongholds made no real dent in Guy of Burgundy's advance to power and in no way did it address the real issue of conspiracy from which, as Count Baldwin suspected, Henry held back deliberately.

Added to that, ironically the king's intervention actually strengthened Guy of Burgundy's position. Instead of serving as a warning to disgruntled Norman barons, it angered them. They may have welcomed the peace Henry's men were supposed to achieve but they were resentful of the methods. Among themselves they muttered that a duke who relied on outside help was himself a traitor, was a turncoat and a coward. Unjustly therefore they held William accountable for the king's actions, and hardened their stand against their rightful lord, turning instead to Guy of Burgundy as the stronger candidate. And since, by promising also to bring peace and by proving through devious arguments that despite his name he was of Norman blood, Guy convinced more Normans still to rally round him. Thus the very means with which William had intended to weaken Burgundian influence actually strengthened it, and increased a hundredfold the task he had set himself to regain his inheritance.

Much of this effect William did not actually discover until he in turn had come back to Normandy. But prior to that return he had had inklings of it, conveyed to him from Conteville where Herluin remained on careful watch. So it was no triumphant William who left Paris after all. Sometimes he felt more like a climber who crawled up a mountain on his hands and knees, only to slither backwards to a point even lower than where he had started. Yet he refused to be downhearted. Like the child who had squared his shoulders at the possibility of defeat, so now the young man called up all those traits of his ancestors to help him, the warlike nature, the endurance, the tenacity of purpose for which the Norman dukes were famed. And of these qualities it was tenacity which best served him, as his friends and enemies were to discover; tenacity, and a trait of his own that set its mark on everything he now did. That was his own brand of high-minded, indomitable courage which did not recognize defeat even when it stared him in the face, and which by force of personality was to bowl over men much more experienced than he was. For in the months ahead it was only by sheer determined courage he could hope to overcome enemies so much more united and cohesive than his own forces.

One last thing. Although the proposed marriage with Matilda was by now an accepted affair, although the king had given grudging approval, or rather had put forth no further obstacles, William was still not satisfied with the results of his wooing. He did not want it said he had to marry by force or drag a bride to the altar as if he were some sort of heathen. Nor could he claim their last meeting had been altogether satisfactory, though he had done his best to charm the girl. It would be no exaggeration to say that rapport was lacking! In retrospect their encounter seemed to him more like a military skirmish in which both sides had received some hurt before calling a temporary truce, leaving the main causes of contention unsettled. That this was partly due to pride – that pride which was to blight so much between them – did not improve his recollection of it.

Matilda's attitude had angered him, but it had also pained him. At the back of his mind was another thought he had never put into words, some lingering idea of what marriage should be about, some memory of the past when his father had been alive, some echo from the partnership of Duke Robert and Herleve which had touched all his childhood; some dreaming over and above the practical reasons he had so succinctly prescribed for his own wedding.

And then there was the lady herself. He tried to tell himself that all she had shown was stubbornness, albeit stubbornness verging on dislike. Yet underneath he had sensed a kind of warming, as if given time she might relent and reveal her liking. And he found her attractive. There, he had admitted it. Her small stature, about which she was so sensitive, intrigued him with its contrast to his largeness, as if she were some delicate creature that, were he not careful, in his rough way he might stamp upon. And the more she was angry the more her beauty shone. When he thought of her eyes, her hair, he knew he had never seen another girl (except that first peasant milkmaid), with such colouring. As for her tongue, well, he had known nothing but its rough side so far. If he could but find the key to unlock that hidden self he had told her existed, he might find happiness. But how? Once more he consulted Golet.

When asked, William's friend tried to hide a smile. 'Look you, my lord,' he had said at last seriously, 'you have no difficulty with other women.'

It was true. William's lovemaking with peasant girls was completely normal; he had no fears of them at all, and they still seemed to like him.

'It means this particular lady is the cause of the trouble. So what makes a difference?' William asked him.

Here Golet had coughed silently, hesitant of what to say next. He found his master's questions painful because of his own past, yet in a way he was moved by them. If it occurred to him that his position was strange, the peasant companion of a duke, he never let such thoughts go to his head, never took advantage, remained what he had always been, a simple man who was a good and loyal friend.

'My lord,' he said finally, 'as in other things you must make your own way. But I think if you could see the lady as any other, 'twould serve. Meet her as you meet with them, without formality. Of course, there are women,' he went on, reminiscing, 'who need to be dominated, who despise men who are not their master in all things. Such was my own wife. That is why she took a lover. Now I speak of matters I know not of, but they say Count Baldwin is himself henpecked. In her own household the Lady Matilda has been set a bad example.'

He would say no more but he had given William plenty to think about. And although William liked the idea of mastery – hadn't his childhood dreams been filled with it – he sensed that for once Golet was not completely right. About the meeting yes, perhaps, but not the rest. It was not exactly domination that Matilda lacked, or if she did it was something more subtle than brute force, was related to some kind of sharing that had existed between his father and mother both and yet had no name in the everyday world they lived in. This conviction was so strong that another meeting with Matilda became of prime importance, another meeting such as Golet had suggested, to explain himself and tell Matilda why he wanted her for his wife. Not for your father's support – he rehearsed the words – nor for your mother's rank, but for you yourself. But those were ideas that only a lovesick boy would use.

He had carefully organized their last encounter to catch her off-guard and in public, so she could not, for shame, create a fuss. She had therefore been bound to listen to him; in short he had ensured that he had all the advantages and she had none. This next meeting must be planned in a different way. He wanted her free to say what was really in her thoughts, which he believed if given expression would reveal that inward loving self she kept secret. A private rendezvous then, if he could persuade her to it, with no one to observe or overhear, just the two of them, alone. And if in truth the idea of privacy suited him better, that was something he did not admit even to himself.

Twice he had Golet waylay Matilda with invitations; twice she walked past, head in the air, having her bodyguard push him aside. Once, shamefacedly, he had a priest write her a letter which surely someone in her household could read to her. Back came the parchment with his seal unbroken; she must have known it was his seal. Time was passing, he was due to leave court; soon there would be few chances left. Too proud to complain to her father he devised another plan.

He had noticed how in the company of other royal ladies she went to church regularly to hear Mass. He discovered that she also went to confession in the evening; although her mother had her own confessor and there were priests a-plenty in the Flemish entourage, Matilda must have preferred to keep her sins from her mother's ears. Much as he was tempted to sit in that confessional box and hear those sins for himself, it was beyond his powers of arrangement. But he could wait for her in the nave beyond, albeit it ran contrary to his own pride to have to skulk and beg for her company as if he were a page-boy.

He chose a dark evening, which an overcast day had enhanced, when the Paris gutters were full to overflowing and dirt and refuse lay stranded on the cobblestones like flotsam. He himself arrived early, unaccompanied, careful that his cloak hid his face and person. Shielded by the gloom inside the great cathedral he secreted himself behind a pillar as if in prayer and waited. He had almost despaired when he heard the main doors of Notre Dame grate open and soft footfalls come down the aisle. As he had hoped, Matilda's bodyguards remained in the street beyond, at a respectful distance, and at her signal her tiring woman withdrew into a side-chapel, there presumably to make her own devotions until her mistress had finished hers.

Matilda's took a long time. She must have much to confess, he thought, and the sharpness of his jealousy surprised him; he had not known he could be jealous. His arm holding the folds of the cloak grew cramped; like a horse he wanted to stamp his legs to take the stiffness out. Careful not to make a sound, careful to keep the pillars between him and those watchful guards, shielded by the gloom, he slid towards the place where Matilda knelt.

She was almost finished. The priest mumbled his final blessing, melted back into the shadows of his inner sanctuary; she bowed her head. What thoughts filled it, William wondered; what hopes, fears, dreads? When Matilda rose and stretched out her hand to light a candle, he was there before her, a tall shape in the semi-dark. She dipped the taper towards the others guttering in their brass holders, let it catch light, the soft wax dripping. Her lips moved. As her hand withdrew his closed firmly over it.

She gave a gasp but did not scream. He wondered if she had recognized him, or if it was someone else she hoped to find. A sudden gleam from the candle she had just lit showed him her upturned face, the glint of her eyes. His fingers touched her hair and he smelled flowers. Suddenly he was back in a Norman meadow, the grass springing beneath his feet, the trees arched overhead. He felt as he had as a child when all was right; it was as if God Himself spoke and told him what to do next.

His hand tight around her waist William drew Matilda back into the even deeper darkness of the nave where he had earlier

179

noticed a second doorway which led out to a side porch. The porch itself was small, seldom used, enclosed on three sides by wooden benches. The fourth side gave on to the street, empty now and dark, the rain washing the cobblestones. It was not the most fitting place for courting but at least they would be undisturbed.

He had thought out carefully what he would say, to bid her take heed, bid her beware of trifling with him, for in trifling with him she played with fire. I am not one of your playthings, he had wanted to tell her. But the arguments and persuasions went out of his head in one great rush, as if some other, greater impulse submerged his thoughts. Again he had no name for that sudden surge of feeling which he had not anticipated, and yet he knew it was why, in secret, he had wanted this meeting to be perfectly private and alone. It made his arm tighten around her and his mouth clamp down on hers.

Pulled up against him, Matilda struggled, tried to push him away, tried to say something, said nothing. Her arms crept round his neck, her lips touched his, opened, breathed.

William drew back first, 'Jesu,' he said huskily. He wiped a hand across his mouth. Where did you learn to kiss like that, he wanted to ask, but some common sense warned him to be quiet.

Her tongue had been warm to start with, soft and gentle, then seeming to take a life of its own, flicking along his lips, then burying inside. And her body against his had been warm, its first limpness reacting to his strength until it too had come alive, pressing against him, like a kitten. He knew enough to know that was what young maids did, that was how virgins were when they were introduced to loving.

The thought excited him almost as much as she herself did. He had been enveloped in his cloak; now he shrugged it off so it was wound firmly around her. Seating himself on one of the rough benches he drew her down on his knees. Under cover of the cloak his hands went exploring along the fabric folds as perhaps, given the opportunity, he had always meant.

The material of her gown was silk, embroidered with rich thread. The touch of it reminded him of the scraps of sleeves with which she had bound up his arm. It was so fine he could trace the lines of her body underneath. Her breasts were small, like apples still not ripe, her waist narrow – he could span it with both hands. Below the waist, accentuated by its high embroidered girdle, the naval dented in; below that again a straight flat line stretched to where she sat primly, legs together, feet together, perched on his lap as if riding side-saddle. He dared not touch below the waist. Instead he moved to stroke her flanks.

Her legs were proportioned to her height; he remembered them as being sturdy like a boy's, did not expect their graceful curves where the thighs stretched up to meet that straight flat line. The shape of her buttocks pressed against him. He kissed her again, and as she shifted her head towards him so he shifted, his hands beneath her now, stroking along those curves from the back, lifting them so that gradually she was facing him, her legs on either side.

Everything went from his mind then, even the proximity of the holy place and the liberties he was taking. All he could feel was the closeness of her body and its secret parts. With one hand he held her at the base of the spine, tiny as a bird; with the other he mapped out the shape of the breasts, cupped them with his fingers. His thumb moved downwards, past the little waist, traced it past the navel down the flat incline, pressed hard, harder.

She spread herself to him, her skirts rucked up, settling back so that he could trace between the folds. Like a flower she opened to him, the bare skin moist like dew. When her body began to move in time with his, he caught her against him so she felt his erection beneath his clothes. Although he could have shucked them off, although he could have thrust himself inside, he did not, merely helped her move at her own pace and will. And when a shudder shook her so fierce that she trembled as if in some sort of fit, he felt a satisfaction in himself that was greater by far than any physical release.

After a while he helped her straighten her dress, rearrange her hair, seat herself as primly as before, all without saying a word, although he wanted to. Never in his own young experience had he known such passion in something so innocent. He knew enough to recognize it for what it was, nothing counterfeit. But William could not speak of it. It was as if something impeded him, as if it would be sacrilege to try to put it into words. And Matilda was as quiet. He had never known her so quiet.

Then she gave a little nod, a brusque kind of nod as one might when settling something with oneself. Again he saw how her eyes shone. They seemed to say, 'That's so, and I agree.'

She stood up without looking at him, her head bowed as a child, or as a girl overcome with shyness. He couldn't be sure but he thought she whispered, 'Beatrice was right.' And as he continued to stare at her, she went carefully back into the church, holding tight her skirts so they scarcely brushed his knees. Still in a trance he watched her continue down the nave towards the main entrance, although he could not help noticing how she felt the pillars for support. When her maid joined her she leaned upon her arm; her guards sprang to the alert as she approached; together they disappeared into the wet streets. Only after Matilda had completely gone from his sight did it occur to William that throughout scarcely a word had been said on either side. And suddenly, leaning back against the wooden bench he began to laugh: so much for his fine arguments. And for a moment there in the empty porch he felt he knew Matilda of Flanders better than anyone in the world.

He crossed himself. Awareness of what he had done, what he had led her into, came back to him; the sense of place, of where he was and the sacrilege he had been guilty of. Yet in his heart it was not guilt he felt, but a great jubilation of the spirit, a certainty of belonging that he now saw he'd lacked ever since his parting from Herleve.

He would have no chance to see Matilda again to plead his suit. What had been between them must be secret. Just as he would never speak of it, he knew she would not. It must be held in abeyance, weighed and judged in his absence. If she still found him wanting he had nothing left to persuade her with. And if he had failed he would give her up, no matter what it cost: the practical considerations and the formal claims would now be nothing in comparison with the private loss.

That was the decision he carried back with him to Normandy, borne like a banner, as he faced the public challenge of his enemies. And in truth in some ways their threat paled beside this greater personal one.

Chapter 14

Mauger of Rouen, the new archbishop, had no wish to be part of any more alliances. Mauger was content. The summit of his ambitions met, his brother in control, he had no further needs except to be left in peace to enjoy his position. He felt no threat and expected none, as he trotted one winter's day along the outskirts of his territory. The year was 1045, the future bright, an ecclesiastical council already in the planning; he smelled success as warm and satisfying as the mulled wine he had just been drinking. On all sides the power of the Norman Church was growing, the number of religious foundations increasing by leaps and bounds; given time, Mauger might also have been allowed to bask in the thought of triumph.

He had been making an episcopal visitation to one of the new outlying abbeys and, having celebrated Mass in all its solemnity, had just partaken of an ample repast. He belched loudly. The air was cold, with a hint of snow, but the sky was clear and the horses clattered merrily over the broad, tree-lined trail. Three riders flanked him on either side, three more rode in front and as many behind; he was well guarded. His own horse was small, a lady's jennet, and carried him comfortably; his cloak was thick, fur-lined; his boots of padded leather. Around him marched his men-at-arms, clanking along in solemn style; all in all a satisfactory escort. Then a cry from the front startled him out of complacency and made him rein back in fright.

The cry itself had nothing of alarm to it or, rather given the nature of the times, was only as alarming as its hearers made it. Advancing towards them along the same track came an equally impressive cavalcade. Knights, armed, helmets down and shields ready; foot soldiers armed, their spears at a slant, flags and banners fluttering, unknown flags; some lord then about his own affairs, on progress through Mauger's domain. The archbishop's unease increased. What lord had business in these parts that he knew nothing of?

The leader of this approaching group rode in its midst, a

cautious man therefore, heavy-set, youngish, his round fleshy face partially hidden by a beard. Not a pleasant face, suggesting an owner at once both weak and vicious. And certainly someone whom the archbishop would have preferred to have passed without incident. But although the path was wide enough for both to continue without halt the other held up his hand in greeting.

'Well met, my friend,' the man said. 'Truly a fortuitous encounter.'

When Mauger, affronted by the informality, tried to stare the man down, he beckoned to his standard-bearer to spread his flag so that the Burgundian markings showed. Again Mauger reined back. He had no desire to meet the upstart who had recently been elevated to so much prominence; the man who, somehow, within scant months, had gained possession of so much Norman land. The archbishop's reply stuck in his throat but nevertheless he forced it out, recognizing Guy of Burgundy by name and pronouncing episcopal blessing. Best enhance the idea of Church sanctity, Mauger thought nervously as he intoned in Latin, but he wished for his brother's presence. The Count of Arques would be better fitted to deal with Guy of Burgundy than he himself. The very fact that the Burgundian could rise so openly on Mauger's own church land was proof of his power, and his contempt.

As Count Baldwin had damned him, so Guy of Burgundy appeared; devious, and deficient in the aggressive qualities that had made Ralph de Gacé and the Count of Arques dangerous, except when he thought his adversaries weak. Then, like all bullies, Guy of Burgundy could show belligerence. Although he wore sword and mail like other men, Burgundy was not a fighter. Nor was he famed for horsemanship. Even the archbishop, himself no great horseman, noted how Guy kept a tight hold on his horse's rein and shifted uneasily when it did. The man's success came, rumour had it, from his ability to persuade. And from his possession of the one advantage which William of Arques lacked, the one which Ralph de Gacé had once warned of: that of not being truly Norman born or bred (although he claimed it), and therefore not so subject to his peers' jealousy. In this way he was freer to act without upsetting his neighbours. As the archbishop continued to mumble out blessings, stringing out the meaning as long as he could, these things darted into his head as he had heard his brother speak of them. And once again he wished for that brother. William of Arques, on first hearing of Guy's advancement, had growled, 'We either fight him or join with him.' Which? That was Mauger's immediate problem.

But Guy was not like Ralph de Gacé, who went straight to

the heart of an issue. He liked to keep his hearers dangling. He therefore allowed the bishop to speak on, then himself intoned as elaborate a reply, suggested even that both ride together to the nearest hostelry to drink wine. Or cider – wasn't Normandy famed for its cider, smooth as honey? And so he spoke, honey-smooth, his full mouth smiling; although his oval-shaped eyes, set close together under heavy brows, never altered their deliberate, calculating gaze, giving the lie to his joviality.

The invitation was worded in such a way as to make the archbishop decline. He stuttered weak excuses, such as the length of the ride back to Rouen, the lateness of the hour. Abruptly Guy broke in. 'You've heard the Bastard's been in Paris?' he asked. He jabbed a finger in the air accusingly but his voice continued calm, flat, almost uninterested. 'How came he there alive?'

Startled into truth, the archbishop again began to babble. It was Ralph de Gacé's fault. His were the men who had planned the coup, his were the men who had failed to kill, who had allowed the boy to return to Conteville to seek his step-father's help . . .

'To a castle left unwatched?' Guy of Burgundy's voice kept its flat tone. 'I heard that was your brother's work.'

He leaned forward on his horse's neck, watching Mauger, sure of him. 'My lord archbishop,' he said in the same off-hand way, 'it is no secret that things have been badly managed. I speak not as an outsider,' he went on persuasively, 'good Norman blood flows in my veins. And since by the grace of God and good luck I have recently inherited Norman lands, I am as desirous as the rest of you to keep my inheritance safe. But to my mind you and your brother have failed, as other men have done, because you have underestimated William. I on the other hand am better placed to deal with him, as my experience and great following show. Which is why I now approach you in person.'

Again the finger jab. 'I have heard,' he said, 'as mayhap you have, that the dukeling seeks to marry. This marriage must not take place.'

A third time he leaned forward, stabbed with his finger at the prelate. 'You are a churchman. Find a way to stop it. Matilda of Flanders is too great a prize,' he said softly, 'and Flanders too strong an ally for a bastard.'

Startled by this turn of events, and by Burgundy's words, all news to him, Mauger began to protest. 'There are always impediments,' Guy said, cutting through his fluster. 'Niceties of law. Previous betrothal; closeness of relationship; descent by blood, consanguinity I think you call it; barriers of that sort.

'That's what churchmen are good at,' he added, a glimmer of contempt showing now. 'And as head of a conclave of Norman lords, I am empowered to order it.'

This talk of ordering was more than Mauger could bear. 'What's this?' he bleated. 'I've heard of no such conclave.'

Guy of Burgundy smiled, and named his lords. He spoke in a curt, precise fashion, as if he were merely counting lands with their worth of corn, their harvest yield, rather than listing names and titles and personalities of such importance as to make his unwilling listener quail. A conclave, he had said, and so he made the roll: Rannulf of the Bessin, Nigel of the Cotentin, Haimo of Creully, Ralph of Thury, Grimoald of Plessis, lords of the Cinglais near Falaise, to say nothing of those clustered closer to home among his own properties along the Seine, those who were once the archbishop's friends and who were therefore a danger to Rouen. All in all they were a large and formidable group, whose holdings encompassed an impressive proportion of Normandy.

'Loyal to me,' Guy said at the end, not without a trace of satisfaction, 'and disgusted with the lack of rule which ruins this fair duchy. To a man they are sworn not to let the Bastard return.'

Mauger knew when he was beaten. Best put on as good a face as he could under the circumstances and pretend acquiescence. He bowed as well as the saddle pommel permitted and raised his hand. 'So be it, my son,' he said, 'although I would protest that as a man of holy orders I have had no part in murder. You malign me, my lord; even the suggestion is anathema. As for marriage,' he added, cunning in his own way, 'if the Bastard is killed there'll certainly be no marriage. Consult first with my brother . . .'

Guy of Burgundy spurred forward and left him speaking to air. His men spurred with him, thrusting unceremoniously through the archbishop's company. And when the drum of their hooves had rolled away into the distance, the archbishop himself gave the word to hasten forward, in a lather of impatience to impart this development to his brother.

One thing alone escaped Mauger, and he mulled it over as he spoke to William of Arques. 'With such goodly company,' he said, 'why should he need us?'

His brother gave him the answer. 'Fool,' he bellowed. 'He doesn't. As we supplanted Ralph de Gacé, so are we now supplanted. Guy of Burgundy has entered the lists and thinks to take our place.'

He lowered his head, the dark hair matted into curls, the dark eyes bloodshot. 'He won't,' he said. 'He shan't. Hold firm, brother. All's not yet lost.'

He eyed the archbishop. 'Now,' he said, 'again, slowly this time, repeat exactly what he said.'

Guy of Burgundy was better satisfied with the outcome of the meeting. Since his arrival in Normandy he too had noted the growth of ecclesiastical power and deplored it, although, long schooled in hypocrisy as he was, he said nothing. It seemed to him that there did not exist a single Norman lord who had not established at least one monastic establishment upon his lands, as if spiritual atonement made up for temporal chaos! His own secret opinion of the Church was almost heretical; let churchmen work for a living and sweat off their lard. He smiled cynically. His 'order' to the fat, dawdling archbishop would certainly have that effect!

He had taken stock of the archbishop and found nothing to be frightened of. Only Mauger's last remark stuck in his mind. Obviously the archbishop had lied about his involvement with previous assassination attempts, but he was right of course that assassination was still the best recourse. Two attempts had failed, a third might succeed. If he could find someone to make the effort! For although Guy of Burgundy despised the archbishop, like the archbishop he did not want murder faulted on him.

Nor had Guy revealed all he knew, to wit, firstly, except for Conteville, how few friends William had, and secondly, how deep resentment against him was because of the king's intervention in Norman affairs. That Guy himself counted also upon regaining Henry's favour if he could, persuading the king to bestow Normandy on him, or failing that at least making the king's interest in the duchy wane, was a secret to be kept carefully hidden. But it coloured his preparations so far as to cause him also to dally in the hope of success, provided of course that William's efforts failed.

The co-conspirators however were not as united as he would have liked to believe. Some did not understand his reasoning and were all for pushing rebellion on. Among these so-called hot-heads was an older man who should have had more sense, Grimoald of Plessis. Grimoald was not convinced by Guy of Burgundy's claim of Norman descent, was loud in his criticism of the Burgundian's dilatory approach, and sceptical of the result. Grimoald himself was a Norman of the old school, like Herluin of Conteville, proud and stubborn. Once convinced of William's unsuitability nothing could make him change his mind. He was not exactly disloyal to his feudal bond, rather was loyal to an old Viking dream of a united Normandy with all men equal beneath an equal law, honour-tied to a leader of outstanding military skill. He and Ralph de Gacé had once been friends; he would have welcomed Ralph de Gacé as duke and had been bitterly disappointed at Ralph's fall from power. To exchange Ralph de Gacé for Guy of Burgundy sat uneasily. And in truth he saw little between William and Guy of Burgundy except that Guy was older and at present wielded more influence. The fact was that most of Grimoald's antagonism towards William stemmed from ignorance. He resented feeling bound to a man half his age and had he actually known William or been otherwise convinced of William's strength he would as readily have supported him. So there was nothing personal in Grimoald's dislike, nothing treacherous; he spoke of defection openly, without regret, as a cruel necessity. And since like Ralph de Gacé he called a spade a spade, he spoke his mind to any who would listen.

'Why wait?' he was among the first to complain. His grey-blue eyes under bushy brows stared aggressively; his chin poked out. 'Waiting we put all in jeopardy. For only fools let an enemy arm himself, if by acting first they might catch him unawares. As for the best way to avoid war, I say cut the bastard's throat and have done with him.'

When his cronies, in whom he confided, backed away, inventing excuses for not joining him, he shrugged them off. He'd act alone and be damned to them. He knew that William was said to be riding through his dukedom, calling up his feudal army, or, as Grimoald put it, 'Squealing for support.' He also knew that the duke's step-father was acting as his nominal advisor – an unnatural situation, he thought, calculated to make the boy chafe at the bit. When William broke, and sooner or later Grimoald knew he would, when William made a wrong step or made a wrong move, then Grimoald would be ready for him. But if William or even Guy of Burgundy could have proved without a shadow of a doubt that they shared Grimoald's dream he would have backed either's cause with the best will in the world.

In his assessment of William's standing with Herluin, Grimoald's guess was partly correct. Since William's return from Paris his relationship with his step-father, never close, had deteriorated. This was entirely William's fault: from the very moment William had ridden back through the gates of Conteville he had offended, though he had not meant to. His chief offence was the result of that very determination to take charge. Unwit-

ting then of Herluin's feelings, he had assumed control of Conteville as he was entitled to as its overlord. Without consulting his
step-father, as if in his own ducal palace at Rouen, William issued
orders and sent off messages near and far; even as far as Flanders
to keep Count Baldwin aware of his progress, even to the king
to remind him of his promise. And although he gave full lip
service to Herluin's place, and although Herluin was impressed
by William's determination, it sat ill with the older man suddenly
to find himself by-passed as if he were a nobody. Moreover all
this coming and going of horses and men put a strain on Conteville's resources. As Herluin had once explained, the castle was
not large; its armoury and supplies were sufficient for its own
garrison, not for all these additions. Then there was the added
difficulty about William's guard, swelled as it was by Count
Baldwin's 'lendings', Herluin had also 'lent' men, had expected
them to return to his service as before, not remain under their
new master's charge – all these were legitimate grievances which
might have made Herluin angry. But it was William's determination to collect an army without delay that caused Herluin to
break.

'He means to summon his levies in person.' Too proud and
loyal to accuse William of other, smaller faults, in private Herluin
permitted himself to air this one just complaint. He and Herleve
were speaking in the privacy of their own chamber, he himself
standing, back to fire, running his sword-worn hands through a
belt thong while his sons, three of them now, played at his feet
with wooden shields and daggers. He lifted his boots out of their
way as they tumbled past him like puppies in the rushes.

'What's to be done, eh?' Herluin asked. 'Oh 'tis true the levies
come slow for all their promises; too slow, I think. Myself, I feel
our Norman barons hang back to see which way the wind blows
before committing themselves. But your son rushes on without
forethought. I could tell him what I've learned in a hard school,'
he went on, 'that the best time to lance a boil is when it ripens.
He'll not listen. He grasps at nettles 'ere they be grown; he sees
no danger to his person. I would fail in my duty to him,' he said
more solemnly now, 'if I did not warn him. For although perhaps
he may win some new friends, to ride abroad, openly, as he
intends, gives chance to his enemies.

'I admit he's changed,' Herluin continued. 'He's grown. Paris
has been the making of him. You may beam for pride,' he
muttered in an aside that was meant for Herleve's hearing, 'your
first-born dukeling. I, who knew his father well, see Robert in
him.' He swung his own second-born son out of reach of his

189

brother's flailing weapon. 'And I know how hard it is for him to be beholden to a mere step-father. I have not that parental right with him.'

His own eyes softened as he looked at his wife who sat darning one of his shirts, her fingers pretending to smooth the seam although he knew in her concern she had already stitched together both sides by mistake. 'So tell me, lady,' he said, 'what are we to do to stop your son's headlong insistence?'

Herleve too had noticed changes in William. She had seen nothing strange or unexpected in that. If he were more forthrightly authoritative, in her eyes as a mother that was part of his character, a natural development from boy to man. And again it had not occurred to her, as a mother, that there should be any difficulty in William's return under his step-father's charge. She herself had been simply glad to have her oldest son safe with her at last. Now Herluin's warnings of danger rang a bell. She stopped her mending, blocked her ears to her son's cries, listened to her husband carefully. She knew Herluin to be honest and just. Underneath his words she sensed his anger that William had overstepped himself. She did not want to take the task of censure on herself, but for the first time she became aware of Herluin's predicament in being faced with William's stubbornness. And in truth she also had a grievance of her own with William which she had not mentioned, partly because she also was too proud to pry, partly because in the scale of things it seemed too personal a matter to raise with him at this moment.

Taking Herluin's oldest son by the hand she went out to challenge William. She found him in the armoury, overseeing the sorting through of the weapons. It was a place that Herluin took pride in. He remembered the name and history of every piece that hung there; the swords and shields of his ancestors had pride of place. She knew it was Herluin's right and duty to be present for the counting. For the first time in her life she almost felt angry with William for supplanting her husband, even in this small thing.

She waited until the job was done. William would find no neglect, she thought, Herluin took too great care for that. When the piles of arrows, pikes, swords and shields, had been arranged to William's liking; when the armourer went burdened off with the few blades needing repair, she came up to where William was bent over, inspecting a line of bridle straps.

'Just like your father,' she said. 'How often have I seen Robert like you now, preparing for war, leaving nothing to chance, even in his own castle taking over from his seneschal.'

190

The rebuke was faint but William heard it. He flushed, put down the straps, stood up. 'I cannot sit idly by and let my enemies gain on me,' he said defensively. 'I also prepare for war.'

'Like your father, then,' she said. 'For neither could he sit idly by. And in his wars what did he win? A dukedom that he did not want, a father's death and a brother's death that were not his fault and yet weighed on him like sin. And so finally his own death.'

She closed her eyes. 'Where is the haste for war?' she cried as if in pain. 'Wait for the king. Until then, Herluin makes you welcome. Nor does he grudge you anything you need. 'Tis you who take advantage of him.'

She broke out, what also had been in her thoughts compelling her to speak. 'You tell us nothing of what has befallen you in Paris, nothing of your true plans, nothing of your intended wife.'

She too flushed. But there, she had said it, the grievance that had eaten at her since William's return. For it was a great sadness to her that despite their closeness he could not even confide in her.

In his preoccupations William had not realized that again he had offended his step-father. Nor that he had displeased his mother. Since his return he had decided to let nothing stand in his way, had devoted every waking moment to plans, counter-plans, decisions, all dealing with preparations for a conflict he knew must come. To that end he had made a personal vow to put all personal hopes out of his mind, including Matilda. 'Just as once I had to put you aside,' he wanted now to say Herleve, 'just as all my life I have to hide what I truly feel.'

'*Ma mie*,' he said, his old name for Herleve slipping out. 'Do not fault me. I have achieved two things that I went to Paris for. I have my knighting, and I have a bride in hand, if she'll ever consent to have me. When the time is right, I promise to tell you all about her, if you would have it so. But not now. Now I have not time for love-making. The third thing I went to Paris for I do not yet have in my keeping, and it is the gaining of that which consumes me.'

He turned on her fiercely. 'Believe me,' he said, 'I should like to sit with you by the hearth and dream of married bliss. And who then will win Matilda of Flanders her dukedom? The control of my lands and the re-establishment of my title is all consuming. There, I have said it, I cannot help myself.'

He added, less passionately, 'Why should I lie to you? It is as if there is a fire in me that burns my very flesh. My enemies' hunger is not so fierce, their lust to kill is less than this desire of mine to prove myself and show what I am.'

Herleve heard the passion; she saw the look in his eyes. It reminded her again of Robert. She had seen that look many times before in William's father, the predatory stare of fighting men who brook no opposition. Viscount Herluin, for all that he was brave and strong, did not have it. She knew it for Robert's heritage to William. William was right, as soon stop a fire as stop him.

It was then that her other son, her little Odo, broke free of her grasp and ran to pull at his tall step-brother's arm. 'And shall you win a battle,' he asked in his piping childish treble, 'and cut off heads? Shall you ride home victorious like Rollo the Viking?'

William laughed, caught the boy up and heaved him in the air. 'There, *mon gars*,' he said as once the men in Falaise had spoken to him, 'from your vantage point tell me what you see?' And as, surprised, Odo blurted out the everyday things of castle walls, soldiers, horses, the serving women with their bread and milk for eating, 'All good and natural,' William told him, speaking through the child to their mutual mother, and through her to her husband. And through Herluin to all the other Normans who, because of weakness or fear of change, or simply out lack of courage, would not answer his appeal to join with him. 'We take such good and natural things for granted. But if I shut myself up here, there will be many who will lack them, who will live and die never knowing what good there is in life. So I go to win it for them. And when my people have it,' and here he smiled at Herleve as he set the child down gently, 'then shall I have it too, and with your help, *ma mie*, find happiness in my own marriage.'

The little boy was silenced, as was Herleve. Herluin was right, Herleve thought, he has changed; he's grown into a man who cannot be stopped, a leopard who cannot be caged. And yet underneath the outward shell he is not so hard as he makes himself appear. And, remembering her long-dead lover, the Robert who, for right and justice, could bring down the whole wrath of the country on him, 'Go then your ways,' she said through smiles and tears, 'like your father again who, when he wished it, could charm the hazel trees into flower or make the sun run eastwards. I see we cannot keep you. I can only pray to God to look after you. But if you have the love of a worthy woman, be she noble-born like Matilda, or base like myself, then I believe thoughts of her will bring you safely home.'

She spoke from her own experience. And William knew it. He wished suddenly that both their lives had been different so that she need not have suffered as she had for that belief, and that he might have indulged in the luxury of it for himself. But he had neither the time nor the inclination to try and explain Matilda, certainly no time to regret the past; he simply smiled again and went back to his sorting.

That evening William laid before Herluin and his mother his immediate plan, namely to ride westwards where much of the opposition against him was centred to force the barons there to declare their allegiance to him. He sensed Herleve was biting her fingers to keep from crying out. 'Why there?' he knew she was wanting to plead with him, 'why in the very heart of your enemies?' Like Herluin himself she listened without comment, knowing there was nothing anyone could do to prevent him.

At this moment Golet was Herleve's only comfort. Before William left, accompanied by his bodyguard formed from his step-father's troops and his small group of Flemings, again Golet sought Herleve out and, standing before her in his ungainly way, made her a promise which she was long to remember. 'You spoke up for me, lady,' he said, 'when the duke left for Paris. And so I went with him to keep his feet on the ground amid the mighty and famous. I made him a good jester when there was nothing much to smile about, but now I shall go with him in my other guise.'

He tapped the bundle on his back where he still kept his axe. 'Do not worry,' he told her. 'Golet will keep on guard, as good as any squire. Nothing can pass me; I shall still be his eyes and ears.'

The place William had selected to shame his barons into loyalty was about the worst in Normandy. True, the castle of Valognes was a ducal property and its seneschal remained loyal to William. The castle, although well-built and strong, was situated some fifteen miles south of Cherbourg, in the very heart of rebel territory. Even for William the journey there was daring, passing through the territories of many known defectors who were not likely to listen to him and certainly not likely at this point to change sides. In his heart William knew Herluin was right; if messages could not convince them, his own presence was not likely to drum up support. But William cared nothing for that, or rather the very fact of it inspired him. It was not just that like any youngster, he wanted to show his independence and prove himself; nor did the knowledge of Herluin's probable total disagreement spur him on. He sensed a wider arena than that. His need to convince the whole Norman world he was still alive had enlarged to include proving that he also did not lack courage, was capable of holding other men in check and making them do homage to him. And once their loyalty was assured then he would claim their military support as his ducal right. So he reasoned. Although well guarded – the least Herluin could do for him – William made no secret of his travels, in fact flaunted them to give warning of who he was.

His request for a hunt within days of his reaching Valognes, was another proof of his determination to force the issue. He knew he had to deal with hard and, for the most part, brutal men, who would only be convinced by extraordinary efforts. A hunt would show how little he cared for his enemies. That he would also be revealed to best advantage – mounted, a rider without peer, a man of arms come to age – might also serve to persuade lords, who up to now had held back, that he was the true duke, the man to whom they owed loyalty. Whatever the effect he hoped for, he certainly went his own way wilfully, putting his life at risk for what at best was mere bravado. But as his spiritual advisors could have told him, in the midst of life is death.

He did not act without some forethought. The day before the hunt, men had surveyed the ground in search of game, with orders to report anything untoward; the men who would accompany him were those he could trust; surrounded by them he would ride the fastest horse the castle could provide. If at night the hounds had bayed in the castle courtyard, William shrugged the ill-omen off.

The day of the hunt dawned bright and clear, the air crisp and the scent keen. When in neighbouring villages and hamlets people stopped their work to stare, to point, to shout, 'Our duke back from the dead', he felt no reason why should make a secret of who he was. He doffed his bonnet, waved, shouted back, a youngster in full flush of life, enthusiastic, rejoicing in his own strength.

'Now,' Grimoald gave the order. 'Make no mistake.'

Armed in his old-fashioned manner, leather coat linked about with chain-mail, Grimoald led his men at a gallop along the forest rides, helmets down, swords drawn. His round shield was blank; he rode without banners – to his mind they were new-fangled inventions; he and his men knew each other too well to need any distinguishing marks. Behind him, again at his order, bowmen slipped through the underbrush, their bow strings looped and ready, the feathered arrows cocked. No one saw them pass, or if they did, they were merely peasants, whose throats could be cut without threat of discovery. Come dusk, an early November dusk, nothing would stop them mingling with the other hunters, or even entering into the castle courtyard. But if they were lucky as he hoped, they would get a clear shot at the target before that, as easily as at any unsuspecting buck.

They caught two men whom God in His mercy did not turn aside, two goatherds with their flocks, who were dead before they had chance even to notice anything untoward. They followed the hunt on a parallel course, waiting for their moment to strike. Only one man did see them, and he himself remained unseen, although their way of riding, their grim determined air, made the hairs on his head rise like a dog's.

Golet had remained with William throughout these past months, he and the duke continuing to complement each other like bread and cream. Since hunting on horseback was a nobleman's right, Golet had followed on foot with others from the castle and, more as spectator then huntsman, had settled himself in the branch of a yew tree, his axe crooked in his arm.

The tree grew out over the path where it made a bend. If a deer had passed within throwing distance, Golet, well hidden by the thick cover, would have had as good a chance of a hit as any huntsman, although probably he would not have dared try his luck, for all his favour with the duke. And, mindful of his promise to Herleve, he could remain on guard. The sound of horses' hooves off the main track alerted him to mischief. Leaning out he saw Grimoald, and although not recognizing the man, recognized at once his purpose.

There was no time for conjecture; on recognition came the act. Golet had selected the yew carefully, not only for its evergreen foliage but also for its position at the bend where there was a view in both directions. Waiting until Grimoald's rear guard had passed beneath the branches, he leaned out and took careful aim. The axe head sang through the air, its blade lightning bright. It caught the last rider just before he turned the corner, cleft through coat and armour without a sound. And without a sound the rider sagged in the saddle, pinned to it. Moving almost as fast as his axe, Golet leapt for the reins before the startled horse could rear aside. One great heave and the dead man toppled; another heave and Golet was in the saddle in his stead. He turned, spurred back. Behind him, confusion broke out as Grimoald's knights milled, not certain what attack had taken place nor who the attacker was.

They rallied soon enough, some continuing onward ever faster after their main quarry, others turning to give chase. Bowmen ran and shot and ran to shoot again, their arrows hissing hail-like among the dead leaves. The riders could not catch the madman, for so they deemed him; one lone man without sense or reason, who dodged and twisted off the path among tree trunks where no real horseman would go at that speed. But one of the arrows must have reached him, judging from the sudden splatter of crimson left behind.

Seeing it then the knights drew rein, conferred. 'Let him go,' was their united judgement, 'he is a nothing, already dead.' They turned, signalled to the bowmen to follow them, and rode back to rejoin their master. Under the trees the horse galloped with Golet still clinging to its mane.

The arrow had caught him high up on his shoulder; his whole side was numb, his arm useless; at every stride he felt the blood pump out. Only when he was sure he was not being followed did he cease his headlong flight while he had strength and tried to tie his arm against him to stem the flood. Then, in one last effort, he wound the reins tightly round his sound hand so that even if he lost consciousness he still could ride. He kicked his heels and drove the beast forward faster than ever in the direction the hunt had taken. All the while his lips moved in silent prayer.

One of the things William had learned from his travels with his uncle was a kind of presentiment of danger. Perhaps it came from noticing small things: the way a tree top suddenly waved and wind gusted where there had been stillness, or birds cried out and were silent, or shadows darkened where before all had been bright. Such a sense now possessed him. He had been in the forefront of the hunt, his horse running well under him; like the Count of Flanders all his joy concentrated in the chase. When suddenly, on some inexplicable impulse, he reined back and let the others forge ahead, he told himself a bridle strap had loosened or a girth needed tightening, but although he rebuckled both they really did not require attention. The sound of a single horse beating its way through the woods off the path heightened the tension. At a bound he remounted, his hand closed about the shaft of his hunting spear. When the horse burst out of the thicket he was ready to withstand it, until he saw who rode it, face as white as the clothes were red.

Golet was almost done; he swayed in the saddle like a reed and the horse itself had lost direction and galloped aimlessly. It took William but a moment to catch it and bring it to a stop, its side heaving, covered with foam, its black coat streaked with blood and sweat. Another moment and he had cut the reins away, was lifting Golet to the ground, was propping him up against a tree bole, searching under the jerkin for the gaping wound from which blood still poured. The eyes which had been closed opened, narrowed, and focused painfully. 'Avoid Valognes,' Golet said, all the last strength he had put into words. 'They come for you.'

His free hand caught William's as if to push him away, his mouth curled in a smile. 'I have made my jester's gallop,' he said. 'See how I ride like a knight.' And as William hesitated, 'Nay, I am spent. Grant me a Viking's death. Ride on before 'tis too late.' He sagged back, the smile gone, his eyes blank.

William laid Golet down as if he were already light as air, as if he were nothing but skin and bones. A great coldness swept over him then as if his bones too had been laid bare, as if part of him had been cut off. More than grief, he felt a severing between him and this man who, despite the vast differences between them, had formed a bond – what had Golet called it? – 'oath-sworn'. A sense of loneliness possessed him, like the loneliness of his childhood when Herleve had first left him, and although he had vowed not to think of Matilda, this unexpected loss brought her to mind. Memory of her gave him comfort. He longed for Matilda's presence, real and alive, as he had once held her, to feel her warmth and passion in contrast to this stiffening cold.

Almost ashamed of the comparison, ashamed by his weakness of self-indulgence, for a long while he remained beside Golet, cupping his dead friend's face in both hands, praying for his soul. Other memories now flowed through him, made him weep, made him smile: Golet teaching him axe play, Golet arriving at Conteville, Golet the 'swan' whose loyalty, given once, was given for ever. Not until later did he remember Golet's last warning, and when he did the shock of it, of that dreaded, familiar warning, strung through him like an arrow barb. As in his old nightmares he felt heavy as lead, unable to move hand or foot, unable to defend himself, crouched beside his dead companion, one more friend dead for his sake.

A second time the thud of approaching horsemen beat through the forest, and it was not until he distinguished them that William was able to break the hold of the past. These were no huntsmen, not dressed and armed the way they were, not riding furiously and sternly onward towards him – bent on murder no doubt.

Carefully he laid Golet down, straightened his limbs. 'Farewell brother,' he said, and gave him the kiss of peace. Once more he leapt into the saddle, dug in his spurs. He heard the cries and shouts waft after him; so shout huntsmen when they sight their quarry, he thought, and it made him ride the faster.

Like Golet, William took to the thickets, ducking under the low branches, leaping his horse over tree stumps. Like Golet, even when sure he was not followed, he continued his wild gallop south, not caring now where it took him as long as he avoided Valognes.

The sun was already sinking when he came to his senses and took stock. Then, as Walter would have done, he turned backwards, back towards his step-father's lands. Who these new assassins were he could not guess, but he knew they must have Guy of Burgundy's blessing and would be as tenacious in their pursuit as others had been. Suddenly all his pent-up anger, a lifetime of it, exploded in one howl of rage. It drove him onward, a true madman's rage.

Through the night he galloped. Across the shallows of the River Dure where the water lapped cool about the horse's hocks, but he did not dare stop to drink; across the estuary of the Vire at low tide where he took a chance of its turning, the horse's hooves crunching over wet sand and weed; along the shore road, past Isigny, its inhabitants sound asleep.

Sometimes he could hear the waves breaking; like voices from the past they called to him. Sometimes he answered them, sometimes he spoke to Golet. I shall miss you, he said to his dead companion. You are the memory of the other half of me, the part which I am always having to keep hidden. He cried out, 'Until those two parts of me are reconciled like my duchy, I shall never be at peace.'

And it seemed to him that his father's voice spoke out of the darkness and told him something, a thought he could not quite comprehend, like a half-formed dream slipping out of his mind's grasp, that if he ever did bring about that reconcilement he would be a greater conqueror than promised in his mother's vision. But often he did not think at all, simply rode on and on.

At Ryes he stopped, his horse foundering. Dawn was just breaking in a swirl of red: red for danger, for blood, for death. It was too early yet for anyone to be about, not one of the village huts showed a curl of smoke and the dogs were too night-weary to bark. From the walls which surrounded the manor house, built of wood and cob, inlaid with flint, a watchman hailed, his voice loud with apprehension. 'Who goes abroad at such an early hour?'

On impulse he said, 'Summon your master. I have news for him.'

And when Hubert, Lord of Ryes, came stumbling to the door-

way, belting on his sword, his shirt unfastened, 'Rise up, lord,'
he cried, 'rebellion threatens. Call out your guard.'

Hubert looked, recognized, and responded. 'Open the gates!'
he cried. 'Come in, my lord.' And he himself came down to
unfasten the locks and make William welcome.

When William had told as much of the story as he saw fit, the
old man cried, 'Do not tarry here, it is not safe. Ride on towards
Falaise; I'll summon up my troops and follow after.' And as
proof of his sincerity he had his three sons roused from their
beds and brought down.

They stumbled into William's presence, bleary, yawning, at
first not sure who the tousle-haired, tired-eyed youth was. At
their father's whisper, they went down on their knees and swore
allegiance to a duke they had only heard of by name. 'We ride
with you, lord,' they said, 'just give us time to dress and arm.'

The oaths of fealty were returned, lands and honours as pledge
for loyalty. Fresh horses were led out, the exhausted one hidden.
Mounted on Hubert's own steed, supported now by three young
men of his own age, William rode on again, forded Folpendant,
heading for Falaise. And on a second impulse when he reached
it, before coming to the castle walls, he turned up the little river
valley where his mother once had washed clothes and his father,
seeing her, had thence wished for no one else.

The square keep glinted white above the village, although no
flag flew as in his father's day. The gates were open, villagers,
men and women, moved in and out about their own business;
there was no treachery here. As he remembered, the guards
leaned on their spears and watched over the walls and the hounds
slept in the great courtyard. He stopped then for a while in the
shadow of the forest, trying to remember, trying to recall all his
past life, and his three companions waited in the shadows beside
him. Then all four rode up towards the drawbridge, crossed into
the courtyard. As men came running and guardsmen went on
their knees in submission he shouted out, '*Dix Aie. Chez moi je
suis bien arrivé.*' I have come home.

He had the gates closed, the seneschal of the castle dismissed;
he sent messengers far and near, a cry to arms. He took time
for only one other thing. He went down into the village once
more, crossed the ford and entered his grandfather's hut. Fulbert
was sitting as he remembered him before the hearth, his gnarled
hands playing with a long piece of wrapping. Light from the
flames glittered on the paring knives laid out in their familiar
rows, cobwebs hung in black loops from the rafters; everything

seemed the same, although now William had to stoop his head under the beams. Walter was standing behind his father, his youngest son on his shoulder. He smiled and William felt his pleasure as warm as any fire. But both waited for Fulbert to speak first.

'So grandson,' said Fulbert, 'they tell me you have grown. Come closer, lad,' he said, 'My eyesight's dimming.'

And when William had come up to him the thin hand gripped painfully about his shoulders. 'Growing's one thing,' Fulbert said. 'What about sense? Do you know they're baying for your skin, boy, like one of my rabbits. You won't get through them without the king's help.'

Walter tried to hush him but the old man shook him off. 'I said it from the start,' he said. 'Ah, if I were but the age I was; why, your father and I fought a battle once and won against a whole army.'

He said, 'Like you I once was an axe-master. And for weapon I know no better. Your swordmen can't withstand it, I've seen swordsmen throw swords and run. But an axe can travel after them, there's no place for hiding from an axe. Well, grandson, if you must fight take this with you. By God's favour I give it with my blessing.'

He held out the bundle in its wrapping although the weight made his hands tremble so that Walter had to put down his son and take it from him. From beneath the many layers a Viking axe emerged, like the one Golet had been so proud of. William held it, hefted it, would have swung it except he feared there was no room.

The little boy crept closer to look, pointed. 'Shall you cut off heads with that?' he asked in his village patois, as fearful and curious as Odo had been. William laughed at him from his great height, then bent down so he could look more closely. 'And when you are grown, so shall you, with your father's permission.'

He straightened up. 'Wish me well, uncle,' he said simply. 'I have not always been as wise as I should have been. But beggars are not choosers. After this, I shall beg no more.'

To his step-father William made no excuse for past folly when Herluin joined him at Falaise, bringing with him the remainder of the Conteville guard. Neither did Herluin mention Valognes, although in truth he had swelled with pride on hearing of William's miraculous escape, a ride no man in memory would have attempted. Rather, each welcomed the other with open arms, as comrades before a war begins. And as William estimated Herluin's worth as a fighter and the worth of Herluin's men, he knew they would be well-suited in battle.

Herluin brought a surprise with him, Herleve and his sons, closely encircled by their escort. When William made as if to question the wisdom of this, Herleve put out her hand to hush him. She beckoned to him to approach, leaning down from the saddle, suddenly taller than he was. Her lips against his were cold. For a moment she held William's shoulders in tight embrace, gazing into his eyes with her soft ones as she used to do when he was a child. 'So again God favours us,' she said, 'to have saved you anew from death. But Golet is dead!'

She hung her head to hide her tears, keeping William waiting. After a while she continued, 'I have prayed for him and will have a chapel built to his memory. But I know already God has him in keeping, for he had a noble soul.'

Yet still she did not descend from her horse although William held out his arms to her. She smiled nervously as if not sure how to continue. 'So it has come, the war you have been wanting for so long,' she said at last, 'the war I have been dreading. For it not only endangers you, it takes with you everything else I love. But before you question why I am here, Herluin has brought us for a purpose, thinking Falaise safer than our home. He has in mind a place of battle if you will have it so, on the open plains beyond Conteville.'

Now she did look hard at William. 'It puts his own castle at risk,' she said, 'for he leaves it undefended. Yet he offers you that sacrifice. So, dear my son, listen when he speaks. He loves Conteville well, yet for your sake will gamble with it to ensnare your enemies.'

When Herluin named the site, on the plateau north of Conteville, and when he argued the benefits, the land spreading to a sandy plain known as Val-ès-Dunes, a place of open aspect where the enemy's advance could be easily seen and where William's cavalry could manoeuvre as easily, William saw at once the advantages and could raise no objection.

'I need no more persuasion,' he said to Herluin. 'Nor does my mother serve as hostage for your good name. Your loyalty to me and mine is beyond all question. As for her, she acts in faith merely to come back here where her happiness and grief began, where so much of her life took place that to return at all must seem a dream. Lodge her and your sons within Falaise, gladly are you all welcome. Only tell her that Golet is the last man I lose. I swear to keep all others safe.'

And to his little half-brothers, watching open-eyed, he said with mock severity, 'Do you, my brothers, watch over Herleve.

To you her charge, as once was mine. For she is a jewel without price. If I ever marry,' and for a moment his smile darkened with the thought, 'may God grant me such a lady wife.'

So was peace made between William and Herluin, and so the place of battle fixed. Now went the messengers galloping with the call to immediate action. 'We draw them out,' William cried, 'we lure them forth. We ourselves shall act as bait for our enemies in a trap of our own making. No more shall we hang back letting them set the pace; we ourselves set it. And he who falters in this hour lives with cowardice; he who runs with me runs to victory.'

He sprang on his horse, the same horse that had carried him on his famous ride; wheeling it, he saluted those who remained behind, and at a gallop thundered down the rise where so often his father had led men on similar enterprises. And watching William in his pride, Herleve, her father, brother and sons, and all those left within the walls, could not but see that Robert the Magnificent was here revived, and William's victory was assured.

From Conteville, from Ryes, from a hundred other small baronies in and around Falaise, William's followers roused themselves. Throughout the cold of the last days of the year they marched towards the meeting place Herluin had suggested, some detouring through the marshes of the Auge and slipping past Argentan to converge at Mézidon. Their numbers could be counted in their hundreds, although each small levy was received with cheers. But still too few, as scant few as Guy of Burgundy had estimated. Only the arrival of the French king's troops could turn the tide. But would the king still come?

Equally, by word of mouth, by disloyal messengers, by all the underhand ways and means traitors learn from spies, William's enemies, foiled in the last attempt on William's life, heard of his place of meeting. They too mounted up and rode to face him. Guy of Burgundy's work was done, to his mind William's cause already lost even before the duke crossed swords with him. Like William, he and his men massed themselves before the same plain, but in their thousands, easily doubling and perhaps tripling William's troops, as they themselves now boasted.

Chapter 15

Guy of Burgundy had set up his quarters on the eastern banks of the Orne, south of Caen, almost due west from Conteville. As the crow flies it was not far from where the original conspirators had held their meeting. From time to time when someone entered or left his pavilion rain drifted in; it seemed to him to be falling endlessly as it had done since the Yuletide, the new year which should have brought better weather lost in this welter of gale and storm. And his advisors had promised that the spring of 1047 would be mild enough for planting wheat, and burying men!

The wind caught the flaps and whistled round the flagpoles. Remembering a hotter, sunnier Burgundy, he cursed this Norman climate. Outside his sentries coughed and stamped, huddled under the awnings. Already there was talk of sickness of the lungs, of dysentery, of plague. It wasn't the loss of life that troubled him – he could spare the soldiers – it was this incessant drizzle, this dampness and cold, eating into a man's bones, while the enemy prepared its puny force, a puppy facing a mastiff. Yet to any who dared grumble in his hearing, he bid them be of good cheer, although marking them for future censure once the battle was won.

'We've much to be thankful for,' was his daily admonishment. 'Compared with the Bastard we dwell in paradise.'

And leaning forward from his carved oak chair he would grin his sharkmouth grin, his sharp nose sharply pointed. 'He may have escaped Valognes with a madman's ride, but you've heard what he's been driven to? Crawled on his knees all the way to Poissy, threw himself before the king, begged with tears and supplications – a ploy more suited to a monk than duke – for the king once more to honour his commitment. As if twice before wasn't enough!'

Again that mirthless grin. 'The king won't like that. I know Henry inside out, he only acts when he's certain of the outcome, and this time he knows who's bound to win! He's had his bellyful of Normandy. That's why he'll favour us.'

A final grin. 'Why man, when the die is cast we'll have Henry on our side. Poor William's battle's lost before it's ever started. The Bastard's finished.'

As for the weather, weren't these January rains good for harvest; didn't late frosts help roots set? He was new-come to farming matters, he must ask advice on that. With his smooth tongue he flattered, soothed, cajoled, but the effect on him was tiring. He yawned, stretched, his nerves on edge. Inside the tent was warm enough, a brazier fire, fur rugs, a warm fur cloak; supplies and forces were plentiful, almost all of the western duchy swarmed to join him. Patience, he told himself as the wind blew harder and the tent sides swayed; a few days more and the battle's ours, Normandy's ours, the dukedom's ours. And if our luck holds, mayhap also the little lady of Flanders, whom William now will never have!

Only to Grimoald of Plessis did he show his rougher side, a flicker, that he also hid under supposed pleasantry.

'Greetings, my lord,' he told the grizzled warrior when Grimoald rode in, surrounded by his followers. 'I see you well, I trust. And I see you come well-armed.' His voice too hid a sneer. Grimoald still was accoutred in ancient style down to his boar-fanged helmet and great round shield; he and his men looking like Celtic warriors. But the old man had not failed to come, had brought his men, a goodly number, not to be despised. The Burgundian however couldn't resist one final jibe. 'All set for victory this time, I trust; success not slipping through our fingers?'

Grimoald grunted and thrust out his chin but, thinking better of it, merely nodded his head and passed on, saving his retort for a better occasion. In privacy he felt the sneer, sharp as a stab; knew its cause and deplored its truth. How William had eluded death still puzzled him. In his mind a thousand times he had re-enacted the assassination attempt. There was no way a victim could have avoided it, yet William had, his flight already passing into legend. What did they call the ford he'd crossed? *'La Voie du Duc,'* as if fleeing for one's life was of itself a virtue! Grimoald knew why Guy mocked; it only added to his dislike and his uneasy feeling of distrust, as if even at this late hour this was a man he could not trust.

Reaching his own tent he swore a mighty oath, vowing to be avenged. In the coming battle he'd show his true calibre; why, he'd been fighting battles so long he'd forgotten what peace meant; let the young cubs take notice how much was due to older men. As for the duke who had indeed 'slipped through his fingers'. . . . 'Tell the French to bring on the boy,' he roared into his drinking horn, quaffing wine like water. 'Tell them to set him up. Like a scarecrow stuffed with straw he shall be unstuffed and scattered to the winds of chance.'

His anger was personal, fuelled by a sense of humiliation, hatred of the duke becoming a sop to failure. As far as loyalty was concerned, whatever allegiance had been sworn had already been fulfilled, for here he, Grimoald, was as proof of it. For the man to whom allegiance had been pledged, the outsider who pretended to be one of them, he cared not a fig, and even less for that outsider's ambitions, let all perish.

In his dislike of the man he was not alone. By now there were others who were equally disenchanted. Splashing to and fro in the rain, watching the river rise, they voiced their concern, although they too hid their lack of confidence. Guy of Burgundy could cajole so far, but his power of persuasion could not compete with what they knew by instinct. All wanted a united Normandy perhaps, a secure Normandy, free of anarchy. But who was now best suited to the task of unification began to appear open to question.

Some claimed they had dallied too long, giving their opponents too much breathing space; some that they had miscalculated both time and place of attack; others that they had misjudged the Bastard's strength and staying power – suppose after all he were to win, such miracles do happen. Like the rising currents along the Orne the whispers floated.

At Mézidon, where the heavens had opened up to pour forth a rainspout so severe as to drown an ocean, William also waited. Daily now he sent scouts to scour the east for news of the French king. When nightly they returned, the horizon empty, he was hard-pressed to maintain his early enthusiasm. He knew as well as anyone that without the king there was no holding the opposition; it hadn't needed Fulbert to tell him that. He reconsidered carefully all the ways in the past he had endeavoured to keep the king on course, and came to the conclusion that the count of Flanders had been correct – King Henry spun like a top; all depended which way the wind blew him. He therefore sent a last urgent message, similar to many previously sent, to Count Baldwin. The least the count could do was to try again to persuade the king to help. But help was at hand, closer than William dared dream of.

By lucky chance or, as William's friends were after to maintain, by God's good grace – for who could have expected so speedy a response – one of the earlier messages sent from Falaise to

Flanders had found Count Baldwin in Paris. The reason for Baldwin's attendance at court was not completely fortuitous, for it was indirectly linked to William, and directly concerned William's proposed bride. In short, Baldwin had come to take issue with the king over the proposed Church interference with the Norman marriage agreement. For when some inkling of Guy of Burgundy's scheme to prevent the marriage had reached Flanders, it had set Matilda into such a state it was almost as if William himself had jilted her. And although she had never openly admitted to anyone her willingness to comply with her father's choice, and certainly not to Baldwin himself, her misery at this news convinced her father of her eventual compliance. That, coupled with Baldwin's own understandable anger, had brought father, mother and daughter once more back to Paris, there to oblige the king to take action against so monstrous an intrusion on their family rights. (Albeit the Princess Adela privately hoped her husband would fail to influence her brother, she herself having no great faith in this so-called marriage alliance and being almost at one with her daughter in Matilda's seeming ambivalence towards it when it was going well!)

Matilda's own position in the matter was calculated to confuse. In public she had seemed to welcome William's departure for Normandy: 'There's an end to him,' she'd said. But as days had blended into weeks, to months, it seemed she had changed her mind, for she grew pensive and restless, as love-sick maids are said to do. By roundabout means, by skilful questions and even more skilful deductions, the count, and hence the countess, had heard rumours of William's appearance to their daughter in the church. Not all the details of course, none of the ones that would have sent the countess into hysterics and the count scrabbling for his sword. Matilda's present maid was discreet: scandal would jeopardize her own position. Nor in truth had she any notion of exactly what her little mistress had been up to in the dark shadows of the church; that would indeed have been scandalous. She had merely suggested that a young man had been seen to greet the Lady Matilda with all due reverence, what harm in that? No harm at all, the count had decided, himself preferring a duke who showed himself in every way a zealous lover as son-in-law. Nor could the countess argue with her husband, both parents secretly relieved that Matilda at last might have met her match in stubbornness. But Matilda had begun to think of the meeting in another light.

Since William had left she had heard nothing directly from him. All his messages were to her father and dealt with military matters; they had nothing to do with her. Her physical yearning for William began to turn into a sense of violation. She had no more qualms about the peasant girls; all the men she'd ever heard of took peasants for bed-fellows, even her father. But she feared that William might now think of her in the same way, had treated her like a serf to be even with her for things she had said of him; had acted towards her as if she were a wanton, a whore, to show her who was master. And in not resisting she had given herself away.

Suppose William never approached her again? Suppose these war messages were all that he would ever send and, assured now of her father's interest, it would transpire that he cared nothing for her? There must be other marriages he could make that would be equally advantageous, marriages with other heiresses as suitable as herself politically and without her unfortunate inability to show her liking.

The memory of her last evening with William released within Matilda a swarm of conflicting emotions. But to have it suggested that a posturing archbishop in Rouen had the right to prevent her marriage turned all into reverse. It was bad enough not to know where William was; to be told she had no right to know raised all her hackles. Without being asked for her opinion, without thinking of the consequences, she had confronted her father and argued that he must again go to Paris, this time himself to ask the king to support William as had been his original intention. And not caring that she appeared so inconsistent, she had demanded to accompany him, if needs be to plead her own cause.

Sight of her determined grief was too much for Baldwin; it touched his kind heart and weakened him. Although aware of the inconsistencies in her behaviour he pardoned them and agreed. And arriving in Paris about the same time as William in Valognes, for once Baldwin minced no words in speaking with the king.

Anger barely held in check, he had forced the king to listen. 'Are we to let the Church ride roughshod over us?' he'd thundered. 'Has papal power the right to interfere in French state affairs? And shall the archbishop of Rouen flaunt his might against your own authority, sire?'

Skilfully avoiding all suggestion of benefit to himself from this marriage pact, and his own part in achieving it, Baldwin kept to the forefront of argument the issue of Church dominance over secular matters, an issue which he knew the king for once was in no doubt about. For if the Church's authority took precedence, where did that leave the king's? Baldwin gave Henry no opportunity to reflect that sometimes royal interests might be best served sheltering behind papal rulings; instead he continued to hammer at the idea of new Norman insurrection, Rouen's audacity being but one more sign of a dukedom's complete disintegration.

When one of the messages from William reached the count, it did not need the tattered piece of parchment with William's mark scratched on it to warn Baldwin of the urgency. A few more days, or weeks at most, and William's cause would be lost and his dukedom gone for ever. Nor could Baldwin conceal from Matilda the gravity of the situation.

Matilda's own face, already drawn with so much worry, paled to faintest white. 'He relied on you, Father,' she said, 'you promised him. And he promised me a dukedom,' she added, 'to make of me its duchess. As God is my witness, how can that happen if he is abandoned to the mercy of his enemies?'

She snatched at the message whose contents, although she could not read them she already remembered by heart. 'And look how he has kept his part of the bargain,' she cried, 'and plans to make a stand at the turning of the year.' (This actual message had been earlier sent, before William's final departure from Falaise.) 'So while we play the Yule away, making merry, he and his men suffer hurt and cold with none to succour them. How can you deceive him?' she cried, her voice shaking with passion. 'How can the king? God will not pardon such callowness. I beseach you to do something. For William must be helped, even if I have to tell the king so myself.'

Something in her voice warned Baldwin that she meant every word. Once more he sought audience of the king and told him the gist of William's plans, pointing out that William had honoured his side of the agreement. He rounded on Henry bluntly, repeating his daughter's arguments. 'We owe it to him to honour our commitment,' he said. 'If not,' and now his gaze slid past the king in furtive fashion, and his round cheeks caved in as if he was holding his breath, 'if not, when papal authority overreaches itself, some of us will side with the Church, even to the breaking of our feudal bond. Just as some of us now are ready to offer William the support his overlord by right should extend.'

It was the closest he had ever come to open challenge and Henry sensed it. It frightened him. Flanders in defiance was a new concept. The king had never really wanted Flanders and Normandy to combine; he had only countenanced a betrothal pact between them because he could find no way to avoid doing so and because he thought Matilda would never accept. But neither did he want the pope to be seen to overrule him, nor Normandy to be under greater obligation to Count Baldwin than to himself. For a moment he swayed on his feet, a man whose dithering could cost the lives of thousands and lose Matilda her duke. Then he gave the welcome words that Matilda had been praying for as much as William. 'Sound the march,' the king said. 'I follow after as quickly as I can.'

One advantage the king had over his vassals. As well as relying, like any lord, upon his normal feudal levies, he usually kept a makepiece mercenary army on full alert. So it was that, even as William reached Mézidon, French troops were already massing along the Norman borders and were prepared to cross as soon as the king joined them. And just as William had given up all hope entirely, outriders came spurring back with the tidings that at last the French army was approaching Val-ès-Dunes with the king at their head, the path of their advance churned to mud like a vast ploughed field. At the same time, they also told of the nature of Count Baldwin's pleas – and their effect on the king – but not their actual content, for that was too delicate a matter to be discussed at such a moment. They also spoke of Matilda and Matilda's insistence. Matilda's influence on her father was much wondered at. As was her determination to save a marriage to which she had never openly agreed, why the father must be besotted and the lady bewitched, begging William's pardon.

Then like a boy let out of school, William leapt from the pavilion where he had been sheltering from the rain. 'As God protects us,' he cried, 'Normandy is saved. Break out my banner, let the trumpets sound.'

To himself he added, 'And praise God for Matilda of Flanders that at last she has meddled to such good effect.'

He vaulted in the saddle with all his armour on, rode out to meet the king, his own 'army' flanking him, his face set in what was to become a familiar frown of concentration as if he no longer saw the immediate and obvious but had his gaze fixed on some far-off horizon. It counted little now in the scale of things that he had so few supporters and the enemy so many. What mattered was Matilda had spoken for him and the king had responded. His spirits soared. Seeing Henry, William could not keep his jubilation from breaking out. 'My lord king,' William cried, spurring forward, his standard-bearer hard-pressed to keep up. 'My lord king, gladly do I give you greeting. Twice before have you ventured here on my behalf and twice have I heartily thanked you for it. Now this third time I myself have come to bid you welcome and of my own will to join with you against a common enemy. But especially am I glad to welcome you back to a place that once you were pleased to say was your refuge. The whole of Normandy is in your debt, sire, and God has you in his keeping.'

He smiled, his smile brilliant. 'But time's a-spoiling,' he cried. 'That enemy lies yonder.'

He wheeled his horse to point where, through the grey sheet of rain, the flat sandy plains stretched north east to the coast. 'Even the weather conspires to help us. The rivers rise; a few hours more they'll be in spate, cutting off their retreat.'

'And mayhap hindering our own progress.' The king was curt. He kept his temper with an effort, made no attempt to match William's enthusiasm, listened with more attention to his bishops' earnest pleas for peace, offering to join them for Mass with a wry expression as if to say, 'Why call on God when we've His very deputy here in this young idiot.'

To his councillors' suggestions of further delay, of need for rest and planning of battle strategy he was equally receptive. 'We bide here tonight,' he said. He shook his cloak so that the raindrops splattered. 'Tomorrow let us pray for respite from these January storms and the confusion of our enemies. 'Tis God who succours us, not we ourselves.' Guy of Burgundy had judged him right, to hold to a decision three times was twice too often.

Seemingly chastened by this royal response, seemingly daunted by the king's prevarication, William dismounted in glum acquiescence. He attended the king at his night's feasting, listened apparently meekly to older men's advice on the arrangement of the forces or their withdrawal as the king decided. In his heart he determined to press ahead with or without royal support, prepared to win all or lose all in one instant.

The next day dawned grey and wet, a typical Norman wintry day, making even the most stalwart shiver. Still holding his impatience in check, William joined Henry at his prayers. The tiny church of Valmeraye was packed to the doors by knights and lords, all dubious of the outcome of their efforts. He sat with head bowed devoutly, the epitome of godliness. But there were those who noted that throughout the service, while the bishop took time with the sermon, he played with his gauntlets and belt, or fidgeted with his weapons, like an experienced huntsman ready to rouse the game and commence the hunt.

The day was still early when they were let out, the rain as heavy, the wind coming in sudden squalls. The mounted men, testing the condition of the ground, again advised delay. Suddenly William rose up from the ranks. 'Delay is ignominious,' he cried, 'only the weak and cowardly hold back.'

Nearby was an upturned cart used for sleeping under. He sprang on it, spread his arms, encompassing the world. And the world, holding its breath, stopped to listen. 'He who claims my lands and seeks my ruin is indeed an interloper, breaking every law for good. What he does to me he can do to all, to you and you and you.'

He pointed from one great lord to the next, to all those of Henry's court who accompanied the king. They shifted uneasily beneath his gaze. 'And he also shows disrespect to you, my sovereign liege.' William pressed home his attack, addressing the king directly. 'You alone bestow my right, from you alone my duchy comes. Fail me and all men will look askance, for once honour is lost nothing is left.'

The watching army again held its breath. This was a challenge, certainly direct, certainly uncompromising. And for a moment William's fate hung in the balance. Win all, lose all . . .

The king heard him, not only his words but the force behind them. He was shamed. It reminded him of William's father whom he had once so admired; it reminded him of his own former self. Stung by the young man's contempt, tired of resistance, he acquiesced, more convinced than ever that one day the young man would do him harm. He gave way with bad grace, muttering to those beside him that if William burnt for glory he should earn it; let him take the lead and bear the brunt. 'Seeing death close to may sober him,' he said. Only the insistence of his more experienced barons made him reverse his command, they arguing that teaching the young man a lesson was not worth the risk of having all founder.

Pushed therefore to battle, the king was finally persuaded to share the honours. William was to lead the left, he himself took the right. And when the call to mount sounded and trumpets blared, as squires held their masters' horses and knights swung into the saddle, for very shame he himself was obliged to clamber on his stallion and order his flag unfurled, even though he had no wish to die on a Norman battlefield for a Norman conqueror who might yet conquer him.

Not so William. He mounted like a warrior god, as if his horse had wings. And he thought, if I am to die, what better way than now, surrounded by my friends in defence of my own duchy?

He had not been disappointed to find there were no foot soldiers, no bowmen available to him; all depended, as Herluin had hoped, upon mounted knights. But they had already pro-

nounced the ground too dangerous. He eyed them. The rain had
doused their spirits, the mud made for slow-going. Resembling
plodding cart-horses, they moved off through the overhang of
cloud and fog. They need a fire to set them going, he thought,
but he held that thought in check, and joined them in their
winding progress towards Bill and Airan and the plain of Val-
ès-Dunes. In spite of all these drawbacks, his lack of leadership
experience, the maddening cautionary approach of King Henry,
he still felt the hand of God at work. And even in this moment
of great peril he allowed himself to remember Matilda, and thank
God for her interference.

Val-ès-Dunes was so called because of the sandstone from
which it was formed. It stretched in a huge monotonous plateau,
a featureless plain that the rains almost obscured, like an enormous amphitheatre in which the greatest conflict of William's life
was to be enacted. And counting the numbers of the enemy that
in turn began to come towards them; noting the scores and scores
of banners like a sea of wheat, those colours and devices which
even the wind could not flatten, estimating the names and reputa-
tions of the lords who bore them, the French king's forces were
themselves flattened, wishing themselves anywhere else.

Their enemy, seeing them falter, raised up a cheer, came
on again more determinedly, exhibiting a confidence which was
abruptly shattered when one of the banner-bearers was seen to
move aside. Followed by a large detachment of mounted men
their master suddenly wheeled out of the ranks, the first defector
from Guy of Burgundy's army. A whisper swelled through the
remainder, 'Ralph Tesson flees . . .'

From his vantage point on the left, William watched this movement with mixed emotion. He recognized the banner, he remembered the man. The treachery came the harder that Ralph had
once been his father's friend. When the knights in their formation
now galloped towards him he recalled Turold's advice and, steeling himself, gave the order to hold firm. As the riders rapidly
approached he bid his men raise their lances to make a wall of
spears although he knew the attack would be heavy: Ralph Tesson's soldiers were noted for their bravery. Only when the voices
began to reach him did he understand what they said.

'Pardon lord, pardon, we will not fight; we ride with you
instead.'

His throat which had begun to close in painful anticipation
suddenly gasped for air; his heart thumped drum loud. He had
barely enough sense left to motion his men to move aside and
make space before Ralph Tesson had reined up. Then the

momentary unease at the prospect of fresh treason turned to triumph, for here indeed were valuable reinforcements.

Seeing William, the old Norman warrior – himself a doughty fighter – threw himself off his horse and knelt on the rain-soaked grass, his short grey hair beaded with wet, his face pale and streaked with dirt, his horse and he splattered with it. 'My lord duke,' he cried in a ringing voice, 'I and mine are at your mercy. But give us your trust; we will not fail.'

William looked at him, the first real traitor he had ever seen face to face, in the flesh. In all his years of nightmares these traitors had taken many forms and shapes, become monsters, exaggerated to gigantic portions. He saw an older man, wet and mud-stained like himself, a man who, whatever his previous faults, now showed genuine contrition. But for a while he said nothing, unable to speak, let Ralph Tesson kneel there until his friends nudged him into reply, anxious for his reaction, afraid he might deny pardon.

Only then did William smile. 'If we were to say what this means to us,' he said, as if speaking to himself, 'we would talk so long, and you listen, that we might miss the battle. We believe you, Ralph Tesson, because we wish to believe you; because not believing would break all honest trust between men. Take up your sword and mount, ride with us as Normans, no need of anyone else. Let us chase our mutual enemy back where he belongs.'

And when Ralph Tesson was again in the saddle William leaned forward and gripped him by the forearm, his blue eyes so intent that afterwards men said they seemed as if they might bore through metal. That look, they said, that piercing look was worse than any reproof or censure, and caused Ralph Tesson, hardened thought he was to treason and its aftermath, to weep.

There was no time for further speech, the rebels were indeed upon them. Like a torrent they swept forwards, seeking to overwhelm by sheer numbers. On the right side King Henry's men were splintered apart under their charge, the king keeping himself well to the rear out of danger. Not waiting for the moment of contact, William gave the word to charge first.

Throwing aside his lance, he drew his sword. Behind him his men did likewise. Hand-to-hand encounter, then cavalry, his horse moving as easily as if it spent all its days in battle. Behind him, William's own knights, strengthened by those of Ralph Tesson, thrust as hard, the days of waiting over. The two sides met with a clap like thunder. Horses reeled beneath the impact, men fell. Swords clashed, sliced downwards. Then as quickly the shock of encounter passed. Opponents who for a moment had faced each other were swept aside by new waves of attackers, were lost to each other and confronted with new dangers. But William's line held.

All through the morning the battle raged, swirling mists and driving rains obscuring the field. Individuals were lost in the confusion, were forced to wander helplessly until they found someone they could identify. Friend or enemy, they welcomed either. Groups of knights who remained together continued to fight together like private armies, detached from the main force. Pressed from the rear, pressed from the front, the two flanks swayed back and forth, sometimes bursting through into the clear, sometimes so caught in the throng of men and animals that even the wounded were held in the saddles. The gaudy banners lost their colours, drooped in the wet like bedraggled birds, were cut to ribbons. Once a cry went up that the king himself had been unhorsed, once that the duke had been killed. In the rear of his own army, like Henry not looking for personal glory, Guy of Burgundy cursed and howled, and from safe distance urged his followers on to greater efforts.

Among the rebels was one reputed to be a famous warrior, greater than any on the field. He was a vassal of Rannulf of Avranches, loyal to his master although perhaps not having any personal interest in the outcome beyond survival. At his master's behest this knight fought with such skill as to surround himself and his horse with a circle of dead or dying men. He had placed himself in a way that blocked retreat, thus holding Guy of Burgundy's army steady and meanwhile preventing William's supporters from making headway against him; as long as he remained in position both sides found it impossible to proceed either forward or back.

In one of the lulls when the wind quieted and the squalls of rain had slackened so that the noise of battle could be heard, William noted him. 'What is that man's name?' he asked. And, when they told him Hardez from Bayeux, 'A hardy man,' he cried, 'and hard it will be to dislodge him.' Without telling anyone, without having even his squire follow him, William rode towards the man. As his horse stumbled and slid on the blood-soaked grass, its hooves treading on corpses, he shouted, 'Hardez of Bayeux, turn and meet me,' even though for a moment, seeing the size and experience of the warrior and the ring of carnage around him, his own courage had faltered.

Then with a mighty effort he raised up his helmet, tore it off so that all men might recognize him, and urged his steed onwards.

His cheeks were bloodstained where a spear had caught him; his hair blew; another burst of rain driving into his face for a second blinded him. Although his sword hilt was slippery, he raised the blade. Twice, thrice, a dozen times he charged his opponent, wheeled, retired, charged again until his arm was heavy as lead and his breath was gone, his armour rent, his leopard-crested shield battered out of shape. Neither could make headway against the other, both were evenly matched.

Hardez of Bayeux too was almost spent. 'Hold back, my lord,' he wheezed, reining up, 'for pity I spare your youth. Go fight another more your age.'

He meant this seriously but William took it for a sneer, and its faint echo of Golet's joke, when they'd first fought, enraged him. Sheathing his sword with its notched and blunted edges, one last time he urged his horse into effort. From his saddle he drew the axe that Fulbert had given him and Golet had taught him to use. Letting the reins dangle he swung the axe above his head. All the years of hiding, of entreaty, all the shame and grief were in that final stroke. Had it failed he could never have recovered to make another. Down swept the axe. It smote Hardez apart, cleaving through helmet, skull and flesh like cutting through wax. And as the body swayed and fell, it seemed to William that all his past rose up to applaud, even to the dark bulk of that fallen Flemish captain, from Hugh the Messenger to Count Gilbert, Osbern and Turold down to Golet, the last, 'Well done, lord,' they cried.

The death of Hardez of Bayeux broke the backbone of the rebel resistance. Seeing the fall of his favourite, Lord Rannulf lost heart and began to edge westwards, the way now clear for retreat as well as for advance. Although in places small groups continued to hack each other, the vast majority turned tail and fled. With Guy of Burgundy now well to the fore, back they went the way they'd come, through Serqueville, William's followers in hot pursuit. The rain hampered their flight.

Those who could not ride fast enough were cut down as they tried to escape; others, throwing away their weapons, begged in vain for mercy. In that hour of victory no quarter was given. At the Orne they hesitated, the river swirling fast, yellow-frothed, choked with trees and logs. As more survivors arrived those already on the banks tried to scramble upwards, slid on the slippery sides until the earth gave way. In their dozens, their twenties, their fifties, they piled upon each other, clawing for purchase, the current washing over them and turning and twisting them like flotsam, their horses struggling for foothold until they too were swept away downstream. There, together with their riders, or what was left of them, they blocked the mills of Borbillon. Of those who lived to reach the river not one in a hundred crossed it, but were either trampled or drowned. So God in His wisdom granted William victory.

Guy of Burgundy was one who did manage to escape. He had got across by a small bridge before the flood tore its timbers apart. In the last moments of his flight he too had been wounded, a glancing blow. A young knight not recognizing him had thrust, half missed and, seeing easier quarry, left, allowing Guy to ride away. The wound made him ride the faster! Once across the river he did not pause to see what had become of the tatters of his army, but continued towards the Caen estuary where a boat was waiting.

The storm had tossed the sea into whirlpools but such was his terror that by bribery and prayers he persuaded the captain to put out into the waves. Once free of the bay the rain clouds hid their progress and, by hugging the coast, the sailors brought him to the mouth of the Seine. From thence, a quick detour took him south to Brionne, where Count Gilbert's castle was strong enough to withstand any siege. And there he went to earth like a fox; he would have to be dug out, if any should dare attempt it. Behind him he left a trail of disaster which his Norman followers, those few who survived the original slaughter, were help less to prevent.

One by one they were obliged to make submission, lay down their arms, plead for their lives with the boy they had despised for so long. To their amazement, he treated them with fairness, not hiding his contempt but appearing more disappointed than angry. Only one man he did not spare, and that was Grimoald of Plessis.

When Grimoald was led before him – half covered with mud, for he had fallen from his horse and been unable to remount – they looked at each other, young man and old; one who had escaped assassination, one who had contrived it. 'What say you, Grimoald of Plessis?' William asked.

Grimoald shook his head defiantly. 'Nothing,' he said. 'I am too old to make amends as others here have done.'

He shot a venomous regard at Ralph Tesson. 'I ask for nothing,' he continued, 'I regret nothing. Except that at Valognes I made a mistake.'

When William's followers cried out at that, Ralph Tesson louder than the others, 'And that perhaps I also was mistaken, for Guy of Burgundy has proved as weak as all the rest. For where in God's name shall this poor land of ours find anyone to put it to rights. Not you, Bastard,' he added, 'you are too green, hazelwood that snaps. Not your peasant stock. That is rotten to the core, and will make of us a laughing stock.'

And he spat.

Even then perhaps William might have shown pity. But the old man held him with his gaze. Spare me, it said, and you show all your weakness. I want no pity, nor expect any. I would not have granted you mercy had I caught you at Valognes.

Faced with such implacable obstinacy, William had no choice but to give the signal. But when, still unrepentant, the old man was led to his death, 'I could wish for such loyalty as that hatred,' William said. He looked about him. As far as the eye could see the plain was littered with the dead and dying. Horses roamed freely, reins dangling. Men nursed their wounds, wept for their friends, searched through the dead for booty, according to their own natures. This then is battle and its aftermath, he thought. His own body smarted from half a dozen wounds. Yet when he rode across the plain to observe more closely, he remembered all his boyhood dreams and how he had vowed to smite his enemies with fire and sword. And he remembered too his first battle with the peasants at Sées. Theirs had proved a fruitless enterprise. Pray God this be not likewise.

Meanwhile King Henry left William to enjoy his victory, and himself retired towards the frontier, vowing never to return to Normandy, convinced that his support of William had made the duke too strong for his own good. 'That young man needs no more help from me,' he said. 'Rather, I shall need help from him.'

He checked his steed savagely, for he had not forgiven it for throwing him. 'By the holy cross,' he cried, 'I have expended more than any man to keep William alive. Yet how will he repay me if he tries to take my crown? Henceforth William of Normandy is no friend of mine. Let those who side with him be warned. Next time we come this way 'twill be a different story.'

Brimful of hate he went back to Paris to plot revenge. But even his hate choked him, for he knew there was no justice to it. And he hated himself even more for giving in to it. But of all the things he hated, envied, despaired of, it was that this very William, this bastard son, so resembled the father whom Henry had admired, that even on the eve of battle William could argue reason as Robert had done, could see another's point of view, could persuade and charm. And in battle itself William had been

Robert's living presence, while Henry, the king who had vowed to surpass Robert, had faltered . . . Henry cowered at the comparison.

In a fit of depression he flung himself down on his couch as once, years ago, he had flung himself down in a grassy Norman clearing and dreamed of things he would do when Robert had won the kingship for him. All those wasted years, those sad lacklustre years rose up to confront him with his own faults. *'A weak man swayed like a reed.'* Had he but known it, so had one of the lowliest of his subjects judged him. And thus now he judged himself, a pithless reed, bent all ways, trying to be all things to all men, trying vainly to cover all contingencies save those caused by his own inadequacy. But for all that, brimful of hate. So much hate that revenge for his own inadequacy had to have its place; he could no more hold back on the need to reassert himself than stop his own breathing.

Chapter 16

They said the hand of God had shown itself, that God must have been on William's side, that with or without the French aid he would have triumphed. Remembering the earliest lesson he had ever learned, William thought, Winning is good if indeed you win. As at that long-ago crossing of the Eure when someone had first tried to kill him, the after-taste was not good: the blood, the wounds, the death and dying. Even the bravest of the brave, the most gallant, the most cheerful can still hang dead and God have no pity on them. As then, so now, the defeated gave victory a deeper dimension beyond the joy of the moment. And just as when he was a child William recognized the horror, now the reality cut at him although he had learned to hide his distaste. But perhaps there had been so much killing in his life that he was becoming numbed by it.

However he had won. Returning afterwards to the group of huts that made up the little village of Caen, he had priests light candles and sing *Te Deums* in remembrance of all the dead, offering to have chantries built for future prayers when the duchy was completely won, in honour of God and God's goodness to him.

All this he promised in pious wise, compensating for that ignoble part of him which at the battle's height had bid him vaunt himself. And on his knees he offered thanks, head bowed, eyes closed, no more fidgeting this time with belt and sword. And after the service was done he still lingered as if lost in thought, as if the numbers of those poor drowned souls, the sheer mass of them, hung on his conscience and he was responsible for them, as if their gathering, their attacks, their very treacheries were laid to his charge.

He did pray for them. But he also prayed for himself and for his own future. He knew that not all the dukedom was at peace and he had lost the king's friendship for ever. Guy of Burgundy was still at large, as were the original conspirators. Moreover William of Arques and Archbishop Mauger of Rouen still loomed like a threat; they too were unfinished business, the more formidable because they worked unseen, in secret. But most of all he prayed for Matilda.

Or rather he prayed for guidance on how to proceed in the matter of their marriage. By now rumours had also reached him of Church interference. To himself he had tried to laugh the rumours off, but no less than Baldwin was he angered. Here in this humble little church with its guttering candles and its stale smell of grease and incense he knew he was powerless to challenge God's right to dictate the conditions of a wedded alliance.

Yet he meant to challenge it. Hence his prayers for forgiveness. For if it were wrong to challenge then God would punish him. But he himself could not believe that God would so demean him as to give him a victory that would be remembered through the centuries and yet deprive him of its greatest benefit.

God did not then give William an answer. But as William now moved about his dukedom, enjoying the fruits of victory, visiting castles, cities and border posts previously closed to him, there was time for further contemplation. The knowledge that, after all, he might lose Matilda through no fault of his, or hers, gnawed at him. And granted all the difficulties that William faced what he finally decided might have seemed foolish, having nothing to do with battles or their aftermath, certainly nothing to do with crushing conspiracy. He disregarded the fact that for a duke even the most private of affairs are affected by and dependent upon public ones. And that even if God is silent He still knows what is being done.

William told no one but Herleve of his decision. After procrastinating as long as he dared, he went to her at Conteville to discuss the matter, as he had promised. He found Conteville in confusion. As Herluin had feared, the enemy had not treated his castle kindly, standing as it did in the path of their advance. Half the walls were torn down and the gate towers in ruin. But already masons were busy piling the used stone for rebuilding, and Herluin himself greeted his step-son cheerfully, accepting William's immediate offer of assistance with monies and men without blame or argument.

William found Herleve in the under-croft, trying to make sense of the ransacked stores. She was on her hands and knees gathering up spilled grain with a short twig brush, Odo and his brothers pulling the torn and ripped sacks out of the way, in their efforts proving more of a hindrance than a help. William remained in the doorway, grief catching at him. He hated to see his mother so work-harassed, it choked him. When she sensed his presence she did not stop her brushing. As simply as if he were a child like the others she asked him to help his little brothers move the sacks so she could sweep behind them. Only when she was sure that she had salvaged all she could did she lean back on her heels and thank him, pushing her hair out of her eyes like a young girl.

'See what vandals they were,' she said, 'nothing taken for use, all for waste and spoilage.'

She did not say to William how great his victory was, she did not even praise God for his and Herluin's safe return, but he felt it there in every move she now made, in the homely act of gathering the spilled wheat, in the modest repast of stewed apples and milk she set before him, in the amusement she got from watching his half-brothers act out the battle.

When he told her why he had come he saw relief and perhaps a flicker of resentment, gone as soon as thought of. No mother likes to hear of a son's marrying. 'Tell me,' she said, leaning her elbows on the table. The sun, spreading through a shattered embrasure, caught at her hair, outlining it with gold. And so haltingly he told her more than he had told anyone else, even Golet, of the infuriating mixture that Matilda was, of his fears that she might not have him, of his even greater fears that she *could* not have him, and of his decision to leave Normandy and find out for himself how things truly stood. But even this he did in fits and starts as if the words were wrung out of him; as if, even with Herleve to whom he had come expressly for this reason, he could not give all away in case he revealed too much of himself.

When he had finished speaking she remained seated, one of her smaller sons on her lap as she fed him bread and milk. William saw in her the young mother he had remembered from Falaise. 'I think,' she said after a while, when the child's mouth had been wiped and he had been set on his sturdy legs to run and play, 'I think you need not fear that God will forsake you. The archbishopric of Rouen has not been kind to us in the past and yet they could not prevent us doing what had to be done. As for your detractors, let them say you are foolish to leave your dukedom. As long as your enemies lie quiet licking their wounds, you can be spared. Nor in such an enterprise do you need help or advice from king or councillors, certainly not from me. But I will give advice nevertheless.'

She smiled at him to take away the sting. 'Firstly I would suggest you learn again to say what is in your heart, not hiding it. Secondly, do not go as a warrior – although no doubt your prowess has gone ahead of you, as indeed it cannot but fail to do.'

She put her head on one side, considering him. 'We cannot hide your shaved head, alas,' she pronounced, 'which I see you now affect like all your soldiers, but I myself will find you clothes suitable for such an expedition, even if I have to rob Herluin's coffers or what is left of them. And thirdly, I would ride in haste, with all the speed that once took you across the Norman countryside, so that Matilda of Flanders need have no reason to be offended by your delay.

'But it seems to me if what you say is true you have no need to worry,' she added. 'The Count of Flanders is your ally; his daughter, despite her indecision, has already demonstrated her feelings. She is young,' Herleve continued with her usual understanding, 'go gently with her. Do not act with her casually, in a take-it-or-not, 'tis-the-same-to-me fashion. She will know whether you speak the truth, as well as I do.'

It was in this way, with Herleve's blessing, and the repeated offer of Viscount Herluin to keep watch while he was gone, that William rode towards Bruges where he knew Matilda was lodged. He rode fast and hard, as might any man with an overpowering mission, or an ardent suitor, desirous to see his betrothed and make her his. What he really thought and felt was as yet held tight in his heart, unbeknownst to any other, save what Herleve had guessed at.

In the city of Bruges, where Baldwin, his lady wife and his family were ensconced, news of William's approach disconcerted the Count of Flanders. The count was like a man with two heads, in two minds what to say or do, in this instance as indecisive as the king for whose indecision he had never had any sympathy. The count's wish for alliance before Val-ès-Dunes had been all positive, had been all sincere as his speaking out before the king gave proof. And true, as far as his own affairs went, Baldwin still welcomed the Norman alliance and after William's victory had less reason than ever to doubt the wisdom of his choice. But neither could Baldwin deny that since then a new obstacle had arisen to give grounds for concern. Nor for once was Matilda the greatest of these.

Since their last momentous visitation to the court and Baldwin's blunt speaking to the king, Matilda could not go back on the impression she had then given; that would have been true folly. Although she had once again lapsed into silence, offering neither yeas or nays when the subject was broached, as it was frequently these days, and although her mother, ever hopeful that the whole affair could now be dropped, construed Matilda's silence as dislike, the count took all with a grain of salt. Echoing poor Golet he would have said women are very contrary, saying one thing and meaning the opposite. It was not his daughter who made the count hesitate to greet William, nor yet his lady wife. Baldwin did not doubt that William, fresh from a victorious battlefield, could easily win as decisive a victory over the ladies. It was this other obstacle, as great as it was unexpected, fresh come to light, that left Baldwin rudderless, like a ship that is tosses and turned upon a stormy sea. An obstacle so great that when the duke actually arrived, Baldwin would find no words to express it, would actually hold back in cowardly fashion letting William discover it for himself, letting William cope with it as best he could, unprepared. In his cunning way Baldwin may have believed that by saying nothing the obstacle might go away, or by claiming it was not his fault throw the burden back on William.

William reached Bruges in early summer. The rain storms which at the year's start had raged with unbated force had given way to drought; the ride was long and hot. He found a landscape baked dry as dust, as flat and dirty dull as ever the countess's complaints had suggested. Yet, entering in the city with all the confidence of an Alexander, William came straightaway to the count's residence without pause or let, made his greetings to the countess as to a royal princess of France and clapped the count about the back, hailing him as an ally and friend. And, again without stop to wash the stain of travel off or change his clothes – all Herleve's careful attention to them thus brought to nought – he at once requested audience of his intended bride.

He called her that, no need now to beat about the bush. 'For with your lordship's blessing,' he said to the count, 'and that of your lady wife, I see no further reason for delay. If she agrees, that is.' And he smiled the secret smile of a man who expects no contradiction.

The countess sniffed and looked away, still too haughty to approve; the count smiled, bowed, gnawed his ring as was his habit. He made a gesture as if to say, 'God knows, your grace, what to do.' He had not the heart to warn of the obstacle that awaited.

William permitted himself a second secret grin. He doubted if Matilda had spoken of their last meeting, or if she had he was certain it had been much censored in the telling. But had she forgotten it? Had she put it aside, pretending it had never happened? Or, as indeed he himself had done, did she hold it close to her heart? He had again prepared a speech. He meant to tell her that although in battle heat there were moments when she came not uppermost, her memory had always been present, that having heard of her intervention on his behalf, he honoured and thanked her. And then, when he had told her of the dangers he'd faced and the victory he'd won, she'd turn pale, pretend to faint, as maids do on hearing of their lovers' peril. And if, as a final touch, he added that all had been endured for her sake, surely she would give way and let him clasp her in his arms as he once had held her. Only then would he broach the subject of their marriage and the difficulties he'd heard that surrounded it.

'By your leave then, I shall plead my suit myself,' was all he said and, bidding his host and hostess a gracious leave, he had taken the steps two at a time up to Matilda's bower, where her mother had reluctantly directed him.

The count's palace at Bruges was very different from anything William had seen so far, a place of residence as well as a fortress. He had sensed the difference even as he rode through the outer city walls. Now he noted the steps as he sprang up them. Stone-made, wide, with a curved stone balustrade: they would have been useless under attack; nevertheless he admired their gracious elegance. Normandy had nothing to compare with it. Nor had Paris, where all had been luxury compared with Normandy. Paris was primarily built for defence. For the first time it dawned on him that just as Herleve had come down in the world to leave Falaise for Conteville, so perhaps would Matilda scorn Falaise as a barracks, not a home.

These doubts did not intimidate him, but he marked and remembered them. Nor did he stay on ceremony. Reaching the door, heavy-framed with elaborate carving round the edge, he waved the guards aside and wrenched open the ornate iron clasp without a by-your-leave. Ducking his head under the arras he found himself in yet another large chamber, hung with embroid-ered tapestries upon which were depicted battles, legends, histor-ies. A great brick fireplace was built into one wall where a fire smouldered, although outside the day was warm. Rugs of woven wool were scattered over the floor instead of the usual rushes; beside an open window, hung with some sort of yellow skin to let in light, Matilda and her maids were seated by their embroidery frames. He suddenly felt as out of place, as loud and noisy as a hound let to run in a convent.

Hearing the sound of the opening door and his boots clanking across the floor, Matilda looked up. While her maids, several of them, all about her age, began to chat, heads together, eyes peeping out at the unwelcome intruder, she remained calm; only the dropping of her needle showing her agitation. Her quietness troubled him. Once he had felt her emotions leap, but months had passed since then. Would she meet him favourably or unfavourably today; he couldn't guess. Nor could he gauge what the interim had meant to her. He waited for her to speak.

She picked up her embroidery needle and went on with her work. He might not have been there, or at best been a page she had summoned and then ignored. William felt himself flush, reduced to nothing by her insolence.

Suddenly it didn't seem to matter what she thought. 'Put that aside,' he heard himself order her, his voice harsh. 'Where is your welcome?'

Again the maids whispered, shocked, tantalized. He thought, I should have better phrased that, questioning shows weakness. Irritated, he rounded on the women. 'Get you gone,' he growled. 'Leave us alone. We have much to talk of.'

They looked from him to Matilda until she casually waved her hands as if to say, 'Go, go, 'tis a nothing.' The girls withdrew reluctantly, lingering near the doorway until a second gesture drove them out. She herself still did not speak, although her eyes flashed as he had seen them in the light of the church. Are we to sit again like mutes, he started to say then, remembering the reason for their previous silence, was abashed. His anger faded. He began to pace about, pretending to examine everything, from the tapestries hung on the wall to the strange skin covering on the window-frame to the elaborately carved coffers underneath, finally stopping at the place where she sat. Her embroidery skeins were spread across the floor and unexpectedly wound themselves round his boots like trailing vines.

When he tried to shake them off he heard her laugh, almost too low to be a laugh, a sliver of sound. She bent down. He felt a tug, her head with its golden plaits but inches beneath his nose. 'No different then,' she said as she straightened up, her voice mocking in a way that was new. 'Time has not made of you a courtier.' As if she had expected it.

And you, he wanted to say, has it made you more tractable?

'You will have heard of the battle six months ago. Your father's men will have brought you news,' he said.

She didn't answer, stayed where she was winding up the unravelled wools. 'And you will remember,' he said, the words he'd so long rehearsed bursting out, 'what I purposed when I left, what our agreement was. Now am I come to see it fulfilled.'

Still no reply. 'Answer me,' he said. He dragged her up, his hands round her waist. The sudden jar sent her head-dress askew, her braids went flying. In exasperation he seized one and flipped it so that it swung to and fro like a bell rope. He could shake a reply out of her, he could break her ribs with a sudden twist as easily as snapping twigs. 'Christ's bones,' he swore. His own face had grown red. Some emotion stronger than anger flooded him. 'Then if you still remain voiceless, may you choke with pride. May you rot in hell, an old maid; may you die in a nunnery for, by God, no one else shall have you.'

He rounded on his heel, pulled her towards him. Held like that, legs dangling, he remembered from before something about her little feet, now clad in leather, green and gold. Their smallness gave him the strangest mixture of feeling: the need to do something violent contending with the need for gentleness. Against his chest he heard her own heart beat in time with his, as loud and as fast, in unison. But when he set her down and tilted up her face he found it was bathed with moisture as if she had been weeping.

'Just as always,' she was saying, her voice high, hiccoughing, 'only thinking of yourself. Once you accused me of it: in you there's no place for anyone or anything else . . .

'I can't fight you,' she was saying. 'You're twice my size. I can't fight father, mother, courtiers, the whole world. You see me as I am, my lord. But you do me wrong.

' 'Tisn't I who won't have you,' she said. She straightened up, almost speaking to herself. 'To burst in on me unannounced, no word of greeting yourself, no thanks, no gratitude. Only a command – do this, do that – as if I were your servant. And never a thought of what happened after last we met. I might have been your whore.

'You've won a battle,' she said. 'Yes, we've heard of it. It's on everyone's lips, a greater battle I suppose than the one you boasted of when you were a child. But never a message to me direct, never a thought of what I feared. Am I stone?'

The torrent of words poured out. He recognized them. Not the actual words she used but the meaning behind them. Why she's as jealous for me as I for her, he thought. It was a revelation.

He stood back, took a deep breath, began again. 'Lady,' he said, ''tis true I do you wrong. God rot my tongue, it comes from soldiers' company. I should do better not speaking at all as I did once. Not speaking there's no cause for quarrel.'

He stole a look at her. She had half-turned, was looking into the fire. He came to stand beside her. 'Shall I tell you what I really was meaning to say,' he said low-voiced. 'I meant to say how much I missed you. Instead I shall confess that although the battle of Val-ès-Dunes gives me my duchy back it is still only half restored. The treasury is empty. Castles I own are still not mine, their revenues go to other hands. Falaise is a heap of stones compared with here. I do not know I have the right to ask you to bear poverty for a while; or ask you to share hardship. But were you there I would show you how beautiful Normandy is, its woods spread with flowers, beautiful like the hangings on your walls.'

She looked up at him. She was wearing a dress of blue; he remembered how Herleve had put on such a gown to do Walter and him honour when they had returned. Her braids had come undone and the fair hair fell in ringlets. 'Why my lord,' she said, and there was real laughter in her voice now, 'perhaps it's just as well you limit speaking. If you were to say so much I would be in Normandy before you'd done.'

Somehow she had crept up under his arm, the top of her head level with his chest. Somehow her hands were about his waist, clasping at his belt. He had to lift her to kiss her lips. Her feet in their green shoes seemed somehow to entwine with his and somehow the woollen rugs became rucked beneath their heels so that he felt himself stumble.

They did not fall, rather seemed to sink until they were lying side by side. And then there was no longer need for words, silence suited them.

How long they stayed like that there was no way of knowing. But presently she stirred, sat up and tried ineffectually to push him off. 'If we are to be wed,' she said, 'we can't go rolling on the floor, like peasants.' Her smile took away the sting of mischosen words. 'Although afterwards,' she said, 'I'd not complain.'

Suddenly her face creased. It was as if a hundred cares had heaped themselves there. Before he could ask what, she had pushed at him again, pulled her dress free, jumped to her feet and began agitatedly to walk back and forth. He rolled on his back, hands crossed beneath his head, watching her. He thought she had never looked so beautiful.

When she said, 'Haven't you heard? Didn't Father tell you? They won't let us be married,' it was as if she were still joking. She had to repeat the words before they began to make sense, the one final thing he had been frightened of.

'Who says?' he asked, pretending he didn't know what she was speaking about.

She made a moue, her lips curled. 'It started with your churchman,' she told him, 'the Archbishop of Rouen. That was bad enough. But it's worse than him.'

She cried, 'While you were fighting battles there's been as great a battle here, although Father thought he'd put an end to it by persuading the king to support him. But the king came back angry from Normandy. What did you do to anger him so? And now he's agreed to side with the Pope and let the Pope have his way.

'Don't lie there,' she scolded as if she expected him to jump up and start a vigorous campaign. 'Just when we thought all settled, first came an envoy from the king bidding us beware, that we were beholden to him by feudal right and must abide by his decisions. Then followed a papal deputation from Rome, with the pope's charter, sealed with his seal, so much wax dripping they scarce could carry it. All to the same effect – archbishop, king, pope – that our marriage is prohibited, God forgive the whole crew.'

He sat up then, listening intently, 'On what grounds?'

'That's the jest of it,' she said; she sounded as if she were crying and laughing at the same time. 'That's the whole joke. That we are related, that like Guy of Burgundy my family is kin to yours. That my grandfather married your grandfather's sister; that I am descended in direct line from some mutual Viking pirate ancestor. So much for your being a bastard,' she said. 'Why, you're cousin to half the world!

'And lots of other things,' she went on when she was calmer. 'That my mother was to have married your father, that we are both too old, too young, too close, too separate . . . I can't begin to tell you all. So much, so little, meaning nothing, meaning everything. And all to keep us apart.'

'And what do you think?' he asked. He spoke nonchalantly. Herleve's advice to the contrary ignored, no one would have guessed how much rested on her answer.

'It doesn't matter what they say,' she said. 'Their very saying so is enough to prevent us.'

By now William too was on his feet, had straightened his sword belt. Arms braced against the chimney he was staring into the fire. He watched her surreptitiously. When she moved she reminded him of a whippet he once had had, fast and thin and lithe, beautiful in her own way. 'What of your father?' he asked.

Again her moue. 'Angry,' she said, 'Blustering, threatening. But silenced in the end. He used his best arguments to force Henry to fight for you. Against this coalition of king and pope he'd none left. And fearful too,' she added. 'For 'tis a fearful thing to stand against God's holy law.'

'Yet for all that he still favours the marriage,' she went on quickly. 'He'd be more than happy to have it celebrated. There's trouble to our south; he'd like to have called for help from you. The German princes this time, pressing hard. But their emperor has the ear of the pope. So there too our marriage plays a part in a struggle having nothing to do with us.'

'Rouen started it, and Rouen belongs to me,' William said grimly. 'I'll burn his archbishopric about his ears.'

He caught her by the hand, forced her to stand and face him. 'And what of you, lady?' he tried a smile. 'If we share a common Viking background, like a Viking won't you take ship with me? We could be off before you were ever missed,' he said. 'Normandy is large, there'd be room to hide.'

Like his mother she smiled and wept at the same time. 'And all those sons,' she asked him, 'all those heirs you wanted to be born in wedlock to keep your line intact? What about your dreams, Conqueror, your vows to get your lands back? You've barely started.'

She took his hands, placed both of them over hers as if making allegiance. 'I'll keep,' she said; the third oath-swearing of consequence he had ever known.

Later that night when the feasting was over, and Count Baldwin had drunk enough to admit to obstacles, when he too spoke of his ambitions and reiterated his need for allies; when the tables had been folded and the singers summoned; under cover of the dancing Matilda came up to where William sat. She had changed her dress, bound fresh ribbons in her hair – in all her appearance and demeanour she looked and acted as if this were her betrothal feast and she an affianced bride.

'Dance with me, my lord,' she said. And when he blushed, not liking to answer he had no skill, she took his hand again and showed him how the steps went, and how to stop and pivot, as grave as a schoolmaster. The fiddlers played and the harpist sang, and the red wine flowed.

'I'll still be your duchess,' Matilda said in his ear; she had to pull at him to make him bend his head, 'provided you win me a duchy. Not part of it. Not this or that in bits and pieces like patchwork but the whole. And when you can send me word that all is done and knotted tight, and the Archbishop of Rouen has been forced to bow to you, then I'll marry you.'

She was little, light on her feet, he followed her lead more heavily until, gradually coming into the rhythm of the music, he spun her round and round. The walls were lit by torches that spluttered; in between was darkness. He steered her into a corner where no one could see. 'Hold me,' she whispered, leaning into his embrace, as free and wild as any peasant woman, as free and giving of herself as ever Herleve must have been. And there in the darkness, with the rich court spinning but feet away, he gentled her as he had showed her before until she cried out softly for longing and buried her face against his chest.

Next day he left. She was not there to bid him farewell but he knew she watched from her window. Before he rode out of the gates he turned round, making his horse leap, then doffed his cap and waved it. Back he rode towards Normandy to fulfil his destiny. And if his enemies gloated to think his plan for personal advancement was finished, doomed to failure, God's curse on it, they did not reckon with the other partner in that marriage contract.

Matilda watched William leave with a heaviness that at the moment nothing he did could have lifted. Like him she had come to know all about waiting and she dreaded it. She had thought leaving him at the church in Paris was the hardest thing she had ever done; to have him return and go again now seemed even harder.

Memory of what she had just promised him made her blush. Yet it had to be said. There was no way she could let him leave still uncertain of her regard. As for the Church prohibition, she crossed herself, prayed again for God's forgiveness. I can't give him up, she told herself, much as William himself had done.

After the battle against Burgundy she had expected William without delay. 'Now blessed be God,' her father had said, his eyes watering for pleasure, 'God be thanked, a great triumph. Worth all our pains.' He had shut himself up with the messenger, intent on every detail. The king's intervention and his own part in it he waved aside. It was the boy's prowess that counted. 'Saw it from the start,' he said, 'you can't disguise military genius. Like his father. He's inherited it from his father, no doubt of it.'

Emerging from those hours of conference he had tweaked her braids, a familiar sign of good humour. 'Now we'll settle things,' he had said. But nothing had been settled. And even if Baldwin had tried it would have been beyond him once the Church officials had taken over at the king's insistence: all those learned arguments, those documents, witnesses, records; a man could be swamped by them.

But I shan't be swamped, Matilda now thought. She jutted out her chin and swung her hair. They shan't catch me with their logic, tied inside out like a bundle of old clothes. Before the dust of William's horse's hooves had settled she had sought audience with her father with a plan of her own.

She found him still in a good mood, if a little bleary-eyed after the previous night. 'You drank my health,' she told him, coming to the issue like a man, 'you toasted me and pledged me to him. So what shall we do to ensure the marriage takes place?'

When her father, bemused by Matilda's change of manner, sat down heavily as if to regain his balance, she smiled. 'Come,' she said in her sweetest tone, no play-acting now, 'you know it must be so. And he will be too great a man to let a combination of monk and weakling stop him.'

She leaned over the arm of Baldwin's chair as she used to do when she was younger and they had been perfectly in accord. 'He'll have all of Normandy,' she told him, 'no doubt about that either. And when he does I'll take it with him.'

Count Baldwin opened his mouth to contradict but she laid her fingers on his lips, the merest touch of her hand. 'Flanders needs him,' she went on demurely, as if offering herself as sacrifice. And although the twinkle in her eyes belied the earnestness of her declaration the set of her lips showed she was serious.

Count Baldwin liked to have her near him; he liked to have her lean on his chair and wait on his every word; he liked even more her smile and her attention and her obvious desire to please him. It had been long since she had wanted to please him in any way. He knew it was no use to lay before her all the arguments of Church and king, unless to explain how powerful both were; she would snap her fingers at them. Her optimism gave him heart, he did not like to be beaten either and Henry's change of heart had disquieted him. Besides, what she said now concerning Flanders and Normandy was what he himself thought. Hearing her echo it was flattering.

'Well,' he began hesitatingly, for not many daughters were capable of discussing politics with their fathers, and even if they were might not agree to do so, holding it unmaidenly to interfere in men's affairs. Matilda smiled at him. 'Well indeed, my dear lord and father,' she said. 'So we are agreed. Now how to achieve it?'

And perching by his side, she put her little hand out to take his. 'I think,' she said, solemn as a monk herself but with again that half-mocking, half-deprecating smile, 'we should do this.

But only when he has all of Normandy . . .'

And not waiting for Count Baldwin's consent she outlined her own plan.

Chapter 17

'Far be it from me, my lord,' the messenger said sanctimoniously, 'to invent bad news. 'Tis not of my own desire and will that I beg for help. I speak in my master's voice, the Lord of Bellême. I do but report these seizures of Domfront and Alençon . . .'

The duke's glance was such to cause the man to lapse into silence, to twitch with discomfort, to wish himself anywhere else than where he found himself, in the great hall of Falaise where the duke himself had but moments before returned, hard on his own arrival. Cautiously, under cover of the darkness, he eyed William. The duke's aged, he thought; these past three years have wearied him. He noted how fatigue had darkened William's face, sunken his eyes. Where the iron helmet had pressed a red weal marked his forehead and his hair around the shaved patch at the back was flattened like any common soldier's. He was still armed with belt and sword, spurred. Dirt was encrusted on his mail coat; his leggings torn. Like a peasant, the messenger thought, and unconsciously he preened himself, his clothes, hair, person immaculate as befits an envoy, detached from the news he brings, a bearer, not a creator of it.

Until that moment William had scarcely noticed what the man was saying, his personal discomfort too great to be bothered with the sort of pin-pricks messengers troubled him with these days. His body ached, ringed with bruises where his ribs had caught so many blows they seemed fused. Yet on the field before Brionne, from whence he had come, he had hardly felt them. His head was aching too, but not from blows. He stood shivering before the fire, the icy winds that had penetrated his cloak as he rode still with him. He felt too tired even to sit down; a danger in sitting that he might never rise again. Suddenly from out the welter of the messenger's words he caught the names.

Only then did the bleatings take shape and form, though he knew their substance already by heart. It was only in the names that there was a difference. You don't bring me news he wanted to say, there is nothing 'new' in your message, either 'good' or 'bad'. In a voice hoarse with shouting orders, counter-orders, he barked, 'And what do you know first-hand of seizure that you speak so readily of it?'

He leaned forward towards the flames. Or what of siege attack, he thought, of assault, repulse? What of fighting in the dark, the pre-dawn raid, the corresponding sortie back? What of men dying underfoot, in your arms, on your sword?

He had been resting his boots on the great hearthstone; now he stood up, took a step forward, sword swinging. He noted, almost with satisfaction, how the messenger backed away. Good, he thought. Let him tremble at what he does not know. Where I've come from is fear itself. A castle under siege is hell, he wanted to say, to shout it out so that he could cast off the memory of it; a hell for those within, a hell for those without, day and night without respite. Like Brionne.

Since his return from Bruges almost three years before, the taking of Brionne had been his main intent. It seemed a joke, one of God's jokes on him, that even now as he came back to Falaise having almost achieved it someone should be waiting for him with yet another similar task. Like the labours of Hercules depicted on Matilda's tapestries, he thought, there is no end: before one is finished another starts.

These last months had seen savage fighting round the castle walls where Guy of Burgundy still cocked his nose. William had been on constant watch, hourly called to arms, sleeping – when he could snatch sleep – on the ground; since he had been a boy when he and Walter had been fleeing for their lives he had never . known such rough living. Look at me, he wanted to say. That dirt you espy is the dirt of Brionne. I am impregnated with it; the castle is inscribed on me. My very skin is engrained with it, with mortar flakes, shards of flint, gravel, mud. Count Gilbert built Brionne to stand; even I, his favourite, cannot enter it or tear it down.

But he did not. Instead his attention was suddenly caught by a large, straggling pile of sticks heaped to feed the fire. With his toe he dragged them out, laboriously knelt, his mail coat hindering him, and began to build, scratching on the stone much as Walter had done long ago before laying the twigs crossways for support. The messenger's alarm increased, especially when the duke impatiently beckoned to him to approach.

'Do you know how siege towers work?' the duke asked. Without waiting for response he went on, 'Or what happens if they aren't built right, if they aren't high enough, or stick in place, or catch on fire? Or how long it takes to design them so they have no faults and men inside aren't trapped, half in, half out, to be toppled fifty feet?'

Bending over the twig model, the messenger registered shock as he listened to William explain in detail the intricacies involved in siege tower use, how the first he'd had made had burst into flames, doused with blazing oil poured from above, how the second had been too short, so low that the castle defenders had been able to shoot down at its occupants. And how now the third might be successful because of wheels, enabling it to be dragged to a better site . . . The messenger nodded his head as if in agreement. He's gone mad, he thought.

'No, I've not,' William said, seeing the look in the man's eyes, 'no more mad than this mad world where men are burnt like logs, or shot arrow-full to look like hedgehogs. But if you've no experience of these siege weapons, don't stand there, puffed with conceit, as if to speak of fairs and their pastimes.'

Painfully he straightened up. 'Nor talk to me of Domfront and Alençon as if they were on the moon. I know where they are. There isn't a castle in my dukedom that I don't know how to defend, how to invest. I've had my bellyful of both.'

'Your news come late,' he shouted as the messenger stumbled off. 'Falaise is full of exiles from the south, Bellême is but last in line. And since your lord has had no thought of us, has failed us often in the past, ask rather why he comes whining for help to us now.'

But William knew why. Left alone, he eased off the mail coat. When presently a page came to unlace the straps, the undershirt was stained red where the collar had chafed at the nape of his neck. And there were other stains, rips and gashes where lance-heads had struck. If they had pierced through, he thought, I should be dead and all these cries, these moans for help, these lies, would be addressed to someone else.

He felt no guilt for his treatment of an envoy who deserved better respect. Guilt would come but for the moment he was too tired. Almost three years, he thought. And then – like the messenger – he thought, I've aged.

Somewhere in the past three years the excitement before and following the battle of Val-ès-Dunes had been lost, to be replaced by what he had learned to think of as a continual fight, a slogging sort of conflict, seldom decisive, never again jubilant. At the end of which, only after months of work, was there any hope of taking Brionne.

Impatiently he kicked his stick model apart, just as his grand-father did when some design had dissatisfied. I might have made the towers out of dust, he thought, for all the good they've done. *When you have it all*, Matilda said. Sometimes I think I've scarce gained a yard.

It was easy to list what had gone wrong, more difficult to know how to set it right. On his return from Bruges he had been on fire to start his rule, eager to begin the administration of a dukedom that now seemed his. His first move, to limit the wars that his barons so readily engaged in, had been greeted with respect. By October of that same year of 1047, he had summoned a council of the Church to proclaim the Truce of God, a master-stroke, he had told himself, prohibiting barons from fighting on certain days, exempting the duke from those prohibitions.

The council had convened at Caen; a fitting symbol; there conspiracy had been formed, there conspiracy had been crushed. But even though he, William, could boast that he at least had summoned it, that in this the Church had been subservient, had cringed and fawned, Mauger the archbishop chief among them, the Church, more shrewd than he was, had outmanoeuvred him. The ban had been full of loopholes, flawed with weakness and deceit; to wit, that if the Truce of God was to be upheld the Church alone had power to punish those who broke its laws. The Church was not likely to excommunicate those it liked – or feared. The Norman barons had not been long intimidated by the Truce, nor had the Truce lasted long, not worth the parchment it had been written on. And conspiracy still flourished.

As for Archbishop Mauger – certainly Mauger had cringed, he had also shown his cunning, pleading ignorance and lack of influence. And an inability to lift that other ban which so bedevilled William and overshadowed his future. Pinning Mauger down was like catching a salmon, he thought; the more you tried to grasp its tail, the more slippery it became.

Thinking of this second failure William began to pace back and forth across his empty hall, a restless stride that his father was said to have had, and his father before him, like a leopard caged, back and forth to wear a furrow in the stones. As no doubt would William's son, if he were ever to have one!

'It is nothing to do with me,' Mauger had said – had lied – but how to prove he lied? 'Why should your Grace heap reproach? It is the pope who is to blame. The new pope, Leo IX, is responsible for forbidding Your Grace's marriage vows. Who am I to withstand the pope?'

And with a glee he could scarce conceal Mauger had intoned the place, the time and date when that main prohibition would come into effect, as if already it were sancrosanct; Rheims, October 1049, when Pope Leo himself would convene with the French bishops on this and other matters. 'But if I, alas, am unable to help,' Mauger had intoned, his small eyes sharp, 'perhaps the king can. Is not the Lady Matilda the king's niece – who more suited than the king to plead for you?'

He knew very well what Henry's position was, and that William and King Henry were estranged. That too was a legacy from Valès-Dunes.

Back and forth now went William's thoughts, keeping time with his steps. The king, having done his promised part, had refused more aid. His fear and dislike increased, he was said to have regretted Guy of Burgundy's defeat, even now to be searching for other allies against Normandy. As for that marriage William craved, although envoys from the Flemish court still made their way to Rome to change the pope's mind, the pope stood firm, as firm as the castle of Brionne – and with the contrivance of the king!

She'd marry me in a trice, William thought; I could persuade her to wed me if only the duchy were all mine. But it isn't. Not while the Church is defiant; not while my barons are uncontrolled and Brionne stands; not while King Henry encourages attacks upon my lands . . . as he does at Domfront and Alençon.

Savagely alert at last, he concentrated on what the messenger had told him. Two castles taken, he had said, naming them, places that the duke could not allow to fall, guarding as they did two important cross-Normandy routes. Alençon, the first, stood on the old Roman road south; Domfront straddled the ridgeway east and west. Both were held by the lord of Bellême, although William Talvas of Bellême had in fact occupied Alençon without permission. Alençon was built on Norman land; Domfront was in Maine but so close to Norman boundaries as to make no difference. And both seized now by the king's new friend, Geoffrey of Anjou.

The pile of twigs was crunched underfoot. When a page approached with a fur-lined gown, with offers of wine and meat, William waved the boy aside. Brionne might have proved a stumbling block, but that did not mean other castles would be as difficult. He might go south, retake, return before ever it was known he was gone. But what of the king if he heard? What of Guy of Burgundy, besieged? What of other malefactors, waiting to rise? Back and forth went William's thoughts, back and forth he paced.

Geoffrey of Anjou was also not unknown to him, although he had never met the man. Geoffrey was a count with ambition.

Stealthily at first, gradually with growing contempt, he had been amassing lands to the south of Normandy. William had spoken truth that in Falaise there were already exiles from his attacks. Gervaise, the archbishop of Le Mans, Berthe, widow of the count of Maine, her children and friends, had more reason to beg William for support than the lord of Bellême. Yet Le Mans and Maine were not important to Normandy in the same way as Domfront and Alençon. And previously King Henry had shown no liking of Anjou. Nor had Anjou need to attack Bellême except to test William's response.

I have no duty towards Bellême, William thought, ever have that family done mine wrong. And cleverly have they held their land from different lords to set us against each other. He remembered Yvres of the same name, the bishop of Sées, who had burnt his city instead of protecting it: he recalled the peasants' abortive raid and his own naïve wish to make use of it. Yvres of Bellême was typical of the whole line, treacherous, double-handed. Yet the bishop's callousness seemed less reprehensible to him now. He himself had known times when to preserve a little one must lose much.

And that was the last thing that had gone wrong since the victory of Val-ès-Dunes, the change in himself. He had grown hard, repulsion and strain taking their toll of him. Sometimes he felt as if he were encased within a calloused shell which hid whatever finer thoughts he had once had. He no longer sickened when he saw the dead, he no longer suffered with each of the wounded. He had learned how to calculate success, measuring it on the battlefield; so many of ours dead, we lose; so many more of theirs, we win. The only thing that softened him was the prospect of marriage. But as it still remained in limbo, so did Matilda herself seem to pale, to fade like the memory of the outline of her face. Even the remembrance of the touch of her pliable body eluded him. At nights now when he felt her lack he had other women to assuage his needs, camp followers, prisoners, hostages, whoever was at hand and convenient. Like dead bodies at the battle's end they were lifeless to him. And he as lifeless in himself.

He shook his head to rid it of such thoughts.

Count Geoffrey of Anjou had a nickname, the Hammerer. And that is how he fights, William thought, no fine gestures, no charging forth with armour bright and sword raised; just dull, crude blow after blow after blow, until walls and gates and towns are split. And if I do not drive him back and defend these gateways to my duchy, William thought, what else will he crave and take? And using Geoffrey of Anjou to achieve his ends, the king will boast he can twist and turn me as he wills. Has taking Brionne depleted me, he thought; am I Atlas to bear the world? As when he was a child he heard his father's voice. 'Upon us the weight,' it said.

More war then, William thought, the Truce of God further off; my marriage again postponed. I still like a man buffeted by contending winds, first east, now south. And the king a scarecrow swung between.

Before dawn, in conference with his new seneschal, who had replaced the long-dead Osbern, he had envoys sent to summon his vassals up, those who still were faithful to him. Praise God, although their numbers had remained small their hearts were sound. Not waiting for their musterings which would take time, he next called out his own household guard. They at least he could be proud of, no knights like them in France, trained by him as he himself had been trained, an elite fighting force which he had formed over these three years . . . Letting others take Brionne, he would leave with them at once, make his stroke like the Hammerer, and with luck return before he would be missed. *There's not a castle I don't know how to invest, defend.* What William had learned in Brionne he would practise at Domfront.

Mindful then of his experience, he had engineers accompany him, summoned carpenters, masons, builders. Remembering also the attack on Sées and Walter's judgement of it, he brought commoners, foot-soldiers, pike-men, archers. At Brionne bowmen had proved their worth in defence; he had learned that even mounted knights could not withstand an arrow's reach. And Walter and his grandfather, seeing him now in full response, marvelled at his efficiency and speed. 'His father's son,' they told themselves. And crossed their breasts in memory.

Within days, as he had hoped, William was on the march before the king and his other enemies knew where he was gone. Behind him massed his knights, solid as a battering ram, trained to charge and stop and charge again, their pointed helmets rising in unison, pennants fluttering from their lances, their shields looped over their arms. Their chain-mail shone. Behind them again stretched a more wavering line. When he turned in the saddle he could see it. Guarded by outriders were supply carts, pack mules and baggage wains undulating along the hill crests. The sight pleased him. He'd have no foraging in his lands; all would be provided for, done neat and trim, food and fodder recompensed when his own supplies ran out. Like Geoffrey the Hammer he had moved fast. Like Robert, his father, he had moved true so the peasants should not say he pillaged them.

Beside him rode two new companions who also pleased him well. They were his own age, high-born, bringing with them their own followers. One was Roger of Montgomery, married to a daughter of Bellême, who thus had a personal interest in the conflict, in retrieving what was lost. The other was William Fitz Osbern, son of his old dead friend, to whom William owed such debt. William liked both men. He trusted them, and more to the point, they liked and trusted him, were young and, like him, receptive to change. Satisfied on all counts he settled back in the saddle, quickened the march, closed off his thoughts and concentrated on the attack to come. The only sounds were the creaking saddles, the jingling spurs, the crackle of the leopard flag. That sixth sense which Walter had honed, his instincts for danger, warned him of it before the next messenger caught up.

This was a different sort of envoy. His horse was lathered with its ride, its sides heaved, its eyes rolled. The rider, grey with strain, held himself upright with effort; his voice trembled as he tried to hail the advancing columns. When William gave the order to halt he lumbered up, seeming more like to fall than give his message, with or without judgement on its contents.

'My lord,' he croaked at last, 'Brionne yields. The traitor, Guy of Burgundy, is fled.'

William said nothing. The hum of approval swelled, then stopped as the messenger went on. 'In his place the Count of Arques challenges you. The Count of Arques will not stay at Domfront, but retires to his own lands. In company with his brother Mauger he breaks with you, renouncing allegiance. No more is he your vassal, lord, but declares himself your equal, master of the Seine.'

William listened stony-faced. 'And what more?' he prompted.

The messenger gathered strength. 'The French king has formed a pact with him. The king gives him accord. And to further your discomfiture, lord, and to strengthen him, the king has promised him all the support that once was yours.'

He made no excuse, no plea for mercy traditional in such circumstances, begged no pardon for such dire report. His distaste for it was written in every line of him, not like that last painted popinjay who had preened at disaster from a safe distance. But of all who heard, only William seemed unmoved.

Perhaps it was because he had learned to leach feeling out of him, perhaps because in truth as he had feared he had no feeling left. All fell upon a hardened shell. ''Tis no more than we expected,' William said.

Suddenly, for no real reason, he smiled as if light-hearted, as if, knowing the worst rather than always have it to come, he could face it better. 'So the scavangers gather,' he said. 'When they have me, let them pick my bones. We continue south,' he said.

And, as the column began its forward march, 'Sir messenger,' William said courteously, no anger apparent, 'take back these words. Say I break no bond nor oath. Say I shall return with fire and sword.'

He clamped tight his mouth and clapped spurs to horse, the mud from the track flying behind him as he galloped off. Strangely the capture of Brionne over which he had laboured so long had no meaning for him now. He did not rejoice or savour it. There was no time. If he thought of it at all it was to assess how it might help or hinder him in this new defection of his step-uncle in the east. By and large he thought it would help, again bringing into the open the treachery he had always suspected of Arques. We can ride all day and night, he told himself, we can still reach Domfront before they suspect. When we have it under siege, I'll make a detour to Alençon to retake it. And then I deal with Arques.

That William of Arques' treachery could have come more conveniently at another time was a thought he held battened down, as he did his anger and chagrin that both his step-uncle and his king should think so lightly of him. But it was a knowledge that ate at him, a canker hidden from the world and therefore twice as dangerous.

Had the castle of Domfront been attacked as he had planned, unprepared, unwatched, events there might have taken a completely different course. Had not an outlook, idly watching the north while he whittled at a tree branch, caught a glitter of armaments through the scanty autumn leaves, and stayed long enough to tally numbers before he fled to raise alarm, William would have burst through the forest and taken Domfront. But, he found the castle bolted up, its battlements lined with men, appeals for help already sent to Anjou, their new master, and fresh reinforcements hourly expected.

If these set-backs daunted William he didn't show it. Relying on his experience at Brionne he embarked upon the elaborate task of establishing new siege works and building an earth enclosure to harbour his own men, searching the woods for trees – the tallest, straightest oaks he could find – lashing them together with the toughest hemp, weaving branches overhead for protection, draping the sides with thick hides until the forest rang with the sawing, hammering and chipping of tower builders.

'Like wood cutters,' Geoffrey the Hammerer mocked when later he observed the scene. A squat, heavily built man, years of deceit and treachery had lined his face, twisted his once handsome mouth. News of William's attack had surprised but not alarmed him; he soon was on the march back to Domfront, prepared to come to the rescue. William's own defences he dismissed, puny gestures, not worth the noticing. What, should a stripling scarce weaned scare the Hammerer? Signalling to the castle to take heart he prepared to mount a counter-attack in the defence of his new possession. He watched from the ridge where he had massed his men as William's knights came out from their earthen fortress and grouped into their fighting wedge. Nothing new in that. And then, as they began their advance, 'Inexperienced cubs,' he sneered, 'full of wind. No trained knight charges uphill.'

He laughed. 'They're young fools,' he told his followers on the ridge, 'wait till they reach the foot. Then trample them. But spare the Bastard if you can,' he gave the order, 'he's ransom money.' And staying where he was, he crossed his arms in pleasant contemplation of how much the ambitious Count of Arques, or the French king, would pay to buy his prisoner.

Below him on the plain William watched Geoffrey, knew him by repute, knew why he stayed up there – not to keep himself safe as Guy of Burgundy had done but to show how little effort it would take to succeed in so slight a skirmish.

Again the thought, having entered William's head, would not let go, burned in him like pitch. Yet he had to hide his anguish. 'Stand fast,' he yelled to his men who were all for advancing. 'Let them come down. And God have you in his keeping.'

It was not easy to stand still and watch the Angevin advance from their position on the hill, nor to wait their charge, a wave of them coming like a tidal bore that sweeps all before it. The shock of meeting was fierce but William's knights held firm. And although the contact was short it was not as sweet as the Hammerer had anticipated. Those 'inexperienced cubs' kept their heads, as stout as his more seasoned followers. William held the forefront, his men braced to let the Angevins run against their points. On either side, his two companions opened the wings, pivoted round and closed them pincer tight so that the enemy was caught without the strength to charge again or make a break and run. Only when they had been neatly dealt with did William give the command they had been waiting for, his 'Charge!' ringing through the trees and setting the woodpigeons fluttering. Like the woodcutters they'd been likened to they hacked through the Angevin reserves, overran the ridge, took control of it. No trained knight charges uphill . . . For the first time in his military career Geoffrey the Hammerer looked on and knew he had been outclassed.

Too angry to speak he withdrew to his camp, established beyond William's, retired in order with his household guard; better to live and fight another day than die in such a paltry episode.

'He would not stand and fight,' William thought, 'next time he shall.'

But time passed and Count Geoffrey did not go away. Yet although he harried William's troops and tried to break through their siege lines, he did not do what William wanted which was to fight with him. And so a stalemate was reached. Count Geoffrey's men could not help Domfront nor bring in the supplies the garrison needed; William could not take the castle nor devote all his time to besieging it, harassed as he was with the Angevin counter-presence. And in all those months, as if to goad his young rival, the Hammerer deliberately kept himself out of William's reach, as if he would not be contaminated by him, a bastard 'pretender' to a title he was not worthy of.

Whether that was what he really felt, whether that was gossip meant to provoke, no man knows. But William felt the slight as sharp as any wound. And like a wound which festers it also ate at him.

Finally, refusing to waste more time, the Hammerer withdrew entirely, leaving Domfront to its fate. And whether because Anjou's dismissal made it seem the less, or because he wearied of so long a siege, William turned his back on it too and made a new assay against Alençon.

By now all Geoffrey's accumulative slights burnt within William with a steady fire, and it needed now only one more insult to fan the flames into an inferno.

At Alençon he found it . . .

They came to Alençon by night, by stealth as William originally intended for Domfront. Dawn found the duke beneath the castle walls which his spies had previously circumvented, searching for those weaknesses which he meant to penetrate. Suddenly Roger of Montgomery held back and caught at William's bridle. 'My lord,' he cried, choking down his rage, 'turn round.' And when William pressed forward, ''Twas never meant. They would not show such disrespect . . .'

He faltered into silence. Above him on the battlements the

guards leaned out to give him the lie and show there was no mistake. Beneath them dangled the fresh hides they had strung out, still steaming, proof of the haste with which they had been hung.

'Go home, tanner,' they called and banged their spears. 'Tan your skins. Skins are what you're bred for.'

William let out a cry. So howls the wolf they say when it scents blood, so cries the leopard. A red rage engulfed him. Not waiting for his friends he rushed towards the gate and hammered on it with his axe which he always carried. The foot-soldiers swarmed after him. Some, feverishly labouring, dragged up a great catapult to hurl stones; others, knowing beforehand the weak spots threw up scaling ladders where outcrops of stone hid them from the walls. The gates gave way, splintered; the battlements crumpled. Within moments the gaps were widened to let in the knights. And seeing them the defenders wavered, threw down their weapons, fled. Now, as at Sées, began the pillage, the rapes, the killings. And for the soldiers who had hung the skins and made the taunts, maiming, even to the cutting off of the hands of those who had perpetrated the insult.

William heard neither the pleas for mercy, nor the screams and the moans. Impervious to them he rode about the vanquished castle, inspected it for damage and planned his own defence, by his very silence giving permission for further butchery. Once in his past he had said, 'Spare them,' to make Herleve happy. Now his hard shell encased him, shutting out mercy. And when his followers cheered him and cried, 'Well done, lord,' he did not smile or feel pleasure in the work. He felt nothing at all.

After Alençon was securely his and its garrison disposed of, William left various of his own men in charge on pain of death to hold it fast, turned and marched back again to Domfront in equally direct fashion. He found the castle in great turmoil, news of the horrors of Alençon running wild and turning all to quivering indecision. Some claimed they must fight on, to surrender would bring like fate to them. Some, crying that they were lost in any case, swore that only submission could give them mercy. Within days came the second fall, Domfront opening its gates of its own volition. William entered as victor without another blow being struck. And so he learned a new lesson, that savagery too can play a part in battle, unmitigated terror becoming an effective weapon. In later years William was to remember this and deploy it often.

If just now he had regrets, if in his lonely hours when thoughts come unwelcome into men's minds he felt remorse, he never spoke of it. That too was something to be nursed in secret, hidden from the world. And if in new nightmares the faces of those murdered men appeared before him, their mouths opened in soundless crying, the bloody stumps of their arms raised in supplication; if he woke with dry mouth and thudding heart, these too were things to hide.

They lessened the triumph. What he might have enjoyed: the defeat of the Hammerer, the retaking of his two border forts and the strengthening of his borders, the enhancing of his fame that Val-ès-Dunes had not been a chance victory, was marred by the loss of his merciful reputation. Yet had he fought as the knight *sans reproche*, the spotless knight of his dreams, he too might have been left to rot with no one to mourn him. In only one thing did he show satisfaction.

At the end of a year which on looking back seemed to have been dominated by messages, he sent a message of his own. This brought only good news, hid the bad. He had it delivered to Bruges where as far as he knew Matilda still waited for him. At its end, after he had listed his achievements in orderly fashion, no false modesty, no false bravado, he added the words that meant most to him. 'All this I have done for you.'

If he did not tell her the sordid details that was because he knew they would soon find their way into every corner of the kingdom. Nor did he tell her what his next labour was. That too she must know. Having fortified the two castles where his enemies had thought to bury him he turned north-east again, back towards Rouen and the Seine, there to face the last coalition against him, even if it meant bringing down the wrath of France upon his head.

In her father's palace, under the embroidered tapestries where ancient gods wrestled with lions, Matilda read his letter, or rather, had read to her the message William had dictated. She was sufficiently her father's child to know the worth of William's achievement, and the intensity of the task ahead of him. *All this I do for you.* So much depends upon it, she thought, too much to take lightly.

She folded the parchment small so it could be concealed in the bodice of her gown. He gambles for greatness, she thought, pray God if he succeed I do not fail. And with swift step she sought out her father. 'Now,' she said, 'although Church and king bar the way . . .'

Chapter 18

Close to Envermeu, where the former Duchess Papia had come from, the castle of Arques could be seen for miles, dominating the promontory above the juncture of two rivers, the Béthune and Eaulne. Its lord, Count William of Arques (now known also as the count of Talou) surveyed the work he was proud of, all he had achieved since first he had begun the building of a fortress there. No stronger castle in the duchy he thought, and made in so short a time – a stout wooden donjon encircled by a palisade, the whole encompassed by a great moat, with two towers guarding the entrance. He patted the walls in satisfaction, looked over their sheer depths down into the murky waters. He knew that since Guy of Burgundy's defeat at Val-ès-Dunes there had been a vacuum in Norman politics which even the Bastard had been unable to fill. Whoever holds this place, he thought, holds the pathway to Paris and controls the waterway of the Seine and thus the balance of the dukedom. Second in importance only to Brionne, he thought. And now Brionne has been lost, taking Guy of Burgundy with it, Arques is next in line. All my life I have been waiting for my chance, he thought. Now I seize it with both hands.

Had he been a more emotional man he would have held them out, those large, square-fisted hands, shaped for gripping reins and hilts, shaped for holding on to things. And just as at Vaudreuil proximity to the king had kept the Bastard safe for a while, so he judged that promise of the king's support for himself would again bring followers swarming, all those too weak, or too afraid, to stand on their own. As their next overlord, he thought, I shall whip them into shape. I do not need the king for that. And after the lands around my castle are secure, an impregnable centre from which to venture forth, I shall make the Seine mine between here and Rouen before spreading out to the distant corners of this land, even to the south where William is boxed in.

Moreover outside the duchy, I have other backers as strong, he thought. My wife is sister to the count of Ponthieu and

247

Ponthieu is a formidable ally. I have a legal son of an age to inherit; that too will count in my favour. Add that in recent years, at Mauger's insistence, a succession of Church treaties has increased my influence with the Church as their frequent request for me to witness their documents proves. It is not only my brother as archbishop who strengthens me, he thought, the whole Church appears on my side. William's brief popularity after the battle has not endured. In short, without the king's support there is no way William the Bastard can hold Normandy intact. I can.

He patted the walls again, liking the texture of the rough-hewn wood, liking the strength and feel of it. Ambition ran wild in his heart as it had not since that meeting on the dunes when Ralph de Gacé had first put the dukedom at issue. The young duke was penned up at Domfront and Alençon; Guy of Burgundy had taken to his heels back whence he came, so was Arques' own claim to the dukedom beyond question; why, he was free to strike as fancy took him. He threw back his head as does a bull scenting blood and yelled his approval.

His mail coat belted round him, sword in hand, he clambered down from the top of the donjon and continued his tour of inspection. Fortress, towers, walls – and the soldiers who armed them – nothing escaped his attention. Methodically he went from top to bottom, as the old duke of Normandy, Richard II, would have done, his father's son at least in this, the father whom he had never known. All was in working order. Good, he thought again; I am prepared. God smiles on me. And then, irreverently: He should, Mauger's prayers alone surely suffice to ensure God's favour to our cause.

The Count of Arques had not yet heard of William's successes in the south, far less by what means he had gained them.

Once Domfront had been secured, William made his way north as fast, perhaps faster than he had first come south. By now autumn had arrived and the weather worsened. He took no notice, camped rough along the way, not wasting time searching for congenial lodgings, but making do with what he found as he had when a child, by his own example obliging his commanders and their retinues to do the same. Again as he rode he glanced continually around him, taking stock of all that went before and behind, like a good baggage-master (which one of the former dukes was reputed to have been). Everything he saw should have pleased him. The baggage train still kept pace, its wagons loaded with what he had found to spare in the border garrisons, enough left to feed those remaining and to accommodate him and his men. Despite heavy losses his army had been increased over the past weeks by others of his feudal levy. Although not large it would suffice to give good account of itself. As for the men who formed it, harnesses polished, weapons gleaming, horses groomed and fed, they looked what they were, battle-honed and ready, showing no sign of disease or disaffection. And since he had left the wounded behind, had seen the dead buried with full honour, in all things he had shown a lord's care and concern for those who suffered or died in his service.

He settled in the saddle, drew his cloak about him, and let his horse pick its own way through the ice-caked mud. Unease still gnawed at him. His step-uncle's treachery, like that of Ralph de Gacé's, was no small thing, not to be taken lightly. That he had been expecting it did not soften the blow. Nor was the king's defection new. Every day it seemed fresh tales of Arques' effrontery reached him, Arques and his brother revelling in their new-found favour, revealing their cruelty to any who dared resist. The fact that any had withstood them, to his own loss, spoke much for William's own reputation. But the cost had been high. He drew his cloak even closer, kneed his horse on. There would be time to answer all these injustices in proper style when this journey was done.

One story in particular had disturbed William, reviving all his latent fears and doubts. Among those who had put up initial resistance to the Count of Arques were two whom William had reason to number among his dearest allies – although it was true he knew of them only by repute and had never met them. They were both sons of a man he once had revered, whom he counted as beloved as his father, Turold, his early 'tutor'. He had never met these sons but knew of them by name: Hugh of Morimont and Geoffrey of Neufmarche. Their stand on his behalf had impressed him. In a subsequent engagement, Hugh had been killed. News of the loss of this unseen friend and his followers, treacherously ambushed in Esclavelles (in which the hamlet of Morimont was situated) had but recently reached him. From it he had learned how Hugh, tricked into parley, had been taken from the rear and overrun. Perhaps the name of Hugh, causing another dead Hugh to rise from his past, had broken a dam of reserve, as if the other wrongs done in the duchy in the name of 'lordship' were encompassed in Hugh of Morimont's death. He grieved for Turold's son as he had grieved for Turold, reliving the moment when Walter had slammed the door shut in Vaudreuil, leaving Turold alone to face the pack of their enemies. Over and over he heard Walter's claim, 'Turold holds.' He heard Walter's mourning . . . 'I have never before failed anyone.' If after all these years he still could not bear to think how Turold had died while he and Walter had made good their escape, it seemed to him that this second death, which appeared equally without meaning, must have some reasoning behind it, must be a call from God to ensure that once and for all William was prompted into crushing the evil in Normandy.

He did not underestimate the danger of the dual alliance between step-uncle and king, in some ways the worst he had ever faced, worse perhaps even than when he and Walter had slid from the privy and thrown themselves into the waters of the mill-race; if not so immediate, equally likely to be deadly. For now, like Turold, he stood alone, without King Henry to back him. Abandoned by the king, who it might be claimed had always offered some sort of protection against utter destruction, like Turold he faced a pack eager to begin its mauling.

That night he made a decision. When darkness and the falling snow forced him to call a halt he allowed the men to find shelter from the worst of the weather; the horses were fed and the camp fires lit and the meagre meal prepared. He himself did not eat, but paced through the horse pickets, stopping to examine the beasts, look at their hooves, ensure they were all groomed and sheltered. For a while he stood fondling the nose of his own charger, sired by that stallion which, years ago, he had bestowed upon the courageous captain of his guard. He watched the little lights of the fires fade, then flare up again in the wind. They seemed like the flickerings of his own hopes.

William's companions stood in a group to one side of the camp, knowing better than to disturb his reverie and yet concerned for him. Ever since Alençon his mood had been dark, severe, foreboding. And he himself appeared a foreboding figure, his tall frame wrapped in a rough soldier's cloak, his head stooped against the storm. Now he strode out into the open, no longer hiding his face. As the troopers scrambled away from the fires, 'Nay,' he said, 'bide where you are. But give me room to warm myself.'

They looked at him warily as he unfastened the cloak. Under it, his coat of mail glittered, his rich belt with the duke's insignia shone in the firelight. He marked their glances. 'When I was a boy,' he said conversationally, instinctively dropping into the homely speech he had learned from Herleve, 'when I was a child, my father promised me toys like these. And dearly did I grieve as children do, that he never came back to bring me them. And dearly did I pay,' he said, 'for my father's death, that my enemies should encompass my ruin. But my mother Herleve, whom some of you know, told me a thing. "It is not where you are born," she said, "but what you are. God in his mercy gives men the right to make of their lives what God has given them."

'God gave me two things,' he said. He had their full attention now. 'He gave me a mother who above all others I honour, a so-called peasant, who apart from birth is nobility itself, a woman like your own, stout of courage and of purpose firm, who taught me how to love this land. God also gave me a father who was duke, to guard and protect the land that we love.'

He looked round him. Silently in their twos and threes the men had drifted closer like the snow; knights and commoners, standing side by side. 'Normandy is not a coin to deal with,' he said, 'not a thing to give away or lose. Nor should we pledge allegiance and then relinquish it. We gave oath to an overlord who, as God is my witness, has no right to dishonour that oath, he should as soon tear his own flesh away. And so neither Arques nor France can usurp what God has given us although we must wrestle them to the ground for it. The battle that comes,' he said, 'will be the hardest we have fought; will take all the skills we have been apprenticed to. I myself welcome it. All my life I have been preparing for it. But back me, lords – for here we are all lords, equals as were our Viking forefathers – and we drive away this threat for ever more.'

Caught in a great silence made up of falling snow, flickering fires and empty space no one spoke. 'He who has no liking for that fight, let him leave,' William continued. He spoke simply, one soldier to another, man to man. 'But he who rides with me now rides to glory with a conqueror.'

Out of the silence a drumming began, the clashing of spears against shields, like the roar of waves across a shingle beach.

None left that gathering that night by choice. They did not stop for sleep; long before dawn they saddled their horses, gathered up their weapons, marched on. And when they came to Arques they burst down from the plateau like a river in flood, to catch Arques and his men unprepared before their walls.

The count was in need of winter supplies, and had been on a foraging raid, for care of his new dependants. The approaches to the moat of which he was so proud were blocked with wains of hay and corn, with bellowing cattle, with herds of sheep driven thither by men-at-arms. The gates were open allowing serfs to rush in and out, laden with wood and sacks of grain. The count was supervising the castle provisioning from a vantage point outside the walls, feeling so secure that he had no watch posted.

251

Taken off-guard, his unarmed soldiers leapt for cover while those mounted screamed a warning. The count pivoted in his saddle, to stare upwards at the wooded slopes as at a vision.

Without faltering in their stride, William's knights plunged down the ravine towards him, a line of lances pointed. It did not take the fluttering banners to tell William of Arques who it was. Yet he was no coward. As his own men drew back in horror he beat about him with the flat of his sword. 'Mount, mount,' he shouted. 'What do you fear, he is but human?' And putting spurs to horse in turn he drove towards the oncoming wave, although it made even his defiant spirit tremble.

Seeing him, William gave the sign to stop and, while his men hauled back on their reins, he proceeded alone, with only his standard-bearer for company. Step-uncle and step-nephew met almost mid-centre between their respective armies, which halted behind them at a decent distance.

They circled each other, like two dogs scenting out a conflict, the uncle tall, broad-shouldered, square-faced, his bull head hidden by its great helmet from which his small eyes glinted; the nephew taller still but lean, quick-witted and limber.

'I have never seen you before,' William said. His voice rang out level, trumpet-clear. 'Nor have you ever seen me. In good conscience I could ask you why, unknown to me, have you hounded me so? What you have done and do strikes at my very being. I can unleash my men,' he said, 'yours are still in confusion. But they have no quarrel with you. I do. Stand you and fight me then. I have waited a long time to meet with you.'

The count was a seasoned warrior. Every moment gained for his men was a moment lost to the duke's. He could hold this boy, this untrained boy, with one hand. 'As your grace would have it,' he sneered and, digging in his spurs, galloped forward while William too urged on his horse. Hate flowed between them like a current, the count's tinged with malice and envy, the duke's unsullied by jealousy.

The two Williams collided with a clash that almost toppled them both. Shields battering, swords swinging, they hacked and parried, passed each other, swung back, hacked again, until the sweat ran down their faces and near blinded them beneath their helmets, until their arms were leaden. All that William had ever learned, all he had gained in these past years since Val-ès-Dunes was put into his every thrust. It was not only for his life he fought or even his inheritance; his reputation, his future good name, hung in the balance. With each stroke he felt the loss of those empty years when this man who should have been his kin had belittled him. 'I kill you or die.' Had he shouted those words aloud, had he hammered them on his uncle's shield, they could not have been made more clear than in the ferocity of his attack.

For his part, the count had thought to strike and run, one stroke was all it should have taken to lay low so inexperienced a youngster. Instead he found a man who matched him skill for skill as any seasoned fighter, who controlled his horse like no other rider he had ever heard of except his own long-dead father, who knew every trick of horsemanship and swordsplay as if they had grown within him without need for learning. And who, young though he was, could not be tempted into error. The count's confidence began to dwindle as he was forced to retreat beneath his nephew's incessant blows. No longer on the attack, obliged to shelter beneath the great triangle of his shield while William battered it, his thoughts darted feverishly, this way and that, as if he were a cornered animal hunting for escape.

By now he guessed that the gateway to the castle would have been cleared, those within the walls would have seen to that. If he could make a break and run he could at least withdraw inside leaving his men to fight a rearguard action. He threw up his shield to take William's down-coming blow, glanced beneath it to ensure his men remained in place, and pivoted his tired horse. Then with a cry he held up his hand, the sword down-pointing, hefted off his helmet, all signs of a wish to parley.

His face was lined now with more than years, sweat and dirt deeply etched, and his ginger-coloured hair was matted to his skull. Through narrowed eyes he squinted at his step-nephew to see how things were with him and noted with disgust that he scarcely seemed to draw breath, his hand did not tremble; the younger William was as fresh and hale as when they had started.

'Nephew,' he began, in a whining sing-song that he copied from his brother, 'there has been wrong between us. Or rather, men have tried to make wrong.'

With every word cunningly persuasive, he drew back a little to shorten the distance between him and his men, watched how William leaned upon his saddle, intently listening. 'I know not why it should be so,' he continued, 'for in truth I knew your father well. And liked him better than any other duke, my own father notwithstanding.'

If he remembered when last he had said such a thing, on the sand dunes before Caen, he beat the memory down. 'I am a man of principle,' he continued, 'it was my duty to hold the duchy steady while you were a boy. And hold steady I did, although other usurpers tried to rip it from you.'

He snatched a quick look around him. Almost there, he thought. 'The dukedom is a prize,' he cried, unconsciously echoing his nephew, 'not easily lost. And not easily won by any passing adventurer.'

One step, two, three, and he was within hand distance of the first ranks of his own guard. 'Nor usurped by any wandering itinerant, without even legitimate claim.'

With one last mighty effort he swung his horse completely round and plunged headlong through the ranks which closed behind him. 'Onward,' he shouted then, urging his followers into action, 'onward. A reward to him who takes the Bastard.'

As the count's soldiers steadied themselves for a charge, William watched his uncle's retreat with almost detached disinterest. He had seen through his manoeuvre and could have stopped it. But something held him back, something that cut through the hate. It was not family feeling, wanting to save a man who should have been his mentor and guide; it was not shame. A more professional impulse than that, it was some soldier's distaste for a cunning that served its own interest like a weasel's. In a flash of understanding it came to him that if this was an example of noble kinship he was well off without it, for in truth it lacked even a pretence at nobility. And with that thought all hate died.

He let the men of Arques plunge towards him, hardly bothering to summon up his own. Here are scum, he thought. And such was his indifference he thrust them aside like flies until his own men, taking the law into their own hands, came down to join him. Together they drove towards the castle, herding their opponents like the cattle that had previously been rounded up, harrying them up to the gates which had closed precipitantly once the count was safe inside. Those who were shut without, knowing their master would show no mercy, and expecting none from William, fought like wolves, but were cut down under those strong walls. On the battlements, as had others before him, the Count of Arques cursed the day that William had been born.

The count was safe at the expense of his men. Arques was shut up. As at Brionne and Domfront William began the now familiar siege. Mangonels were dragged up for hurling stones, towers were built, dykes dug and earth walls raised to cut the castle off, all within so short a time it seemed as if some demon aided him. His father had earned the nickname of Robert le Diable; perhaps a devil possessed the son! When reinforcements from the outside tried to break through they too were utterly destroyed. The count of Ponthieu was killed and the French king's forces reduced to a rabble and easily hacked to bits.

This successful ambush of the French and Ponthieu relief forces at Saint-Aubin broke Arques' resistence. That night, ignominiously, he escaped and fled to Boulogne, there to be sheltered in disgrace. Without further fighting, William entered the impregnable castle and took it for his own. Faced with loss of his own troops, faced too with loss of his integrity, King Henry of France himself was forced to intercede, even though to make so strong a stand without an ally to hide behind went against his nature. Preparing two armies of equal strength, he vowed his intent to invade Normandy and bring its young duke to heel. Let the 'Conqueror' know who was master! Yet before his troops could arrive a third invasion took place, of more lasting importance than either of these two.

After William's journey to Bruges three years ago, Matilda had told her father what she meant to do, with or without his help. In the intervening time she had not changed her mind, in this showing herself as strong as rock, as stubborn as William. Her 'now' was nothing new and had long been predetermined. She had to argue of course, Count Baldwin being loath to lose her and seeing danger on all sides. William's successes helped her, while the French king's change of side at least clarified the position. She knew now who was friend, who enemy.

She used all her guile, playing upon her father's fears. Never had she seemed so loving as when she hung about the count's neck and persuaded him that he could live without her. She kept private her own thoughts – how she could not live without William and was desperate to marry him whatever the consequences. How at times her body craved his. Once she had realized this she had accepted it, and time had not made any difference. She did not speak of it but it coloured all her subsequent actions. And Count Baldwin, having weighed the consequences and found them wanting against his daughter's firmness of purpose, had finally agreed to her departure, despite the many risks involved (not least the dangers inherent in the travel itself).

'Father,' Matilda had said, her eyes glowing, 'you will not regret my loss. For I am not really lost as I would be in a nunnery. And in a convent surely I shall be immured if you forbid me. I must go, father,' she went on, 'I owe him it.'

When her father, puzzled, shook his head as if to say you owe nothing, 'Nay hear me out,' she said, 'for it is so. When last we spoke I promised to come only when he controlled his duchy. That was ill-done and I am ashamed to have put so great a burden on him.'

She said, 'In his endeavours I shall be a strength, a stop to his enemies, an encouragement to his friends. And my presence in Normandy will strengthen you. Once there I shall implement your own plan to form a pincer east and west, with Flanders and Normandy the prongs to catch the king. Besides,' her eyes darkened for a moment like Baldwin's own, 'the king, my uncle, puts shame on me by encouraging the pope to ban this match. There is no real cause as well you know; all is for spite, to hinder you.'

Some said the words were put in her mouth by others of her father's retinue who were all for Flanders defying the king and uneasy at the king's attempts on Normandy. No maiden, however strong-willed, could have invented those ideas on her own. Others, remembering the child, remembering what Count Baldwin had always said of her, saw her as their best ambassador. But those who knew Baldwin best swore he agreed for love of Matilda herself, not having it in his heart to refuse her request now she had revealed the depth of her desire.

Whatever the truth, in the end what Matilda wanted she achieved. The Flemish entourage that wound its way across the northern countryside had no military purpose in mind, but had its sights set upon that 'closer alliance' William had first spoken of.

It moved slowly, ponderously, flanked by heavily armed Flemish soldiers and followed by its own baggage-train. Seen from a distance it might have seemed a war column on the march. Baldwin would not let his jewel be lost for lack of force. It travelled in secrecy, the matter delicate in the extreme, to be kept hidden from the king and, as long as possible, from the Holy Church whose ban still stood. Nor did the countess's protests prevail although she, torn between husband and brother, cried she could see no advantage in an alliance against which her brother was now locked in bitter conflict. The countess's querulous protests echoed all the way from Bruges, and summed up what was best not said: what if the king attack; what if the Church say no; what if William lose?

Ensconced within one of the carts Matilda suffered the bumpy, laborious ride without complaint, aware that if she were recognized the purpose of her mission would be jeopardized. She allowed herself to be born along in a fashion she had always despised, forgoing all her previous pleasure in riding freely alongside the men; she suffered the journey to be drawn out, the route to wind and double back following hidden, minor paths. For the first time in her life she bedded down in humble style at out-of-the-way hostelries where food was scarce and bed bugs bit. She did not mind. In strange fashion she accepted, welcomed hardship, in this small way partaking of William's past. It made her feel closer to him.

Her journey took her along the coast where few ventured at this season. Winter storms delayed her progress, the sea beating against the shore with such force that sand and stones, all the flotsam of the Channel, littered the path, sometimes blocking it until it was cleared. Only when she came to the border with Normandy did she sigh with relief as once, coming from the other direction, Herleve had sighed.

And there, close to the border river, the Bresle, where William had suggested she wait for him she halted beneath the beech trees beside St Martin's Priory to say her prayers and take stock before venturing on to meet her lord.

Chapter 19

Alerted by messages from her father, sent also by secret means, William had arrived in the same region before she did. Although beset by rumours of the French invasion force he was not unduly afraid, believing with good cause that his new-won control of the territorially vital Arques would stand him to great advantage. The news that his bride was prepared to leave her homeland to marry him before he had achieved his part of their bargain touched him deeply. He therefore left the Seine, and, avoiding Rouen, where Mauger still held sway, rode towards the north-eastern border where his messengers had directed the lady.

The closest town to the Bresle was Eu. Having reached it, he was received by its count and, throwing off for the time his warlike cares, prepared to meet his bride.

He had not bathed or shaved in weeks; he had no clean clothes. Those on his back were soiled and torn, infested with fleas. He relied on the castle garrison to find him gear that would fit his lanky frame, hoping to be cobbled hastily into some robe meant for a man his size; would have been content to watch from the castle walls as he was had not the count of Eu, in friendly wise, hummed and hawed at his side, screwing courage up.

The Count of Eu was a simple man, of simple ideas and faith, overwhelmed by this visitation. Not until William had arrived had he heard of the duke's matrimonial plans and he was overcome by the magnitude of the honour bestowed upon him and his little town. He had fallen to his knees, kissed his overlord's hand, welcomed him as he ought. But in his heart was constraint.

Accustomed to war and fighting he had small use for words and knew not how to make his feelings known. Finally William, taking pity on his predicament, rescued him.

'Come, my lord,' he said impatiently, as if to someone his own age, 'you twist like a gallow's corpse (an apt if unflattering comparison). What troubles you? The lady comes of her own free will with her father's blessing. Once married I take her back to Falaise. We make no imposition on your hospitality nor will trouble you further than necessary . . .'

The count bristled at the idea of inhospitality. ''Tis not of imposition I speak,' he said at last. 'God knows I make you welcome. But . . .' Again he hesitated, unsure of how to frame the thought, began again.

'Good my lord,' he said, twisting himself in truth very like a man who swings from a rope, 'my good lord, my very good lord, have you not noticed a lack? At least my wife calls it such,' he added hastily, 'although in truth to fighting men it may seem more like relief.'

William gazed about him. It seemed to him all was very well arranged, the castle small but efficiently guarded, its garrison alert. Within the hall the fire was lit, food and drink prepared, the count's own bedchamber had been vacated for his use; he found no fault.

The count took heart. He wiped his forehead. 'True Eu is small,' he said, 'but ever are we at your service. So if I mention things unmentionable I ask your pardon.'

He swallowed hard. 'Your grace, have you not thought how these walls should be bedecked? My wife,' again he sheltered behind that absent wife (who for all the gold in Christendom would not herself have ventured an opinion aloud), my wife says 'tis disgrace that they are bare, that for shame they should be hung with coloured scarves, with banners gold and ribboned flags. And so should the church, as is fitting for a state marriage of such importance. And so should you. You need something better than the leavings of Squire Matthew's saddle-bags; should be already in the saddle to escort your bride back with all due ceremony. But say I, if your lordship will forgive, what point to any of this folderol if there be no church where you can wed. Or, if a church be found, no one will marry you.'

And he wiped his forehead again, more ready to brave a thousand spears than speak of all these difficulties.

William was taken aback at these last statements, both by what the count intimated and his unknowing reiteration of what Matilda had said. In fact, in his excitement these were details he had quite overlooked. Heartened by the young man's silence, the count warmed to his real theme. 'For, since the archbishop refuses you, if you break his ban he may excommunicate you. Or if he does not, the pope will do worse. The pope could put us all under interdict. And if I may speak my mind,' he went on, having begun now loath to stop, 'I say for my part no wife is worth such pain.'

He did not have to enlarge on what he meant. Excommunication was bad enough, the forbidding of speech, of food, of drink, of company, to the condemned man, the cutting off from society, the closing to him of all churches, the denial of comfort of the Mass, the rites of birth and death . . . what sane man would put his immortal soul at risk? But excommunication was punishment for one man's sin and he alone was punished. Interdict was worse for it fell on everyone; the whole world paid. The count of Eu had no wish to be party to any interdict.

'By God's balls,' William paled. He swore a mighty oath. 'Then they do not know my mind. Nor less that of my future wife. Clothes I care not for, and to ride a horse in welcome comes not as hardship. But I swear by my forefathers that if I must, I marry her with or without the church.'

He clasped the count of Eu by his mailed arm. 'Hang out your banners,' he said. 'Enrich your halls. As for a suitable marriage place . . .'

He looked again over the walls. 'What building stands there?' he cried, pointing to a square wooden structure that dominated the centre of the village. And when the count reluctantly answered him, the priory of St Martin, 'No better, Our Lady's Church, blessed to the memory of my ancestor, the Viking Rollo, first duke of that name,' he said. 'Now all that is needed is a priest.'

At the word 'priest', the count held back and bit his lip. That's sacrilege, his expression said.

William noted it and his face darkened. 'Any will do,' he said. 'Somewhere within those holy walls a tame one lurks. You yourself have paid your dues,' he cried, 'you've given alms. Chanceries have you and your parents made for their souls when they're dead. You are owed thanks. And since I have done as much myself, why man, there's not a church in this land whose priest is not beholden to me. Now let that debt be repaid. Get a priest to say the rites, or by God I sack your town to find me one.'

The count of Eu was no fool. He had heard of Alençon. He also knew when a man was driven to his wit's end. He bore the young duke no ill-will, wished to do him good not harm. He crossed himself. 'On your head be it,' he said. And when the duke in turn swore it was so and that he alone would take the blame, much relieved, the count gestured to his men to drag out coffers, which perhaps his wife had had prepared. Their contents spilled, the courtyard blossomed with silks and lace, blues, crimsons, golds. By the time the Flemish entourage was espied the bolts of cloth were all unwound, the walls and hall all cheerfully hung, the church nave strewn with dried reeds and flowers as befitting a bridal day. Hauled from some obscure parish church, a frightened priest was bullied into his dirty cassock, while messengers galloped forth to find somewhere a more suitable bishop. With light heart William leapt upon his horse to give his lady welcome.

By now his own entourage had enlarged to include others loyal to his service. They too rode after him towards the Forest of Eu where the priory was set.

The grey of the sky foretold rain, the grey trunks of the beech trees closed behind like mist. As the horses passed, dead leaves rustled underfoot making them shy. From time to time a startled buck leapt from the bushes and fled and lone birds cried out their warning notes. Only the glitter of armour and weapons, the swirl of cloaks, gave colour to their passing.

Seated within a wagon, hidden beneath its leather coverings, Matilda had been waiting in front of the priory gates for leave to enter. She heard the jingle of armed men's approach and her own guards' swift response to arms and for a moment her face paled with alarm. She parted the skin curtains and peered out.

A horseman had drawn level with the wagon, was bending down to look at her. Knowing herself dirty and dishevelled she felt herself blush as she had done when a child and hung her head. From beneath her eyelashes she glanced up at him, taller than ever on his horse.

'Ah, there you are,' the familiar voice teased, 'up to your old tricks, spying on men. For shame, lady, I told you I would not have my wife play games with me.'

She had planned to have had time to prepare herself in the priory guest chambers, to wash and don one of the many new robes she had brought with her. As if he guessed her thoughts he held out his hand. 'No need for finery,' he said. 'They string out all we need in Eu church. But I take pity on you if you have endured such close confinement all the way from Bruges. Come ride with me, lady, and enchant the world.'

He held out his hand. It would have been churlish to refuse it. One swift spring and Matilda was seated before him, his arm close about her waist, while the other controlled the restless tossing of his charger at the unexpected extra burden. To the cheers of his men and hers, he wheeled round to return to the town.

As they rode she recovered enough to swivel in the saddle, taking in her freedom with great indrawn breaths. The cold air reddened her cheeks, the rush of wind loosened her hair and

sent the plaits bobbing over her shoulders, the hem of her crumpled gown flapped against the horse's sides. She felt William's
gaze fixed on her. 'Sit still,' he said, 'and hold firm your skirts.
Else you'll have us both in the dirt . . . Well, you look no different either from what I remember of you, an urchin scrambling
in the straw.'

His assessment was not flattering but she had become used to
his blunt way of speaking. She held her head on one side and
observed him, had she but known making him catch his own
breath from her unexpected likeness to Herleve. The expression
on his face did not change though, showed neither smile nor
frown. He's older, she thought, tired, more than three years have
taken their toll. Then she laughed. 'Whence came your clothes,
my lord?' she teased him back. 'Look, the stitching under the
arm is already come undone. You need a wife to look after you.'

He grunted. But she knew he was not displeased at the
thought. It excited her. I have come as I said I would, she wanted
to say, before time. What she did say, hesitatingly, was even less
advised.

'My lord duke, I have a thing to confess. If you would be so
kind as to set me on my feet, in private I will tell you it.'

He waved his men on, although a sickness took him at what she
would say now. When they were alone, slowly he dismounted, all
the spring in his step gone, as slowly he helped her down and
seated her on a tree stump. Slowly he drew off his gauntlets and
held them by his side, now and then striking them against the
bark as if to assure himself that it at least was real.

She took a breath. 'My lord,' she said, 'have you ever thought
on what we did when we were younger and you first showed me
the ways of men?'

When he did not immediately reply she stole another look.
Can it be he blushes, she thought. It made her smile to herself,
suddenly feeling older. 'It should be spoken of,' she said, 'at
least I think so. Beatrice told me long ago that in the affairs of
the heart nothing should be kept hidden. So I will speak first.'

She might have been the forthright brat who had rescued him
in the stables, except now he knew enough to see the honesty
beneath. 'I have a confession,' she said. 'I told my father I came
for reasons of state, and to a certain extent that is so. I bind you
both together against a common enemy. And although once I
was foolish enough to say neither of you had the right to expect
it of me, I admit I spoke hastily. Of my own free will now I offer
my help, if help it can be called. But after our meeting in the
church when God, and you, know I was an innocent, I have

often remembered what we did. And I have prayed to God to forgive the sin. These past years,' she said, 'there has been time enough for praying.'

Tears had beaded her eyelashes but she was too proud to wipe them away. 'I have come in good loving faith,' she said, 'although you will say that not always was I generous or loving. And true, those are faults of mine. I have abided by my promise because I felt wedded to you. That is the truth of it. And if you, in the meanwhile, have changed your mind, or if that evening in the church porch has been superceded, or in any way I have been supplanted, why there still is time to part and let me return home.

'No one shall fault you,' she added, 'my father will still be your friend.'

Of all the things in his strange and unusual life William felt he had hitherto never witnessed anything so unusual. He did not know what to reply, like the count of Eu he was too overcome for words. At last he said, 'Lady, I accept your confession if you will call it so. Now hear mine. In all these days of danger and warfare I cannot always swear that you were uppermost in my mind. But you were there somewhere like a light to turn to when all else was dark. And if you have come all this way to marry me when I still am not full master of my proper inheritance, then by God we shall be married, let the pope do his worst.'

He took her hands in both of his as men do when they swear oaths. 'If we have sinned in the past,' he said, 'they say a greater sin awaits us. Does that trouble you?'

She smiled at him. 'That too is something we shall live through,' she said.

The marriage then was hastened on, the makeshift finery, the home-made banners giving lustre to the plainness of the service, the Norman Church rallying round for all that Archbishop Mauger thundered anathema from Rouen. That night the young couple slept in the count's castle, although in the end they did not turn the count and his wife from bed but made do with a tiny chamber recessed in the walls.

'Your mother was satisfied with as little,' Matilda reminded him. 'And as I am small myself it befits me well.'

They lay naked together, wrapped in William's cloak for the night was cold. Whatever there had been of horseplay at the time of bedding had been speedily got through, it obvious that both bride and groom were anxious to be alone. She had wrapped her fingers through his hair and was pulling at it, causing it to spring back in curls. Already her curious hands had discovered all his wounds, those scabs and scars that he had become so used to he scarcely noticed them. And with patient zeal he had revealed to her the mysteries that she had dreamed about, the foretaste of which had kept her constant. Will it always be like this, she wanted to ask, will we always have time for each other?

William whispered, '*Ma mie.*' The name he gave his mother had never been used for anyone else and sounded strange so he said it again, '*Ma mie*, we must remember this and hold tight to it. For I still have a battle to win and a king to conquer before we can be alone.'

'And an archbishop to dispose of,' Matilda laughed, remembering the haste with which the clergyman had gabbled through the service as if certain that before he was through his spiritual master would appear to forbid it. Then she sobered as he spoke more seriously.

'And what if God turns his back on us,' he said, 'what if you and I be put outside the Church? What if the duchy be brought to a standstill by papal interdict?'

She considered. 'Then we are put outside,' she said, 'we are set to naught. Whatever difficulties, we can overcome them. But I do not believe God will turn against us. Has He not already shown you that you are destined for great things, to be a conqueror?'

Her faith in him also touched him. 'Listen,' he said, 'how the wind blows through the trees. It sounds like the sea. When I was a child my father took me to walk upon the strand. He told me that as we had come from the sea in the first place so one day we would return, that there were lands to the north worth the taking. Alas, poor heart, he died far to the south, where he never should have been.'

After a while he added shyly, 'They say that you and I are kin. Then we must share in some part of that Viking blood. Perhaps that explains your attraction for things warlike. Perhaps like a Viking maiden you will fight with me.'

Eagerly she clung to him. 'Only do not send me away. We have been apart too long. Where you go I will bide with you. Even to the battle's edge.'

And when, relieved at her answer, he mocked her further, reminding her of her past inquisitiveness, that she had wanted to see how boys fought, 'I do not speak for myself alone but for your sons,' she said. 'They should grow to be like you, in every way, from the start.'

Again he was surprised at her ability to grasp at a thing close to his heart. Sons, he thought, to pass inheritance to, to train and form and yes, love, as he himself remembered for the short time he had known such a life. He could not yet bring himself to tell her that, it would be shown rather than told.

'And if they are daughters?' he teased her to hide his emotion.

'Well then, daughters,' she said, more primly, 'if it be God's will.'

He held her plaits, pulling them to pay her back for her pulling his hair, unbraiding them so that the flaxen tresses spread over the pillows. 'It matters not to me, sons or daughters,' he said, honest in that. 'Save that there be both. And that there will be more women in my life to subdue.'

He rolled on his back drawing her with him. 'Why else am I called Conqueror?' he said.

The wind soughed through the bare branches, the waves beat on the shore. His destiny was still before him, still unfinished, still to be played out, but that night William and Matilda gave no more thought to it. With the morning they rode away back to Falaise. And the joy in their union gave such colour to their journey even hard-hearted men took note of it.

Epilogue

In the February of the year 1054 the French king finally invaded Normandy. By all accounts this was the strongest expedition he had ever led, backed by many of his leading lords and drawn from all over France. William met it at Montemer in the east and so complete was his victory that the king and his army fled. William was officially confirmed in the land belonging to William of Arques, who never more returned; Arques' brother, Mauger, was deposed and a new archbishop appointed in his stead. Most important of all, William's army was swelled by most of the leading Norman barons, including the count of Eu, who helped smash the French advance.

Montemer was not to be the last battle William fought against his so-called overlord, but it was the summit of his youthful struggle to maintain his hold upon his rightful inheritance. As long as Henry lived his envy continued to arouse unrest, even again to having the count of Anjou attack on his behalf. The king's death in 1059 ended hostilities for a while, and Count Baldwin's plan became fact at last when he was named guardian to the young new king, Philip.

With Mauger's departure, the ban upon William and Matilda's marriage, their excommunication and the interdict inflicted on the whole of Normandy were removed. In return he and Matilda both built monastic houses as atonement. The Abbaye aux Hommes, and the Abbaye aux Dames at Caen were witness to the strength and endurance of their marriage. By then they had children of their own, including sons, to rule after them. William's control of his duchy was secure. And if the young lords from the ducal nursery at Falaise ran and played with their older peasant cousins, and if their beloved grandmère herself rocked them on her lap, as she used to do their father, no one made cause for complaint, certainly not the Duchess Matilda.

Seven years later, in 1066, William once more put all at risk – wife, children, home and happiness – to gain his greatest prize, the kingship of that northern country of England.

It was this English invasion and triumph, as perhaps had been foretold, that gave the reality to his name, the Conqueror.

Author's note:

The death of William's father, Duke Robert of Normandy, while on pilgrimage to the Holy Land, left the duchy in turmoil. William, his heir, was only a child, and illegitimate. Other members of the ducal family had as good a right to the dukedom and were of an age to enforce their claims. William's childhood therefore was marked by violence, conspiracy, and attempted murder, to such an extent it is a wonder he survived at all.

The source of much of this book comes from contemporary records, from monkish chronicles and documents whose conflicting legends I have attempted to put together in a logical sequence. During such a confusing period it is not surprising that chronology (always a difficulty for historical novelists) presented special complications. In a few instances I have rearranged episodes to make better sense, or selected ones which best show the various facets of the turbulence through which William lived. In no place have I underestimated the way in which, as a young boy, he learned to overcome his enemies in circumstances which might have daunted most grown men, nor have I exaggerated his courage and determination.

I should like to take this opportunity to thank both my editor and agents for their patience and support, and my friends and children for their tolerance, especially my son, David, without whose help and expertise with computers and printing out of my MS I should have been truly lost. I would also like to express the pleasure I found in visiting and revisiting Normandy itself.